Fallen Angel

Naughtiness streaked through her, making her wonder if he could actually lie beside her and not take her into his arms.

"I'm sorry if I'm bothering you," she said, trying to keep from laughing. "Any *normal* man wouldn't be able to stand this. But you have an iron will."

He squinted one eye in suspicion. "Are you pulling my leg?"

"No, I'm trying not to touch you, much less pull anything on you." She widened her eyes. "But then you're as cold-blooded as a fish, so I don't have to worry. I could get closer, right up against you..." She snuggled into him, pressing her breasts against his chest. "You're not even thinking how nice it would be to wrap your arms around me and...?"

"Jussie Drussard," he said, "you've got the devil in you."

"Not yet," she murmured, "but I will soon."

DEBORAH CAMP is the winner of
Affaire de Coeurs'
GOLDEN CERTIFICATE OF EXCELLENCE

Other Books in
THE AVON ROMANCE Series

CAMELOT JONES *by Mayo Lucas*
DEFIANT HEART *by Nancy Moulton*
HEARTS BEGUILED *by Penelope Williamson*
LADY MIDNIGHT *by Maria Greene*
OUTLAW HEART *by Suzannah Davis*
PASSION SONG *by Catherine FitzGerald*
VIOLET FIRE *by Brenda Joyce*

Coming Soon

SCARLET RIBBONS *by Judith E. French*
SILVER SPLENDOR *by Barbara Dawson Smith*

Avon Books are available at special quantity discounts for bulk purchases for sales promotions, premiums, fund raising or educational use. Special books, or book excerpts, can also be created to fit specific needs.

For details write or telephone the office of the Director of Special Markets, Avon Books, Dept. FP, 105 Madison Avenue, New York, New York 10016, 212-481-5653.

Fallen Angel

DEBORAH CAMP

AVON BOOKS ◆ NEW YORK

FALLEN ANGEL is an original publication of Avon Books. This work has never before appeared in book form. This work is a novel. Any similarity to actual persons or events is purely coincidental.

AVON BOOKS
A division of
The Hearst Corporation
105 Madison Avenue
New York, New York 10016

Copyright © 1989 by Deborah E. Camp
Inside cover author photograph by Robert Eilers
Published by arrangement with the author
Library of Congress Catalog Card Number: 88-91379
ISBN: 0-380-75741-9

All rights reserved, which includes the right to reproduce this book or portions thereof in any form whatsoever except as provided by the U.S. Copyright Law. For information address Lowenstein Associates Inc., 121 West 27th Street, Suite 601, New York, New York 10001.

First Avon Books Printing: July 1989

AVON TRADEMARK U.S. PAT. OFF. AND IN OTHER COUNTRIES, MARCA REGISTRADA, HECHO EN U.S.A.

Printed in the U.S.A.

K–R   10   9   8   7   6   5   4   3   2   1

He thought she was his'n.
He learned he was her'n.
—cowboy saying

Arizona is no place for amateurs.
—Wyatt Earp

Chapter 1

"**O**h, Beauregard! Feel my heart beating just for you!" Justine Drussard pressed the young man's hand to her lush bosom, which was partially exposed by her low-cut bodice.

Catcalls and moans rose up to drown out his response, but Justine knew it by heart anyway.

"Yes, my love," she shouted. "My heart belongs to you, and now that Papa is on the other side, the gold mine is ours. You, my brave one, have slain the dastardly Dudley Fishbine, and we have nothing but rainbows ahead of us." She looked off, above the cowboy and derby hats in the front row of the Silver Nugget Theater, to the darkness beyond. "Nothing but rainbows, my love!"

Justine looked up to watch the heavy, red velvet curtain fall and separate her from the rowdy Tombstone, Arizona, crowd. As soon as the gold tassels along the hem of the curtain touched the stage's planked floor, Justine grabbed "Beauregard"'s wrist and peeled his hand off her pillowy bosom. When he resisted, she cut him with a flinty glare.

"Take it off or I'll break it off, Carter Hendricks,"

1

she warned, drawing a nervous laugh from the actor.

He dislodged her hand from his wrist and ran his forefinger across his sparse blond mustache. "Those drunken miners wouldn't be so envious if they knew how stingy you are with your affections." He faced front, staring at the curtain. "We're ready for our curtain call," he said, directing his comment to the little man standing in the wings, rope in hand.

Justine stood beside Carter and fixed a smile on her face as the curtain went up again to thunderous applause and whistles. Executing a low curtsy, Justine tried to ignore the man in the front row who swayed toward her, thick lips pursed, eyes tightly shut, his friends bullying him on. Disgusting animals, she thought, then wished she were in a *real* theater where such behavior wouldn't be tolerated. What was she thinking? In the legitimate theater these monkeys wouldn't even be allowed in the front door!

She stepped back, out of range, and comforted herself with the reminder that this was the last show in Tombstone. Come morning Monsieur Bonsoir's Traveling Thespians would move on for a run in a Bisbee theater, then on to relative civilization in Tucson.

That's when I quit this mule team, she thought with conviction. She'd had it with traveling shows that were more circus than theater. She had to get back to her roots—Shakespeare and other classics. No more plays written to entertain drooling dogs. Sure, the money was good and the work was steady, but Justine had learned from experience that she'd rather be a supporting player in a reputable company than receive top billing in a poorly written and performed melodrama.

The players took their bows, then the moth-eaten curtain fell again. Justine let the smile slip from her lips, and her shoulders slumped as she wove around the stage settings and other actors to the backstage area. The theater owner had provided three rooms for the troupe to save them hotel bills. Being the leading lady, Justine had taken over one of them. No more than a tiny closet, it was at least private, and she made her way to it gratefully.

Privacy was a rare commodity in traveling shows. Even modest young women became accustomed to dressing in front of the other women and, occasionally, in the company of stagehands. Justine tugged at the front of her dress, hating the way it rode so low on her breasts. She was eager to be out of it and into her nightclothes, and to scrub the greasepaint off her face. Bone tired, she wanted nothing but a good night's sleep so that she'd be ready to travel tomorrow after breakfast.

A parchment calendar was tacked to the door of her makeshift dressing room. She paused, her hand on the doorknob, to examine the calendar page, realizing that she'd lost all track of time. When had she joined up with this company? she wondered, thinking back to the summer. June, wasn't it? No. July. The week after the celebration of the Fourth. The summer had been one disappointment after another as she'd narrowly missed out on key acting roles, making her jump at the offer from Monsieur Bonsoir. And now it was fall already. Fall, she thought, staring at the top of the calendar, where big black letters spelled out OCTOBER 1881. She looked at the numbered boxes, ticking them off one by one until she found Tuesday the twenty-fifth, then she projected her thoughts forward to Thanksgiving, when she'd be in Tucson and finished with her obligation to this company. Not too far off, she thought with a resigned sigh. At least she'd have something to be thankful for on that holiday. She'd have her freedom and more than enough money for a ticket to St. Louis or Chicago. Some city that appreciated fine theater.

Justine pushed open the door and stepped inside. Closing it, she reached for the lamp she'd set on the table nearby, but she froze in midmotion when she saw an unfamiliar hulk on her narrow bed. The hulk smiled, flashing pearly white teeth.

"What are you doing in here, Elmer?" she asked her oily-haired boss.

"The name is Monsieur Bonsoir," he corrected through clenched teeth.

"You'll always be Elmer Bragg to me," she said, leaning back against the closed door and eyeing him with suspicion. "Once again, what are you doing in my room?"

"Your room through the goodness of my heart," he said, illustrating his point with a jab of one fat, stubby finger. "Now it's your turn to show your appreciation to me." His French accent sounded about as real as the four-carat "diamond" ring on his finger. "Do you not recall that I told you I would collect soon?" The bedsprings sang out in relief as he stood and took a step toward her. "The room is *ours* tonight, Jussie Drussard."

She shook her head, sending her dark curls bouncing around her shoulders. Stiff-arming him, Justine pushed Elmer away. "Not another step," she said. "You might bed every other woman in this company, but not this one. I'd rather sleep with a desert lizard."

"That can be arranged," he said, smiling, then batting her hand away. "Submit or I'll throw you out on your pretty little ear."

"You've seen too many melodramas, Elmer," she said, turning away from his pursed lips, then slipping sideways. "Now, out with you before I get really mad."

"Oh-ho!" His brown eyes glistened amid the rolls of skin surrounding them. "I like zee woman with fire!"

"Zee woman is going to fire you with a good swift

kick if you don't back off right this minute!" She tried to sound mean and ornery, but she trembled inside as she sized up her opponent. Elmer weighed at least 280 pounds, she guessed, and she barely tipped the scales at 100. Her only advantage was her brain, since Elmer's was soft from disuse.

Elmer lunged, fingers wiggling and eyes glinting piggishly, and Justine struck. The flat of her hand stung his flabby cheek, leaving a bright imprint. He stared at her for a moment, his eyes watering and drool slipping from one corner of his thick lips.

"Elmer-r-r-r." Justine let his name ring like a warning bell. "Keep your distance."

With a massive grunt, he threw himself at her again, this time plastering her against the wall. He squeezed the air from her lungs, and his lips left wet marks on her neck and chin.

"Stop it!" Justine pushed at his round shoulders. "Get off of me!" She stamped one foot, burying the heel of her shoe in the top of his, then brought her knee up hard, finding the juncture of his trunklike legs.

Howling in pain, he doubled over, giving Justine enough room to slip away from him and head for the door. She paused to look over her shoulder, then cried out when his hand shot out and grabbed a handful of her ebony hair. He jerked her head back and spat in her face.

Justine blinked and pressed her lips together to keep from retching.

"Get out, you bitch! If you sleep in this room to-night, you sleep with me!" He gave her a vicious shove, sending her spinning and slamming against the door.

Crying and wiping the vile man's spit from her face, Justine wrenched open the door, grabbed her valise, and stumbled out into the corridor. Elmer slammed the door behind her.

The door across the hall opened a crack, then all

the way. Della Beecher propped one hand on her slim hip and tipped her head at a curious angle.

"What's all the racket about?" Della asked in a voice as hoarse as a bullfrog's. "Did Monsieur Bonsoir finally get fed up with your uppity ways?"

"The snake," Justine said, running a hand down her face and wishing for a pan of hot water and a block of soap. She shivered and glanced toward what used to be her room. She'd been lucky to get out of there without any bruises, she told herself, drawing a deep, quivering breath. She fixed the other woman with a woe-is-me expression. "Della, let me stay in your room tonight," she begged.

"It's not just mine. It belongs to all us girls, and it looks like you just became one of us. No more Miss Queen Bee for you. Come on in and join us worker bees."

Justine entered the room, smiling shyly at the other two women. Besides Della there were Annie Lee and Beatrice. Both were making beds for themselves on the floor.

"Grab one of those quilts stacked on that trunk and make yourself a pallet," Della instructed, pointing to the corner of the room where a mound of dirty quilts lay atop a rusty trunk. "After a night on the floor, you might decide to give Monsieur Bonsoir a little lovin' so's you can sleep on a real mattress again."

"Not on your life," Justine said, grabbing a quilt and throwing it to the floor. She sat on it and opened her valise, shoving aside several articles to find the jar of French milled face cream she used to remove her theatrical makeup.

"Honey, you was told when you was hired on that every gal in the company is the property, at one time or another, of the monsieur," Della said, arranging some quilts for her own bed.

"Why do you call him that ridiculous name?" Justine said, smearing the cream onto her face, then trying to find her hand mirror in the bottom of her valise. "His name is Elmer Bragg, and it fits him perfectly. That Monsieur Bonsoir nonsense is okay for the poor fools who pay to see our pitiful excuse for theater, but we all know better."

"Whatever you call him, he pays your salary," Della said, sitting down and tugging the quilts into a better pallet. "If you don't lie down for him, you're just asking for trouble. Am I right, girls?" She looked at the other two women and they nodded, then Annie Lee sighed and closed her eyes while Beatrice turned her back to them. "They're tuckered out," Della whispered.

"Aren't we all," Justine said, pulling her silver mirror from the valise to stare at her shiny cream-smeared face. She found a soft cloth, already discolored with cosmetics, and used it to dab away the face cream and makeup. Down her elegant nose, straight and short bridged, with nostrils that flared slightly, and across her rounded chin, she wiped with the cloth to reveal her own pale, flawless skin.

She was a beauty, she knew, and she used her striking looks to get the attention of directors and theater owners. Once she had them looking, she could make them sit still long enough to reveal what she considered her best asset—her ability to become someone else, *anyone* else. Acting was her life and had been since she was a precocious ten-year-old, singing and dancing for pocket change on the streets of New Orleans and acting as if she hadn't a care in the world.

With her lustrous black hair, her striking gray eyes set in a small, oval-shaped face, and her petite, hourglass figure, Justine Drussard knew she was packaged well, but she didn't rely on her looks, and she never let men take advantage of her because of them. At twenty, she was a virgin and intended to remain so until a desirable gentleman offered her a wedding ring and a ceremony to go with it.

Until that day came, she was perfectly happy in her quest to become the most respected actress of her generation.

"That's a pretty mirror, dearie," Della said, admiring the antique silver handle.

"Thanks. It belonged to a woman I used to know in New Orleans. Jasmine Broadwater." She smiled, seeing the woman's wrinkled face in her mind's eyes. "She gave me this ivory comb and brush, too."

"Oh, my! What fine material. Ivory, you say?"

"Yes, real ivory from Africa. Jasmine Broadwater was a voodoo queen and had roots in that dark continent." Justine took them from Della and packed them carefully in her carpet valise, where she kept her other treasure, her lucky rabbit's foot. "Della, do you really think Elmer might cut my pay if I'm not nice to him?"

"He's done it before."

"But, surely you haven't . . ." She let the rest trail off when she saw Della's twinkling eyes and quick nod. "You have?"

"Of course." Della shrugged. "Why not?"

Someone knocked at the door, making Justine gasp and turn wide eyes on Della, but the other woman waved aside Justine's alarm.

"It's not the monsieur. Don't worry." Della pushed herself up and went to the door. She exchanged whispers with an Oriental boy, then took a steaming teapot from him. Turning to face Justine, she held up the pot and giggled. "Hot tea. Want some?"

"Yes, I'd love some. It'll settle my nerves." Justine held out her hands to Della. They were trembling. "That fight with Elmer upset me more than I thought."

Della gave a slow wink. "This'll do the trick, dearie. I'll get the cups. There are a few in this old cabinet over here. I spotted them last night." She shuffled to the back of the room, out of sight. When she came back, she held a tray with the teapot on it and two cracked china cups and saucers. She'd already poured the tea, and she handed one of the cups to Justine. "Drink up, dearie. Drink up!"

"Thanks, but first I'm getting out of this dress." Justine set the cup and saucer to one side while she wiggled out of the tight blue dress. She flung it across a trunk, then removed her petticoats, corset, shoes, and stockings. Clad only in her chemise, she slipped under the quilt and picked up her tea. "Ahh, that feels ever so much better. That dress is torture, I tell you. It squeezes my breasts until I think they're going to pop right over the top of the neckline. And the waist pinches so, even when I wear a corset." She sipped the tea. It had a peppermint taste and sent warmth spiraling through her. Propping herself on her elbows, she relaxed with a long sigh. "I'll sure be glad to see the last of this town, won't you?"

"Tombstone is a rough-and-tumble place," Della observed. "There are a lot of bad men here, I'll wager."

"Saloons and brothels," Justine said. "That's what makes up this town. Oh, and mines. I've never seen so many working mines."

"Tombstone wouldn't be here if it weren't for them mines." Della took a long, gulping drink of her own tea. "But at least there's some culture."

"Where? I haven't seen it."

"Why, there's theaters all over this place. 'Bout near every saloon has a stage in it, too. And didn't you see that brand new place—Shief something Hall?"

"Yes, I saw it." Justine shrugged off the signs of civilization. "But I haven't seen many decent people around. Just a bunch of drunks."

"I've played worse places."

"I haven't, and I don't want to. I took this job because I was down to my last few dollars, but come

Thanksgiving I'm heading for the big city. I must return to my original calling."

"Your what?" Della asked.

"The legitimate theater," Justine explained. "I'm an actress, not a saloon girl. I want to perform in front of an appreciative, *civilized* audience, not a bunch of smelly miners."

"Miss Queen Bee," Della mumbled.

"I don't mean to sound so," Justine said. "But I *have* trained under Edward Stinnet."

"Who?" Della made an unattractive face.

"Mr. Stinnet," Justine repeated. "He happens to be one of the country's foremost drama coaches. I trained under him in New Orleans, but he coaches in New York City now. He said I was one of his most promising students."

"Did he now?" Della drawled, then laughed under her breath. "Maybe he said that to every lass with cash in hand."

"He did not!" Justine finished her tea, shaking her head when Della offered to pour more. "I'm tired. I'm going to sleep."

"Suit yourself, dearie," Della said with a smug smile. "Suit yourself."

Justine turned onto her side, away from the other woman's jeering grin. She's just jealous, she told herself. She doesn't have an ounce of talent. In fact, she's lucky to get work, period. If it weren't for her limited success at playing piano and croaking out a song or two between acts, Della would be plying her trade in Tombstone's brothels.

Wincing at her own hateful thoughts, Justine doused the lamp. Della looked like a big heap of blankets in the darkness.

"Thanks for the tea, Della," Justine whispered.

"Don't mention it, dearie," Della whispered back. "Sweet dreams."

"Same to you." Justine found a more comfortable position on the pallet and then felt as if a curtain was lowered over her mind. Hers was a dreamless, fathomless sleep. Like death.

When she awoke, she couldn't tell if she'd been asleep minutes or hours. She stared at a trunk across the room, wondering where she was and how she'd come to rest on this lumpy bed so close to the floor. No, not close . . . *on* the floor.

Sniffing at the musky scents of old wood, yeast, and bad whiskey, Justine pushed up on her elbows and peered at the trunks and barrels and broken bits of furniture. Oh, yes, she thought as the fog cleared from her brain. The back of the theater. That's where I am. In with the other girls. The others . . . ?

She sat up, pushing the dark curtain of her hair off her face and looking around for Della, Annie Lee, or Beatrice. Black imps danced behind her eyes and pounded her temples with iron-headed mallets. Justine placed a hand to her forehead and fought off a wave of sickness. When the room had righted again, she struggled to her feet, throwing off the dusty blankets and flinging her long hair over her shoulders.

"Della?" Her voice was as dry as kindling. Justine swallowed back the cottony texture in her mouth and tried again. "Anybody here?" She squinted into the dusk, detecting no movement, no sound except her own ragged breathing. "Where is everybody?" she murmured, turning in a slow circle to locate her valise. It rested on its side, its mouth gaping open as if in shock.

"No . . . oh, no!" Justine bent over and snatched it up, moaning when she felt its light weight. She turned it over and shook out the meager contents. A dress, two skirts, a blouse, undergarments, her old pair of shoes. No money. No ivory and silver accessories. No jewelry. No toiletries. "Robbed." Justine's voice was a sob as she peered into the empty valise, then shook it again, hoping against hope that her precious articles would tumble out and make a mockery of her panic. When nothing but lint waltzed in the faint light, Justine dropped the valise and took a few moments to rein in her fury. She looked around, eyes smarting, heart pounding furiously, hands clenching and unclenching at her sides. Robbed and . . . deserted?

Fed by anger and humiliation, Justine stuffed her few remaining articles into the valise, leaving out one dress. She put it on, tugging at the snug waist, tight sleeves and cuffs, and low neckline. Given to her by a chorus girl two years ago, it was the one she wore only when everything else was soiled because its ready-made lines hugged her figure too closely for Justine's tastes. She could hardly breathe in it without popping stitches. Combing her hands roughly through her hair, she stepped over the grimy quilts to the door. It opened, making her sigh in relief. At least she hadn't been locked in!

She marched, valise tucked protectively under one arm, to the front of the deathly quiet theater. An elderly man stood near the front door, broom in hand, dust dancing around his feet. Her approaching footsteps sounded like cannon fire, and he looked up. Then his eyes widened. He stroked his generous mustache and tipped his head to one side, regarding her as if she were an oddity in a medicine show.

"You still here? I've heard about beauty sleep, but—"

"Where are they?" Justine demanded, stopping in front of him.

"Who?"

"The company I'm with, of course. Where are they?"

He glanced toward the louvered doors. "Miles from here, pretty Miss. They left an hour before sunrise, and it's done past noon. You being such a slip of a thing, they must've overlooked you."

"Not likely." Justine dropped her valise on the

floor. "They didn't overlook my possessions. I've been robbed. They even took my money, and Elmer owes me a month's salary!"

"Elmer?"

"Elmer Bragg." She cast him an impatient scowl. "Monsieur Bonsoir to you. That rat. That slimy, smelly rat! When I get my hands on him—" She throttled thin air, making the old man laugh. "I mean it! Where's the sheriff's office? I'm going to light a fire under him. He's got to put a posse together before that bunch of thieves gets too much farther down the road."

The old man's mustache twitched. "Don't think you'll find John Behan at his office, ma'am. He seems to be busy this day."

"I don't care how busy he is, I need to talk to him." She sighed and laid a hand across her forehead. "Penniless again. I can't let them get away with this. I just can't! I've got to get out of this town and—" She pressed her lips together, realizing she was lamenting to a perfect stranger. "Could you please tell me how to find the sheriff's office?"

"He's not there." The old man shrugged helplessly and started sweeping the floor again.

"How do you know?"

"I saw him heading down the street a little while ago—hold up, there!" He grabbed her wrist when she started for the door. "He's gone. Went toward Fly's Studio."

"What's that?"

"Fly's . . ." He shook his head. "Third and Freemont. You know where the OK Corral is?"

"Yes, I saw it on the way into town." She nodded, recalling the livery in the heart of Tombstone. "Is he getting ready to head out somewhere?" she asked, wanting to catch him before he left.

"Don't think so. Just the same, I wouldn't charge after him just now."

"Why not?" Justine asked, wrenching her wrist from his grasp.

"'Cause there might be some trouble brewing over there." He nodded toward the doors. "I know the sheriff. Me and him go back a few years, don't you know, and he had a full head of steam when he went past here. Told me the Clantons are in town, and the Earps are just itching to—"

"Pardon me," she cut in impatiently. "This is all very interesting, but I've got troubles of my own and can't be concerned with anyone else's. The OK Corral, you said?"

"Yes'm, but you ought not go there. You don't look well, ma'am. Why not rest a while longer?"

"I *do* feel funny." She put a hand to her head, testing for fever. "Like I've slept for days and days." Giving her head a good shake, she cleared her vision.

"Better stay here a spell, ma'am."

"No, I've cooled my heels long enough. It makes my blood boil to think of Elmer and his merry troupe spending my money, wearing my clothes, and selling my things along the way." She thought of how Della had coveted her mirror and ivory comb and brush. "They're nothing but a bunch of sneaking coyotes, and I'm not going to let them get away with it."

"Ma'am, you'd best not . . ."

Justine turned a deaf ear on the rest and strode from the theater, valise in hand, scarred shoes making dusty tracks in the street. She glanced down at her old shoes, the tips showing red where the polish was worn completely away, and she thought of her brand new pair that either Della or Beatrice or Annie Lee was no doubt wearing. She should have seen through them, she thought. Should have known they'd stoop to any level to knife her in the back. When she'd spurned Elmer, she'd sealed her fate, she knew, but her hindsight was much clearer than her foresight had been.

Third and Freemont... She checked the weathered signs and turned a corner. FLY'S PHOTOGRAPHY STUDIO, a sign proclaimed, squeaking back and forth on rusty hinges. And... yes, there it was, the OK Corral.

She lengthened her stride, skirts swirling around her as a breeze kicked up and threw sand in her eyes. Closing in on the corral, she saw several men standing at the entrance a couple of feet apart from one another. They seemed to be absorbed by something just inside the corral, out of her view.

"Sheriff Behan!" she called, hoping one would turn around so she'd easily be able to identify him. "Excuse me, but which one of you is Sheriff John Behan?" she called, closing in fast.

A movement to the side caught her eye and slowed her progress. She looked at the man standing on the boardwalk, hat in hand, his face in shadow. He was plastered against the front wall of an assay office building, and he seemed to be waving her aside, motioning her back with his black hat. She frowned and dismissed him with a tipping up of her chin as she came closer to the grouping of men. One of them held a cane. She caught the glint of metal. Their long coats were blown back, and two of the men wore stars on their chests.

"Give it up!" one of them ordered, addressing someone inside the corral. "Put them down."

"Don't be a damned fool!" another shouted.

"Sheriff," she said, rushing forward, her hand outstretched. She caught sight of other men inside the corral. Young men. Old men. Gun-toting men.

Justine stopped just behind the tallest man, the sight of drawn guns cracking her stony single-mindedness and letting in a healthy dose of fear. Get out of the way! a voice screamed inside her head. Run while you're still able!

But then it seemed that the whole world exploded around her. In the blink of an eye, other guns and rifles flashed into view and fire shot from them, bellowing and belching smoke and bullets. She stood only two feet from one of the men, close enough to see him catch a bullet, whirl, and go down on one knee. Justine screamed, or was it someone else screaming? She didn't know. She couldn't be sure of anything. Then she thought she'd been hit by gunfire as her body was flung backward. She started falling and tried to catch herself, but her fingers clutched nothing more substantial than air. Something struck her head near the base of her neck, and then blackness covered her, shutting out all sound, all sight, all pain, everything, but not before she glimpsed a face. A man's face, blurred, the features unclear except for his eyes. Eyes as blue as the sky ... blending into the sky, then floating away on a dark, smothering cloud.

Chapter 2

⟨ ━━━◦◦◦━━━ ⟩

"Gunfight at the OK Corral..."

"...three dead."

"Billy...and Frank and Tom McLaury...naw, I'm fine as a frog's hair."

"...York Masters...handsome son of a gun..."

"He didn't know her, just...got out of the way and..."

"...lucky girl. What was York doing there?"

"Just nosing around. He figured something was up...tried to talk us out of it, but we...Virgil and Morgan both got hit, but Wyatt escaped harm."

"And the sheriff tried to arrest Wyatt?"

"Tried, but didn't."

"Doc, honey, look in her valise for—wait a minute."

"Is she awake?"

"Almost. Hey there! Can you see me, girlie?"

A face swam into view. Justine squinted, trying to focus. Was it *that* face? The one with the sky blue eyes? No, not that one, she thought, focusing on a large nose, beady eyes, and dark hair pulled into a severe bun.

"Can you see me now?" the woman asked.

Justine started to nod, but pain shot up her neck and exploded in her head. She moaned and closed her eyes, trying to remember what she'd been doing.

"Doc, what do you think? Maybe a shot of whiskey will kick her back into this world."

"I'll pour it," a deep voice rumbled. "Think I'll have one myself. What about you, Kate?"

"Yeah. Don't mind if I do. Bring the bottle over here."

"Kate . . ." It was a low warning.

"I'm not going to get cockeyed. Just bring me the damned bottle!"

It seemed a long time before something cold and hard touched Justine's lips. She frowned, then felt liquid splash inside her mouth and flow down her throat. She coughed, sputtered, sucked in her breath as fire spread through her belly. A coughing fit seized her. She sat up, hacking and crying and wondering if she might die.

"Whoa, little lady," a man said, then a hand slapped her back, and Justine thought her teeth had been dislodged. "You don't seem to be used to good whiskey. Maybe she's a *real* lady, huh, Kate."

"In Tombstone?" The woman whooped. "And maybe I'm the queen of England."

"I've seen her before. Still can't remember where. Lady . . . Miss? What's your name, Miss?"

"Jussie." Justine coughed and fell back, her head pounding. "Justine Drussard."

"Fancy, huh?" the woman asked.

"Hey, you were in that play last night at the Nugget!" Fingers snapped, resounding in Justine's head like gunfire.

Gunfire? There had been gunfire, hadn't there? On the street . . . looking for the sheriff . . . the man with the hat, waving her aside . . . face in shadow . . . blue eyes swimming overhead . . .

"It was him," she said, not recognizing her voice,

but feeling it in her throat nonetheless. "He was warning me, motioning for me to stay back and then he must have shoved me out of the way. I was looking for the sheriff. . . ."

"Yes, dear, that's right," the woman said, smoothing Justine's hair from her forehead. "You got in the way of a shoot-out at the OK Corral. Remember that? You got pushed out of the way in the nick of time, but you hit your head. How you feeling, honey? Got yourself a headache?"

"Who . . . ?" Justine's voice deserted her.

"I'm Kate Fisher."

"John Henry Holliday here, ma'am, but you can call me Doc."

"A doctor?" Justine asked, opening her eyes just enough to see the man with the dark blue eyes and wing-tipped mustache.

"Not that kind. I'm a dentist, retired. How about another swallow of whiskey to clear your head? Give her a sip, Kate."

Kate poured the liquid fire down her throat again. Justine batted the bottle away and propped herself up on her elbows as her memory returned, setting the world right again and making her see the two strangers clearly.

Kate Fisher was in her thirties, heavyset but not unattractive. Doc, tall and lean, bordered on good-looking, but there was a cruel glint in his eyes that his smile couldn't tame. Justine looked around, touching her fingertips to a swelling on her nape. She was in a parlor, on a medallion-backed sofa.

"Is this your place?" she asked Kate, and the woman nodded. "How did I get here?"

"I carried you," Doc said, hooking his thumbs in the pockets of his silver vest. "Why were you looking for the sheriff?"

"I need a posse." She glared at them when they laughed at her. "I was robbed and deserted!"

"That so?" Doc Holliday rocked back on his heels. "Who did the robbing?"

"Elmer Bragg, also known as Monsieur Bonsoir. He owes me a month's salary, and he took all my valuables. Or somebody took them. I'm sure Elmer's behind it all." She laid a hand to her forehead, wishing she could stop the ache that pounded away at it like a sledgehammer.

"Back up," Doc said, pulling a piano stool forward and taking a seat. "This Elmer Bragg headed up that acting troupe?"

"Yes, that's right."

"And why would he take your things?"

"Because I . . ." She looked at Kate, then back to Doc. "He tried to take advantage of me but was unsuccessful," she said, selecting her words carefully. "When I rebuffed him, he swore vengeance. I awoke to find that the company had left without me, and all my valuables were missing. My money, too." She looked toward the lace-draped windows. "What time is it?"

"Getting toward dusk," Kate answered.

"Oh, no." Justine ran a hand down her face. "They're miles and miles away by now. They're heading to Bisbee for an engagement. Can't they be arrested there?"

"Maybe, but we've got a little problem," Doc said. "City Marshal Virgil Earp and one of his deputies, Morgan Earp, were both harmed in that shoot-out earlier. That leaves one deputy, Wyatt, and Sheriff John Behan, who's got his hands full right now, to keep law and order in Tombstone. In other words, ma'am, they can't be concerned with your troubles today. They've got bigger fish to fry, if you get my meaning."

"But what about you? Aren't you a deputy or something?"

"No, just a friend of law and order." He glanced at Kate and exchanged a silent message that Justine couldn't decipher. "Today's events will keep folks pretty busy for a few days, ma'am. It's a bad time for you to be wanting a posse. We just don't have the manpower or the inclination. There might even be an uprising over this."

"An uprising of what?"

"Scum," Kate offered.

"Outlaws," Doc added. "Some of their brethren were killed in the shoot-out, and they'll be looking to even the score, I reckon."

"But what about me?" Justine asked.

Doc shrugged. "Looks like you're way down on the list of things to get done. Sorry, ma'am."

Kate sat on the couch beside Justine and handed her a damp cloth. "Put this on your forehead. That's it. You think this Elmer was the only one out to hoodwink you?"

"I don't know . . . no." Justine frowned, recalling Della's shady behavior. "Della—she was in the troupe—showed a keen interest in my ivory comb and brush last night. We had tea, and then I went to sleep. When I woke up, it was afternoon and everybody was gone."

"Sound sleeper, are you?" Doc asked.

"Not usually. I don't know why I slept so late. I was in the same room with the other women, but I didn't wake up when they were getting ready to leave. I never heard anything." She sighed, feeling weary and heavy limbed. "I slept like the dead last night."

"You said this Della and you had tea?" Kate asked, exchanging a glance with Doc. "Who prepared the tea?"

"I don't know. An Oriental boy brought it. Della served it. Why? Why are you looking at me like that?" she demanded, noticing Kate's sly grin. "What do you think happened?"

"Knockout drops," Kate said, getting a nod from Doc. "I'd bet all the tea in China on it. That gal put them drops in your tea so you'd sleep sound while she robbed you. I used to do that sort of thing myself." She traded smiles with Doc. "Remember, honey?"

"I remember it got you in a heap of trouble that I had to get you out of."

Kate laughed, hooked an arm around Doc's neck, and gave him a smacking kiss on the mouth. "Well, you ought to be good for something, John Henry!"

"I feel so weak," Justine said, weaving back and forth like a Saturday-night drunk.

"You lie down," Kate said, taking the damp cloth from her and giving her shoulder a push. "Get some rest. You can stay with me tonight."

"Maybe you should fix her something to eat," Doc said.

"I will later."

"I've got to get. I'll be at the Crystal Palace if you need me."

"Let me know how the Earps are faring," Kate instructed. "Come on back here, and I'll feed you supper later."

"Be back around eight. Thanks for taking her in, Kate. I didn't know what to do with her, and Masters had his hands full with . . ."

The man's voice diminished as he walked to the door until Justine could no longer hear it, and she dozed, dreaming of flying and floating. When she woke again, she saw that the woman was standing over her, a dinner tray held between her big hands. The aroma of biscuits and ham brought Justine wide awake. She struggled to a sitting position, only then realizing that she was no longer on the sofa but in a big, soft bed.

"How did I get in here?" she asked, looking around the cheerfully appointed bedroom.

"My houseboy carried you up here an hour ago," Kate said. "It's time for you to eat something."

"How long have I been asleep?"

"Only an hour or so," Kate said, placing the tray over her lap. "Don't fret about it. Those blackout drops," Kate Fisher said, bustling to the window to pull the shade and draw the draperies, then back to the bed, "they put you down for hours and hours." She propped her hands on her hips and surveyed Justine with sharp eyes. "Your color's coming back, but . . . you are naturally pale?"

"Yes, I'm afraid so."

"Nothing to be afraid about," Kate said with a laugh. "I'd like to have porcelain skin myself, but I've got a touch of Indian blood in me, so I'm brown whether I'm in the sun or not. You're welcome to spend the night here, but stay in this room. If you wander about, one of the men might see you and want you." She sighed and regret lined her face. "We don't want to build up a man's hopes and then squash them like bugs, do we?"

"No, I suppose not." Justine cocked her head to one side, struck by a queer notion. Was she in a whorehouse? "Kate, are you saying that this is a . . . that is . . . are you a . . . I hope you don't take offense, but are you—"

"This is a brothel, and I own it," she said, answering all the unasked questions. "Of course, now that me and Doc have an understanding, I don't take on clients personally, but I've got five girls here who are more than willing." Kate sat on the side of the bed and looked over the dinner on the tray: scrambled eggs, ham, biscuits, and grits. "Got a good cook on the payroll, too, so eat up."

"It's kind of you to take me in. I don't know what I'll do tomorrow."

"Worry about tomorrow when it gets here." Kate crossed one leg over the other and let out a whoop of laughter. "That's how I make it from day to day, so I don't see why it won't hold you in good stead. I bet your headache has lessened up, hasn't it?"

"Yes, it's almost gone."

"See, what did I tell you?" Kate flashed her a superior smile. "I know what I'm talking about."

"Do you still use knockout drops?" Justine asked before taking a forkful of the eggs into her watering mouth.

"Lordy, no! I almost got thrown in jail over it. If it hadn't been for John Henry, I would have been in a mess of trouble." She leaned forward to whisper. "John Henry's got connections, you understand."

Her mouth full of biscuit and ham, Justine could only nod.

"But the drops were good to have around for those cowboys who occasionally got to thinking women were just like horses and could be rode to death or given a whipping if they misbehaved." She plucked a piece of ham off Justine's plate and popped it into her mouth. "That's tasty," she said with a grin. "I bet it feels good in that empty stomach of yours." Her mood changed from bright to dark, and she stood and paced near the bed. "John Henry's still mad at me, you know."

"Why is he mad?"

"Oh, I got drunk and said some things to the wrong folks. I told some lawman that John Henry had a hand in a stage robbery."

"He robbed a stagecoach?"

"Well . . . not exactly, but he knows who robbed it. I was mad at him because he hadn't been paying much attention to me, and I decided to get back at him. So I got drunk and started telling things that were on the quiet. Things I'd been told never to repeat." She looked aside for a moment as if she were struggling with a strong emotion. "Doc said he couldn't ever trust me again." She waved a hand to dismiss her behavior. "Him bringing you here kind of melted the ice around his heart, but I still can't reach him. I don't think he loves me anymore. Not like he used to. I was hoping we—" She closed her mouth so quickly that her teeth clicked. Sending a disquieting look toward Justine, she squared her shoulders and seemed to gather her defenses. She returned to sit on the side of the bed, prim and proper as a lady in church.

Justine was glad, not wanting to hear any secrets or share troubles with this woman she barely knew. She had enough worries without taking on Kate Fisher's.

"Anyway," Kate said brightly. "The way I figure it, that girl slipped some drops in your tea and cleaned you out the next morning. That Elmer fella probably helped her. You don't toe the line, they replace you." She shrugged her round shoulders. "I guess acting is a lot like whoring that way."

Justine managed a tight smile, disagreeing with Kate's comparison. She knew many people saw work on the stage and the boudoir business as nearly the same, but she wasn't one of them. Acting was an art; prostitution was merely a shame.

"Where did you get your knockout drops?"

"From China Mary," Kate said with a glimmer in her eyes. "That's what tipped me. You said an Oriental boy delivered the pot of tea?"

"Yes, that's right."

Kate winked knowingly and gave a decisive nod. "I'd bet a silver dollar he works for China Mary." She let loose another whooping laugh. "Of course, *every* Oriental in this town and in Bisbee works for her, but she's the only one I know of who keeps a supply of knockout drops. She's got drugs of all kinds. I hear tell she even has a drug that makes men fall in love with women. She calls it a love potion."

"You believe that?" Justine asked.

"Never gave it much thought." Kate fluffed her starched black skirt and rustled the petticoats beneath it. "I never needed any potion to get any man I ever set my sights on."

"Does China Mary live here?"

"Yes. In Hop Town."

"Where's that?"

"At the end of this street, Allen Street," she said. "That's Hop Town, and China Mary's is right on the edge of it, but don't you go poking around down there. It's full of bad men and shady ladies. There are opium dens all around there, too. Never know what you might run into when you're in Hop Town." She raised her brows in mild reproach. "Speaking of shady ladies, I've got some of my own to run roughshod over." She chuckled and stood up, smoothing her long skirt. "I'll take that tray if you're finished."

"Yes, thanks." Justine let Kate lift the tray off her lap. "It was delicious. You've been so kind to me."

"Well, I've got my reasons." Kate shrugged one shoulder. "I couldn't turn John Henry down with him all mad at me, you know. He asked me to see to you and I did. It's that simple." Kate went to the door, then stopped and turned back to Justine. "You could find a job around town. You're good-looking. Any house would hire you." Looking down at the empty plate, Kate sighed. "You could work here, if you've a mind to. I need the business, and you'd sure bring it in." She looked up and smiled. "Think about it, honey. All you've got to do is act like you like the men who like you. You can manage that, can't you?" Without waiting for an answer, Kate slipped out the door, closing it behind her.

Justine sat statue still as a plan formed in her mind. It was a desperate plan and a dangerous one, but these were desperate, dangerous times. Closing her eyes, she saw herself executing it.

In a room like this one, she'd wait for a man to come upstairs to her. She'd fix him a drink and mix a few of those magical drops in the whiskey. He'd drink it and sleep soundly. In the morning he'd awaken to her story of what a powerful beast he'd been in bed and how she'd enjoyed him *so* much. He'd leave full of himself and with a lighter money pouch.

It could work! Justine's eyes popped open, and she had to press her lips together to keep from laughing aloud. She'd ply her dirty trade just long enough to get money together for a stagecoach ticket out of this hellhole. That shouldn't take long, she told herself. No more than a few weeks. She could hold out that long. She was a good actress. She could fool the birdbrains in this town for a few short weeks with no trouble at all!

Looking around the room, she saw her valise atop the bureau. Justine threw back the covers and sprang from bed. The night was still young, she thought, especially in Hop Town.

Her reflection made her want to hide under the covers again. She looked a sight! Hair all mussed, face as pale as a ghost's, and her poor, wrinkled, bedraggled dress! Oh, she was positively pitiful looking. Justine grabbed the hairbrush from the bureau and brushed and swirled and twisted and braided until she had tamed her thick, black hair into an upswept style leaving a few wisps to fall along the nape of her neck and at her temples. Then she washed her face and arms and feet. The cool water revived her, lending her a burst of energy. Slipping into the only other dress she owned—a dress too plain and drab for an actress, but respectable for a young wife or a woman with no imagination—Justine pinched her cheeks pink and tried on an enchanting smile, then a friendly one, and then a shy one. The shy one, she thought. She'd use shyness first, and if that didn't get her what she wanted, she'd try to enchant China Mary.

After tugging on her stockings and hose and garters and all the other coverings a lady had to wear before stepping one foot on a public street, Justine checked herself in the mirror. She gave a nod of approval, then spirited herself from the upstairs room, down the back staircase, and out the door, leaving no one the wiser.

Kate's house wasn't fancy. It was situated on Allen Street, right in the center of a row of saloons and brothels. A block over was Toughnut Street, where even more saloons and houses of ill repute stood, giving that section of town the dubious title of Rotten Row.

Moving cautiously along the sidewalk and keeping to the shadows, Justine was reminded of her adolescence in New Orleans, where she'd learned to attract attention only when she wanted it. Times had gotten better for her when she took up with Old Shoe Black, a banjo player and former slave. He made the banjo talk while Justine danced and sang and acted like she was performing on a stage in New York instead of a corner in the French Quarter. She and Old Shoe Black lived by the river in an overturned hull that nobody seemed to want anymore. Her partner taught her about the bumps in life and how to avoid them. He also pointed out that she was pretty enough to get her way if she was careful.

"Don't gib nuthin' away, whut you want to keep for yosef," Old Shoe Black had said most every night after they'd climbed underneath the ship's hull. "An' don't gib nuthin' away, whut you can't get back if'n you want it agin. Thems the rules. If'n theys broke, thems the regrets."

But she didn't understand, not until right before Old Shoe Black was taken from her. One night he explained further in a voice that sounded like distant thunder.

"Wemens got somethun special, liddle Jussie. They gots it when theys borned, an' theys gots to keeps it safe. Gots to gib it to one man they thinks should hab it. Once theys gibs it away, they can't neber gets it back. Mens ain't made that way somehow. But it's whut makes wemens special."

Blinking away the memory, Justine focused on the

light and noise spilling from nearly every doorway in Tombstone. Men wove along the sidewalk, bleary eyed and drunk. Women cackled like hens, and the stench of whiskey hung in the air, overpowering the smell of horse dung in the streets. This Wednesday night in Tombstone was as busy as a Saturday night in any other town.

"What a pigsty," she murmured, then caught sight of her destination across the street. The sign was small and tacked to the outside wall, just to one side of the swinging doors. CHINA MARY'S.

The building was two-storied and full of red light. Justine sprinted across the street and stood to the right of the doors, listening to the tinkling of piano keys and the low murmur of voices. Men. Women. A smattering of an Oriental language. She stood on tiptoe and peeked over the top of the batwing doors. The place wasn't as packed as the others had been, but China Mary's was doing a brisk business nonetheless. Twenty or thirty men milled inside, keeping the ten Oriental girls plenty busy. The two men behind the bar were Oriental as well.

Having a working knowledge of saloons, Justine went around to the back and found a door painted bright red. She knocked, hoping the decisive rapping was loud enough to demand attention. Almost before her hand fell back to her side, the door swung open and a tall, reed-thin man with slits for eyes peered down at her.

"Yes, miss? What you knock for?" His voice was as soft as a feather bed, almost feminine in the way it caressed her ears.

"China Mary," Justine blurted. "I must see her."

The Oriental man raised his hairless brows. He wore a collarless orange jacket and black silk pants and shoes. His smile was chilling.

"Who knocks, Ah Lum?" a woman asked from within.

"One demanding young girl," he answered, then

stepped back and swept an arm across his midsection. "Come," he said, still smiling. "Come, come."

Feeling as if she were walking into an elaborate jewelry box, Justine stepped inside the dimly lit room. An oil lamp glowed, muted by a red shade. Behind the lamp sat a woman, small and plump, with a wizened, painted face. She sat in a big overstuffed chair, and her feet, bound in black platform shoes, didn't touch the floor. To one side of her was a tea table, to the other a table full of strange objects —cards, saucers, spoons, tiny bottles, matchsticks, and smoking pipes. A sweet, sickening odor pervaded the room. From behind the far wall came the sounds of the saloon, muted by the carpets that hung on every wall and covered the floor.

Beyond the lamplight, Justine noticed other parlor furniture and a desk situated in one corner. Other than the thin man and this woman, Justine was alone in the red-lighted room behind the saloon.

"Come closer," the woman said, her voice high and girlish. "She not a girl, Ah Lum. She a woman. You woman, yes?"

"Yes." Justine took another hesitant step closer. "Are you China Mary?"

"Sure. Oh, sure." China Mary's face was a white moon floating in a dark sky. Her red mouth contrasted with the white makeup, her lips painted only in the center. Her eyes were lined in black, and several combs sprouted from her black, intricately styled hair. Her dress of red-and-gold satin hugged her body like a second skin. She wore not even one petticoat! Gold earrings dangled from her earlobes, and gold and rubies and emeralds sparkled on her fingers. She was a tiny woman with the presence of a giant. "And who you be?"

But before Justine could open her mouth to answer...

"Actress, perhaps? Abandoned, yes? You make believe instead of facing life, my French beauty?"

"I'm...not...French," Justine said, having to push each word out because China Mary's revelations had taken her breath away.

"Of French history," China Mary said, then looked miffed with herself. "How you say? Grandparents French? Yes, but also father. Just because you never saw face not make him vanish from earth."

"How did you...?" Justine pulled herself up, suddenly frightened and feeling woozy. "Who are you?"

"China Mary, I say." The small woman released a high-pitched giggle. "Do not fear so. I of no harm to you, Jus-*see*." She laughed at her own pronunciation. "I like," she said with another giggle. "Jus-*see*. Nice name. Sound like bird calling." She tipped back her head and crooned, "Jus-see, Jus-see, Jus-see!"

"Stop it!" Justine discovered that she was trembling, and she told herself it was from anger, not fear. "How did you know my name? Has Doc Holliday or Kate Fisher been here already?"

"You told me." She touched one long, red fingernail to her temple. "There are words not spoken, but said just the same. I hear them." She waved one hand. "Ah Lum, a chair for her. She ready to faint."

"I am not!" Justine fell into the chair Ah Lum brought forth, admitting to herself that she was a little dizzy. "I just want the truth."

"You tell me what true and what not," China Mary said. A pure white cat jumped into her lap, causing not even a startled blink from the old woman, but making Justine jump in fright. China Mary smiled and stroked the cat. It settled in her lap and closed its green eyes. "You want something from me?"

"What?" Justine pulled her gaze away from the purring creature and looked at the other, more mysterious creature. "Yes. I want something. But you seem to know everything, so why should I ask for it?"

"I cannot give what not asked for," China Mary said, her smile becoming cunning.

"Blackout drops," Justine said, surrendering since she knew China Mary would beat her in any game she cared to play. "Kate Fisher said you had them, and I need some."

"Dangerous," China Mary whispered, looking at the cat. Her long fingernails snaked through its white fur, leaving winding trails through a blanket of snow. "But you in dangerous place at dangerous time, yes?"

Justine felt her eyelids grow heavy. There was something about China Mary's voice, now not so high-pitched but instead low and musical, that made her want to curl up like the white cat and sleep.

"How much you need? One bottle?"

"Yes, that'll be enough." Justine fortified herself by sitting as straight as an ironing board. "I won't need much."

"And how you pay?"

"Pay?" Justine sighed and worked a note of pleading into her voice. "That's a problem. I was robbed, and I have no money. But if you give me the drops now, I promise to pay you in a day. No more than two days. You have my word on it."

"Word of stranger useful as kite with no string." One hand fluttered up, up, and away.

"I'll repay you,' Justine argued. "Look for yourself." She dropped her valise on the floor near China Mary. "That's all I have left in the world. If I could pay you now, I would, but as you can see I've been robbed of all my valuables."

"I see without looking." China Mary closed her eyes for a few moments, then she grunted softly and stared directly at Justine. "I give you drops, but you repay me later with favor."

"A favor?"

"Favor." She smiled, her mouth seeming abnormally narrow because of the strange way it had been painted. "I ask favor one day, and you grant it. It how I do business sometimes. Some favors worth more than gold, more than money." China Mary's eyes glittered like black jewels. "I do this because I like." She dipped her chin, nodding toward Justine. "I like Jus-see. It okay? We have deal?"

"Yes. It's a deal," Justine said, rising from the chair and extending her hand. Why not? She wouldn't be around more than a week or two, so she'd never have to worry about repaying China Mary with a favor. She realized the woman hadn't made a move to shake her hand, so she let it swing back to her side.

"So sorry," China Mary crooned. "Clasping hands never appeal to me." She flicked a glance past Justine. "Ah Lum give you drops on way out. Use carefully, Jus-see. One drop, no more. More can make man sleep forever-r-r-r." She laughed, having rolled that *r* until it sounded like a death rattle.

Justine grabbed up her valise and backed halfway across the room, loath to turn her back on the woman. When she sensed she was near the door, she whirled, took a vial from Ah Lum's cold hand, and dashed out the open door, cringing at the sound of Ah Lum's laugh and China Mary's earsplitting giggle.

The back room of China Mary's on a Saturday night was crowded and intense.

There was no loud laughter here or men trying to feel up women's skirts. No, none of that. In the back room there was faro, played with a vengeance. Two tables, ten chairs, all business.

The dealer at one of the tables was a man with burnished blond hair and robin's-egg-blue eyes. He sported no facial hair, but the hair on his head was plentiful, and many an envious glance had been cast his way during his thirty years. His complexion bordered on being ruddy but just missed, lending his skin a flushed, sun-kissed coloring. His hands had known hard work, but not lately. Square-tipped, his fingers moved lightly over the cards, displaying a grace and finesse often missing in men. When he was standing, he usually topped the other men in the room by an inch or more, being over six feet. His body was wide at the shoulder and narrow at the hips, braced by sturdy long legs and feet that could have been a size larger but weren't considered too small for a man of his proportions.

He had a smile that curled women's toes and made lesser men want to take him out and shoot him. In an age where straight, white teeth were coveted, this man had a royal flush. His smile made a fella want to loosen a few of them just to keep things even.

But he wasn't just another strutting peacock, found among most card dealers and gamblers. No, this fellow was the kind of man men liked to know because he could be counted on in a fistfight. In a town like Tombstone, the man was an asset, and China Mary was lucky to have him on the premises.

On this Saturday night he concentrated on the cards, flicking them across the table, flashing his smile to coddle the losers and buck up the winners. He was having a good night, almost forgetting that ugly scene a few days ago, the consequences of which had taken up most of his week. The townsfolk were still jittery after what had happened at the OK Corral, and who could blame them?

He jumped slightly when a hand landed on his shoulder. Twisting around, he saw that it was Bucko, one of the other dealers.

"China Mary wants you," Bucko whispered in his ear. "I'll take over for you."

"Gentlemen, I've been summoned by the lady herself," he told the card players, sliding back his chair and offering a smile of apology. "Bucko here will take my place. I assure you, I'm not taking any good luck with me, but only the bad sort. Good evening." He dipped his head, swept his coat from the back of his chair, and strode toward the door tucked in the far corner of the smoke-filled room.

Tapping it once, he opened the door and stepped inside the red room. China Mary was sitting behind her desk. Far East, the white cat, was stretched out on top of it, purring loudly. The man removed the garters from his shirtsleeves, tucked them into his pants pocket, then slipped into the jacket.

"You pretty enough, York Masters," China Mary said, waving him farther into the room. "Come and sit. I have happy news."

He obeyed, dropping into the upholstered chair and fishing a thin cigar from his vest pocket. He lit it, savored the first mouthful of smoke, then cocked a sandy brow at her.

"So? What's the happy news, Mary?"

"I found girl of your dreams, York Masters." She smiled, keeping her lips closed, as was her custom. York had never seen her teeth. At times he doubted she had any, but Ah Lum had told him once that Chinese women didn't display their teeth. The white makeup they wore made their teeth look yellow in comparison, so the women were taught as young girls to smile without parting their lips.

"The girl of my dreams?" He chuckled, shaking his head. "How's that?"

"She of French blood," China Mary said, eyes gleaming when he showed more interest. "She been here three, four days, and I keep watching eye on her. She at Big Nose Kate's."

"In business, is she?"

"Of a sort." China Mary laughed, lips sealed, body moving up and down, a high-pitched sound gurgling in her throat. "She here for sleep potion. Blackout drops, she call them."

"Is that so?" He lost interest in the cigar and leaned forward, elbows on his knees, his gaze locked on the woman's white face. "Do tell."

"She a beauty." China Mary rolled her dark eyes. "Stunning." Touching one long fingernail alongside her nose in a gesture of knowing, she nodded. "She the one. Of this, I certain. This woman the one you wait for. Answer to prayers, York Masters. She in tight place, at mercy of fate. Perfect one for your plan. I can pull strings and drop her like puppet into your lap."

York reached into his inside jacket pocket and removed several silver dollars, which he dropped, one by one, onto China Mary's desk. The sound of them clicking and tapping made Far East leap from the desktop into a chair across the room from them. "A token of my gratitude," he said.

"There something you should know about her," China Mary cautioned. "This fallen angel has interesting way of satisfying customers." She giggled, her eyes filling with tears. "Oh, yes, and she owe me favor."

York smiled, pleased by the news. "Does she now?" He mulled over what he'd heard. "Good. I'll pay her a visit, and if I like what I see, we'll call in her debt to you. Is that to your liking?"

"Yes." China Mary reached for one of the pipes in the rack on her desk. "Her name Justine Drussard, but we call her Jus-see."

York nodded. He liked the name.

Chapter 3

Thursday night at Big Nose Kate's was as quiet as a church compared to Saturday nights, when every buck with an itch from miles around hightailed it to Tombstone's Rotten Row.

York had chosen a weeknight because he wanted to make sure he'd get his pick of the girls. Standing outside the front door, he went over his plan again, rehearsing every detail as he'd done often since China Mary had told him of Jussie and her scam. He meant to catch her in her own trap.

Before announcing himself, York removed his black hat and ran the flat of his free hand alongside his head, taming his hair into its side part. He hooked one finger on the stiff, white shirt collar and pulled it away from his neck. He checked the shine of his boots, then arranged an indulgent expression on his face before yanking the bell rope. A Chinese girl opened the door, bowed, and escorted him into the main parlor without a word. He smiled and she smiled back. He knew her. He knew all the Chinese in town, and they knew that he was China Mary's

friend; that in itself afforded him respect in Tombstone.

Five women lounged on twin medallion-backed
sofas of olive green with gold tassels. The room was
dimly lighted—for good reason since a couple of
Kate's working girls weren't spring chicks, and one,
Buck-toothed Tessie, was downright ugly. Curiously,
Tessie was the most asked for. York had heard
around the gambling tables that she could do amaz-
ing things with her mouth.

Kate had her back to him. Standing at the liquor
sideboard, she sensed a newcomer and turned
slowly, an automatic smile stretching her rouged
lips, her smile becoming genuine when she recognized him. She braced her hands against the polished oak sideboard and laughed silently, her breasts
heaving up and down beneath rustling black taffeta
and stiff chiffon.

"Are my eyes playing tricks on me?" she asked,
bugging them at him. "I sure never thought I'd see
the day when *you'd* pay a visit to *my* place." Her gaze
swept him up and down and back up again in open
speculation and feminine appraisal.

"Evening, Kate." York walked his fingers around
the brim of his hat and looked toward the other
women. "I'm feeling restless tonight."

"What are you drinking?"

"Whiskey, thanks."

"What's wrong, can't China Mary keep you supplied with enough able-bodied women to suit you?"
Kate asked, pouring the liquor into a squatty glass,
then extending it toward him.

"I wanted a change," he said, moving into the
room to take the proffered drink from her. "I heard
you had a new girl, but I don't see any strangers."
He glanced at the women on the sofas again, giving
a nod of greeting. He knew them all. Tombstone was
a small town. Nobody got past him without notice.

"My new girl is over there," Kate said, jerking her

chin toward a far corner. "Take a look and take your pick. You can have more than one if you think you can handle them. Spend the whole night. It's your money, your time."

He smiled absently at Kate's sales talk, trying not to stare too obviously into the gray corner where a wing-backed chair was tucked. His gut tightened, and he squinted, trying to seek out that pale face across the room from him. Was she shy, or had she decided he wasn't worth any effort? Kate noticed his straining posture and motioned impatiently, waving the girl forward.

"Come into the light, Jussie. The man wants to get a better look at your merchandise," Kate ordered, her voice gruff.

The girl uncurled from the chair and rose like a plume of smoke, then floated into the light supplied by the twelve candles burning in the overhead chandelier. York's heart lurched when he saw that she wasn't a stranger, after all, but the one he'd shoved out of harm's way at the OK Corral. He watched for any sign of recognition, but there was none. She didn't know him from Adam. Good. He relaxed and tossed the whiskey to the back of his throat with a flourish of satisfaction.

Dove gray eyes stared boldly into his. The tipping up of her chin and the flexing of her petal-soft throat as she swallowed a knot of nerves endeared her to him. He caught his breath, then grappled for his sense of mission. Damn it, man, you're not here to court this delicate beauty! You're here to trip her up and make her do your bidding!

Sure, she looked as soft and as innocent as a baby, but he knew better. The information he'd gathered since his conversation with China Mary had dispelled any qualms he'd suffered about luring her into his trap. She could take whatever he put on her plate. An angel she wasn't.

But his stern inner lecture had no effect on the

stirring in his belly and the burning in his loins. His eyes hungered for her every enticement; the way her hair fell like glossy raven's wings past her shoulders and the swell of her breasts and hips beneath the loose, belted wrapper of dusky peach made his throat dry. Her mouth was coral pink and gracefully bowed. More than anything, he wanted her.

"I'll take her." He hardly recognized his own voice, it was so deep bodied and scratchy. A stranger's voice coming from a place inside him he couldn't control.

"Fine. Good choice. She needs a good breaking in." Kate pressed one shoulder against his and whispered, "You'll be a good match for her. So far she's just been with a couple of quick draws, if you get my drift."

York nodded. "I want her for the night." Again, that voice. That growling, throbbing voice.

"You've got her." Kate beamed and motioned Justine forward. "Take him upstairs, dearie, and be nice to him. Real nice."

Justine smiled fleetingly and sashayed toward the stairs. The scent of crushed rose petals trailed behind her. "Follow me, sir."

"York."

"York," she said, glancing back at him. For an instant her brow puckered as if his name sent an arrow of recall through her, but then it was gone, and she faced front again, taking the steps slowly and smoothly. "And I'm Jussie." On the landing she turned right and opened a door halfway down the hall. She swept inside, leaving him to close the door behind them. "Would you care for a drink?"

"Yes," he said, starting toward the bureau where a tray held bottles of whiskey and shot glasses.

"No," she said, almost leaping forward. "I'll fix it for you. You just relax." Her smile was meant to put him at ease. "Make yourself comfortable."

The furnishings were sparse. The white bedspread with pink rosebuds was incongruous, but it beckoned nonetheless. He sat on the side of the bed, unknotted his silk tie, and placed his hat on the bedside table. He shrugged out of his jacket and dropped both it and the tie onto a low bench against the wall. He noted with interest how careful she was to place her body between him and the whiskey tray so that he couldn't see her pouring his drink.

She thinks she's so clever, he thought with amusement. Well, he'd let her think she was a sly spider attracting him to her web where she would sink her poison into him. Yes, he'd let her think that for a while, and then he'd turn on her and make her *his* victim.

Justine stared at her hands, willing aside their tremor as she finished swirling the powerful drops into the amber whiskey. She recalled the two other men who had been in this room with her. Her plan had worked perfectly with them, but this man . . .

She had noticed the difference the moment he'd stepped into the downstairs parlor. She had burrowed more deeply into the shadows, sensing that he was no sex-starved miner, easily led and swiftly pleased.

Listening to the bedsprings creak, she figured he was growing impatient. She reminded herself that no harm would come to him and that she only needed a few more dollars. Not much longer, she chanted to herself, already thinking ahead to the day when she would board the stagecoach and leave Tombstone behind . . . forever.

Armed with that dream, she spun slowly to face him, drink in hand and a fetching smile on her lips, but she froze and the smile dropped away.

He'd removed his shirt while her back was turned, and his suspenders hung loosely at his sides. Her gaze locked involuntarily on his chest; smooth skin stretched across bone and muscle, and a mat of hair grew thick in the space between his flat nipples, then thinned to a narrow line at his puckered navel. Her body responded to the sight of his. Her belly muscles fluttered, and her skin tingled hotly. In another time and place she would have flirted with him, hoping to win more than just his attention. Fate was cruel to send him to her as a victim instead of a prize.

Lifting her gaze to the brilliant blue of his eyes, she felt a dull stab of remorse. With iron resolve, she extended the glass toward him, silently urging him to take it from her. She felt rotten, soiled, sinful. Not for the first time, she wondered if Tombstone had changed her . . . hardened her.

York took the drink from her, but set it to one side on the dresser. Her gaze followed the glass, so he curled a finger under her chin and brought her face around to his again. Apprehension dulled her eyes and tightened the muscles at the corners of her mouth. He ran his fingertips lightly down the column of her throat, smiling when she swallowed convulsively. He sensed her confusion, divined her struggle for control. He hooked his arm around her nipped-in waist and brought her flush up against him.

"I want to taste you before whiskey further taints my tongue," he said, and bent his head to run his lips down the neck he'd saved. Her skin was warm and smelled of roses. He licked a trail, wetting her skin and making her shiver. She tried to squirm out of his arms, but her efforts only served to inflame him.

He wrapped his other arm around her waist. She must have felt his desire because she stilled and her gray eyes collided with his blue ones. As her lips parted in surprise, York swooped to take advantage. His mouth covered hers in a hard, lusting kiss. A groan worked its way up his throat. She made a sound of protest, and her hands balled into fists at his shoulders. Then and only then did he realize he was not as in control as he thought. Desire dizzied him, drugged him, shamed him. He loosened his hold so that she could catapult from his embrace. Her eyes were wild with panic, her mouth blushed from his rogue's kiss.

"Slow down," she ordered, her husky voice breaking as if she were on the verge of choking. She ran the back of her hand across her lips and her gaze accused him. "If you're one of those men who likes to manhandle and hurt—"

"I'm not," he said, bemused by her innocence. If she thought his actions were savage, then her experience had to be minimal. "But what if I were?" he taunted. "What could you do about it?"

"I'd call for Kate." She inched up her chin in a challenge.

"And?"

"And . . . tell her that you're a brute."

He shook his head, laughing under his breath. "As long as I pay, Kate wouldn't care what I did to you, short of killing you." He gripped her upper arms and jerked her to his chest. "You've chosen a risky business, Jussie. Lucky for you, I mean you no harm, but what about the next man? He might not have a shred of kindness in him."

"Don't you want your drink?" She cut her eyes sideways, staring longingly at the glass.

He looked at the whiskey and sighed his regret, deciding to get it over with. "Right. I need a drink." He saw relief fly across her face as he lifted the glass to his lips and drank the contents. He tried to taste the added element but couldn't because the whiskey was so strong it killed any other flavor. York set the glass on the dresser again. Instantly, Justine changed her tune, snuggling close and rubbing her cheek against his chest. Her fingers teased his flat nipples, making them pucker and strain forward. She pressed a kiss to one, and York thought he might explode into a hundred pieces.

She caressed his bare back and turned her face

into the reddish gold nest of chest hair. She pressed a kiss into the very center of his chest, and he groaned deeply as his hands came up to clamp her shoulders and push her away from him. He was sure he was floating, lifting from the floor and soaring to the ceiling. He no longer felt his own body. He was a spirit. A curl of smoke. Yesterday's dream.

Justine recognized the signs. His eyes were half closed and his blue irises were rolling up, showing mostly white. His head lolled back on his neck, and his hands slipped away from her. His mouth fell open. Justine gently led him to the bed. Just as she got him positioned with his back to it, his knees buckled and he fell. The bed groaned but accepted his weight.

Justine gazed at him, disturbed by her own deluge of guilt. She'd pitied the others, but this time she felt sorry for herself. Crossing her arms against her tender breasts, she tipped her head to one side and appreciated his every perfect feature. He had the most beautiful hair she'd ever seen on a man: brassy gold, straight, and silky. He parted it on the side, and it swept across his forehead and lay in feathered layers above his ears. His sideburns weren't long, but instead were cropped shorter than the present style dictated, adding to the clean lines and close-shaven look of him. And the wicked way he used his china blue eyes—squinting with suspicion, glinting with deviltry, widening with amusement, narrowing with desire. His prowess had scared her. Remembering his rough passion, she trembled and tried to deny the heat building between her thighs.

"You *are* gorgeous," she whispered, smiling down at him and feeling that irritating tug of self-pity again. "But this is the way it has to be, I'm afraid."

She bent to her task, tugging off his boots and socks, then his trousers. Positioning him more naturally on the bed, she arranged the spread over him and only then removed his underwear, careful not to

peek beneath the bedspread as she did. Even so, she
blushed as her shaking fingers encountered satiny
flesh with the hint of heat beneath it. When she was
finally finished, she went to stand near the window,
her back to him and her eyes staring straight ahead
as she fought her own sense of shame.

Had she really thought this would be easy? she
wondered dismally. Was she so naïve that she
thought she could act like a whore, dupe strange
men, take their money, and not feel dirty for doing
it? Maybe if she were a woman like Kate Fisher, with
no integrity, no sense of fairness, it would be easy as
pie, but she was a woman of honor and ideals. Stealing, lying, and cheating were disgusting to her, and
pretending to be a woman of ill repute wasn't her
idea of a challenging role.

Those poor men, she thought, closing her eyes as
tears welled behind her lids. They came to this place
for companionship, and were given a vile potion that
made them pass out cold before they received even a
proper kiss. Only to be lied to in the morning and
told they'd gotten their money's worth.

"I'm leaving tomorrow...somehow...some
way," she whispered, then moved quickly to the
bureau. She opened the top drawer and took out a
knotted handkerchief. Untying it, she counted the
coins inside. Not enough for a stagecoach ticket, but
maybe she could find a man with a wagon or buggy
who would be willing to take her to Tucson for a
dollar or two. "I must try," she whispered aloud. "I
can't do th-this any longer. I just c-can't!"

The man on the bed stirred and mumbled something. Justine spun around, her heart in her throat,
her breath held captive in her tight chest. She
waited, watching the man warily and wondering
what she'd do if he awakened now. But he didn't
move again, and his breathing was slow and deep.

Justine put the money and handkerchief back into
the drawer and covered it up with the other linens,

then she closed the drawer quietly and turned to face the man again. Slowly, hesitatingly, she moved closer.

He looked vulnerable in repose. Enchanted by the way his lower lip protruded ever so slightly, Justine bent forward for a better look. She could count his dark blond lashes and the scattering of freckles along the bridge of his nose. She swayed even closer, indulging a flash of feminine fancy.

She kissed his soft and pliant mouth. His lips parted, so she slipped her tongue inside, touched his slick teeth and then dampened his lips with her own. He tasted of whiskey, and his skin had a spicy fragrance that stirred her, made her want to snuggle closer. Her lips trailed across his rigid jawline, down his neck, over his shoulder.

This place had made her bold, she thought, rubbing her mouth upon his again and loving the shield of control. This must be what it feels like to be a man, she thought. To render another powerless, to put yourself first and not even consider the other at all. But she inched away, suddenly finding the act distasteful. She knew how it felt on the receiving end—to writhe with discomfort, to cry out with fury, to succumb not to the man, but to the law of nature that the weak shall be crushed by the strong.

The weak shall inherit the earth, she recited in her mind, shaking her head slowly. Not in her lifetime. Tombstone was a glaring example of how untrue that biblical prophecy was in this age. Blood dotted every street corner. Power was found in the fastest draw or in the most wicked person. The weak and honorable hid in their homes after dark and dared not look anyone in the eye in the daylight.

So she could not take enjoyment from these moments of superiority. While his slack mouth was a temptation, his defenselessness offended her.

Justine went to the window and sat in the chair near it, training her eyes on the dark sky and wishing for morning. Her lids became lead weights, and her thoughts as thin and flighty as the clouds racing across the moon.

She dreamed of Old Shoe Black, lying on a heap of rubble beside the great Mississippi, his grizzled head crimson, his eyes milky with death. He had died for her, died to save her from those who had wanted to break her, brutalize her, and brand her a grown woman before her time. While she slept, tears stained her cheeks and she sobbed softly, world-wearily.

York stirred restlessly, his head pounding, his ears picking up the sound of a frightened or wounded animal... far off, far away. He turned his cheek into coolness and rubbed his scratchy whiskers against it. Gradually, he became aware of a terrible taste in his mouth. Cotton doused with bitterweed? He made a smacking noise, testing his tongue. It stuck to the roof of his mouth. He grimaced and forced one eye open.

A sledgehammer of light drove into his eye, and he shut it again. He moaned as pain ricocheted through his head. He decided not to move. Not ever.

But that blamed animal whimpered again, and curiosity superseded York's paining head. He pried his eye open again. The light speared him, but he persevered and opened the other eye. Fluttering, lacy draperies reached out and caressed his hot face, then fell back against the window ledge with a contented sigh.

Releasing a gut-burning groan, he sat bolt upright and stared bleary-eyed at the unfamiliar room. God, what had happened to him? Was he still in Tombstone? Had someone found him out? He blinked aside the blur, making his eyes focus enough to see the woman slumped in the chair near the other window. Who the hell...?

His memory caught up with him, zigzagging into his brain like lightning.

"Ah, yes," he whispered to himself. "Dear, deceiving Jussie." A smile stole across his face as he swung his legs over the side of the bed, then stared down at himself with numbing surprise. "Well, I'll be damned. She stripped me naked." His gaze bounced back to her, this time tinged with admiration. The little liar had gall. His grin came back as his thoughts skipped ahead to what lay in store. Morning had broken. It was his turn to pounce. Yes, ma'am, he thought with a growling chuckle, every dog has its day, and this one has my name on it.

He located his underwear, pulled it on, and then donned his trousers before padding barefoot over to her. Jussie sat sideways, her legs brought up so that her cheek rested on her knees. She'd made a loop of her arms around her legs, and her fingers were knitted together, hanging against her ankles. Her hair spilled across her legs like a shadow, leaving her face exposed to the pinkish light of morning.

What bad dreams had pulled her mouth into such a mighty frown? And were those the tracks of tears on her face?

York ran the back of his forefinger down her downy cheek. Regret burrowed into his heart, making him look askance for a few moments while he reminded himself why he'd come to this place for this particular woman. He needed her. Desperately. And his desperation was born from his heart, not his loins.

He pushed his fingers through the side of her hair, curled his fingers around the black ropes of it, and brought her head back sharply. Her eyes opened in alarm, and she released a startled cry. York kissed her flush on the mouth, then let her witness his beaming smile.

"Good morning. I don't know about you, but my head is killing me. Why are you in this chair? Did I kick you out of bed? I admit, I don't recall much of last night."

He admired her recovery; cunning swiftly replaced surprise.

"Good morning to you, handsome." Her voice was as sweet and thick as maple syrup. She uncurled from the chair to stand before him, gripping his wrist and pulling his hand from the tangle of her hair. "You don't remember? Why, I'm insulted!" Her mouth formed a pretty pout. "You were an animal, honey. A beast! I've never been in bed with a man more powerful, more masterful!" She swayed forward, and he caught her by the shoulders. "Honey, you were a raging bull last night, and I loved every minute of it."

"Then why did you sleep in the chair?"

"The chair?" Her mask slipped ever so slightly. "You were thrashing around after you finally dropped off, and I decided to let you have the bed. I wasn't that sleepy anyway." She smiled and rested her hands flat against his chest. "I was tired—you wore me out—but I was too *blissful* to sleep. I guess I dozed off just before dawn." She sighed and closed her eyes for a moment, then moved so quickly that she was out of his grasp and across the room before he could make a grab for her. "Y'all come back any old time, honey, and be sure to ask for me. Y'hear?" She tossed him a come-hither glance over her shoulder. "I hate to bring up business, but we need to square your bill. All night, that's—"

"Since I had such a good time last night, how about a repeat performance this morning?"

"Wh-what?" That spun her around to face him again, her mouth hanging open, at a loss for words.

"Another go-round," York said, taking two long strides. He slipped his arms around her waist and hauled her close, then bent to nuzzle the sweet-smelling skin of her neck. "I'll pay double. Come on, sweet thing. Take this off"—he pushed the wrapper off one shoulder, exposing gardenia-petal skin—"and let me see you in the morning light."

"I . . . no, I can't."

"Sure you can, and so can I." He grinned, loving the charade and her blooming panic. "You can be on top. Did we do that last night?"

"No . . . I mean, I've got other . . . I'm not working now." Her voice rose an octave, and she pushed at his shoulders, no longer the seductive vixen. "Rules of the house. Now, let me go."

"Don't worry." He gathered handfuls of her ebony hair and held her head securely, making her wince when he gave a tug. "Kate will gladly bend the rules if the price is right, and I'm willing to pay whatever I must for you. This time I won't drink. I'll be clearheaded. I'll remember *everything*." He took her mouth, driving his tongue between her lips, punishing her with swift, uncaring strokes that made her gurgle on her fury. She squirmed, then gave a closed-throated cry when he yanked her hair. He ended the kiss only when it suited him. "Now, take this off and make it quick. I'm ready for you." He untangled one hand from her hair, gripped her wrist, and brought her hand against him. "Feel that? It's all yours."

Justine gasped and jerked free, her face crimson with embarrassment and seething anger. Her lips trembled. Tears lent a brilliance to her gray eyes.

"How dare you!" She was so furious she could hardly speak. Her voice was hoarse with self-righteous anger. "*I* decide when, where, and with whom, and you've had your time with me. Get out before I have you thrown out!" She extended one arm, pointing a shaking finger at the door.

The order incensed him. York caught her wrists and forced her hands behind her, holding her prisoner. "Understand this—I'm dealing the cards from here on in, Ma'm'selle Drussard."

"What?" She grew still, staring wide-eyed into his face. "How did you know—"

"That's right. I know your name. I know a lot about you. I know you didn't bed me last night. You slipped some knockout drops in my whiskey, and I'm not the first man you've duped." He whirled her around, twisting one of her arms behind her and keeping her immobile against him by clamping his other arm across her shoulders. "Be still!" he ordered, blasting the side of her face with his hot breath. "The game is over, Jussie. I've got friends in high places. The sheriff, Doc Holliday, the Earp brothers. All I have to do is tell them what you've been up to and you'll find yourself in a jail cell for a very long time."

"Let go of me," she said through gritted teeth. "You can't prove a thing! You're just talking through your hat."

"If you don't do exactly as I say, you'll find out how wrong you are." He fondled her breast. "I own you from this moment on, unless you'd rather waste away in a prison."

Much to his surprise, she tipped back her head and screamed at the top of her lungs. It seemed to take the roof off. Cursing, he glued a hand over her mouth, cutting the scream short.

"You stupid little—"

The door popped open, and Kate Fisher blew in like an ill wind. Before York could blink, she had rested the tip of a revolver against his right temple.

"Let go of that girl or kiss your ass good-bye."

"Kate, listen to me. This little hellcat drugged me last night before I could even get undressed and now she wants me to pay her." York cut his eyes sideways to examine the pearl-handled Colt. Justine took advantage of his preoccupation to escape his hold.

"He's lying," she said, slipping behind Kate.

"He better be, 'cause if you've been doping my customers, you're in big trouble, missy." Kate sent

Justine a murderous glare. "I run a clean house, you know that." She looked at York again. "And so do you. If either of you point the law in my direction, I'll tell John Henry and he'll fill you full of holes." She pressed her face close to York, keeping the gun steady at his head. "Doc Holliday would lay down his life for me if it came to that, so don't think he wouldn't send you straight to hell if I asked it of him."

"And China Mary would do the same for me," York said smoothly, staring straight ahead at a water spot on the opposite wall. "So put that gun away."

Time slipped by as Kate Fisher sized up the situation. China Mary's name had given her pause and altered her decision on how to handle the problem. Finally, she sighed and lowered the gun.

"I want you out of here, and I don't want you coming around my place again. I don't need your kind of business."

"Let's talk about this. I'm sure we can find some —hey!" He looked over the top of Kate's head, then quickly around the room. "She's gone, damn it all!"

Downstairs a door slammed. Kate shrugged and flung out her hands in a futile gesture.

"Long gone, I hope. Now it's your turn. I've got a feeling you came here to do something more than just scratch an itch." She held up a hand to silence him. "And I don't want to hear about it." She turned her palm up and wiggled her fingers. "I believe you owe this establishment a night's fee?"

"But she drugged me! I didn't get anything but a headache, and I'm sure as hell not paying for it."

Kate stared holes through him, her mouth set in stubborn lines. "Pay up," she snapped.

"To hell, you say." York reached past her for his shirt and tie. Frustration writhed in his gut and he was in no mood to be browbeaten by a whore. He struggled to keep his voice low and emotionless.

"Kate, believe me, you don't want to get on my bad side."

Examining the ruthlessness in his expression, Kate backed away, giving him a clear path to the door.

He dressed hurriedly and carelessly, throwing on his shirt and jacket and stuffing his tie and personal articles into his pockets.

"You came here just to get her, didn't you?" Kate asked, watching his every move.

"Maybe."

"Who are you, York Masters?" she asked, folding her arms at her waist but keeping the Colt in plain sight.

He started for the door, stuffing his shirttail into his waistband as he went. "Somebody you don't want to tangle with." He stopped long enough to deliver a look that could melt iron. "You just keep this whole thing quiet, and you won't have any worries. If I hear that you've been sounding my name, I'll make your life a living hell. You follow?"

She nodded, swallowing hard. When he was gone and she heard the front door slam shut behind him, Kate Fisher slumped onto the bed and released a low whistle. She was mighty glad not to be in Jussie's shoes.

Chapter 4

Crouched between two pickle barrels behind Tombstone's general store, Justine caught her breath and took stock of her current situation. An expression of despair covered her face as one layer of bad luck fell upon another.

No money. No job. No clothes. Nowhere to stay. No one to care.

"Damn him," she whispered, blaming the hateful man who had brought all this bad fortune upon her head. Who was he anyway? How had he known about her? she wondered, balling her hands into fists of frustration. Just when things were going her way, he had to ruin everything.

"What's with this town?" she asked, throwing back her head in a plea. The patch of sky visible between the buildings made her yearn for freedom. Melancholy stole through her. Tombstone, she thought with an aching sigh. Was it to be her epitaph? All she wanted was to see the last of it, but it and its inhabitants had a stranglehold on her, keeping her against her will. Drawing up her knees, she rested her forehead on them and tried to think of a way out of town. She wouldn't get far with no money and nothing on her back except a dressing gown.

Would Kate let her get her things and her money? she wondered, but she knew that was improbable. Kate Fisher wasn't the kind of woman to relent once she had somebody at a disadvantage.

Surely, there was someone in this dusty excuse for a town who would give her a helping hand without expecting her life or her honor in return. Some kind soul who'd take pity—

"China Mary?" she wondered aloud.

The queen of Hop Town wasn't exactly a kind soul, but she might give her a job. She hadn't been mean before, just odd. Being in the theater business, Justine had learned to deal with all forms of human oddities. If she stumbled over to the woman's place, bedraggled, crying, and jabbering a story about how she was raped and thrown out by Kate Fisher without her clothes or her hard-earned money, China Mary might be persuaded to help her get back on her feet.

"What have I got to lose?" Justine asked herself. She couldn't stay squeezed between two pickle barrels all day and night. She wrinkled her nose, catching a strong whiff of vinegar and spices.

Getting her bearings before darting from her smelly hiding place, Justine hurried down the back streets and alleys to Hop Town. China Mary's was closed up as tight as a clam, so Justine went around to the back and pounded on the red door as she'd done before.

Ah Lum opened it a crack, pressed one eye to the narrow space, then opened the door all the way.

"She wait for you," Ah Lum said, motioning her inside.

"She . . . who?" Justine asked, entering the cool room. She gave the towering spindle of a man a wide berth. "Do you remember me? I'm—"

"China Mary know you. You sit. I tell her you finally here." He went to a curtained wall, pushed the heavy tapestries aside, and disappeared behind them.

Justine eased onto a footstool, ready to spring up and make a run for it if things turned worse for her. What was Ah Lum talking about? China Mary couldn't be expecting her. Stupid man. She wouldn't be surprised if he was simple-minded, probably since birth and—Her unkind thoughts were shattered when the heavy draperies moved. They parted and China Mary passed through, resplendent in topaz and gold brocaded satin. Ah Lum followed two steps behind her. The dramatic entrance threw Justine for a moment, then she remembered that she was supposed to be forlorn and near hysterics.

Tears sprang to her eyes, and she made her lower lip tremble. "Oh, China Mary! I hate to bother you, b-but I had nowhere else t-to turn!" She clasped her hands in a beseeching gesture. "It's terrible . . . wh-what he tried to d-do to me!"

China Mary's white face was an impenetrable mask. Her expression wasn't unpleasant, but neither was it encouraging. With mincing steps she went to the chair behind her desk. Ah Lum helped her into it, then stood behind her, a dark column with glittering eyes lurking just over China Mary's shoulder. A protective shadow.

The Oriental woman's movements were precise, calculated. Her shoulders didn't touch the high back of the chair. Instead she sat erect, alert, in charge of the room and its occupants. China Mary crossed her arms and her chubby hands disappeared into the sleeves of her otherwise form-fitting dress. She said nothing. The silence was broken only by the ponderous ticking of a clock.

"Excuse the way I look," Justine said when the silence roared too loud in her ears. She smoothed the wrinkles in the inadequate dressing gown and frowned at the flimsy carpet slippers on her feet. "I had to run for my life. I was at Big Nose Kate's and a horrible man tried to hurt me. He was big and brutal. I left my money and my possessions and..." Justine let the rest fade, seeing that China Mary was unmoved by her dramatic story. "Don't you believe me? Don't you care? Of course, there isn't any reason why you should care about me, but I was hoping you'd take pity on a poor, downtrodden girl and give me some work."

"Here?" China Mary asked, her lips barely moving. "You work here?"

"That would be wonderful. I don't care how much I'm paid. I need a place to sleep and some food."

"No can do."

The white cat jumped up on the desktop and crouched at China Mary's elbow. His purring almost drowned out the ticking of the clock. New tears stung Justine's eyes, but these were genuine. She had no earthly idea what she'd do outside this room. She could throw herself on the mercy of the sheriff, she supposed, but what would that accomplish? She'd seen enough of this town to know that the sheriff was little better than the outlaws he rousted from the gaming halls.

She hadn't realized she'd stood up and was turning away from the other woman until China Mary's voice reached out and grabbed her.

"Where you going, Jus-see?"

Justine looked down at her pitiful scuffs and tears dropped off her cheeks. It had been a long time since she'd felt such desperation, so bereft of hope. Not since the day when Shoe Black... Shaking her head to erase the memory, Justine released a moaning sigh. "You said you wouldn't help me."

"Didn't say that. Said no can hire you for my place." China Mary nodded toward the wall shared by the saloon. "Only Oriental girls work here."

"Couldn't you make one exception?" Justine

waved her hand to stop China Mary's negative response. "I don't have to work in the saloon. I could be your maid. I could cook, clean, whatever you need done." She moved closer to rest her hands on the edge of the desk. She sought out China Mary's deep-set eyes. "I have no one else to turn to in this town. Please, you must help me. Can't you give me something to wear and a little money? Just enough money for a ticket out of this town. I'm begging you."

"One so pretty should not beg," China Mary said smoothly, then reached out to stroke the cat. "You not like working for me."

"Yes, I would."

"My girls do as I ask or they"—her gaze flicked up and down like the movement of a whip—"regret," she said, purring the word like a big Siamese cat. "You no soiled dove. You say you soiled dove, but you just low-flying one. Flying low to ground because spirits are sinking." Her hand soared over the top of the desk, banking right and left along an S-shaped route. "But you not low enough to get soiled."

"That's why I had to run away from Kate Fisher's," Justine said, trying for a little sympathy. "I couldn't go through with it. But this man tried to take me against my will, and Kate was all for it! I ran for my life, but where can a woman alone go? I thought you might—"

"No more, please," China Mary interrupted. "I busy woman. No time for make-up stories." She made a sweeping gesture. "You see stage here, girlie? No stage. No act."

"I'm not . . ." The rest died, withered by China Mary's flinty glare. Justine shrugged. "I don't care what you think. A man *did* try to rape me."

China Mary made a disparaging sound. "In pleasure palace, no such thing. What you do to him first? No need answer. I know." She touched a red nail to her temple. "I know all. You sit. Me and you got business."

"Business?" Justine asked, sitting on the low stool again. "What business?"

"The favor." China Mary slipped her hands into her full sleeves, and her lips tipped up at the corners. Her mouth appeared impossibly narrow, since only the center was colored by red rouge. "You owe me."

"But you just told me that you don't want me to work."

"Yes, but I want favor repaid."

Justine shrank back, not liking the sound of that. China Mary was solemn, almost ominous. The cat rolled onto his back and waved his feet in playful abandon. Receiving no attention for his coquettish act, he righted himself and jumped off the desk. China Mary never blinked, never took her eyes from Justine.

Clearing her throat nervously, Justine fingered the ends of the sash circling her waist. "I can't imagine what kind of favor I can do for you. I have no money, no possessions."

"What I want, you have."

"What's that?" Justine asked, almost against her will. She wasn't sure she wanted the answer.

"Your time." China Mary's eyes glittered darkly, like ebony struck by sunlight. "You can afford, yes?"

"I suppose," Justine said slowly, uneasy in the velvet-lined trap. What was this painted woman up to? Paying back a favor couldn't be so easy, especially when one was paying a woman like China Mary.

"I got friend," China Mary said, her lips tipping up at the corners again. "I want you to spend few minutes with friend."

"And do what?"

"Talk. Listen." Her shoulders moved up and down. "That all. Easy, yes?"

"Too easy." Justine knitted her brows, disturbed by Ah Lum's cagey smile and China Mary's simple request. "What else is involved?"

"That all. Just talk. Just listen."

"When? Where?"

"Now. Here." She jabbed a lacquered nail at the ceiling. "Upstairs."

Justine looked up, wondering what awaited her. "Is your friend male or female?"

"You find out quick enough."

China Mary picked up a fan, spread it out, and looked over the top of it. The fan had a scene of pagodas, peacocks, and . . . Justine narrowed her eyes and leaned forward for a closer inspection. Was that? Yes, it was, she answered herself. In the foreground of the lavishly detailed picture, a couple copulated in a field of exotic flowers. The woman was on top. Justine sat back, rolling her eyes and feeling again like a bird mired in black gumbo. China Mary laughed, her low chuckle grating on Justine's already raw nerves.

"You go with Ah Lum. He take you upstairs. I busy here." China Mary was suddenly all impatience and bristling orders.

"But who is it? What am I—hey!" She jerked her elbow from Ah Lum's clawlike fingers. "Don't handle me! I've had enough of being pushed around by men."

"You go," China Mary ordered. "You pay debt. No questions. You go." Her expression was shuttered, and Justine knew it was useless to argue or object.

Ah Lum opened the door leading into the saloon and gave her an arched look. Justine puffed out a gust of breath and moved as nobly as possible across the room and out the door. She felt vulnerable and foolish in her inappropriate frock.

The spindly man escorted her up the back stairs to the second floor. He showed her to a room that had a gold door and was flooded with sunlight.

"Wait here," he said in that soft, feminine voice.

"For how long?" Justine demanded, but Ah Lum closed the door on her question. She was relieved, although she felt like a prisoner.

The bed was a four-poster, the two chairs upholstered in gold satin. A black-lacquered Oriental screen provided a place to dress unseen. Justine sat in one of the chairs and drummed her fingers on the polished arms. Her mind whirled as she considered her options, the possibilities, China Mary's peculiar request.

A friend. Talk. Listen. That's all.

"Something stinks," Justine whispered to herself. "What's she up to? What kind of trap is this?"

She looked around, trying to find something amiss, but her nerves were all tingly and made her mind wander. Jittery, she twisted in the chair, unable to sit still. Was this where China Mary's girls plied their trade? Justine sighed with agitation, wishing she could find a room in Tombstone that wasn't part of a brothel.

The sound of footsteps made her rigid with dread. Justine held her breath as the footfalls sounded closer until they boomed like twin cannons. The heavy feet stopped outside the gold door, and the porcelain knob rattled, then turned. The door swung in on oiled hinges. Justine's fingernails bit into her palms and her heart hammered her temples. York's familiar, cocky grin sent shivers along her arms and down her spine.

"You!" Justine bolted to her feet and dashed forward, hoping to take him by surprise and knock him off balance, but he stepped neatly into her path. Anticipating her next move, he caught her wrists before she could land any blows.

"I hate you," she cried. He laughed and she spit in his face.

With a growl of fury, he flung her backward,

sending her sprawling across the bed. She stared at him, regretting her impulsive action as she watched his face contort with rage.

Now you've done it, she thought as a stab of fear penetrated her protective armor of fury. He'll kill you for sure now, you numbkull.

His hands trembled as he removed a handkerchief from his pocket and dabbed at the saliva on his face. Never releasing her from his vengeful gaze, he replaced his handkerchief, then propped his fists on his hips, holding his jacket back in a pose that spoke of casual superiority.

"Why don't you leave me alone?" Justine asked, angry at the whine in her voice. "Please, just let me go. All I want is to leave Tombstone. That's all I want."

"Fine with me. I'll gladly pay for your coach passage."

She sat up and smoothed the long robe over her legs, covering herself from his unrelenting stare. "Sure you will," she said, tossing off a sneering smile. "And what do I have to do for it? Lick your boots?"

"Do as I ask, and you'll go free."

The bastard. In a town full of them, he was the reigning king, she thought.

"You've followed me all over town just to get under my skirts?" She shook her head. Anger grew inside her like jimsonweed, wrapping around her heart and climbing up her throat to choke her. Weariness mixed with futility, and she was barely aware of the hot tears falling down her cheeks or the tremor coursing through her body as she found her feet.

"All right!" she screamed at him, arms held out from her sides in stiff submission. "Jump on me and get it over with! But let me tell you something." She thrust her face close to his. "You can take me, but you'll never own me." With one slow step back, she squared her shoulders and lifted her chin in a gallant gesture. "So, hurry up. Just don't expect any cooperation from me. Frankly, I'd rather be bedded by a rutting goat."

His expression never changed throughout her tirade, but when she'd finished, one corner of his mouth twitched. He pursed his lips to keep the grin at bay. "Frankly, so would I." He arched a sardonic brow at her gasp of injured pride. "I don't want to bed you, I want to talk to you. So, have a seat and pay attention."

She measured his degree of seriousness, then sat in one of the chairs, pulled her wrapper more tightly around her, and waited to hear him out.

York paced in front of her. Elegant in a pin-striped suit and charcoal vest, he cut a fine figure. Goes to show you can't judge a present by its wrapping paper, she observed wryly. She'd met her share of bizarre men, but he took the prize. Following her all over town just to talk!

He stopped pacing to fish a thin cigar from his vest pocket. He lit it, dropped the burned match into a flower vase on the bureau, then leveled his dark blue gaze on Justine.

"You're an actress."

"Yes." It wasn't a question, but she'd felt compelled to answer.

"Then you're used to being an outsider."

"Y-yes," she said, drawing out the word.

"And you know by now that Tombstone isn't just another town. It's not like Tucson or Phoenix or even Bisbee. It's like a weasel, small and mean."

"I'll go along with that, " she agreed readily.

"And you want to leave this small, cruel outpost."

"Exactly."

"And so you shall," he said evenly.

"I'm ready. When's the next coach?"

"But first you have a debt to pay." He drew long and lazily on the cigar, sending up a single curl of blue smoke. His lean cheeks caved in and relaxed as he struggled to get the cigar going.

"What debt? Are you talking about me owing China Mary?"

"You owe me."

"Ha!" Her bark of laughter was brittle. "I don't even know you, so I sure can't owe you."

"You drugged and cheated me," he reminded her, his tone polite and even-timbred, although his eyes had grown icy.

"That's what *you* say. I'll tell the sheriff that you're a lousy lover and a liar. I'll tell him you tried to beat me and make me do unspeakable things. I can make him believe anything," she said, squaring her shoulders in a show of pride. "I'm an actress."

The cigar had gone out and he flung it aside. He moved with the speed and power of a cougar. Before Justine could fathom his next move, his hands clamped on the chair arms, and she was his prisoner. His nose was a mere inch from hers. His lips pulled back in a snarling semblance of a smile.

"And we both know the kind of woman who becomes an actress, don't we? Ask anybody and they'll tell you those theater people are trash. Actresses are nothing but flashy whores."

"No!" She moved to strike him across the face, but he was quicker. He gripped her wrists painfully and pinned her arms to her sides. "Stop. You're hurting me," she complained.

"Sheriff Behan happens to be a friend of mine, along with the marshals and one of the most important men in this town, Doc Holliday. Now Doc isn't too pleased that you took advantage of his and Kate's good nature by doping Kate's customers and then lying through your teeth about it. No, ma'am." He shook his head. "They aren't happy about that at all."

She wiggled and whimpered when his fingers threatened to crush the delicate bones in her wrists.

"Sit still and listen," he commanded, and she had no choice but to obey. "You're in hot water up to your pretty neck. You know that?"

"Yes."

"The sheriff and the Earps are still sore at you for getting in the way the other day at the OK Corral. If I hadn't knocked you to one side, you'd be as dead as great-grandpa's pee pistol."

"You!" She sucked in her breath, her gaze running over the golden head and then locking on the blue eyes. This was the man who had rescued her! She frowned as another thought pricked like a thorn. *This* was her knight in shining armor. She sighed. So much for flights of fancy.

"Yes, it was me. Are you going to thank me, or didn't your mother teach you any manners?"

She started to tell him her mother was incapable of teaching her anything as highfalutin as a lady's manners, but she decided the less he knew about her past the better. She shrugged, unwilling to bestow on him even the simplest expression of gratitude.

"No manners," he said. "That's what I thought. Theater people." The last was meant as a slur.

"What do you know about theater people, you pompous, self-important blackmailer?" she flung at him, anger rising in her like bile. "You're no better than us. We're all on the bottom rung. So you've rubbed elbows with the lawmen in this pigsty. So what? If I show them a little ankle and jiggle my breasts under their noses, they'll be my friends, too."

"Go on, then!" He hauled her to her feet and pushed her roughly toward the door. "The jail cell is ready, and the sheriff and his deputies will be more than willing to take turns humping you. Go on!"

She leaned against the door and rubbed her stinging wrists, but his version of what awaited her outside the room chained her to it. When he glared at her, she shook her head and tears flew from her eyes.

"What's keeping you? Vamoose," he ordered, shooing her with one hand.

"No, I . . . what is it you want from me?" She swallowed hard, amazed she could force the words past the lump in her throat.

He came closer, took her wrists gently in his hands, and lifted them to inspect the angry red marks he'd put there. Then he led her to the chair and pushed her down onto it.

"I'm York Masters."

She nodded.

"I'm a faro dealer here at China Mary's."

"Why am I not surprised?" she mocked.

"But not just a faro dealer," he went on as if she hadn't taunted him.

"No?"

"No."

She hated to think what else he might be. A slave trader? An opium peddler? To what other vile, horrible work did he lay claim?

He crossed the room and opened the closet door. As he bent over to rummage through the shoes and other items on the floor beneath the rack of shirts and suits, realization dawned and Justine sat straighter.

This was his room!

Seeing it from a new perspective, she noticed for the first time the scent of lime and sandalwood hanging in the air and the reading material stacked on the table next to her. She craned around to examine the spines and was shocked to find that they were leather-bound volumes of Shakespeare, Dickens, and Hawthorne. Further inspection produced more surprises; a pipe stand and ashtray on the bedside table (why hadn't she noticed those before?), three stylish hats swinging from a tree (one black derby, one pearl gray cowboy hat, and a similar

one in black beside it), and shaving utensils beside
the pitcher and bowl on the lavatory stand (she must
have been blind not to have noticed those!).

His room. His room at China Mary's. What was
the relationship between them? she wondered. Was
he intimate with the Oriental boss lady or just one of
her faithful employees? Justine sensed that his connection went deeper than simple employment, but
she couldn't imagine him as the woman's lover.

"Here it is." He straightened and backed out of
the closet. His hair was mussed and he raked one
hand through it, pushing it off his brow. He held out
a leather wallet, then flipped it open to reveal a
square of thick white paper with some official black
letters printed on it. "Can you read?"

"Of course." She sent him a stinging glance before
returning her attention to the card housed in the
leather wallet. Her lips moved as she started reading, but she stopped midway and her gaze flew to
catch his. He was smiling.

"What's this?" she asked, taking the leather case
from him and not believing her eyes.

"You said you could read," he rejoined smoothly.

"You're a . . . that is, you're with . . ." She looked at
the card again and read aloud, "Pinkerton Detective
Agency." She shoved the wallet back into his hand.
"Impossible!"

Chapter 5

Pocketing the identification, York regarded her curiously. He chuckled to himself at her flat refusal to accept his credentials. She wouldn't even look at him, preferring to stare sideways at the sunlight pouring through the sheer curtains.

"Why impossible?" he asked, dropping to his haunches in front of her, making it doubly difficult to be ignored.

"Because..." She glanced at him, then away. "You, a private detective?" She wrinkled her perfectly shaped nose in derision. "What a crazy notion. You think I've never heard of Pinkerton? Well, I have." This last she said with quiet authority, as if it answered all the questions in the universe.

"Good for you." He propped his hands on his knees, his arms akimbo, and let his sarcasm sink in. He knew it had when she set her full lips in a line of reproof.

"They wouldn't hire a two-bit card dealer. Detective work is dangerous. It takes brains," she explained, as if he had none. "Men who work for Pinkerton are the cream of the crop." Her next glance was insulting. "You are hardly that."

"And *you* are hardly an expert." He exchanged insulting glares with her, but his had more power behind it. She looked away first. "Just what do you know about me?" he demanded. When she didn't speak, but instead sat stubbornly before him, lips pressed into a straight, stern line, he raised his voice to get a reaction from her. "I asked you a question, woman!"

It worked. She jumped nearly a foot before her startled gaze locked on him. Her composure slipped back into place with effort.

"I know you're not a gentleman," she returned primly. He laughed and she threw daggers with her eyes. "Pinkerton men don't go around telling everybody that they're detectives." She crossed her arms haughtily. "They wouldn't be *private* detectives if they announced themselves all over town, would they?"

"Since when are you, China Mary, and Doc Holliday *everyone?*" he asked with a jeer. "There goes your theory. Want to try another?"

"Why tell me?"

"Because you're in *my* camp now."

"Why me?" She leaned back, uneasy and wary of him.

"Now we're getting somewhere," he said with satisfaction. "I take it you do believe I'm with Pinkerton?"

"Not entirely," she admitted. "That card in your pocket's probably a fake. I met a man once who carried a card that said he was an English earl, but he was nothing but a broom salesman from Charlotte."

He bowed his head to hide his smile, but when he looked up again the remnants of it glistened in his eyes. "I don't know what to do to prove it." His voice was lighter, more friendly. "I've been with the agency for five years. I was headed to law school when I was sidetracked by Pinkerton. I decided to become a detective instead of a lawyer. Not as much money, but infinitely more interesting."

"Not to mention more dangerous," she added. Folding her hands in her lap, she stared down at them, her wing-shaped brows inching together in a fretful line. "How come you're dealing cards in a place like this?"

"It's my cover. You're not the only one with an act." His teasing grin was there and gone. "And if you tell anyone outside this room that I'm not a shiftless card shuffler, I'll send you packing—to a federal prison," he tacked on when her face lit up with joy. She frowned mightily at him. "Like it or not, you're under my thumb." He illustrated this by balancing one thumb on his bent knee. "Cross me and I'll squash you." He ground his thumb slowly into his knee and bared his teeth with savage satisfaction. "Understand?"

She nodded jerkily. Shiny beads of perspiration dotted her forehead, caused by an outbreak of nerves. "What's your real name?"

"I told you, York Masters." He stood up, towering over her. He was so tall that he made her feel miniscule. "And you are Justine Drussard, struggling actress, dumped here in Tombstone penniless, homeless, and hopeless."

Not caring much for his description, she pulled the sides of her dressing gown closer together, lapping them more securely, and shifted onto one hip as if confronting him was too uncomfortable.

"You are of French blood, deserted by your father when you were an infant and on your own at an early age. You lived on the streets and by your wits like a—"

"How do you know that about me?" she demanded, her gray eyes glassy with grief. "How could you possibly know those things?"

"I'm a detective," he reminded her. He stuck his thumbs into his vest pockets, his long, blunt-ended fingers dangling across the watered silk. "And I'm a careful man. I don't buy a pig in a poke. I investigate first and then make my purchase."

"You have not bought me," she stated emphatically. "You haven't enough money, I assure you."

"Money has nothing to do with it. I've given you a choice; prison or me. I believe you chose me, am I right?"

She didn't answer, but instead just glared at him.

"Am I right?" he repeated loudly.

"Yes," she hissed. "And you needn't shout. I'm not deaf!"

"Just dumb, huh?"

That did it. She bolted from the chair and flung herself toward the door, shoulders back and arms swinging. But when she would have jerked open the door in a dramatic sweep, it wouldn't budge. Locked. She hadn't seen him do that. Sighing, she turned slowly to face him, her eyes glimmering with hatred and her nostrils flaring like those of a spirited thoroughbred.

"I should like to leave," she said, each word enunciated separately, succinctly.

He thought her utterly engaging. She'd be perfect.

"If you're choosing prison, then I'll have to make some arrangements. There's Sheriff Behan to notify, and the Earps must be told so they can bring formal charges against you. Wyatt or one of his brothers will gladly escort you to Tucson. I'll wire the prison officials to expect you. Any preference? Would you rather be incarcerated in this territory or back East? Perhaps somewhere near New Orleans since that's your home, so to speak. Which will it be then? Or shall I choose one for you? All the cells are relatively the same—small, dark, damp, and thoroughly unpleasant—so I don't think one would be any better than another."

"You wouldn't," she said, her voice not quite as

strong as it had been. "You wouldn't send me to prison."

"Why would you doubt it?" he said, his smile deliberately unscrupulous. "You certainly wouldn't be the first, my dear. And you won't be the last, I assure you."

Like a shadow moving swiftly across the landscape, her mood changed. No longer the brisk order giver, she was now the seductress, taking sinuous steps toward him, hips swaying, hair brushing her back, breasts thrust up and out, eyes heavy lidded.

"We can work something out," she assured him, laying her hands upon the front of his vest. "Don't be cross. Be nice. Can't you be nice? I can be *very* nice to you."

He caught her wrists and pulled them down, pinning them to her sides. She winced and the softness in her eyes hardened to stone.

"You forget I've already experienced your idea of being nice. I still have a bit of a headache to remind me." Tired of her ploys, he jerked her roughly, making her stumble against him. "Enough of this nonsense. Are you going to do as I say, or do I throw you to the Earps and let them deal with you?"

She considered her options, recalled how the Earps had gunned down men in the street with no compunction whatsoever, and decided this Pinkerton man was probably the lesser evil.

"Oh, all right," she snapped, trying to free herself. But his fingers closed more tightly for her efforts, and she sucked in her breath. "Owww! Stop hurting me. I told you I'd do as you ask."

He let her go and she examined her wrists. Red marks braceleted them and they stung. She stuck her wrists right under his Roman nose. "Look what you've done. It takes such a big, bad man to beat up on a woman."

"Listen, you," he said, batting her hands aside and thrusting his face down to hers. "I've been better to you than you deserve. You're lucky I didn't slap you across the room when you spit in my face." He brought up one hand and held her chin in a vise-like grip. Her eyes grew round with fear. "Never doubt that I could break your bones as if they were made of chalk. Never doubt that. But if you mind your manners and do as I say, you'll be on a stage-coach out of here soon enough. I'm not a ruthless man, but I won't have a cheap little shrew spitting in my face, either." He pushed her away and sat in one of the upholstered chairs. With a quick, almost angry nod, he indicated the other and that she should sit down in it. She did.

Watching surreptitiously as he lit another of the thin cigars, Justine marveled that a man so hand-some could be so worthless. But wasn't that usually the case? Most of the good-looking men she'd known were as empty as overturned buckets. All show, no substance. York Masters was of that ilk. She figured he had a brutal streak, and he enjoyed lording it over the wretched masses. Bastard, she thought unkindly. If she were a man, she'd fly into him and teach him a lesson he wouldn't soon forget. But remembering the strength in his hands when he'd clutched her wrists and chin withered any such ideas of retribution. He was deceptively strong. In his city slicker clothes, he seemed as calm and gen-teel as a day in May, but beneath that veneer was a man of brute strength and weak conscience.

He held the cigar in his hand, its tip glowing or-angy red and smoke billowing up to the ceiling. Ex-amining the fiery end, he smiled.

"You speak French."

"Uh, a little," she said, thrown off-guard by yet another tidbit he'd spaded from her past.

"Fluently," he corrected. "Let's not lie to each other. It's useless. I know about you, Jussie, so don't bother to hide."

"If you know, why ask?" she sassed.

"I didn't. It was a statement. Your knowing French will come in handy. I need a French girl for this assignment."

"And what's the . . . assignment?"

"I want you to help me trap a murderer." His gaze slid to witness her loss of color. "Yes, there's danger involved, but you're not a stranger to it. You've run on fear before, haven't you? If fact, I imagine you're a woman who is used to living on the brink of disaster. So far, you've kept your balance. I'll help you keep upright this time around, too, Jussie. We're in this together."

"In what together? You said something about m-murder?"

"Yes." He worried the cigar, puffing and huffing until it was smoking again. "I'm on the trail of a man who works for the French Syndicate. You've heard of that?"

"Yes, but I don't know much about it. Crime isn't one of my interests."

He smiled, watching the sputtering tip of the cigar but thinking how versatile she was at accents. Sometimes she sounded like an East Coast-bred, snotty little bitch, other times like a languid, smooth-talking southern belle, and every so often like a ma'm'selle with roots deeply embedded in French soil. An actress, he thought. Well, that would come in handy. Might make all the difference in his scheme.

"Then you've heard that the French Syndicate is a ring of organized crime headed by some unscrupulous Parisians. They make some of their money legally—through gambling and houses of ill repute—but they're also involved in darker dealings like cattle rustling and train holdups. The man I'm after is known locally as the Count. He drifts into Tombstone every two or three months to collect money from the French brothel. Sometimes he replaces the older, less-spirited working girls with new, fresh faces. Those he replaces are sent to other towns and pleasure palaces—or so the story goes. But I think the Count kills them." He crossed one long leg over the other, shifted onto one hip, and looked directly into Justine's smoky eyes. "I'm certain he's murdered one woman, maybe as many as ten. Twenty, even. While ill fame is legal in Arizona, murder is not."

Justine moved restlessly, trying to find her place in this sordid tale. "Murder," she murmured, mostly to herself, then stiffened against a shiver.

"If you do *exactly* as I say, you won't be in any danger," York assured her. "I'll watch over you. I want to catch the Count red-handed," he continued. "I want to put that monster away where he can't hurt anyone ever again."

"And what am I supposed to do?" Justine asked, hoping his request would be simple and accomplished quickly.

"Ever heard of the Establishment?"

"Here in Tombstone?" she asked.

"Yes."

"I've heard of it," she allowed, "but I don't know anything about it. It's another brothel, right? God, this town is chock-full of them!"

"It's not just another brothel. It's run by the French Syndicate. The boss lady is one Madame Chloe Le Deau."

"How terribly French," Justine observed with a laugh. "Sounds like a stage name. Not much better than Monsieur Bonsoir, is it?" She chuckled again at the ridiculously false names.

York watched her with eager eyes, momentarily hypnotized by the backward tilt of her head and the sparkle of her almond-shaped eyes. Ravishing, he thought, smiling despite himself. Lust spread in the pit of his stomach, and he fidgeted with agitation. Working close to her would be a test of strength. She unwittingly lured him, fascinated him, made him hot with desire for her, but he knew that mixing his

personal life with his professional life only compli-
cated matters. Still, this time . . . this time . . . He had
to tear his gaze away from her creamy complexion.
This time was different, and he'd need the willpower
of a monk.

"I'm sorry," she apologized, bringing her merriment under control. "Go on with what you were
saying. This Madame Chloe Le Deau, she's with the
syndicate?"

"She works for them," York said, forcing his
thoughts back to business. "The Establishment is the
finest in the territory, and she runs it with an iron
fist. She has a keen business sense, and she's loyal to
her employers."

"I guess she has to be. From what I've heard
about these crime peddlers, you don't cross them
unless you're partial to pain and death," Justine observed dryly, earning a warm chuckle from York.

"Yes, they're not to be toyed with," he agreed.

"But that's what you're up to, isn't it?" she de-
duced. "You're out to trick the Count and Madame
Chloe?"

"Not trick them so much as catch them. I'm not
interested in Chloe," he said with an indifferent
wave of his hand. "She's a pawn. I want the main
player. I want the Count." His midnight blue gaze
swept to her and held. "And you're going to help me
get him."

Justine fought off a tremor of fear. For all she
knew, her part in this scheme might be miniscule,
she counseled the coward within her. So she'd hear
him out and then make her final, fateful decision.
She certainly wasn't going to display her pretty neck
for him or the Count to chop in two! At least in
prison she'd be alive.

"You'll be hired by the madame, and you'll be my
inside informant, keeping me abreast of any news of
the Count and how he operates. I've tried talking
with Madame Chloe's girls, but they don't confide in

outsiders. I'm hoping you can gain their confidence. They *must* know something. They're not deaf, dumb, and blind. I think they're afraid to talk, but they'd open up to a kindred spirit." He smiled with simple satisfaction. "You can handle that, can't you?"

"I don't mind being your stool pigeon," Justine returned tartly, "but I'm not going to become Tombstone's newest soiled dove."

He stared at the tip of his cigar and grinned. "Soiled dove. How quaint. I thought you wanted to get out of town."

"I do!" She twisted in the chair, deciding to try something drastic—the bald truth. "Look, no more dancing and sidestepping. Let me be perfectly honest."

"This should be novel," he commented dryly, casting a sullen glance her way.

Justine gritted her teeth in dislike, but pressed on. "I came here to entertain, but things went wrong—through no fault of my own," she emphasized.

"I know all of this, Jussie," he said in a bored tone.

"Okay, okay! Do I have to put my life on the line for a damned stagecoach ticket?"

"Aren't you being overly dramatic? And such language!" He clucked his tongue like a maiden aunt. "No one said anything about putting your life on the line, Jussie. You're going to spy and report to me what you've seen and heard, that's all."

She sat up straight, her back arched, her chin high and handsome. "I'd rather die than become a whore. If that is my option, then have mercy on me and shoot me this minute. Through the heart."

He started to laugh in her face, but the chaste sheen in her eyes stayed him. She was serious. He saw something else in her gray eyes and in her tremulous expression: fear of the unknown. York looked away quickly, uncomfortable with the growing certainty of his realization.

Justine Drussard was a virgin. He'd stake his revered reputation as a man about town on it. But how could it be? His information had painted her as a woman of experience, a street urchin who begged for crumbs and probably wasn't above picking pockets. But there it was, the clear-eyed gaze of a young woman with a clean reputation and firm belief in romantic love.

"You can't expect me to compromise my morals for weeks, perhaps months, for a few dollars," she went on. "Not for *any* amount of money. I won't do it. I will not sell myself."

"You won't have to," he said, his voice coming out gruff, hoarse even, because his throat had tightened and his chest seemed to be filled with a clawing sweetness he couldn't name. Suffocating, it was, and not a little unnerving. Her refusal to lower her standards touched him, drew a healthy measure of respect from him. He cleared his throat and tried again. "I have a plan."

"What?" she asked, hooked.

"China Mary is trusted by Madame Chloe. The madame recently lost her secretary and bookkeeper. The woman ran off with a silver miner who struck it rich. China Mary has already told Madame about you."

"What about me?" Justine demanded, incensed to know she was being talked about behind her back.

"That you're a young woman of French origin who has a head for numbers and knows how to be discreet. Madame Chloe will hire you with China Mary's stamp of approval."

"Does China Mary own this town?"

He grinned crookedly. "Only Hop Town, really, but she's powerful. Very powerful. Anyway, all you have to do is make a good impression when you're interviewed by Madame Chloe. The position is temporary, since all the girls have to be approved by the Count himself." He favored her with a quick but kind smile. "Think you can shine like a gold nugget for Madame Chloe?"

Justine shrugged. "Why not? Making a good impression has never been too difficult for me."

"So I thought."

Her gaze clashed with his, and something in his expression made her heart pound like a triphammer. Did he think her desirable? she wondered, and blushed. The warm tide rose up into her cheeks, and she ducked her head, hoping he couldn't decipher her thoughts. Did he have a woman of his own? Someone special? As beautiful as he? Oh, yes. He was a handsome, a beautiful man. He must have a woman in his life. She looked around the room, trying to find something feminine.

"You live here?"

"Yes," he answered, scrutinizing the area as if seeing it after a long time away. "I stay here. Comes with the job."

"Where did you live before?"

He seemed to consider her question carefully before he finally answered. "St. Louis."

"Oh, that's a lovely city. I played there once in a drama called *Asa's Revenge*. I was the chamber girl." She tilted her head to one side, then righted it in a quirk of self-consciousness. "Anyway, I enjoyed that city. You'll go back there when your business here is completed?"

"Yes. Where will you go? New Orleans?"

"I don't know. New Orleans used to be my home, but it's been a couple of years since I've been there. Maybe I'll go to New York or Boston. Someplace with more than one theater in it."

He stood and crossed to the bedside table to knock the ash from his cigar into the porcelain ashtray. When he turned back to her, it was to give her a slow appraisal that made bumps appear on her flesh.

She squirmed in the chair, feeling stripped and vulnerable. Every place his gaze touched burned. When he stared for long, trembling moments upon her parted lips, Justine rose shakily to her feet, unable to withstand another moment of his unrelenting examination.

"Do we have a deal?" he asked, his voice low and scratchy.

Her mind whirled, dissecting and weighing her chances. What was so terrible? a voice taunted within. You'll have a place to stay, a salary, a job that doesn't threaten your morals, and you'll be given enough money to get out of Tombstone. There was risk, but it was no more risky than a prison term. Finally, she nodded, sealing her fate.

"Yes," she said clearly. "We have a deal."

"Good." He held out one hand. "Let's shake."

Forcing one foot in front of the other, her carpet slippers whispering on the wood floor, she approached him and put her hand in his. His hand was twice the size of hers, and she was again struck by his stature. He was a big man. All man. He shook her hand once, then, his eyes seizing hers, bent his golden head and pressed a lingering kiss on the back of it.

Justine couldn't stop the small gasp of surprise that escaped her parted lips any more than she could deny the ribbon of pleasure that fluttered through her at the brief contact. His eyes had closed for a few seconds, but they opened as he straightened to enjoy her high color and the rapid rise and fall of her breasts beneath the inadequate covering. Her nipples stood out, straining against the thin fabric. His mouth went dry, and he released her hand as if it had suddenly become a hot coal.

"Fine, then." He sounded brusque, off balance, baffled. He tried again, hoping for a disguise this time. If she knew she could stir him so easily, he'd be lost. "Then the next order of business is to try and make you look halfway respectable."

His tactic worked. Her face crumbled as if she'd just been slapped hard enough to bring tears to her luminous eyes. She turned away, mumbling something incoherent.

"Come on. China Mary knows more about this sort of thing than I do." York strode past her, brisk and unfeeling, but inside a voice called him every kind of fool for hurting her, for bringing even one single tear to her eyes. Those lovely, smoky eyes.

Chapter 6

Bathed, powdered, and perfumed, Justine stood on a low footstool. Clad only in lace-and-cotton undergarments, she waited for China Mary's return. She ran her fingers lightly over the corset ribs, soft chemise, and pantalets that ended in a deep ruffle below her knees. She sniffed appreciatively, thinking that she smelled like a June bride, all flowery and fresh and bursting with sunlight. Releasing a deep sigh, she decided that there was nothing like a long, warm bath to revive the spirits and make the world seem less tawdry.

The door behind her swung open, and Justine glanced over her shoulder, a ready smile for China Mary claiming her mouth. She gasped when York Masters entered on the other woman's heels. In a purely instinctive gesture, Justine crossed her arms, pressing them against her front and rounding her shoulders to conceal what she could of herself.

"Get him out of here! I'm not decent," she complained to China Mary, who was paying her no mind.

"Don't worry," York drawled, "neither am I." He

chuckled, his insolent gaze running over her. "You've seen me buck naked, so it's a little late to play the role of an innocent."

"I have *not* seen you na—" she gritted her teeth, unable to say the word—"unclothed."

"Oh, really?" He stroked his shadowed jaw. "I seem to recall waking up without a stitch on in that room at Kate Fisher's."

"I undressed you under the covers," she explained, straightening slowly since it was obvious he wasn't going to leave the room. "I didn't peek."

"Maybe you should have," he said around a grin that would have looked natural on a wolf. "I wouldn't have minded."

China Mary released a peal of laughter, and Justine blushed to the roots of her hair. York had shed his jacket and vest. His shirt of charcoal gray stripes was unbuttoned to midchest. Reddish gold hair sprang through the deep vee, drawing Justine's attention when she would rather have looked anywhere but at him. His shirtsleeves were rolled up to just below his elbows, displaying powerfully muscled forearms. Justine was once again struck by the size of him. He made her feel delicate, diminutive even. She didn't like it. He slouched against the side of China Mary's desk, arms folded, ankles crossed, straight hair falling tantalizingly across his forehead.

Her gaze slipped lower to the rise between his muscled thighs before she dragged her eyes away from him, furious with herself for looking at him *there*. What in the world was wrong with her? She'd *never* stared openly at a man's forbidden place, so why was she changing her ways now? Why now, when she wanted to show him how tiresome she found him? Justine released a huffy breath of indignation, her discomfort at being partially clothed forgotten in the heat of her other thoughts. She planted her hands at her hips and faced him squarely.

"Can we get on with this? I'm tired of standing here like a hitching post."

"Patience, patience," China Mary scolded. "You got to look the part." Dresses were draped across her arms, and she began peeling them off one by one, holding them briefly up to Justine, then whisking them away. She tossed each into a chair like so many cleaning rags.

"Wait, wait!" Justine gripped China Mary's hand before she could fling aside a creation of lemon silk and black lace. "This is beautiful. Oh, my! This one is . . . oh, and that one, it's . . ." Words failed her as China Mary shook off her hand and continued the rapid-fire fashion display. "They're all beautiful. Where'd you get them?"

"Never you mind." The woman took two or three mincing steps backward to examine Justine with eyes of onyx. "What color, York? What look good on this little bird?"

What wouldn't look good? he thought, but he didn't speak. Instead, he straightened from his slouch and went to the chair where the dresses lay like a fallen rainbow. His fingertips brushed over creations of pink, yellow, white, and blue fabric. They lingered on a dress of plum rose, then closed on the sleeve of that one and pulled it out from the others. He held it up, running critical eyes across the heart-shaped neckline, puffs of sleeves, and pale pink piping down the skirt.

"This one," he said, handing it to China Mary for her approval. "It will show off her goods, but it's something a lady would wear. I want Madame Chloe to think she's a real lady, with schooling."

"I *am* a lady," Justine informed him, taking the dress from the other woman and giving it her own thorough inspection. It was gorgeous, probably her favorite, but she'd rather cut out her tongue than tell him so. "And I have schooling, for your information."

"I know. Public schooling in New Orleans until you were fourteen."

"How do you know these things?" she demanded, furious that he had her at a disadvantage in more ways than she could count.

"School records," he said with a casual shrug. "Simple snooping, my dear. I'm like a bloodhound, catching a scent and following it until my quarry is uncovered. Completely uncovered." His gaze was intimate, and his smile was meant to set her nerves on end. It succeeded. "Put on the dress. We're wasting time." He resumed his lounging posture against the desk.

She stepped into the dress and shimmied it up her body. "Public records couldn't tell you everything. Who have you talked to about me?"

"Why is it so important? What are you hiding?"

"Nothing." She stood still while China Mary buttoned up the back using a sturdy hook. "I just don't like the idea of a stranger knowing so much about me. It's spooky."

"The acting troupe you were with knew quite a bit about your past. Evidently you didn't mind telling them about your upbringing in New Orleans and the hard times you knew there."

"You talked with people in the troupe?"

"An operative of mine did."

"Did this . . . this *operative* see Elmer?"

"Elmer?"

"Monsieur Bonsoir."

"Oh, yes." He nodded.

"And nobody arrested him?"

"What for? He was cooperative."

"He's a thief!" she charged, jumping down from the footstool and turning a deaf ear on China Mary's command to stay put. She stopped in front of him, thrusting her face up to his, straining forward on tiptoe. "He took my money and jewelry! He left me with nothing, and you let him get away with it? How dare you!" Fury pumped through her, looking for a release. She flattened her hands against his chest and gave him a mighty push that barely moved him. "I could . . . I could just—"

"Whatever it is, don't," he cautioned, capturing her hands and forcing them away from him. "Your problems with your former boss are of no concern to me."

"You're a pig!"

"And you're skating on thin ice." His eyes narrowed to slits. A muscle twitched just below his left ear, drawing her notice.

"Back off, Jus-see," China Mary advised. "You going to cut throat with own tongue." Landing a hand on Justine's shoulder, she dragged her away from the face-off. "You sit. I get one of my girls to do your hair and paint your face. And you"—China Mary sent her flat gaze to York—"you go somewhere else. You underfoot."

"But I'm going to—"

"You go now," China Mary interrupted with an icy voice. "Come back when I say."

His gaze warred with China Mary's for a few moments, then he cursed under his breath. "Go easy on the face paint," he ordered, then strode out of the room.

Justine gave a sniff of contempt. "I hate him."

"No, you not hate." China Mary said, plucking a thread from the shoulder of the plum rose dress. "You just trying to put out fire."

"What fire?"

China Mary's smile was more cunning than comforting. "You don't treat China Mary like fool, and she not treat you like one." She touched a long nail to the tip of Justine's nose. "I send in girl to do your hair."

She'd never looked so beautiful.
Standing before the full-length mirror in a room

off China Mary's office, Justine gazed at herself and couldn't help but feel proud. She had been shown behind the heavy curtain that led to the parlor. A black lacquered door kept her closed off from the other parts of the living quarters.

York had been right in selecting the dress of plum rose, she thought. It flattered her, outlining each line and curve of her body, contrasting alluringly against her pale skin. Sweet Sue, one of the saloon girls, had spent nearly an hour brushing Justine's glossy hair and sweeping it up into curling profusion, securing it with three strategically placed ebony-and-ivory combs. It made her look more mature, she thought. Less like an ingenue.

She heard the office door open and close. Stepping through the curtain, her attention on the way the folds of the dress whispered against her starched petticoats, she spun around in circles to let China Mary take in the full effect of the stunning creation.

"Look, China Mary. See how it shimmers? I think it's positively gorgeous, don't you?" She stopped spinning and gasped. Her hands covered the area over her hammering heart when she saw that she'd mistaken her caller.

"Yes, simply gorgeous," York Masters agreed, grinning around the thin cigar clamped between his full lips. Then the grin turned upside down. "Just one problem . . ." He came toward her, his frown intensifying when she shrank away from him. "Come here and quit acting like a scared rabbit," he ordered, reaching out to catch her elbow and pull her into the fading sunlight slanting through a domed skylight. "The hair is all wrong. Sit over here and let me at it." He manhandled her down into a chair beside China Mary's desk.

"Don't touch it!" Realizing that he was about to destroy Sweet Sue's work of art, Justine wrapped her arms protectively around her head. "It makes me look older . . . mature."

"Hogwash. It makes you look fussy and vain."

"I like it."

"I don't. Juss-e-e-e-e." The last was a drawn-out warning that was as effective as the clattering rustle of a rattler's tail.

Justine's arms fell away, and she issued a sound of rebellion, which only made him chuckle.

"Let's see now..." His voice trailed off. His fingers slid into her hair, right against her scalp. He freed the combs and tossed them disdainfully to the desktop, sending the white cat sailing off the desk and across the room. "For crying out loud, Far East, you'd think I'd shot you. Come back over here, silly."

The white cat eyed him for a few moments, then her tail went up like a flag and she strutted to him. She rubbed against his pant leg and purred contentedly.

"That's better."

Justine thought he was speaking to the cat, but he patted the top of her head approvingly and stepped in front of her to examine the results from another angle.

"The cat's name is Far East?" she asked.

"That's right."

"Is she yours?"

"No, China Mary's. But like most females, she likes me."

Justine didn't miss the smirk in his tone; she simply chose to ignore it. "Are you finished mussing my hair?"

"Relax." He moved around her, out of view.

"I can't," she said peevishly, but she closed her eyes as his callused fingertips slipped under her hair to massage her neck. "I'm going to meet Madame Chloe tonight and give the performance of my life."

"You'll do fine. Especially once I'm through with you. Your hair's so pretty, it needs no adornment or fancy styling." He curled a finger under her chin and lifted her face to his lambent gaze. "Much better. Go look for yourself."

Justine examined his work in the parlor mirror. All he'd done was return her hair to the way it had been before—long, loose, the sides drawn back and held in place by a single comb at the crown of her head. She pulled a few curling strands over her shoulders, then caught his reflection behind her. The cigarillo was clamped in one corner of his mouth, and one eye was squinted against the smoke. His eyes were sending out other smoke signals that she could easily decipher. She looked down at her new high-button shoes and wondered why she couldn't think of one intelligent thing to say to him. Finally, when the silence became almost tangible, Justine released a shaky laugh and whirled to face him.

"So, will I pass the exam?" she asked, blatantly fishing for a compliment.

He lifted one shoulder in an indolent shrug and ground out the cigar in the ashtray on China Mary's piecrust coffee table. "How are you with numbers?"

"Okay, I guess," she mumbled, turning back to the mirror to shield her disappointment from him.

"Two plus two is?"

She spun around, eyes flashing, her disappointment vanquished by irritation. "I've had just about enough of your insults!" She marched toward him, stopping toe to toe. "I can add, subtract, multiply, and divide, and I can also tell when I'm being made fun of and treated like a whore. I'm not an imbecile, and I'm not a guttersnipe."

"You two still hissing like cats?" China Mary asked, parting the curtains and moving into the room with a rustle of satin. She was followed by the glum Ah Lum.

Justine flopped into the nearest chair, furious, her breath coming in quick gasps. She stared into the near distance and tried to think of a way to slip the noose York Masters was trying to put around her neck. Why had she agreed to this foolishness anyway? He probably wouldn't have thrown her in jail if she'd called his bluff. She shot a glance at York's hard, glittering eyes and immediately amended that thought. He had about as much compassion as a volunteer henchman.

"She's all yours," York announced, already moving toward the curtained archway. "I've got to change and get ready for work. When is the appointment?"

"Tomorrow morning."

"Tomorrow?" He turned to frown over his shoulder, and China Mary extended her hands in a helpless gesture. "What happened to this evening?"

"Chloe just sent word," China Mary explained. "She too busy tonight. Says she'll see Jus-see come morning."

"You mean I did all this for nothing?" Justine asked, looking down at her shimmering gown.

"Oh, well." York waved a hand, dismissing the hitch in his plan. "Tomorrow's good enough. We can consider this a dress rehearsal." His glance toward Justine was on the stingy side. "Get a good night's rest, and don't try anything stupid like running away from me." He stepped through the curtain, but his voice floated back to her. "You can't run that far."

Justine made a face, then saw that China Mary was regarding her with amusement.

"I don't care what you think, I *know* that I hate him," Justine said, sliding up into the chair and straightening the skirt of her dress. "He treats me like a whore."

"He know better. He like to squirm under your skin," she said, illustrating her point with a sinuous movement of her hand. "Ah Lum, show this one to room upstairs. You stay here tonight, Jus-see, then you go to Madame Chloe's tomorrow after breakfast. I tutor you in what to say, how to act, but later. You go now. I send up dinner tray. You eat. I got business to run."

"But I—" Justine gasped as Ah Lum, moving like a shadow, came up beside her and grasped her elbow. She was pulled straight up as if she weighed next to nothing. She stared at Ah Lum with shock, realizing he was far stronger than he looked. He forced her from the parlor, deaf to her sounds of protest.

The room she was shown to was located directly across the hall from York's. After Ah Lum left her, Justine inspected the accommodations before pressing her ear to the door to listen for any movement. Was York in his room? She backed away, shaking her head. She didn't care if he was. He was rude and lewd. He might wear fancy clothes and talk like a city lawyer at times, but he was no better than most of the animals in this town, and she wanted nothing to do with any of them.

Strolling around the pink and cream room, she admired the furnishings, which were delicate and inlaid with ivory and jade. Even the bed's headboard was intricately carved and adorned with mother-of-pearl to create a picture of lotus blossoms. It looked nothing like a brothel, nothing like a whore's room. And for that Justine was thankful.

"I'm an actress," she whispered, reassuring herself as she went to stand before one of the two tall, narrow windows that looked out onto the street.

Leaning against the window frame, she looked through the sheer pink draperies at the canopy of stars overhead. The sound of mines was constant in Tombstone. Night and day, one could hear the rumble of heavy machinery, the pounding of hammers and picks, and the clack-clack-clacking of the mining cars along the rails. It never stopped. If it ever did stop, Tombstone would live up to its name: the town would die.

Hop Town was hopping. It was still early, just an

hour past dusk, but a crowd was already gathering. Shouts and barks of laughter rent the night.

A door opened across the hall. Justine whirled to face her own closed door and held her breath, expecting York Masters to barge in at any moment. But his footsteps sounded along the hallway, growing dim until she could hear them no more. Justine slumped forward, flexing her fingers and realizing she'd been gripping the window ledge behind her as if she might fall through the floor at any moment.

"Silly," she scolded herself, breathing normally again and rubbing her hands together to encourage the circulation and relieve her tension. "What's wrong with you lately, Justine Drussard?" She sucked in and released a long, calming breath, then smiled. "That's better."

The knock at the door sent a jolt through her that jarred her from head to toe. She clutched her breast, feeling her heart slam painfully in her chest.

"Wh-who is it?" she croaked, knowing it was York. But why hadn't she heard him approaching her door? Had he tiptoed?

"Ah Lum."

She lifted her gaze heavenward before opening the door. The Oriental man entered, a dinner tray held between his long, skinny hands. He set it on the bed, then left with nary a glance in her direction.

Justine tucked into the food, filling her empty stomach and improving her disposition. When she was finished, she found several nightgowns in the bureau and slipped into one. Climbing into the bed, she curled onto her side and ruminated on the events of the past few days until she fell asleep. It was well after midnight when she heard York Masters and his woman outside her door. Justine sat up, wide-eyed, eager eared.

"Ummm, York, honey, kiss me again." The voice was slumberous, seductive, blurred at the edges. A whimper followed. "Oh, yes, honey. Get me inside before I drop to my knees right here in the hall."

"I don't mind, if you don't mind," York said, laughter threading through his voice.

"You awful thing." A giggle, high and girlish. "I will not do such a thing where just anybody could walk up and see me."

A doorknob rattled. Hinges creaked.

"After you, darlin'."

"Come on in here, handsome. I've got something for you."

"I've got something for you, too, Satin. It's long and hard and—" The door closed, muffling the voices so that all Justine could hear was an occasional deep rumble answered by a higher trill.

Half an hour later she heard a woman's cry of ecstasy. Justine plastered her hands to her ears, squeezed her eyes shut, and gritted her teeth in agony. Jealousy ran through her heart like a sword through a soft center. The rest of the night passed with images of York Masters with another woman—naked limbs entwined, mouths roaming hot and free, hands caressing and carelessly stroking.

Was that what lovemaking was like? she wondered, perplexed that she had such visions. Before York Masters had stormed into her life, she had given little thought to such intimacies. Someday a husband would tutor her, she had told herself, and until that time she would expend her energies on her acting talent. But York Masters made her think, made her wonder, made her squirm with a feeling she couldn't identify.

The woman across the hall cried out again, chanting York's name several times before her voice faded.

Justine plunged under the covers and wrapped a pillow around her head. She called York hateful names, chanting her own litany until sleep finally rolled over her in a wave of mercy.

Chapter 7

Sprawled in bed, York Masters delved his fingers through the damp mat of hair covering his chest and frowned at the morning sunlight waltzing across the ceiling.

Stupid jackass, he called himself. What the hell were you trying to prove last night by bringing Satin up here? Is your head so full of that little actress that you can't think straight anymore?

He made a fist, wincing when his fingers closed around clumps of curling hair and tweaked his chest. He'd brought Satin to his room just to make the girl across the hall jealous. Hell, she probably didn't even hear him come in last night. She was probably fast asleep and couldn't care less who he bedded, or when, or how often. But last night he'd drank one too many brews and invited Satin Doll to come to his room instead of going to hers, as was their custom, on the off chance that Jussie Drussard might hear them.

As usual, Satin had left at daybreak, and since then York had lain awake, staring sightlessly and

trying to figure out when he'd caught calico fever.
He'd been around enough to know that a bachelor
couldn't straddle a fence. He either had to build one
or tear it down.

"Build one," he said to the silent room. "Build it
high and strong to keep that gray-eyed hellcat away
from you or you'll be sorry, son. Real sorry."

Then he remembered how he'd seen Jussie's face
when he'd made Satin Doll moan beneath him last
night. He'd thought of Jussie Drussard! Holy Moses,
he was in trouble. Big trouble.

He'd investigated the Count for too long to let *any*
woman divide his attention. Day by day, week by
week, month by month, he had stayed in the background and learned more and more about the Count
until he was certain of his facts. He despised the
man. Bringing him down was the most important
thing in York Masters's life. Women were necessary
occasionally, but they weren't important. They
weren't permanent. Personal involvements were
something he couldn't afford. Not until the Count
was behind bars—or dead.

Yet, Jussie Drussard haunted him. What he had
learned about her stoked his interest. She'd led a
hard life, but she wasn't a hard woman. He'd expected her to be as tough as boot leather, but she
was soft, vulnerable, innocent in so many ways.
Maybe that was an act, it was hard to tell with her.
She was a damned good actress—all his sources said
so—and she might just be playing a role to gain his
sympathy. Could a man ever be sure of such a
woman? No wonder folks likened actresses to
whores. You never knew whether or not they were
putting on a show.

Think of her as one of your operatives, he cautioned himself, just one of your pigeons. Nothing
more. And for God's sake, keep your eyes off her
lips, her breasts, her legs, her backside, her . . . Just

keep your eyes off her, he instructed himself, then swung out of the bed. He had to get dressed and talk with her before she went to meet Madame Chloe.

Having finished her breakfast, Justine was returning to her room to fetch her gloves and bonnet when the door to York's room swung open and he stepped out into the hall, directly into her path.

"Did China Mary talk with you?" he almost barked at her.

"Yes, I'm just going to get my things, and then I'll be on my way," she said, reaching to open the door to her room.

He looked grumpy, and Justine was glad. She hoped he had a splitting headache. After making all that noise last night, he deserved it. She spun around in alarm when York started into the room after her.

"Excuse me, but this is *my* room," she informed him icily.

"I've got to talk to you before you meet Madame Chloe."

"Not in here."

"In here." He pushed her across the threshold and closed the door behind him, leaning against it in a blatant threat. "This will take only a minute. I just want to go over a couple of things with you."

"Make it snappy." She grabbed the lacy white gloves off the bureau top and pulled them on with angry, jerky movements.

"I want you to tell the truth."

"About what?"

"About everything. I've found it works best. You won't be tripped up if you keep your story straight. When Madame Chloe asks what you've been doing in Tombstone, you tell her about the acting troupe and how Elmer robbed you and left you high and dry. Tell her you resorted to working at Big Nose

Kate's, but you didn't like her or her clientele. That'll take care of any rumors Madame Chloe might have heard about you. Understand, so far?"

She answered by directing a cool, flinty glare at him. He looked away, and she considered it a battle won.

"Tell the truth and play up your French blood. Madame is snooty about being French. She thinks her Parisian ancestors give her a leg up on other women. Probably the best thing you can do is not offer any information you're not asked to give. Think you can handle it?"

Again she extended a cool glare.

"What's wrong? Cat got your tongue?"

"I can handle Madame Chloe," she said with quiet authority. "Don't worry about it." She stood before the free-standing, oval mirror to angle her wide-brimmed mauve-and-cream hat to one side in a saucy tilt, then tacked it in place with two pearl-tipped hat pins. As she smoothed her hands down her tiny waist, she saw York's expression floating behind her.

The naked desire in his eyes worked on her like fire on ice. Every cold, hateful, vindictive feeling she had for him melted away. She forced her gaze away from his reflection, afraid she might do or say something she'd regret; something that would expose her hand to him. That would be the worst thing she could do. He was a gambler, after all. If he sensed her deep feelings for him, he'd use them to up the stakes and make his winnings all the more enriching. He'd taken enough from her already, she thought, grabbing her beaded purse and moving quickly toward the door and its moody sentry.

"I should leave now, or I'll be late for the appointment." She was glad she had the purse to occupy her hands and her eyes. She opened it to check its contents while waiting for him to move aside.

"Beautiful."

That brought her head up, widened her eyes, made her heart leap into her mouth.

"Wh-what did you say?" she asked, begging him to repeat it so that she could treasure the compliment all the more, but when a shuttered expression dropped over his face, she knew she'd just as soon ask for the moon.

"The dress," he said, so low she could barely hear him. "It's beautiful."

"Oh. Yes, it is." She stared holes through him until he was forced to lift his gaze to hers. For several charged moments their eyes did battle. His surrendered. He moved away from the door, swinging it open and dipping his head in a silent request that she precede him across the threshold.

Justine shunted past him. His call of "Good luck" as she marched along the hall elicited a mouthed, "Go to hell" from her.

Asked to wait in the front parlor of the Establishment, Justine used the time alone to gather the cloak of another character around her. She conjured up pride for her French blood, recalling a woman she'd admired once because of her dignified airs. The woman, a fellow actress in a production of *As You Like It*, had impressed Justine to such an extent that Justine had hung on her every word, gesture, and affectation. She had studied the woman so diligently that now, two years later, she could recall her in rich, ripe detail.

I'll be her, she thought, selecting the character, slipping into it, snuggling into a better fit, finally feeling right at home as a worldly, self-confident version of Justine Drussard.

By the time she was summoned into Madame Chloe's white-and-gold office, Justine was no longer a dock rat from New Orleans. She was bouffant with good breeding and as French as a brioche.

"Madame Chloe," she said, ladling on the French inflection as she held out one gloved hand to the woman rising from the chair behind a small, delicate desk. "It is good of you to see me. Merci, merci, Madame."

The response was immediate. Madame Chloe's smile, at first stiff and polite, thawed into a genuine welcome. She took Justine's hand and squeezed it lightly before releasing her. Extending a hand toward the white-and-gold upholstered chair beside Justine, she inclined her head in an elegant instruction to be seated.

"You come highly recommended from China Mary," she said when Justine was perched on the edge of the chair cushion. "Highly recommended. Which is odd. China Mary rarely endorses anyone who isn't from the Orient."

Justine had never seen hair like Madame Chloe's. It was white, a pure, angel-wing white, and piled high upon her head in a profusion of stiff curls and upswept swirls. It reminded her of cotton, and it was all she could do not to stare. Despite her snowy hair, the woman was no more than thirty, Justine surmised. With eyes as dark as coals and a triangular face of perfect symmetry, the French madam was a stunning woman to behold. A beauty mark rode beneath the right corner of her mouth, drawing one's eye to the red bow of her lips. Her figure, full at the hips and breasts, enhanced her allure. She was a woman of substance. Not a frail flower, but an exotic blossom seeded in French soil and pruned by a precise hand.

"I'm flattered," Justine said. "China Mary has been most kind to me." She offered no more, recalling York's advice to curb her tongue whenever possible.

"The position open here is that of a bookkeeper."

"So I was told."

"You worked for Big Nose Kate?"

Justine nodded.

"Why did you leave there?"

"Kate and I didn't get along. Besides, I didn't like the work."

"Hmmm." Madame Chloe regarded Justine for a few moments. "You could not do the work? That is what I heard. The talk around town is that you cheated the customers and Kate."

"Madame, I could make a living flat on my back, but I choose not to. I did not cheat anyone. I simply left because I felt my talents were being wasted." She withstood the woman's unblinking scrutiny for several moments before adding, "I have a fine brain in addition to a fine bosom and derriere."

The older woman lowered her gaze and smiled. "And where did you tutor this fine brain?"

"New Orleans."

"Ah, a beautiful place. So different from Tombstone. What brought you here?"

"I traveled with an acting troupe. The showman left me here when I rebuffed him." She shrugged one shoulder. "It is just as well. I was growing tired of his tacky idea of theater."

"So, you're an actress?"

"I have been many things, but acting is one of the things I do well. Bookkeeping is another." She put iron in her voice to discourage any misgivings Madame Chloe might harbor.

"So, you are quick with numbers?"

"Quick and meticulous," Justine assured her. "I want very much to be in your employ, Madame. Otherwise, I must leave Tombstone soon as there doesn't seem to be much here to amuse a woman of my standards."

Madame nodded. "It is not Paris."

"No other city is," Justine said, and passed a look of shared memories to the other woman, who passed it back with a smile. "It is a jewel among glass baubles."

"When were you there last?"

"I was but a child, but I remember it vividly."

"I was there only recently. I hope to go back in a year or two."

"How nice for you."

"Oui." Madame Chloe's thoughts seemed to drift from the room, from the country, from the continent to distant Europe. It was a full minute before she returned her attention to Justine. "Pardon. Back to your request of employment. Have you a lover here?"

"A lo . . . no."

"I don't want to hire another faithless woman who will leave me with no notice as the last one did." Madame looked aside, her face momentarily contorted by a painful memory. "That bitch. Taking off as she did . . . with that grimy little runt. Disgusting!"

"If I wanted to run off with a miner, I could have done that days ago," Justine informed her. "I am here to work, Madame, not to snare a husband or a lover."

Madame regarded her again, but Justine could see that she wasn't completely convinced. "So, you are eager to work?"

"Yes, when could I start?" Justine asked, trying to press the woman into a decision.

"I will let you know in a day or so."

Justine's hopes plummeted. York Masters wouldn't like this. He expected her to be hired on the spot. "A day or so?" Justine perfected a pout. "I see . . . well, if that's all you can offer . . ."

"It is, ma'm'selle. I must think on this. I don't make decisions on a whim. I'll let you know by the end of the week. It is a promise."

"Merci."

"You'll be at China Mary's?"

"I hope so, but I don't know if China Mary will

extend her courtesies. I was only offered a room for one night."

"Do not worry," Madame Chloe said, rising from the chair to signal an end to the meeting. "I will send word to her. She will allow you to stay in her house until I've made a decision." She nodded her cottony head slowly in a gesture of farewell. "Au revoir."

"I can't believe this! I ask you to do one thing— *one thing*—and you can't manage it." York paced in front of her, his boot heels snapping against the floor, his arms gesturing wildly.

"Madame Chloe didn't say no, she just said she'd let me know in a day or two. She strikes me as a prudent woman."

"Oh, is that how she strikes you?" he jeered, pausing long enough to issue a sarcastic sneer. "You can't tell me anything about that woman I haven't figured out for myself."

"So, you know she's no more French than you are a gentleman."

Doubt dulled his eyes for a moment, then he swept it aside with an impatient gesture. "Don't be stupid. She was in Paris only a year ago. Stayed there nearly six months before she came back to the U.S."

"Many people visit France, but that doesn't make them French." She pretended to study her nails, buffing them against her skirt and admiring their shine as York continued to glare at her. "I happen to know an acquired accent when I hear one." She smiled briefly. "Owning one myself as I do." She glanced up and caught the barest hint of amusement in his cornflower blue eyes.

"What makes you think her accent isn't genuine?"

"Several things." She folded her hands in her lap and brought her gaze up to his. "Mainly, she pronounced Paris, Pair-iss. Any native of France would pronounce it Pa-ree." Justine rolled the *r* and shrugged smartly. "Also, I think she's as attracted to women as she is to men."

He fell back a step, struck by her powers of observation. On *that* point he knew Justine was right. Madame Chloe didn't discriminate in bed. It wasn't common knowledge, but York had spoken to several women who claimed to have shared intimacies with the madame. But the fact remained, he reminded himself, that Jussie had failed to get in the door. No matter that she could ferret out bits of information from afar, he wanted her right under the madame's nose!

"I know she grazes on both sides of the fence," he said, just so Jussie wouldn't think she was too far ahead of him, "but you didn't go there to play a guessing game. I sent you there *to move in!*" His voice rose to a roar on the last three words, making Justine flinch.

"You hush, please," China Mary said, sweeping aside the curtain and bouncing into the room on her small, platformed shoes. "What you shouting about?"

"She's still here, *that's* what I'm shouting about." York pointed an accusing finger at Justine, then turned his back to her as if the sight of her made his stomach lurch.

"That okay. She can stay in same room. No problem."

"That's very kind of you," Justine said. "Madame Chloe said she would contact you about me staying here another night or two."

"She send houseboy to ask. I say okay." China Mary step-hopped to her desk and eased into the high-backed chair. "York Masters, you lower voice and temper. No need for fireworks."

York fell into a chair, making the wooden joints creak. Legs stuck out in front of him, his head cradled in one hand, he stared broodingly at Justine until she felt like screaming.

"We wait one day," China Mary said, raising a single finger. "Then I let rumor fly across town." Her hand became a bird's wing, graceful in an unfelt breeze. "Rumor say I might hire this French girl. I break my own rule for her, she so smart, so loyal, so rare." China Mary's giggle scaled upward. "Chloe hire her quick then." She nodded sagely, her ornately sculptured hair bobbing but not one strand stirring. "If China Mary want, Chloe throw caution to wind." Again, the hand fluttered.

"Why is she hesitating?" York asked, sliding up off his spine.

"She careful woman," China Mary said. "Just 'cause this girl French not mean she belong at Establishment. Madame Chloe want to sniff around like hound." She wrinkled her button nose to demonstrate. "Want to smell for anything rotten."

"In other words, she's wise to us."

"No, York Masters. She just careful. Once she hear I want Justine, Madame will snap her up."

"Then put out the word today," York said, but China Mary shook her head. "Why wait?"

"Don't want to tip hand. Patience, York Masters. Patience. It is virtue, yes?"

"I wouldn't know. Virtue hasn't interested me in years." His insolent gaze slid meaningfully to Justine.

"Don't worry, girlie," China Mary told Justine. "Things work out. I give you different dress to wear. Save that one for Chloe's place." The woman inched forward across the desk, her thin brows pulling together. "Why you frown, Jus-see?"

"I . . . well, I feel like a beggar. No clothes, no place of my own. Nothing! I'm tired of it. I'm used to making my own way. I've never accepted charity. Never."

"Not charity," China Mary insisted. "You working for York Masters, yes?"

"I guess."

"You guess right," York assured her, rising to his feet and stretching like a lazy tomcat. "Can you fix her up with some clothes?" he asked China Mary. The woman nodded. "Good, then I'll leave you to it. I'm going upstairs for a nap." His eyes touched briefly upon Justine. "I didn't get much sleep last night."

Justine sent him a less than sympathetic smile. "What a shame. I slept like the dead. Must have fallen asleep the moment my head hit the pillow."

"Bully for you," he said, almost snarling. "I wish you were as good at impressing Madame Chloe as you are at sleeping and eating."

"I told you I did my best!" Justine said, jumping to her feet to stand before him, quivering with outrage. "I don't know what you're griping about anyway. I'm the one who's sticking her neck out while you have a fine old time playing cards and compromising women!"

She wanted to bite her tongue for letting that last slip out, especially when York lowered his chin until he was looking at her through dark blond brows. A bothersome smile curled up one side of his face as he folded his arms against his chest as if to trap the laughter there.

"Slept like the dead, did you?" he taunted.

"Even the dead would be awakened by that racket," she rejoined sourly.

He winked one blue eye. "When she comes tonight, I'll stuff a rag in her mouth."

Although her face flamed with embarrassment, Justine managed to inject venom into her voice. "You do that. Put one in *your* mouth while you're at it."

He chuckled, obviously delighted with the turn of conversation, then sauntered away, shoulders shak-

ing with merriment. When he was out of earshot,
Justine whirled to face China Mary.

"Tell me one thing, will you?"

China Mary extended her hands, palms up. "If I
can."

"Who is this woman he calls Satin?"

Chapter 8

Satin Doll was aptly named, Justine thought.

Hair as black as night fell down her back like a bridal train and cupped her small rump. Her dress fit like a satin glove. No petticoats, bustle, or lace, just sleek material—a rich emerald color patterned in gold. She had creamy skin, a compressed, pouty mouth, and slanted black eyes that glistened like almond-shaped onyx. Her figure was doll-like; she had small breasts, a tiny waist, the mere suggestion of hips. Satin Doll was a treasure, every man's fantasy, and every madam's answered prayer.

But Satin Doll wasn't for sale.

She worked for China Mary as a show girl, and the Oriental madam had explained that Satin bedded for pleasure, not business.

"She too special to sell," China Mary told Justine, then she nodded toward the saloon. "You see for yourself. She on stage tonight. She my number-one girl."

Was she York's number-one girl as well? Justine wondered as she stood in a shadowy corner at the front of the saloon and watched Satin Doll's show.

107

Beery men whooped and hollered, but many were
mesmerized into silence by the Oriental beauty on
stage. Satin used a large black-and-red fan to entice
and suggest, hiding half her face before letting the
fan flutter alluringly across her breasts. The fan hovered at the tops of her thighs like a curious butterfly,
then soared back up, dragging reluctant gazes with
it.

She made promises with her eyes and suggestions
with her fan, making the men crowd closer. Graceful
as a bird in flight, she swooped across the boards,
arms and hands telling an age-old story of desire and
conquest. Two other Oriental girls backed her up,
but they were merely decoration—two pearls on either side of a multifaceted emerald. They could have
had faces as ugly as sin and no one would have noticed.

Although Satin looked as if she'd just stepped off
the boat from Peking, she didn't sound it. China
Mary said she was born in China, but was raised in
San Francisco. She talked like a native. Justine remembered the voice outside her bedroom the pre-
vious night. No broken English. The woman that
night had sounded as American as the Star-Spangled
Banner.

York came into the saloon just as Satin Doll finished her show. The applause was loud and long.
Satin blew kisses to the most ardent spectators, then
disappeared behind the curtain.

Perfect timing, Justine thought, keeping her eyes
trained on York as he closed the door to the gaming
room. He flicked down his turned-back cuffs and removed the gambler's garters from his shirtsleeves.
Advancing into the saloon, he shrugged into his
black suit jacket and stuffed the garters into the
pocket. He adjusted the hang of the jacket by jerking
at the wide lapels as he sauntered toward the long
bar, pausing once or twice to acknowledge greetings.
Justine recognized Wyatt Earp, the lawman the peo-

ple of Tombstone both loved and hated. Even China
Mary gave the brothers Earp a wide path.

"They shoot, then think," Mary had said of them.
"They men of few words, many bullets."

York ordered a whiskey. One elbow propped
against the bar and his drink in hand, he swiveled
sideways to survey the room. Justine squirmed farther into the corner, shunning interested gazes with
her constant scowl. Only one man had approached
her, and she'd sent him sailing off with a curt, "Forget it, mister. I'm not interested, and I'm not for
sale." Hidden away in the corner, few noticed her.

Satin Doll emerged from backstage, sans fan. She
went directly to York and brushed a kiss on his waiting cheek. York handed her a drink, then led her to
Wyatt's table, where only one chair was vacant. York
sat in it, and Satin sat in York's lap.

Justine made a sour face. It was just like him to
court one show girl while condemning another for
being one. Hypocrite, she seethed, her eyes narrowing to smoky slits as she glared at him.

He wore no hat, and the overhead candelabras
spread burnished light through his wheat-tipped
hair. He would no doubt smell as good as he looked,
Justine thought. Damn him! Why did he have to
have so many fine qualities? Why couldn't he be all
bad so she could hate him without complication?
She'd never been around a man who smelled so
wonderful—a citrus scent mixed with aromatic
woodsmoke. Clean, bracing, woodsy. Such polish,
but he wasn't just a pretty boy. No, not York Masters. There was a ruggedness beneath those fancy
clothes and a ruthlessness at the corners of his sensual mouth. And in his eyes Justine had glimpsed an
occasional glint of steel. York Masters was a man of
many layers, many moods, and much arrogance. His
taking advantage of her bad fortune galled her and
made her wary of him, even as her heart pounded
furiously when he was near and blood warmed her

most private parts. He couldn't be trusted, but what was worse, he didn't expect anyone to trust him.

Insolent bastard, she thought unkindly and half-heartedly, for she couldn't deny her attraction to him and her envy of Satin. The woman sat comfortably in his lap, slim arms draped around his neck, eyes flirting with his.

Justine had to look away for a minute until the pain subsided. The ache squeezed her heart and made a sham of the hateful thoughts she'd directed toward him. She didn't really want to compete with Satin, but a part of her rose to the challenge. Gathering her defenses, she swung her gaze back to York. He was laughing at something Satin had whispered in his ear, then he kissed her small, full-lipped mouth. A quick, hard kiss.

The memory of her own sneaky kiss when he'd been unconscious wormed into Justine's mind and made her tingle.

Wyatt Earp lifted a hand, waving at someone who'd just entered the saloon. All eyes tracked to the front of the saloon, where the batwing doors flapped on creaking hinges. The newcomer was Doc Holliday. Doc saw Wyatt, gave a nod, and started toward the table. Justine held her breath as Doc strode past her, no more than two feet from her nose, but he didn't notice her. She released her captive breath and returned her attention to York and his number-one girl.

Everyone at Wyatt's table was busy glad-handing Doc Holliday. Everyone but York. His ice blue eyes were trained on her, unrelenting and uncompromising. Justine felt like a rabbit suddenly exposed to a hunter's bead. Instinctively, she wedged deeper into the corner, then realized how futile her efforts were. She couldn't escape him so easily. His eyes told her so.

Satin chose that moment to run a long-fingered hand through his hair, pushing it back from his forehead so she could place a kiss there. Envy changed to jealousy, stabbing Justine through the heart. Her eyes watered, and her breath caught in her throat. Deserting her shadowed corner, she burst into the open and shoved through the bodies crowding her path. The distance to the door beside the stage, which gave access to a short hallway and the staircase, seemed a mile long instead of a few hundred feet. She made it through the door and had her hand on the railing when York overtook her. His big hand clamped down on hers, curving around it and holding her in place.

"Where's the fire, Jussie?" he drawled.

"What do you want?" she asked, almost hissing at him like a cat with its back up.

"What are you running from?"

"Not from you. I was just watching the show. It's over and I'm going back to my room."

"Watching the show or checking out your competition?"

"You really think you're the cock of the walk, don't you?" She gave an incredulous laugh, then jerked her hand free and gathered up her skirts. "She can have you. Night after night, for all I care."

She took the stairs by twos. York was right behind her, then beside her, then ahead of her. He checked her progress on the landing. His hands closed on her shoulders and pulled her up on her tiptoes.

"Let go!" She struggled, but he held on. "Your insufferable arrogance makes me want to swear off men forever!"

He laughed. "What are you so mad about, Jussie? I haven't done anything to you—lately."

She gathered the moisture in her mouth, and her lips puckered involuntarily, but York's look of warning dried the spittle in her mouth and sent caution slicing through her anger.

"Don't even think about it," he warned. "You spit in my face again and I'll backhand you, I swear I will. Besides, you don't want to fight. You want to be kissed, good and hard."

"You're drunk," she accused, but she knew better.

"Not by a long shot, honey."

Hot words deserted her, and the battle cry became a whimper. "Don't call me that. I'm not your 'honey.'"

"And I'm not buying this act, Jussie." He brought her up to his smiling mouth. "Shut up and kiss me."

"No. Go slobber on your Satin Doll and leave me alone!"

"You're jealous."

"You're crazy."

"You want me."

"You disgust me." She struggled, but he wrapped one arm around her waist and held her chin with the other hand, effectively keeping her mouth within kissing distance.

"Remember the night we spent together?" he taunted. "The night you slipped me that knockout potion?"

"Let go." She didn't want to remember, not now. Not when he was holding her so close that she could feel the beating of his heart, the warmth of his breath, the swell of his manhood.

"You had fun, but I didn't. I figure you owe me one."

"I don't owe you piddly-squat!"

He laughed, baring straight, perfect teeth. "That's not how I see it."

Justine let fly with a vicious kick. He sucked in his breath and let go of her to massage his paining shin.

"Goddamn it!" His chest rose and fell, and he looked at her from beneath lowered brows. "Big mistake, Jussie. Now I'm mad."

Justine dashed into her bedroom and tried to shut the door, but York popped it open with one thudding whack. She put the bed between them and faced him in a partially crouched position, ready to spring when he pounced. But he didn't pounce. He simply closed the door softly and propped the heel of one hand high on one of the four bedposts. He stared at her at his leisure, amused, looking as if he could remain so until the end of time. After a minute Justine straightened but remained wary.

"Now what?" she asked. "What have you got up your sleeve this time?"

"Not a damn thing." He shrugged indolently. "I'm just giving you a firsthand view of what can happen in this town to a girl with more mouth than brains. As you can see, I'm in your bedroom, and you're at a distinct disadvantage."

"That's how *you* see it."

"That's how it is, sweetness. Any time I want, I can grab you, tear that dress off you, and have you every which way. If you want a demonstration, I'll be glad to oblige."

"No." She puffed out a sigh and propped her hands at her waist. "So, what's the point: Is this just another demonstration of your brute strength? If it is, it's wasted. I know you could beat me to a pulp, big man." That last remark was a sneering taunt that brought him away from the post to stand on his own power. Justine tensed, regretting her hasty remark.

"When you get over to the Establishment, you'll be on your own for the most part," he said, his voice and jawline tight with checked irritation. "I'll keep an eye on you, but I can't watch you every single minute. If you sass the wrong man over there, you won't get another chance. *That's* the point."

She lifted one brow, seeing through his lesson. "You didn't chase me up here with that in mind. I'm not as dumb as you think."

"Then why did I chase you up here?"

"To rub my nose in it. You saw me watching you with that show girl, and you decided to make darn sure I understood that you and her are sharing sheets." She thrust her head forward with belliger-

ence. "Well, I don't care who you tussle with in bed,
York Masters, as long as it's not me!" Her finger
stabbed the air, emphasizing the point. "Just one
thing. Don't go turning your nose up at me because
I'm theater people when you can't keep your hands
off that fan dancer. She and I are cut from the same
pattern; the only difference is that I'm cut from better
cloth."

"Ha!" He threw back his golden head to laugh at
that, but she could tell he wasn't amused. "The difference between you and Satin is that she doesn't
pretend to be something she's not. She's just a show
girl; a girl who makes a few bucks by flouncing
around on stage and giving men something pretty to
look at. You"—he jabbed a finger at her—"do the
same damn thing but you call it *the-ah-tah!*" He made
a disgusting swipe with his hand. "Bullshit!"

His low opinion of her stung. She had known a
lifetime of being slapped down, stepped over, and
spit on and had developed a tough skin against it,
but York had penetrated her armor so convincingly
that it frightened her. He was dangerous in too many
ways to count. Her lower lip trembled, but she managed to hang on to a thread of composure.

"What do you really know about me?" she asked
in a broken, breathy voice. "How can you stand
there and judge me?"

"I've touched a soft spot," he observed smugly.

"That's what you wanted, isn't it? To hurt me,
make me bleed, make me hate you a little more than
I already do?"

"That's what I wanted." He moved around the
bed and lifted her chin up and around with his
thumb. His eyes changed, liquified. No ice, just
warmth. He dipped his head and brushed her lips
with his. When she made no response, his mouth
tensed with regret, and he withdrew. "You *do* hate
me, don't you?"

"Completely."

"Good." His hand fell away. A muscle spasmed beneath his ear. "Let's keep it that way."

He went to the door, jerked it open, and swung to face her before stepping over the threshold. "Our plan worked. Madame Chloe sent word that she'll hire you. You're expected over there first thing tomorrow." Then he was gone, leaving Justine to gape at the closed door.

Through the grimy panes of Satin Doll's room in Hop Town, York could hear the tinkle of piano keys. Probably coming from the Crystal Palace, he thought. Music from the Establishment couldn't float that far. He took in a deep breath, then coughed it out as the incense-laden air irritated his throat and lungs. Incense and something else, his nose told him.

York turned to face the bed where Satin Doll was curled like a kitten on her side. Her naked skin gleamed with a patina of perspiration. The night was warm and enveloping. The water in the bowl of the opium pipe bubbled as Satin took another long drag off the snaking tube. Her eyes rolled back, showing the whites, and she exhaled the smoke with a singing sigh of contentment.

"Come to bed and love me," she said, her voice as smoky as the room. "What did you come here for if not for that?"

He looked down at himself and saw disinterest. First time for everything, he consoled himself. "I'm not good company tonight, Satin. I'll get dressed and head out."

"Don't be in such an all-fired hurry. I can get a rise out of you if you'll just haul it over here and give me a chance." She crooked a finger and smiled, then patted the mattress next to her. "Put yourself in Satin Doll's hands, baby."

He sat on the edge of the bed, and Satin's cool palms washed over his back and around to his thighs. She flattened her small breasts against his back, coming up on her knees to fondle him intimately. She kissed his shoulder blades, his neck, his backbone. Her tiny teeth nipped his skin. She had always stirred him, but not tonight. He closed his eyes and saw Jussie's face. Groaning, he lurched off the bed to escape Satin's urging hands.

"It's nothing personal," he said, essaying a smile. "My mind is everywhere but in this room. I'll see you tomorrow night."

Satin tipped her head to the left, and her long, silky hair fell like a black waterfall to pool on the white sheet. Reaching for a silk robe, she put it on. "Does this have something to do with that woman staying upstairs at Mary's? What's her story anyway? She's not moving in on my territory, is she?"

"No. She's going to work at the Establishment tomorrow." He dipped his head to button his shirt and shadow his face from her wise eyes.

"So, you managed to get her inside, did you?" She lifted her thin brows. "I'm glad. Maybe she can find out something."

"Do you think the girls will talk to her?"

"Most likely. She can't do any worse than you and I have done. We couldn't get any of those girls to give us the time of day. Talk about some tight-lipped gals—woo-ee!" She smiled, shrugging her narrow shoulders. "Frenchy's going to whore for you?"

"No. She's going to be Madame Chloe's bookkeeper until a permanent one can be hired by the Count."

"Is that so? Are you thinking of moving up in the world? Thinking of trading in this show girl for a whore's bookkeeper?" She shrugged indifferently. "Do what you want."

"Don't I always?" he said, matching wickedness with wickedness, then tossing off a grimace of reproach. "What are we doing, Satin? Fussing like a couple of kids? It's stupid. Beneath us." He touched a fingertip to her button nose. "Tell me something."

"What?" Her eyes were luminous in the candle-
light.

"Have you ever been in a play? You know, acted."

"Legitimate theater?" She laughed softly, shaking
her head until her hair flowed like dark water
around her shoulders and down to her waist. "I'm
not trained for that. Why, they'd laugh me right off
the stage."

"They who? I can't think of any man who would
laugh at you. You're beautiful, Satin. You know you
are."

"Yes, but in the theater beauty only gets you on
the stage. Talent keeps you there. Those women are
trained. They are classically taught. Me? I'm a graceful bird who can do a few dance steps, but that's it.
The rest is illusion."

"Did you ever think of the theater?"

"Sure, what show girl hasn't? But you learn quick
that those doors are closed unless you've got something to back up your looks. I know you lump us all
in one pile, but there *are* differences," she said, leaning forward to kiss his chin, his cheek, his mouth.
"None of the girls at China Mary's could do my
show. I'm a cut above them. And theater actresses
are a cut above me." She ran her fingers through her
long hair and sighed. "I wish I could have helped
you more, York."

"You've done enough for me." He pulled her into
his arms, letting her snuggle against him. "You
never asked questions. You just jumped right in and
did everything I asked."

"That's because I fell for you. You know that. One
smile and you owned this Satin Doll."

He trailed his lips down the side of her face. Her
skin was fragrant and petal soft. "You're the best
friend I have—you and China Mary."

"You trust me, don't you?"

"Sure." He leaned back to look into her face. "Why? Don't you trust *me?*"

"Of course. It's just that . . . well, I heard that Doc Holliday gave Kate the boot. It's hard to believe. They've been together so long and she made one mistake—one mistake—and he kicks her out of his life. That's not fair."

"They might still mend the fences, but you've got to admit Kate's mistake was a doozy. She pointed the finger at Doc. Told some marshal that he robbed a stagecoach, for Christ's sake. She signed an affidavit that stated he not only robbed the coach, but that he killed the driver. Hell of a mistake, Satin."

"But she took it all back later," Satin pointed out. "She was drunk when she signed that statement. Drunk and probably scared. Don't you ever get scared and do crazy things, York?"

"Not that crazy. I wouldn't betray someone I loved . . . someone I cared about."

Satin pushed away from him and reached for the tube again. As she inhaled the concoction, tears glazed her eyes. "Sometimes life isn't so simple. Sometimes you can't make the right choice."

He regarded her with concern, not liking her melancholy mood. "Satin, you should go easy on that stuff. It's not good for you."

"Neither are you." She smiled and closed her eyes. "Or maybe I'm the one who's not good for you. Maybe I'd be doing you a favor if I went away, left you alone."

"Don't talk like that." He gave her a kiss and made her look into his eyes. "You know my leaving early tonight doesn't have anything to do with you, don't you? It's me. I'm tired. I've had a long day. You understand?"

"Sure, sugar. You go on and get some rest. I always want what's best for you." She made a shooing motion. "Get going. I'm fine. I'll just smoke a little more, and then I'll drop off to sleep."

"See you tomorrow," he whispered, then closed the door behind him and wondered if she could really handle her habit. He'd told himself it was like smoking tobacco, but he knew better. Satin was getting worse, he thought, striding away from the one-story tenement and along the predawn streets. She was depending more and more on that damned opium pipe. Or maybe his lack of response had made her turn to that smoky comfort. I shouldn't have visited her tonight, he thought. Not after that run-in with Jussie.

Jussie.

God! He had to get that woman out of his mind! He slammed one fist into the other, cursing hotly under his breath and wishing he could beat the hell out of something.

It was just that sometimes she reminded him so of Lizzie. Both dreamers. Both thinking they could handle any situation. Both too brave and too stubborn and too beautiful for their own good.

Sweet Lizzie. He saw her enchanting face in his mind's eye, and his heart ached. His eyes blurred with tears. She could have stayed in St. Louis with him, but she'd been to the theater and had gotten it into her fool head that she could be a stage performer. She could have men at her feet and make money of her own. His pleas that she stay with him had fallen on deaf ears. She'd left him, headed for unknown territory. One postcard came from Boston with a brief message: "Dearest York, I'm an actress! Performing on stage every evening! The Count—he's my new friend—says I have something special. He believes in me. Will write again. Your Lizzie."

Theater. Acting. York rolled his eyes. She'd been a novelty act, not an actress. The Count had wrangled jobs for her in French Syndicate-owned saloons and dance halls.

She hadn't written again. He'd heard nothing from her. Nothing. He'd tracked her to Tombstone and lost her trail. But he knew the Count figured in somehow. The Count always figured into women disappearing from Tombstone. That bastard had blood on his hands. Lizzie's blood? And what of Jussie? Was she being led to her own slaughter?

"Lizzie. Jussie." He shook his head as his vision turned inward to the worry he carried like a second heart.

"Got a burr under your saddle, son?"

York whirled at the sound of the voice, then relaxed when he recognized Doc Holliday's long frame. Doc stepped closer, stroking his full mustache as his light blue eyes sent out sparks of amusement.

"'Evening, Doc." York stuffed his hands in his trouser pockets and propped one hip against a hitching post outside the Crystal Palace Saloon. "Caught me talking to myself."

"I won't tell." Doc fired a match and lit a cigarette. "Want a smoke?"

"No, thanks." York tipped back his head to stare at the starry night. He wondered if Jussie was sleeping soundly.

"Heard around town that the French madam has hired herself a new bookkeeper."

York nodded.

"Got your pigeon in the cage, huh?"

"As of tomorrow, yes. Of course, it's temporary. The Count has the final say."

"I 'spect he'll be riding into town within another month or so. Don't you reckon?"

"If he keeps to schedule, yes."

"Think the girl can find out anything?"

"She's sharp as barbed wire, Doc. A lot sharper than I thought. Nailed Madame Chloe cold."

"How's that?"

"She said Madame Chloe wasn't particular about gender and was about as French as Kate Fisher."

Doc chuckled, then sobered too quickly. "By the

way, Kate's gone. Took the stagecoach out this afternoon."

York took a moment to study Doc's face and detected regret there. "She's gone for good, is she?"

"Yep. I sent her away." Doc blew smoke at the moon. "She done me wrong once too often. I can't bed a woman I don't trust."

"I'm sorry you couldn't work it out, Doc, but I understand. A man's got to be careful, especially in a town like this."

Doc studied the end of the cigarette as if it were a crystal ball. "Women can sure tie men in knots. I'm glad Kate's gone. Sometimes I didn't like myself much when I was with her."

"I hear you," York said, feeling it in his heart.

"Got yourself woman problems, son?"

"Nothing I can't handle."

Doc trained his gaze on York. "You sure this young filly can keep a cool head around the madame? Chloe's no dumb-butt, you know."

"I know. Neither is China Mary." York's mouth twisted ruefully. "And Jussie can wrap Mary around her little finger."

"You, too?" Doc's sly grin was about as pleasant for York as the kiss of a buggy whip.

"She's on *my* lead rope, I'm not on hers." York pushed away from the hitching rail and started across the street. "See you around, Doc."

"Who set fire to your tail, Masters? Was it something I said?" Doc's laughter fell on York like rain from hell, scalding and hissing and blistering his usually tough skin.

Chapter 9

"**I** want the money box, if you're finished with it."

Justine looked up from the ledger as Madame Chloe came into the office. The madame yawned and covered her mouth languidly.

"Yes, I'm finished." Justine handed the iron box over to her. "Every dollar is accounted for. Here are the tabulations for your inspection." She gave the woman a long sheet of paper. "You did well last night. I bet this house brings in more than any other in town."

"Mmm." The older woman glanced at the total and nodded. "Not bad."

"Will your boss be pleased?"

Madame Chloe afforded her a brief, chilling glance. "I please myself and the rest falls into place." Still studying the sheet, she left the office for her private rooms at the front of the house.

Justine sighed, feeling blocked at every turn. Five days had passed since she had been summoned to the Establishment, and she was beginning to relax around the French madam, but she hadn't uncovered one bit of useful information.

She'd been given a room—small, but adequate—and shown to a desk in Madame's spacious office. Madame's own delicate desk backed a bay window. Justine's was sequestered in a corner beside a pair of French doors. The arrangement and routine had fallen into place with nary a hitch.

Mornings were spent in blissful silence since everyone—except the jovial cook, Peachy—was asleep. Justine savored the time alone, dawdling in her bedroom and going to the kitchen in the late morning for a peaceful breakfast before beginning her bookkeeping. Madame Chloe usually made an appearance shortly after noon, still wearing one of her many silk wrappers and no makeup. Without cosmetics she wasn't as attractive. Her skin was blotchy, her eyes puffy lidded. She was a night creature, for as the day wore on and dusk approached, Madame Chloe's beauty emerged. By nightfall, she was ravishing.

Having known a few actresses with that same timetable, Justine knew how to get along with her new boss. She said little and stayed out of her way until late afternoon. By that time Madame Chloe was more sociable. After supper, served promptly at five and with every Establishment resident in attendance, Justine retired to her room behind the office. Sometimes she and Peachy played a few games of checkers before Justine turned in.

Madame ran her house efficiently and with an iron fist. The first-floor parlor was the greeting place where the girls, in their transparent dresses and handmade, filmy underwear, charmed the prospective customers. The air was redolent with imported French perfume and the finest whiskey and rye. The middle floor was reserved for "private" entertaining, and the upper floor for high-paying customers who were spending the night or required special services.

The soiled doves were required to bathe at least twice a week, and several wore falsies under their slinky gowns. Justine had seen these in the theater, but was fascinated nonetheless. The false breasts and bottoms were made from fine wire covered with fabric and woven into alluring shapes.

The girls were encouraged to drum up business. One girl, Blond Babette, delivered printed cards around town that announced, "Elderly gentlemen would do well to ask for Babette at the Establishment. She is adept at satisfying the needs of those of advanced age."

Wednesday was token day. Customers were given trade tokens to be exchanged at the general store for items of their choice. This was meant to appease angry wives.

The Establishment residents were cordial, but Justine had little in common with them. She liked the piano player, a wiry young man named Ivory Sparks who hailed from the Carolinas and had a toothy grin and big freckles. He was a friend to all the girls, teasing and complimenting them at every turn.

Justine had asked about the Count—last night at supper when his name came up—but she'd gotten little information.

"Does the Count come around often?" she'd asked.

"Several times a year," Madame Chloe answered.

"What's he like?"

"His privacy," Madame answered smoothly, purposefully misinterpreting the question.

The tension at the table had been so thick it was choking, but Ivory Sparks relieved it with entertaining palaver. Justine dropped the subject, deciding it was too soon to press for details. She couldn't arouse suspicion, and ill-timed, persistent questions tended to do just that.

Justine's thoughts were interrupted when Peachy brought in a tea tray, then left to see to Madame

Chloe's noon breakfast. Sipping the savory tea and sampling Peachy's oatmeal muffins, Justine worried about her lack of success. She wished the Count would ride into town and end the suspense today or tomorrow, not next month. More than anything, she wanted to be free of York Masters.

The irony of that wish wasn't lost on her. She smiled with rueful understanding, realizing that her scourge was no longer Tombstone, but one of its residents. York was fire, and Justine was afraid of being burned.

At night she thought of him, dreamed of him, tossed restlessly in bed for want of him. She wished she'd peeked under the sheet when she'd undressed him at Big Nose Kate's. She *wanted* to see him naked. The shame of it! The man had made her a tart!

Shoe Black would be ashamed of her. He'd done everything in his power to keep her unscathed and unsullied. But one man, one golden-haired, blue-eyed man, had undone all of Shoe Black's good teaching. Justine had been courted by many, but she'd wanted none of them with anything akin to what she felt for York Masters. He had pried open the lid of her womanly desires, and she couldn't seem to get that lid nailed back down again.

Of all the men in the world, she hated the thought of succumbing to him. She wanted a man who respected her, and York had made it clear that, in his eyes, she was no better than a whore.

York made no distinction between women who walked the streets and those who trod the boards. He should know better, she thought, wondering why a man of his intelligence was so sadly lacking in that one area. It didn't make sense. Why was he being so mean to her, almost *forcing* her to despise him? Maybe he sensed her growing attraction to him and wanted none of it. Yet if that was so, why did he keep taunting her, backing her into corners and making her blisteringly aware of his own arousal?

Realizing that she was sitting at her desk staring into space, she finished her tea and placed the tray outside the office door for Peachy to retrieve. She made herself concentrate on righting Madame's meticulous ledgers. Work had piled up since the last bookkeeper left, and her predecessor hadn't been all that accurate or conscientious. Obviously, Madame Chloe had been enamored of the woman's other assets.

It was late afternoon when Madame Chloe came into the office again, with York Masters at her heels. Justine stood up, shaken to the soles of her shoes by York's unannounced visit. The amusement in his eyes and his barely suppressed smile brought bright color to her cheeks.

"Justine Drussard, I would like you to meet—" Madame began, but York interrupted her, coming forward to grasp Justine's hand and lift it for a butterfly-soft kiss.

"Introductions aren't necessary, Madame Chloe. Jussie and I know each other."

"Oh?"

"We met at China Mary's," he explained, releasing Justine's limp hand.

"But of course."

"In fact," he said, turning to face Madame Le Deau, "it's Jussie I've come calling on, although seeing you is always a pleasure."

Madame Chloe looked from York to Jussie's rosy-hued face, and a knowing smile touched her rouged mouth.

"I see." She bowed her white head. "Then I'll leave you alone with my bookkeeper, but you can't keep her long from her work." She arched her painted brows in reproach. "Perhaps from now on you can arrange your visits in the evenings when she's at leisure?"

"Your point is taken to heart, Madame Chloe." York saw her to the door and left it open a crack. He tread lightly to Justine, and his tone was little more than a whisper. "Are you surprised to see me or have you been struck dumb since we parted?"

"What are you doing, coming in here and making her think there's something going on between us?"

"There *is* something going on between us. We're partners. We shook on it, remember?" He tossed his hat onto her desk as if he meant to stay awhile.

"Shhh!" She tilted sideways to see past his broad frame to the doorway. "Do you want someone to hear, you fool?"

"Simmer down, I know what I'm doing."

"But you made her think we . . . you and I . . . that we're—"

"Lovers," he finished with relish, letting the *l* roll off his tongue as if he hated to part with it. "Or, at least, close to being so. That might work to your advantage. Perhaps Madame Chloe won't try to seduce you if she thinks I've beaten her to the draw."

York strolled around the room, stopping to snoop at Madame Chloe's desk, then moving back to Justine. He made a comical face at her frowning countenance.

"So, how have things been for you here? Anything to pass on to your partner?"

"No. Nothing. I asked about . . . him, but Madame Chloe cut me down. It seems that subject is forbidden territory around here."

"Well, keep prying."

"But I don't want Madame to think I'm too nosy."

"Madame isn't the only one around here who's met the Count, Jussie. Find someone with a loose tongue and set it wagging."

"Right." She nodded, seeing a new trail to explore and glad that York had pointed it out to her. "The piano player and the cook are really friendly. They both like me."

"Atta girl." He winked, then came around and sat in her desk chair. He hooked her around the waist and hauled her into his lap, laughing at her sounds of aggravation. "Be still, Jussie. Enjoy the moment."

"I'm not your Satin Doll, so quit handling me like I am."

"If you were Satin, I'd be undressing you right now."

His growling tone quelled her frantic struggles. She cut her gaze to him, searing him with it. The teasing lights in his eyes blinked out.

"Listen to me, this is important." He brought his lips close to the delicate shell of her ear. His breath warmed her neck and set her senses whirling. "We need a code. A way to contact each other. Where's your room?"

"Back there," she said, nodding toward the door.

"On the first floor?"

"Yes."

"Show me." He released her, lending a steady hand and then keeping hers in his. "Lead the way," he urged when she made no move toward her bedroom.

"I can't take you in there," she protested. "Madame Chloe might come looking for me and find us. She'll hit the roof."

"Just show me, Jussie, and quit acting like a spinster in a whorehouse."

She shrugged, controlling her burst of anger. "What does it matter? This is *your* play, not mine." With that, she went across the room and opened the door to her small room.

York strolled in, glancing around quickly and making a face of contempt. "Not much, is it?"

"The best rooms are reserved for the evening trade."

"How delicately put," he said with a smirk. He went to the window and smiled when he swung around to face her. "Perfect," he declared. "Anytime you need me, you put a lighted lantern in this window, and I'll come running. When I need you, I'll do the same. You know which window is mine, don't you?"

"Yes, but why would you need me?"

He smiled wickedly. "I might get lonely some night."

"Don't put a light in your window for that. I don't need you wasting my time."

"If you get lonely, you can light a lantern for me."

"If I get lonely, it won't be for your company."

"Hard-hearted Jussie," he teased.

"No, not hard-hearted, just choosy."

His smile vanished, and he gave her a look that made her heart tremble in her breast and time stand still. She knew he was struggling to keep from saying something by the flexing of the muscle in his jaw and the rapid blinking of his expressive eyes. When his lips parted, Justine held her breath, wanting to catch whatever words he fought against.

"Choose me." Hoarse. Pleading. Heart stopping.

For a joyous few moments, she let herself believe. A smile nudged the corners of her mouth, but suspicion slammed down hard like a fist. She turned away from what she wanted to believe and closed her eyes to find reality. He came up behind her and ran his fingers down her back, tracing her spine. She grabbed one of the bedposts to keep from dropping to her knees.

"Please, don't."

"Don't what?"

"Don't prop me up only to slap me down." She spun around, indignation lending her strength. He was regarding her with a mixture of confusion and concern, softening her heart even as she strove to shield her reaction from him. "I know you don't care anything for me, so don't go acting like you want my attentions."

"I wouldn't mind your attentions," he allowed.

"And neither would you honor them. This town has spoiled you by making you think you can have any woman you want just for the asking. Well, not *this* woman. I might not have much, but I still have my pride, and I won't have you dancing a jig on it." She marched past him, back to the office where she felt more secure. Her bedroom implied an intimacy she didn't want with York Masters.

He followed her but didn't leave as she'd expected. Instead, he ambled toward her and traced the pattern in the rug with the toe of his black boot. Justine sat at her desk and opened the ledger, trying to hasten his departure. She was jittery having him so near and so obviously reluctant to leave. She handed him his hat.

"I understand the signal," she said, prompting him to go.

"I'll check on you every few days," he said, eyes still trained on the white-and-gold patterned rug, hands running aimlessly along the brim of his black hat.

"Fine. Give my regards to China Mary."

"Sure thing. I guess I should go."

"Yes, please do."

He turned on his heel and strode toward the door. Justine focused on the work before her, but then she heard the thud of his boot heels come closer again. She looked up just as he reached her. His face was a blur as his mouth, open and thirsting, covered hers. His tongue lay heavily upon hers for a moment, then curled to tickle the roof of her mouth. Justine moaned, knocked senseless by the gale of his sudden passion. One hand cupped the back of her head, the other rested lightly upon her breast. Her willpower fell away and let her body rise up into his waiting arms. She hugged his lean waist, urging him to deepen the kiss and drive the lingering doubts from her mind.

But he set her away. His breathing was ragged as he faced her, eyes darkly blue and lips glistening. He shook his head, making her doubts rise up to mock her.

"You..." He shook his head again, as if befuddled. "You defeat me."

"I don't know what you're saying," she confessed. "I don't know what you want. One minute you're ridiculing me, and the next thing I know you're kissing me."

"You want to know what I want?"

"Yes."

"I want you. Under me. Naked."

She couldn't check her quick intake of breath or the widening of her eyes. She wished she could take back the question because the answer was destined to haunt her.

"But we don't always get what we want," he said softly, already moving toward the door. "And, mostly, that's for the best. You'd do well to stay out of my reach, Jussie."

"Easy to say. Not so easy to do." She took a step toward him, still feeling the fire of his kiss. "You don't make it easy for me. You know that. Maybe we should talk to each other instead of arguing and trying to hurt each other. It's not getting us anywhere. I know that deep down you don't want anything to do with me. You don't want to dirty your hands."

"No, you're wrong about that."

"Am I?"

"Yes." The steadiness in his eyes confirmed his answer.

"Then explain yourself. Do you like to push me this way and pull me that way? Playing with my feelings, is that your idea of having a fine, old time?"

"No." He ground his teeth in aggravation. "I don't mean to... God! I don't know what I'm doing anymore. I know one thing for sure, though. Wanting you is getting in the way of"—he glanced through the crack in the door, his face tensed, then he put a smile on it—"your work here. I'm certain

Madame Chloe is coming in this moment to send me
on my way."

"I warned you, Monsieur Masters," Madame
Chloe said, sweeping past him into the office. "Jussie is on *my* time now."

"Yes, of course. Forgive me for keeping her from
her work." He dipped his head and his gaze touched
Jussie's for a naked instant, telling her there would
be another time, another meeting. "Good day,
ladies."

Justine turned aside as he left the room, pretending to straighten her desk while she rearranged her
visage. Lifting one hand, she touched her tender lips
and felt for any telltale marks of York's kiss.

"How did you do it?"

Looking toward Madame Chloe, Justine raised her
brows in inquiry.

"Throw a lasso around York Masters," Madame
Chloe clarified.

"He's a man, and I'm the new girl in town," Justine said, shrugging. "It's nothing, really."

"That is wise. He's a maverick. He doesn't travel
with the pack, and I have always found loners to be
trouble. Bear that in mind, won't you."

"Of course. I agree." Justine sat at the desk and
bent over her work. "It's only a flirtation." She sent
the other woman a smile meant to disarm her.
"Harmless."

Madame Chloe's eyes narrowed slightly as if she
was seeing past Justine's smile to the truth behind it.
Justine faced her work again, warning herself not to
underestimate Chloe Le Deau. She might look light
and airy, but she was just the opposite.

In the woman's dark doll's eyes, Justine had
glimpsed a carnivore.

Cherry Vanilla looked like her name. With red hair
and white skin, a ready smile and an infectious giggle, she was one of Madame Chloe's most requested

girls. She was the only girl at the Establishment with
no French background, other than having been
highly recommended by a French Syndicate madam
in Kansas City.

"I've worked here for two years." Cherry's coppery eyes widened with amazement. "Saints preserve us! That's a long time for me. I've got itchy
feet." She plucked a red rose from the arrangement
on the upright piano. "I'm going to wear this tucked
in the bodice of my dress tonight. Won't that look
fetching?"

Justine nodded, thinking that Cherry didn't need
such enticements. She walked into a room, and the
men in it wanted her.

"Do you like it here?" Cherry asked.

"Yes, very much. Everyone's been so kind."

"People are right nice here. Of course, this is the
best house. I've heard other houses aren't nearly so
fine. You were at Big Nose Kate's for a while, weren't
you?"

"Only briefly."

"She left town, you know."

"No, I didn't." Justine's knees gave way and she
sat on the piano stool, swinging back and forth on
the rotating seat. "When did she leave?"

"A few days ago. Doc Holliday paid her passage.
That's the gossip, anyways. Guess he finally got a
bellyful of her."

Justine felt a twinge of pity for Kate, recalling how
she had been hoping Doc would forgive her for
whatever wrong she'd committed. Well, at least he'd
given her enough money to get out of town, she
thought, wishing she had been so lucky.

"Were you ever in the pleasure business?" Cherry
asked, breaking into Justine's musings.

"No, not really. I tried, but I wasn't very good at
it."

"It takes a certain talent." Cherry spun the rose by
the stem, letting its perfume spiral up to her nose.

"I'm mighty glad for the work. My mama kicked me out when I was barely fourteen. What was I to do? I didn't have any romantic prospects, and I wasn't going to marry just any old thing." Cherry's round chin jerked up. "I got my shopping list, and I'm not settling for secondhand merchandise, if you get what I mean."

"I understand," Justine assured her. "Like you, I have no intention of settling for less than the best."

"From what I hear, you won't have to." Cherry grinned mischievously. "York Masters has been calling on you, right?"

Justine averted her gaze and shrugged, trying to appear coy.

"Lucky girl." Cherry spun in a tight circle, hands clasped to her round bosom. "He's a king of hearts, that one. I've been hoping he might stop in and like me, but he stays mostly in Hop Town. I heard he was messing with one of China Mary's girls."

"Satin Doll," Justine supplied.

"You've met her?"

"I've seen her."

"Is she pretty?"

Justine positioned her hands on the keys and sounded out a C chord. "I suppose." She wrinkled her nose in distaste at the turn of the conversation. "It doesn't matter." Looking up, she engaged Cherry's full attention with a friendly smile. "Have you ever met the Count? What's he like?"

"The Count?" Cherry tucked the rose behind one ear and sighed. "Oh, he's a gentleman. You'll like him. All the girls do."

"When do you think I'll meet him?"

"When he gets here, most likely."

"Yes, but *when* will that be?" Justine asked, knowing she was pressing hard but taking the chance since Cherry didn't seem too nimble minded.

"Let me think . . ." Cherry turned reddish brown eyes upward for guidance. "Soon, I guess. A couple of weeks. He comes around to collect the profits you know. But he always spends time with each girl."

"What do you mean? He spends time with every girl? Does he talk to them or . . . ?"

"Well . . ." Cherry gripped the edge of the piano lid and rested her chin on her knuckles. Her eyes grew bright. "I can't speak for the others, but he took—"

"What y'all doing to my piano? Giving it a polish with your rumps and elbows?" Ivory Sparks asked as he loped into the room.

"I'll tell you later," Cherry whispered to Justine before bussing Ivory's cheek. Justine managed a strained smile, feeling as if the innocent piano player had just pulled the rug out from under her. She stood up, giving over his stool.

"Sorry to interrupt, but I need to limber up me fingers before the place starts fillin' up." He sat at the piano and popped his knuckles one by one.

Cherry looked to the mantel clock and let out a playful shriek. "Saints preserve us! I've got to wiggle into my dress and put on my face. See y'all later!" She sprinted from the room, her bare feet squeaking on the hardwood floor as she turned the corner and dashed for the stairs.

"Cherry, Cherry, Cherry," Ivory chanted with a good-natured grin. "Always a day late and a dollar short. Bless her heart. Was she telling you about her sad childhood?"

"About her mother kicking her out of the house?" Justine nodded, finding the story too familiar to be interesting.

"A shame, ain't it? These poor chickens have all been kicked around. Some are blinded by love, others betrayed by family." His fingers moved expertly, picking out a fitting melancholy accompaniment. "The world, it's full of woe," he half sang. "Full of heartbreak and lost chances."

Justine studied him for a few moments. He was

speaking from experience. She started to ask him about himself, but she tamped down the impulse. Everyone had a sob story, but she wasn't at the Establishment to offer a shoulder to cry on.

"I was talking to Cherry about the Count."

The mournful tune stopped midstanza. "What about him?"

Edging around the piano, Justine trailed a fingertip along the hinged lid. She crossed her arms on the top and looked over them at Ivory's guarded expression. "She was telling me that he's a gentleman and spends time with each girl when he visits."

"Cherry wouldn't know a gentleman from a billy goat," Ivory answered with a grimace. "That weren't kind, but more truth than not. The Count ain't no *gennaman*," he said, sneering the last word. "How could he be? He hires out women like they's buggies to be ridden and then put away for the next man."

"You don't approve of the women who work here?"

"I don't approve of the men who make a livin' off 'em," Ivory corrected, then began picking out a happier tune.

"I want to make a good impression on the Count," Justine said, watching Ivory's feeble attempts at disguising his hatred for the man.

"Why care about him?"

"He'll have the final say on whether or not I keep this job."

"Don't go fretting 'bout that. You're pretty and Madame Chloe likes you, so the Count'll letcha stay."

"It's that easy?"

His eyes met hers. "I wouldn't get too friendly with the Count," he advised in a lowered tone. "Be nice, but not *too* nice."

"Why? Do you think he's dangerous or something?"

Ivory's expression hardened to stone. "I think

he's . . ." He shook his head and pressed his lips together in a stubborn line.

Justine went to his side and placed a hand on his shoulder. When he looked up at her, she smiled. "Everyone puts their troubles on your shoulders, so why not put yours on mine? Tell me, Ivory, tell me why you hate the Count. I want to help."

"Naw." He looked at the piano keys, and Justine squeezed his shoulder. "I got my reasons for hating him, that's all."

"What are they?"

Ivory glanced around to make sure they were alone, then he swiveled to face Justine. "Because of Shelley," he whispered, his eyes shimmering with tears. "That's why I hate him. He took away my dear, sweet Shelley. . . ."

Chapter 10

Twilight bathed Tombstone in a purple haze. A swift dry breeze winged in from the desert, bringing with it the faint perfume of hearty blossoms and spreading a dusting of sand on every surface. The breeze sent the sign hanging above the barber-shop door swinging and singing on its rusty hinges.

Keeping to the boardwalk along Allen Street, Justine moved in a sprightly manner. The tapping of her heels sounded like hammers. The leather soles on her boots ground the sand to dust, and the breeze sent the dust flying behind her billowing skirts. She ducked her head, angling the brim of her bonnet to shield her stinging eyes from Tombstone's grit. The streets were nearly deserted. Merchants had closed their businesses, and saloon keepers had not yet sent theirs into full gallop. Shifting her bulky parcel from one arm to another, Justine glanced inside each saloon she passed, comparing them to China Mary's. Most were common, except for the Crystal Palace, which was quite grand with its chandeliers and gilded walls. On the next block another saloon or music hall was under construction. Tombstone was still growing, but in one direction. Everything being built was meant to store or sell liquor.

How many drunks can one town support? she wondered, then admitted to herself that she'd been in many towns like Tombstone. Young towns built churches and saloons first, then feed and dry goods stores, stables and schools, usually in that order. Tombstone was no different from any other mining town, springing up from necessity and thriving as long as the silver held out. Miners were interested mostly in three things: a filling meal, a bottle of whiskey, and a willing woman. By that standard, Tombstone was paradise.

Entering Hop Town, Justine went to the back of China Mary's place and knocked softly. Ah Lum peeked at her, closed the door for a few puzzling moments, then opened it wide to her. He didn't waste words, but merely inclined his head in a silent greeting. China Mary sat in the big, upholstered chair, her tiny feet dangling above the floor, Far East curled in her lap. The remains of a chicken and fluffy rice sat on a low table, and Justine realized she'd interrupted China Mary's dinner.

"I'm sorry. I can come back later."

"No, come sit." China Mary motioned her farther into the room. "We finished. Take this away, Ah Lum."

Ah Lum obeyed, taking the tray and himself out of the office, but the savory aroma of the roasted chicken hung in the air. Justine looked toward the curtained passageway.

"Is Ah Lum a relative or just a friend?"

"Both." China Mary's eyes sparked with humor. "He husband."

"Husband? I never thought—I mean . . . well, I'm surprised. I never thought of you being married to him."

"Married many, many year." Her gaze shifted to

the parcel balanced on Justine's jutting hip. "What you got there, girlie?"

"The clothes you loaned me." Justine held them out, wrapped in newspaper. "I've purchased a few things of my own, so I want to return these and thank you for your kindness."

China Mary nodded to the chair near her. "You sit. Put clothes down. Tell me about Madame Chloe. She treat you good?"

Justine sat opposite her and placed the clothes beside the chair. "Madame Chloe has been very good to me. I think she likes me, but I'm sure she doesn't trust me."

"She trust no one."

"Yes, I think you're right."

"Something else?"

Justine met China Mary's wizened gaze and wondered if the woman really had the power to read her mind, to see her future, her past, her best-kept secrets. "I don't trust her, either."

"It good you don't. She viper."

"Yes, that's true. She's kind, but she keeps everyone at a distance. One thing bothers me."

"What?"

"She keeps hinting that I should work downstairs at night and make extra money. I don't want to be backed into that corner again."

China Mary released a high giggle. "You no like being paid for?"

"No, not in that way. I made a promise to myself long ago that I wouldn't turn to that kind of life. That's why I've studied so hard and put up with so much."

"You study?"

"Acting," she said, waiting for derision, but China Mary's expression was one of interest. "I studied drama with several teachers, one of them quite famous. I've spent the past two or three years getting as much experience on the boards as possible, and now that I'm a seasoned performer, I'm going to approach one of the larger troupes for an audition, and then I'll . . ." Her voice trailed off. "I'm sorry. It's just that it means so much to me to be taken seriously, to not be laughed at or looked down on. I've had a lifetime of that, and I'm sick of it."

"I know."

China Mary's assertion was so strong that it sent Justine's gaze to hers. In the Oriental woman's sunken eyes, Justine saw insight and wisdom. She *did* know, Justine thought. She *did* understand.

"You cloaked in shame," China Mary said in a singsong chant. "But it not your shame. Your mother's shame. Yes, your mother. You ashamed of her."

"My mother's dead."

"I know, but you keep her shame alive in you. Let it go, Jus-see. Your mother forced onto rough road. Had to stumble and fall. You fall, too, on that road."

"I wouldn't have been on that road," Justine said, following China Mary's circuitous talk.

"You too hasty to point finger. If you have little baby crying for food, you walk any path to find it."

Justine shifted irritably. "I should go. I have things—"

"You stay and talk."

"I don't want to."

"You will." China Mary stroked the lazy cat in her lap, the limp movement of her hand belying the strength in her eyes. "It time we spoke of these things."

"Why? My life is nothing to you."

"Not so. You stumbled into my world. You now part of it, and I part of yours. When you leave your mother's home?"

"My mother never made a home for me."

"When you leave?" China Mary repeated, ignoring Justine's bitterness.

Justine sighed her resignation. Why was this

woman so insistent? Her life wasn't all that interesting or different. Everyone had a sad story somewhere in their past, and hers was of no consequence in the overall scheme of things. "I left her when I was thirteen," she answered sullenly.

"So young."

"New Orleans is a big city. I was lucky enough to meet a couple of good people who watched over me." Justine looked squarely at the other woman. "I never had to sell myself to strangers like my mother did."

"And what of father?"

"He left when I was a baby. Took off without a word. He was about as upstanding as a snake."

"He French, like mother."

"Immigrants," she said, nodding. "I suppose dear Father decided he could do better for himself without a wife and child claiming him, so off he went. My mother never heard from him again." Uncomfortable with the memories crowding into her mind, Justine made a face of displeasure. "You don't want to hear about this. It bores even me."

"I want to hear."

"What about you? How did you end up in a place like this?" Justine looked around at the dark furniture and the glint of the jewels in the lids of snuffboxes and embedded in goblets and vases. "Did these things come from China?" she asked, picking up a delicate lacquered box inlaid with ivory.

"Yes. All from China."

Justine opened the box and studied the silver balls inside. She looked to China Mary for an explanation.

"Helps in lovemaking," she explained with a sly grin. "No need man to know 'little death' when you got those. They do all the work. You get all the pleasure." She laughed, high and loud, when Justine snapped the lid shut and put the box away from her. "You so innocent, yet so full of knowing. Who take care of you back then?"

"Old Shoe Black, mainly. Him and Jasmine Broadwater." She smiled, remembering her old protectors. "Shoe Black had a face like a raisin and a heart of pure gold. I don't know why he decided to be my guardian angel, but I'm awfully glad he did." She didn't try to hide the tears shimmering in her eyes. "He put my life ahead of his. Nobody had ever done that for me, and nobody has since."

"One has."

"Who?" she challenged, blinking away the past. Tears licked her cheeks, and Justine wiped them aside.

"York Masters. At corral. Remember? He push you out of bullet's way. Could have got shot for trouble."

"Oh, yes." Unsure of how she should respond and why she had conveniently forgotten that incident, Justine stared off into space. York had pushed her to one side to save her life although she was a stranger to him. Why had he done that? He couldn't have known then that she would fit so perfectly into his deception. "I wonder why he did that."

"He has good heart, too."

Justine sent her a dubious look. China Mary laughed, her body moving up and down with mirth.

"You not believe?"

"Not entirely. He's more devil than saint."

"Tell me more of Shoe Black."

"Oh, I thought of him as being as old as Methuselah, but when I think back now, I realize he wasn't. Maybe in his fifties. He had white and gray hair. Woolly hair. And eyes as bright and shiny as new buttons. He lived in a boat hull on the docks, and he let me live with him when he noticed me wandering in the area day after day. I was sleeping under bridges or in courtyards, but Shoe Black gave me a home. His home. It felt like my place more than anyplace I lived in with my mother. It was just me and Shoe Black. No one else. At my mother's, I never

knew who might barge in during the middle of the
night. They always scared me."

"Who, Jus-see? Who scare you?"

"The men. My mother's men. They stared at me.
Sometimes they tried to touch me, kiss me. My
mother fought with one over me. He was big, and I
knew my mother was no match for him. He'd get to
me sooner or later. That's when I left. She was frail,
weak. She didn't have much fight in her."

"She all fought out maybe."

"Maybe, but she was the sort of woman who let
things happen to her. She . . . well, she drank." The
stab of pain that her admission caused surprised Justine. How could it still hurt so badly after all this
time? she wondered, looking away from China
Mary's probing eyes. "As far back as I can remember, my mother drank too much."

"Sometimes life so hard it go down easier with
whiskey."

"My life hasn't been a church social either, but I'm
not a drunken whore." She extended a hand in an
appeal. "Please, don't defend her. I knew her, you
didn't. I defended her for years, until I was old
enough to put away my childish notions and really
look at the woman. On stage I play make-believe
people, but away from it I face the truth, no matter
how ugly. My mother talked about starting over,
having a better life. She talked and talked about it."
Sighing, Justine recalled the futility she'd known living with her mother. "But a wishbone is no substi-
tute for a backbone."

"Your mother pretty like you?"

"She was beautiful once. And she wasn't simple-
minded. She could have found other work. She
could have been a maid, worked as a clerk, maybe
even taught school. She was smart, but she was
weak. So weak."

Justine shook her head sadly, recalling the discov-
ery of her mother's character. It had been painful to

stop pretending that her mother was a shabby pod that would someday burst into glorious flower. Her mother was drunk most of the time, barely sobering up enough to attract men. She stayed sober for that only because the men brought money or bottles. It was commonly known that Jackie Drussard would do anything for a swig of whiskey.

"Jus-see, even the strongest will weaken under four hundred blows," China Mary said, her tone gently scolding. "What she did not to harm you. Why you wish harm to her?"

"I don't. I just don't sugarcoat her, and I certainly don't want to be like her. Shoe Black taught me honor and morals. He told me of love and of lust, and how to resist the latter."

"Why resist? Lust good!"

Shifting her startled gaze to the Oriental woman, Justine was even more startled to see that she was serious. Her stroking of the cat became caressing.

"Lust make heart beat fast."

"No, that's love," Justine corrected her, making China Mary issue a short laugh.

"What you know, girlie? I in business. You on outside looking in."

"Shoe Black wouldn't lie."

"He man. I woman. Woman to woman, I tell you straight."

"Shoe Black wouldn't lie!" Justine asserted.

"Who say he lie? I say he shield you from harm by making you fear unknown. That good. You girl child then, but you woman now. Time you got wisdom. Can't hurt you now."

Justine rocked onto one hip, unbalanced by China Mary's insistence on speaking of things Justine felt were better left unsaid. She barely knew this woman! She certainly didn't fancy hearing a discussion of the private doings between men and women from this odd brothel owner.

"I should be going," Justine said, already making

a movement to stand, but China Mary's rapping voice stayed her.

"You sit! You listen! You rude to walk out when I talking to you, girlie! Did Shoe Black teach you no manners along with teachings of sin and sacrifice?"

Falling motionless, Justine gave the woman her full attention. She understood now how this short, round woman could control every Oriental in Tombstone. When she adopted a commanding air, she could control an entire brigade of rowdy soldiers, Justine wagered silently, waiting for the woman's next words.

"You working in pleasure house now, girlie. Need to know about woman-man business."

"I know."

"You know nothing. You think lust bad?"

"It is."

"It good. Every woman, every man lust. Nothing wrong with it, so long it controlled. Can be master of lust, but not love. Love is own mistress."

"I . . ." Justine shook her head, feeling rattled. "I don't understand."

"'Course not. Told you so, didn't I?" China Mary's smile was so smug that Justine felt as if she'd been slapped across the cheek. "Man and woman feel lust, but don't have to act on it. Can hold back. Beat down." She buried a fist between her breasts as if keeping her heart on a tight rein. "But love goes own way. Takes no orders. Once you in love, you in love. No fighting it. It wins always. Maybe you get heart broken, but nothing you can do. Got to let it mend. Got to take punches, roll with them." China Mary studied Justine for a few moments. "You silent, Jus-see."

"Do you love Ah Lum?"

"Yes, but our marriage arranged when we children. That is our way. We fall in love along the way. We lucky. Some husband and wife not so lucky. Never love."

"And the girls—girls like Satin Doll—do they love?"

"Not for money. Love money can't buy. Can buy lust, sometimes. Not always. Mostly girl just satisfy man, glad to get money, but feel nothing else. Lust born from here." She touched her forehead. "And here." She flattened her hand below her stomach. "Love born here." Her hand rose to cover her heart. "When both happen, whole being joins whole being of loved one. That magic." Her eyes shone brightly, and she looked past Justine to the room's far corner as if her memories were there. "That best hand life can deal. Make you big winner."

"But lust is what animals feel."

"No, girlie, that instinct. That nature. Nothing to do with heart or head. Just in heat, a cycle. All things of nature got cycle. Even us, but love and lust don't happen certain time of year or month."

Justine nodded, grudgingly agreeing that the woman made sense. But something Shoe Black had said stuck in her head, refusing to let go.

"But men will lie to get their pleasure. They'll say they love you just to get you on your back."

"Sure, sure, but you don't bed 'cause of what *he* feels. You bed 'cause of what *you* feel, Jus-see. Only then it good. Only then it honorable for you."

Pinpoints of light began piercing Justine's mind and soul, lighting her way and putting words on her tongue. She wondered if this was what it was like to have a mother to talk to, to learn from, to share the secrets of womanhood.

"But what if you love him and he *says* he loves you, and you have . . . well, you're personal with him? Then he admits he was only fooling, only talking pretty words. How can you live with the shame of being taken and given nothing in return?"

"Shame not yours. Shame his," China Mary explained with maternal patience. "You honorable. You spoke truth. He one who lied."

"Yes, that's right." It seemed clear, seemed right. But it was hard to accept. It was hard to let go of Shoe Black's teachings. "But a man won't respect a woman who gives herself to him out of wedlock."

"Maybe that true. Depends on man and woman." China Mary's narrow lips curved into a grin. "Sometimes, Jus-see, respect is not what woman seeks. Sometimes woman just want to be close—close as can be to man she loves. She *want* to give herself to him, no matter what tomorrow bring. Respect she can give herself. Being one with man she love, she no can give herself. See, Jus-see? Life not always so simple. Life usually like trading. You give this for that." She rocked her hand back and forth. "Sometimes trade good. Sometimes bad. But just looking at pretty stream won't quench thirst."

"You've given me a lot to think about," Justine said. "But why? Why did you want to talk to me about these things?"

"Any time I can give knowledge, I happy. You ignorant for too long. Time you get wise like me." China Mary's laugh plucked the stinger from her words. "You need to know these things. Need to know some men honorable, some not. You got bad habit of slamming door in man's face before he knock, Jus-see. It just human nature for man to flirt with woman. Not shameful. Not sin. Just nature."

"Yes, I see your point."

"You been taught to fear men. That good back then, but no more. You woman now, Jus-see, and woman need man. Nothing wrong with that."

"But I don't want to be cheap. Not like my mother."

"You only cheap if you sell yourself short. It up to you and got nothing to do with getting pleasure from man you love."

Not totally convinced but interested enough to ruminate on China Mary's ideas about love and life, Justine gave a sharp nod.

"Tell you what . . ." China Mary brushed the white cat from her lap and leaned forward with intensity. "I like you. You good girl. I give you piece of luck."

"How will you do that?" Justine asked, amused.

"I give you little money, enough for stagecoach ride tomorrow. You send money back when you can. No rush. I trust you. What say, Jus-see?"

Justine didn't know what to say. Stunned, she could only stare at the woman, knowing she shouldn't stop to question China Mary's generosity, but finding it impossible not to do so. A stagecoach ticket out of town! It was too good to be true.

"No fooling? You'd really do that for me?"

"Sure. I good woman."

"Yes, but why didn't you do this before when I begged it of you?"

"'Cause I not know you so well then. Want ticket money or not?"

"Yes!" She smiled, then frowned. "No." She could see York's face floating in her mind, and it reminded her that she'd struck a deal with him. Damn it!

"No? Why you not take?"

"I . . . I want the money," she said, almost wailing, "but I promised York Masters I'd help him with this —this dumb, old Count hunt of his. Oh, piffle!" She struck one fist into the other open palm. "I gave my word."

"Break it."

"No, I can't do that." She sighed, hating herself for being so damned honorable. "I can't go back on my promise. I might have made a deal with the devil, but I did so willingly and I must honor it." She shrugged, then extended a pitiful smile. "Sorry, China Mary. Thank you all the same." Justine stood and extended her hand to the woman. "I simply must go. Talking with you has been interesting."

China Mary made a face at Justine's extended hand, but clasped it all the same. "You come back soon, Jus-see. We talk again. I tell you about my love potions and those silver balls."

Justine shook her head in amusement. "Good night, China Mary." She started for the door, then stopped and turned back to the woman. "Oh, I almost forgot. Is York in his room?"

"No. He not in room."

"Oh, well, I'll see him another time. I saw a volume of Shakespeare in there, and I wanted to ask him if I could borrow it. My evenings at the Establishment are rather dull, and Madame Chloe has no library."

"You come back tomorrow," China Mary suggested.

"Yes, I'll do that. Good-bye for now." She let herself out the back door.

When Justine was gone, China Mary looked to the far corner again and raised her thin brows.

"Well, what say? She still trustworthy?"

"Seems so." York stepped from around a black screen and came into the light. "What do you think?"

"She woman of honor. Her whole life been spent seeking respect. She want to be lady."

York nodded, recalling the fervid quality in Justine's voice when she'd talked about her mother and her own struggle not to be like her. He ran a fingertip lightly across China Mary's lily white cheek. "As we both know, life isn't about holding a good hand, but about playing a poor one well."

China Mary's smile transcended friendship. It made him feel like family.

Chapter 11

Leaving China Mary's, Justine took a less-traveled route through Hop Town that wound amid narrow back streets and gave her a glimpse of how the Chinese lived when they weren't working.

Their world was dismal. The colorless one-story buildings reminded her of the shantytowns she'd seen all across the south. Lanterns burned in a few windows, their light filtered by the grimy panes. Gray-lumbered buildings stood like a long row of scraggly Confederate soldiers, and tattered canopies hung above crumbling stoops, poor shelter from the sun.

Sand collected in every corner. Nothing grew in this section, not even cacti. A dozen or more children, none older than eight or nine, galloped like wild mustangs in the street, but they scrambled to their one-room homes when they spotted her white skin and Caucasian features. Skinny dogs followed Justine, wagging their tails weakly and sniffing at her heels. She hurried on, anxious to leave this place, where she was a conspicuous outsider.

"Hey there, French gal!"

151

She turned toward the voice. A woman stood silhouetted in a doorway. Hazy red-orange light filled the space behind her.

"Are you talking to me?" Justine asked, wanting to be on her way.

"That's right. What you doing in this part of town?"

"Leaving it. Good night."

"What's your hurry, Frenchy?"

Justine studied her, noting her sloping curves. Then the woman gave a toss of her head and a long curtain of hair swished down her back. "Oh, it's Satin Doll, isn't it?"

"Sure is." Satin leaned a shoulder against the door jamb. "Been at China Mary's?"

"Yes." Justine took a step toward her, drawn by an avid curiosity. "Aren't you working tonight?"

"I am, but later. Come over here so I don't have to shout at you. This is a nosy neighborhood, and I like to keep my business private."

"I didn't know we had any business with each other," Justine said, moving close enough to make out the woman's sultry smile.

"We've got a couple of things in common. We both work on the stage, and we've both taken a shine to York Masters."

Justine shook her head, refusing to be drawn into such a discussion. "Is this where you live?" she asked, craning her neck to see past Satin's shoulder into the dusky room.

"Yes." She turned sideways, sliding her spine against the splintered door frame and giving Justine a better view of the room. A trunk sat at the foot of a bed. Clothes of bright, rainbow colors were strewn across the floor. "Come on in, why don't you."

Justine hesitated, then went inside, her curiosity getting the best of her. The first thing she noticed was the opium pipe and cloying odor in the room. Satin had been smoking—heavily and recently. Justine faced her and was struck by the Oriental woman's exotic beauty.

"How do you like living at the Establishment? Are you fitting right in?" Satin asked.

"It's very nice," Justine said, looking up at the paper-shaded lantern above her head. Her gaze wandered across the bed to the gold crucifix at the head of it. A string of rosary beads dangled from it. "You're Catholic?"

"Yes, I was schooled by the good sisters. You, too?"

"No, but my mother was raised Catholic." Justine sat on the edge of the trunk and folded her hands in her lap, feeling out of place and uneasy under Satin's keen scrutiny. "I never went to church. Sunday was just like any other day to me when I was growing up."

"Not me. My folks are devout. They came to this new country and embraced everything—the country, flag, customs, and religion. I went to Catholic school when I was six and stayed there until I was sixteen."

"So you got a good education?"

"The best money could buy. See what it got me?" She extended a hand to indicate the cramped room and lack of valuables. "Their money was wasted..." Her voice trailed off, and sadness darkened her eyes.

"China Mary thinks you hung the moon," Justine said, wanting to lift that mantle of despair. "She goes on and on about you."

Satin shrugged. "She's family." Noticing Justine's startled look, she laughed. "She hasn't told you? I'm her niece. Mary doesn't tell anybody anything they don't ask to hear. I suppose we could all learn a lesson from that."

Justine nodded. So, Satin and Mary were bound by blood. No wonder China Mary thought Satin was special, better than any of her other employees.

"What about you? Got any family?" Satin asked.

"No. I've been on my own since I was a child. What about your parents? They're both still living?"

"Yes." Satin lolled her head toward the shadows, hiding her face from Justine. "But I'm dead to them. I died when I ran off to become a show girl." She sighed wearily. "They're well off and hold to the old ways. My father owns a big fish market in San Francisco. Ever been there?" Justine shook her head. "No? It's a great place." She sighed again, smiling to herself, then the sadness overtook her once more. "When I defied them and left with a traveling show, I cut all ties. I knew I was doing it, but I was too young to understand that I might long for family one day. I'm lucky to have Mary." She glanced at Justine. "You've got no family? No aunts or uncles or cousins?"

"None."

"That's a shame."

Justine felt her opinion of Satin Doll change and grow. Satin wasn't just a lovely, shallow creature. She was a woman filled with regret, with a melancholy that wafted about her like a perfume. What had made her spirits droop? Did York Masters have anything to do with it?

"How did you meet York?"

A cunning smile claimed Satin's pouty mouth. "Mary introduced us. We hit it off from the start. It was as if we'd been good friends for ages. He treats me like a lady."

"Why shouldn't he? You are, aren't you?"

Satin looked surprised, then pleased. "Yes, but most people don't see that right off. York did. He never took things for granted. He asked first." She laughed again, bowing her head. Her long, straight hair fell forward like a silky curtain. "Of course, I was ready and willing to give him anything he wanted." Her smile waned, and an expression of regret pinched her doll-like features.

"What's wrong?"

She tossed her hair back and seemed to gather her composure, crossing her arms almost defensively against her chest. "Oh, I was just thinking of poor Lizzie."

"Who's that?"

Satin regarded Justine with surprise. "York hasn't told you about her?"

"No." Justine leaned toward Satin, sensing that she'd stumbled upon something important.

"He sure is keeping you in the dark." She gave a short, harsh laugh.

"You tell me," Justine urged.

"Why should I? Ask York."

"I'm asking you." Justine held Satin's gaze for a long moment. "Please. Is Lizzie one of the missing girls? Do you think she's dead?"

"Yes, yes." Satin straightened and nodded toward the open door. "But I'm not going to betray—" She stopped and swallowed hard. "If you want information, ask York. I'm not singing like a bird for you."

"Why won't you tell me?"

"Because it's not my business . . . just ask York."

"I'll do that." Justine moved toward the door, brushing past Satin. When she was outside, she turned back to face her. "So, you're part of his investigation, too?"

Satin nodded. "I was. Now I'm just his woman. What does that make you?" Her smile was chilly. "When you're flirting with him and loving up to him, remember me. Remember that I saw him first."

"You've got it all wrong, Satin. He doesn't want me, and I don't want him. He's blackmailing me into helping him, and as soon as I've paid my dues I'm long gone."

"Is that so?" She studied Justine for a few moments, and her expression became more friendly, as if the threat Justine posed had passed. "You make him tell you the whole story. You've got no business staying in the Establishment without knowing what you're up against. Tell him I said he shouldn't blind-fold you."

"Thank you. I will." Justine looked past her into the foggy room, wondering if the melancholy that hovered around Satin had anything to do with her opium habit, or if it went deeper than that. "Take care of yourself, Satin."

"You, too." Satin drifted backward into the embrace of shadow and smoke. "Give York a kiss for me." Her laughter floated on the still air and then faded away.

The man with the gold tooth didn't take kindly to losing, and his partner in the red long johns and bib coveralls wasn't too thrilled either.

Noting this with instincts long honed at the poker table, York dropped the deck in the center of the table and caught Bucko's eye.

"Gentlemen, Bucko here has come back from a short break, and he'll be dealing the next game." York extended a hand toward the deck and a broad grin to Bucko. "It's all yours, pal. I'm long overdue for a swill of tonsil varnish." This quip rarely failed to win chuckles, but it failed this time. Gold Tooth and Long Johns just stared holes through him.

"Where I come from, it ain't right for a dealer to duck out when he's been holding the winning hands," Gold Tooth said.

"Maybe your luck will change with a change of dealer," York said, trying to keep it friendly.

"You saying you don't cheat?" Long Johns asked.

York was standing, but at that he rested the flat of his hands on the table and leaned into Long Johns' ugly face. "Mister, I hope you're not accusing me of cheating."

"What if I am?"

"Then we'll have to ask you to leave," Bucko broke in, shouldering York away from the table. "And that would be a damn shame. York, go on and get yourself a good stiff one. Me and the gentlemen will continue with this friendly game of poker." Bucko sat down and took control of the deck. He motioned for the Oriental bar boy. "Drinks at this table, Lo Chen. On the house."

York went into the saloon with new respect for Bucko. The man was a wizard at soothing ruffled feathers, and York wished some of Bucko's polish would rub off on him. He knew he had a tendency to go off half-cocked, especially when some weasel was accusing him of dirty dealings. Stupid bastards. If he'd wanted to cheat them, they wouldn't have a cent in their pockets, or pockets at all for that matter! Sure as hell didn't take much smarts to hoodwink a couple of jackasses like them.

He went directly to the bar, ordered a whiskey, then ordered another and another. He was drinking too much lately, he knew, but he didn't want to think too clearly. When he was clearheaded, he thought about her and worried that he might have placed Jussie in harm's way. What if the Count saw right through her? He might be too late getting to her. The Count might make Jussie vanish like the others before he could get to her and save her. And if anything happened to her... well, he could barely live with Lizzie's disappearance. He'd buckle under the strain of another.

He'd thought Jussie was worldly, being an actress and on her own for so long, but he'd misjudged her. She was a babe in the woods—untried and unblemished. At first he'd tried to convince himself it was an act, but he had to listen to his heart, and his heart told him she was surprisingly pure, and as exasperating as one of Mary's confounded Chinese puzzles.

God, he was dwelling on her again! He slammed a hand down on the bar in frustration. The barkeep jumped to refill his shot glass.

It was bad enough to dream about her almost every night and wake up sweaty and aching. He couldn't do a damn thing about his dreams. But he could keep himself from being obsessed with her while he was awake. He tossed the liquor to the back of his throat and heard a faint buzzing in his ears. He smiled crookedly, giving himself over to the numbness.

"Hello, love," Satin said, sidling up to him and running a slim hand up the back of his jacket. "Going to watch my show tonight?"

"Guess so." He glanced at her, taking in the tight gold dress and sniffing at the evidence of opium that rose from her. "Satin, honey, you're getting whipped, and you don't even know it."

"What are you talking about?" she asked, standing on tiptoe to kiss his square chin.

"That stuff you're smoking. It's going to be your undoing."

"It's what keeps me happy." She widened her eyes and laughed. "It and you, of course. You make me happy."

He shook his head. "You just won't listen."

"I'll do whatever you want. You know that, don't you? You know I'd never do anything to hurt you."

"Yes, I know." He sent her a befuddled glance. "What's wrong? You seem all wrung out."

"I saw Frenchy earlier."

"Frenchy? Oh, her. So?"

"So, you should be ashamed of yourself for sending her into that snake pit blindfolded. How come you didn't tell her about Lizzie?"

"Did you?" he asked, more sharply than he'd intended.

"Simmer down. I mentioned her, and Frenchy asked a passel of questions, but she didn't get any answers from me. You're not doing her any favors by keeping her stupid, you know."

"Let me handle it my way."

Satin shrugged. "You're the boss, but you're wrong. I don't like the idea of her being under Madame Chloe's nose and not knowing the playbook line by line. It's not right, York. You've sent her into a gunfight without any weapons."

"I said I'd handle it. I don't want her to know about me and Liz."

"Well, you can at least tell her about Lizzie and the Count, can't you?"

"Satin..."

"Okay, okay." She held up her hands, surrendering to his warning tone. "Come by later tonight."

"I don't know..."

"I promise not to nag." She kissed his cheek and sauntered away, dropping smiles like tokens among the admiring men lining the bar.

After another whiskey, York grew warm. The saloon was loud, raucous. The noise reverberated in his head. He left his post at the bar and went toward the swinging doors and the fresh air on the other side of them. Stumbling onto the boardwalk, he stepped off it onto the street and stood there for a full minute, head flung back, lungs filling with desert air, eyes gobbling up the stars overhead.

"Star light, star bright," he recited, remembering how his mama had taught him to believe that the stars were angels who granted wishes to good boys and girls. "Wish I may, wish I might, have this wish I wish tonight." He closed his eyes, saw Jussie's sweet face and her luminous dove gray eyes, and pursed his lips to speak her name.

But a hand clamped over his mouth, imprisoning his wish. York grunted in surprise as he was jerked off his feet and dragged backward, his boot heels making furrows in the dusty street. His instincts were slowed by the liquor. He didn't begin to struggle until he was pulled into the alley beside China Mary's and slammed against the outside wall. The back of his head bounced against the barrier, and he saw a different kind of star.

"You don't steal a man's money and then just

walk away," a voice rasped. Hot, stinking breath fanned his face and made his eyes water.

When his vision cleared, York saw a gold tooth glinting in the dark. That's when he knew he was in a heap of trouble. He tried to pitch himself forward, elbows swinging back into the wall and pushing him upright, but Gold Tooth shoved him off balance again.

"Grab hold of him," Gold Tooth ordered. "It's time he was taught a lesson."

That's when York noticed Long Johns standing nearby. Long Johns' hands felt like vises around his biceps as he wrenched York's arms until his elbows met at the small of his back.

"What's the big i—" That was all York got out before Gold Tooth slammed a fist into his gut and knocked the breath out of him. He tried to lift his legs and get in a good kick, but the flying fists took their toll. His gut hurt so bad that he hardly felt the uppercut to his chin or the fist slamming into his ribs. A red haze blinded him, and he tasted his own blood.

"What's going on?"

He heard the voice, but his confusion fooled him into thinking it was in his head, repeating what he'd tried to say.

"Get away from him, you cowards!"

That wasn't a voice in his head, York told himself as he slipped down the wall, realizing as he fell that his attackers had backed off.

"Who are you?"

Footsteps sounded smartly, coming closer. "His wife. Who are you?"

"Shit."

"What have you done to him?"

"He cheated us at cards."

"So you ganged up on him? Get out of my way."

"Hey, lady! Don't go pushing me like I'm some—"

"Forget it," Gold Tooth said. "Let's get out of here. We taught him his lesson."

"Yes, get out of here before I scream for the sheriff. He's right inside the saloon, you know. All I have to do is—"

"We're getting."

"You keep your mouth shut, you hear? Cheating son of a bitch . . ."

York looked around just in time to see a boot swinging toward his face. He ducked and knew a moment of delight when the boot slammed into the wall, and its owner cussed a blue streak.

"I said *go!*" It was a woman's voice . . . an angel of mercy. He knew the voice, knew it well. "You bastards!" she called as they took off. "That's right, run! Run like the cowardly rabbits you are!"

"Jussie?" York forced her name past his lips.

"York?"

A pleasant aroma settled over him, and he looked up into smoky eyes and the face of an angel. Sweet Jussie.

"Can you stand up?"

He decided to try sitting up first. With effort, he righted himself and tried to smile reassuringly at Justine. He spit out a mouthful of blood and shook his head. Some of the fog lifted.

"Should I go get the doctor?"

"No." He coughed and rested a hand against his tender ribs. "I'll be okay. Just let me catch my breath." The night air cleared the cobwebs from his brain. "What are you doing out here at this time of night?"

"Looking for you."

"Lucky me."

She frowned at him. "Well, I did save your ornery neck. The least you can do is—"

"I mean it," he broke in. "Lucky me." He smiled, but it hurt. He touched the stinging corner of his mouth, and his fingers came away bloody. "Ouch. Help me get to my room."

"Put your arm around my neck."

He did and tried not to depend on her strength, but finding his feet was a struggle. Justine groaned but didn't buckle. Once he was standing, he leaned against the outside wall and rested a minute before letting her help him to the back entrance and up the stairs to his room.

"Who were those men?"

"Sore losers." York sat on the bed and motioned for Justine to close the door. "Good thing you showed up when you did, or I would have killed those fellas."

She smiled, then laughed with him. "Is that the story you're going to tell?"

"That's it. Got to save face, don't I? Did you tell them you were my wife?"

"Yes. I thought that might shame them into leaving you alone."

He chuckled and looked at her fully, realizing she was dressed to kill, all mint green silk and white lace. Her matching bonnet was out of kilter, pushed off center by their struggle up the stairs.

"Aren't you a pretty thing," he whispered, caught by her charm. "Did you get all gussied up just to come looking for me?"

Bright pink colored her cheeks. "I was going to wait until tomorrow, but something told me I should find you tonight."

"Thank heaven for a woman's intuition."

"It's more than that. I knew I wouldn't get a good night's sleep if I didn't see you."

"Keeping you up nights, am I?" He wiped his mouth with the back of his hand, smearing blood. "I didn't know you cared."

"I don't, but I *do* care about my own skin." She pointed a finger inches from his nose. "You're holding out on me, York Masters. I want to know about

Lizzie—about everything—or I'm not going to tell you what Ivory Sparks said about her a little while ago."

"Ivory talked about Lizzie?" He forgot the pain and shot up from the bed to grab Justine by the shoulders. "This isn't a game, Jussie. Tell me!"

"You're right," she said, looking boldly into his eyes. "It's not a game, so why are you playing around with my life?"

Chapter 12

"**S**urely you knew that this business wasn't a church picnic," York said, turning away from her to pour water into the bowl on the washstand.

"You said I would be safe if I followed your instructions."

"That's right, and you will be."

"But you're not telling me everything. Satin says I should know about Lizzie."

"Satin's got a big mouth."

"I think she's more concerned for my welfare than you are," Justine charged, stepping closer while he washed the crusty blood off his lips and chin. The skin under his left eye was red, but Justine knew it would change to blue or purple by morning. "Are you going to be okay?"

"Yes." He removed his shirt and pressed a hand to his ribs where the skin was faintly discolored by the blows, then he tipped up his chin to examine the redness there. "You came along in the nick of time. Now that my head's clear, I'm feeling more like myself. I think I drank too much."

"I *know* you did. You smell like a whiskey bottle."

She wrinkled her nose to further illustrate her point.

"Well, pardon me all to hell. I didn't expect female company tonight." He tossed her a black look, then reached for the lump of soap by the basin and worked up a lather. "You can leave now. As I said, I'm fit as—"

"I'm not leaving until I get some answers," Justine interrupted. She sat on the bed, fluffed her skirts, and made herself comfortable.

He rolled his eyes heavenward. "All right. There's not much to tell, and it won't help you any to know it, but..." His shrug said the rest. He sponged off, running the washrag over his muscled torso and under his arms. "Lizzie was the last girl to disappear from Tombstone. She was a show girl just like you."

"I'm not a show girl. I'm an actress."

"Whatever," he said in a dismissive tone. "She thought of herself in those terms, too. The Count made her believe he was going to make her famous, then he told her he was going to marry her. Pretty promises that brought her to Tombstone and its pleasure palaces. She had some kind of act and was booked into one of the theaters here, but her act didn't play well, I guess. The Count decided he could make more money with her in a pleasure palace instead of a theater. That's when he moved her into the Establishment and turned her over to Madame Chloe."

"Did the Count take her away later?"

He nodded. "She didn't stay long at the Establishment. Just a couple of weeks, I'm told. The Count left with her six or seven months ago. Satin told me Lizzie was with him on the last night she was seen in Tombstone. She told Satin she didn't like..." He gargled and rinsed out his mouth.

"Didn't like what?" Justine prodded.

"Whoring." He winced, but Justine couldn't tell if it was from physical or emotional wounds. "She rebelled, refusing to stay at the Establishment. The

Count took her with him when he left. Headed to another town, or so the story goes. Only problem is I can't find her. Lost her track completely."

"And you think she's dead," Justine finished for him.

"I hope I'm wrong, but that's exactly what I think." Finished with his toilet, he faced her. "I've come clean," he said, grinning at his double meaning. "Now it's your turn. What did Ivory say about Lizzie?"

"That he loved her. She was a good friend of his, and he wanted to help her. He said she was unhappy at the Establishment."

"When did he say all of this?"

"Earlier this evening, before the customers started arriving. I brought up the Count, and Ivory made no bones about the fact that he despises the man."

"Did he say why?"

"Because the Count took his ladylove away."

"Lizzie?"

"No, a girl named Shelley. Ivory loved her and was going to marry her, but the Count took her away to another town. Then, when Ivory made friends with Lizzie, the same thing happened. Lizzie left one night without even saying good-bye."

"And he believes that's all there is to it?"

Justine shook her head, staring at her clasped hands and recalling the haunted expression in Ivory's eyes. "No. He thinks they're both dead. He said Shelley wouldn't have left willingly, and she would have written to him if at all possible."

"But he has no proof."

"Well, he didn't offer any. I think he might know more, but he's cautious. He's opening up more and more to me, but not all the way. I like him. He's a sweet, uncomplicated man."

"Is that how you like them?" York asked, grinning crookedly. "Sweet and uncomplicated?"

She let that pass, deciding it was too dangerous to

trade flirtations with him when he was partially undressed. "Ivory doesn't trust Madame Chloe either."

"Who does? I can be sweet and uncomplicated if I put my mind to it. Want to see?"

"Ivory told me to watch my back around her," she said, pointedly ignoring him. She had a sneaking suspicion that Ivory wasn't the only one who was withholding information.

"You can watch your back, and I'll watch your front." His gaze drifted down to her breasts.

Growing tired of his cavalier attitude, she rose from the bed to face him. "Are you interested in any of this? Sometimes I think you only care about yourself. Take poor Satin, for example. . . ."

"What about her?"

"She thinks you really care for her."

He rolled his eyes again and barked a laugh. "Well, hell, I really do. What's that got to do with the price of tea in China?"

"She's messing around with that opium pipe too often and you know it, but you do nothing to help her. As long as she's available to lick your boots and warm your bed, you turn a blind eye to everything else about her."

"That's not what's got you as hot as a stove's lid." He stepped right up to her, forcing her to tip back her head and look at him. "You're full of piss and vinegar because you want me to care about *you*. You don't give a damn about Satin's problems."

"We're not talking about me. We're talking about you."

He made a move to embrace her, but she ducked under his arm and circled behind him. Swiveling around, he crooked a finger seductively. "Come here, Jussie."

"No." She shook her head and made her voice firm. "Not on your life, buster."

"The chase is over, honey," he whispered. "You done gone and got caught."

He made another dive, but she skipped sideways, laughing as he lunged at thin air and came up with an armful of it. Despite her best intentions, she felt the pull and tug of him. Delicious naughtiness glimmered in his eyes and lit his smile. Her heart reacted, beating fast and hard.

"Stop it," she begged, still laughing. "You just got clobbered, remember? You're in no condition to play cat and mouse."

"I'll be the judge of that."

"No." She stiff-armed him, her hand flattening against the mat of hair growing thickly on his chest. "I've gotten what I came for, and now I'll just be on my way." Backed against a table, she reached behind her for support and encountered a stack of books. She edged around the table, putting it between them, and selected the volume of Shakespeare. "May I borrow this? I miss the theater, and I thought that in the evenings I could—"

"You could spend the evenings making love to something else besides a volume of Shakespeare." He made his eyebrows go up and down, and Justine laughed in spite of herself. "If you're gentle, I'll let you love me."

She was sorely tempted, but she kept thinking about her assurance to Satin Doll that she didn't want to be York's lover. Was it a lie? she wondered, looking into his teasing eyes and admiring his wicked grin. Was she only fooling herself by insisting she wanted nothing from York except his absence?

"I think Satin sees me as competition," she threw out, wanting his reaction.

He smiled, not having to say anything since it was more than obvious that Satin was right.

"Why do you want me?" Justine put the book down and sent him a stern look. "I mean it. Why me? You've made it clear you only want to use me. Is that how you get through life? Using people, then tossing them out with the wash water?" She saw that she'd succeeded in taking the humor out of the situation. York was no longer smiling. "I want more than that from a man, York. I think too much of myself to allow you to treat me like a . . . well, like you treat Satin." She swallowed, finding it difficult to bare her soul for his inspection. Feeling stripped of all pretense, she stood before him, trembling.

"What do you know about how I treat Satin?" he charged, his tone indicating she'd struck a nerve. "Did she say I mistreat her?"

"No, but she's not happy and—"

"And you figure I'm her problem? She's a grown woman, and I can't tell her what to do or what not to do."

"What about China Mary? Satin told me Mary's her aunt—another thing you forgot to mention." She frowned at his sigh of aggravation.

"Mary's the one who gives her the opium. The Chinese see it differently than we do. Look, what do you want from me, huh?" Propping his hands at his hips, he dipped his head to glare at her straight on. "You want me to cry and beat my chest and wail against the injustice around me? What good would that do? I'm a professional." He jabbed a thumb at his chest. "This is no place for amateurs, sweetheart. I thought you understood that."

"I do. The problem is I like you, though I can't imagine why!" She blinked, surprised by her own outburst but nearly exploding with a need to be honest. She wanted him to agree with her, to tell her she was right to trust him with her most private self. Averting her gaze, she listened to his telling silence. "Every once in a while I get a glimpse of a nice, caring man, a man with a heart. . . . and I like him . . ." She lifted her gaze to his and saw that he was rapt. "I like him very much."

"How much?" His voice was hoarse with longing.

"Enough to want him . . . to hope he wants me."

She smiled when his eyes sparked with hope. "I pray I'm not just a foolish woman with a wild imagination."

"You're not." He reached for her, pulling her into his embrace and lowering his mouth to hers.

The seductive movement of his mouth and the insinuation of his tongue between her lips fired her anew with divine passion. She held his head between her hands and kissed him back, living only for the moment, only for the man.

"You can trust me," he whispered, then pulled back to lock gazes with her. "I won't hurt you, Jussie. I want to be the man you see in me. God help me, I do. You believe me, don't you?"

Looking to the clear pools of his eyes, she saw only his goodness. Her heart ached to be loved by him, to open up to him. She nodded, realizing he was worth any risk. Maybe tomorrow would be full of woe, but she would have this night to cherish, and she knew in her heart she'd never regret it.

"I believe you, York. And I *do* want you. More than anything in the whole world, I want you to love me tonight."

He caught his breath, as if taken aback by her bold admission, then he gathered her to him again for a kiss with commitment behind it. She could feel the fire in him and the heat rising from his skin, fragrant and maddening. He was a flame and she was kindling, too long put up and left to dry. Slowly, she caught fire as his mouth and hands set off sparks and left her gasping. Fire and desire, she thought incoherently. Fire and desire.

He moved with her to the bed, and they fell upon it, letting their hands tug at clothing, loosen ties, and free buttons until there were no longer any shields. York pulled the sheet over them, and it whispered across their bodies. Rubbing his back, she looked into his eyes, and desire looked back at her, cobalt blue and shining.

"I don't ever remember hungering for a woman like I hunger for you," he said against her parted lips.

She could only moan in response. Her body throbbed with a thousand pulses, creating a roaring in her ears. She'd fancied how he must look, but her limited knowledge of the male anatomy couldn't do him justice. For he was beautiful, and the sight of him increased her passion. Turgid and proud, he beckoned her to investigate. She touched him, and that slight contact made him shiver with longing. He closed his eyes for a brief moment to let the sensation play itself out. When he opened his eyes again, they were glazed.

He was so different from her. She, all curves and valleys; he, all planes and ridges. His large hands spanned from beneath her arm to her hipbone, making her feel tiny, delicate. It was all so new to her; the friction of his crisp body hair against her virgin skin, the intense heat of his flesh, the weight of his lower body upon hers, and the intimacy of hard, pulsing muscle against her soft belly and sensitive inner thighs. His kisses, open mouthed and hungry, allowed no room for doubt or fear. She caressed his shoulders and the indentation of his spine as she returned his kisses. Her tongue parried his, learning and mimicking, then finally inventing and augmenting.

They rolled as one, changing places so that she was now sprawled upon him. She rained kisses over his face, placing them carefully upon his bruised skin, then lifting up a little to rest her hands lightly on his battered ribcage.

"I don't want to hurt you," she whispered, winning a smile from him.

"Then don't leave. That's the only way you can hurt me now." He framed her oval face in his hands. "Jussie, you're one beautiful woman. How many men have told you that?"

She felt herself blush as she kissed his glistening mouth. "You're the only one I've ever wanted to hear say it."

"And you're smart, too. Mighty damn smart." A laugh rumbled in his throat, then changed to a growl with an appetite behind it. He nuzzled her breasts, his lips and tongue joining forces to make her dizzy with desire.

She stretched onto her back again while he explored sensitive patches of skin on her stomach, the undersides of her breasts, and the sides of her waist. The sheet was pushed aside, no longer required. The pressure built within her until she had to voice it, softly moaning York's name. A corner of her mind quivered in the face of the unknown, but wanting overrode the fear. She wanted to walk into the fiery heart of him and be cleansed by it, changed by it, reborn in it.

Like a tongue of flame, he entered her. Her virginity held for only a fleeting moment before melting away to allow him to engulf her from within and spread his heat without. She panted, caught up in the storm, unsure of her part in it. York's labored breathing and his hoarse chant of her name told her he was responding in a way she had never dreamed was possible. He was out of his head.

Flesh grasping flesh, she arched up, testing the connection and shocked by the hot friction created by York's swiftly grinding hips. The white disc grew red-hot. It was the sun. His release shot her toward the ball of flames. With his last powerful thrust, he buried his face in the side of her neck and a shudder racked him, then gusted through her, blowing out the firestorm and leaving glowing embers in its wake.

She cleaved to him, feeling the changes in her body. Justine closed her eyes, letting her breathing slowly return to normal as her body took its time, tingling here and quivering there.

"Did I hurt you?" he asked after a while.

"I don't think so."

"Think? Don't you know?"

"Not yet."

He raised his head to look at her. "I didn't disappoint you, did I?"

"I believe you're angling for a compliment," she said, smiling.

"Maybe I am." He nuzzled her breasts, and his breath warmed her skin. "So tell me. Ease my mind, honey."

"I'm not hurt, and I'm certainly not disappointed." She sighed, loving the caress of his lips. "What about you? I bet I don't stack up too well beside all the ladies you've—"

His kiss stopped the rest. "This bed is just big enough for two, so don't go hauling a bunch of other people into it. It's me and you and nobody else."

She shook her head, laughing. "I'm not letting you off the hook that easy. You've got to tell me— are *you* disappointed? Do you wish you were still wondering about how I'd be in bed? Sometimes the wanting is better than the getting."

"Not this time." He inched up until his face was poised above hers. "I'll never forget you. Not even when I'm old and gray without a tooth in my head." He kissed her, his mouth lingering lightly. "Loving you is about the easiest thing I've ever done."

She lifted her arms and draped them over his shoulders. His kisses were lazy, and she was content to savor each one. Loving him wasn't so easy, she thought, but it was impossible to fight. She'd tried to deny the attraction, and she'd fought her feelings for him every inch of the way, but now she was glad to surrender, happy to be his woman.

"And when I'm old and gray I'll have a faint recollection of some fellow with a funny-sounding name. . . . " She laughed when he bit her shoulder. "Ouch! What's that for?"

"You'll remember me." He narrowed his eyes playfully. "Women never forget their first man."

"York," she whispered, sounding his name with deliberate seriousness. "When I'm asked who taught me to love, that's the name I'll say. York." She pulled his mouth to hers possessively. She never wanted to let him go. She wanted to grow old with him.

York lifted his head, his expression serious. "I hope you don't end up hating me for what happened here. For whatever it's worth, I'm grateful."

She flinched involuntarily. Grateful? That's all? she cried inside. That's all you feel? She mocked herself for imagining he would feel anything stronger or more lasting.

He rested his head on her breasts and was quiet for a few moments. Justine denied the sadness slowly invading her. So he didn't love her. She knew that, but that didn't mean he'd *never* love her. There was always tomorrow, and the next day. Love took its time. It didn't always happen in a rush.

"I wish you could stay the night," he said, breaking into her inner dialogue.

She looked at him from the corner of her eye. Anything *but* that had never entered her mind. What was he used to? Did his women pleasure him, then slip away into the dark like a bad dream?

"I *am* staying," she assured him, not liking the turn of events. Didn't he understand that this changed things for them? "What's more, you'll escort me back to the Establishment come morning. I'm not easily won, nor discarded, York Masters. Just because I've slept with you doesn't mean I've surrendered my self-respect."

"And it doesn't mean our arrangement has changed, either. I'm still the boss, and I don't think it's a good idea for you to spend the night with me."

"A few minutes ago you thought it was a grand idea."

He lay on his back, staring gloomily at the ceiling.

"Jussie, don't be this way. I was hoping you'd behave."

"Behave?" She shot up, grabbing the sheet and tucking it high under her arms. "What's that mean, behave? I'm not a child! Don't worry, I'm not staying. And not because *you* don't want me, but because *I* don't want to lie beside a man so...so unfeeling and...and—"

"Oh, stop your fussin' and fumin'." He sat up, insolent once again and cockily in control. He actually grinned, as arrogant as a lone rooster in a pen full of laying hens. "You don't have to jump and run. Come back to bed, and I'll see you home before daylight."

His suggestion didn't even give her pause. Fired by indignation, she yanked on her clothes. She wanted to wad up the dress he'd thought was so fetching and throw it in his face, but she put it back on, knowing she'd never wear it again. He'd ruined it for her.

"I knew you'd be this way as soon as your hunger was sated," she said, speaking mostly to herself, venting her fury so that she wouldn't drown in its poison. "Yes, I wanted you, but I knew in my heart of hearts that you'd treat me like a common whore as soon as you'd spilled yourself inside me."

"For God's sake!" he said, rolling his eyes with a dramatic flair. "Will you listen to yourself? You sound like a character in a bad melodrama."

Bad melodrama! She glared at him...oh, damn his blue eyes!

"Speaking of which," she said, snatching up the volume of Shakespeare and taking careful aim, "I don't want this. I don't want anything that will remind me of you!" She let it fly. The book sailed through the air, pages fluttering, and would have flattened against York's forehead if he hadn't raised an arm to take the blow. "Damn your eyes and damn you for making me feel like a fool!" She stormed from the room, slamming the door behind her with a vengeance.

Smarting from wounds she'd never felt before, Justine left China Mary's and hurried to the Establishment. She let herself in the back way, skirting the main rooms where the girls and their customers drank spirits and traded shallow conversation. Once she was safely in her room, she slumped against the closed door and let the tears flow. It was the contradictions that hurt, that warred inside her. On the one hand, she had grasped a slice of heaven; but on the other, she had been dropped into a private hell.

"Don't blame him. You knew good and well that he was about as softhearted as a peach," she scolded herself, wiping aside her tears and shielding her heart and feelings once again.

She'd learned early on how to roll with the punches. She'd been schooled on the streets of New Orleans and had been a quick study. Squaring her shoulders, she moved resolutely to the window and opened it to let in the cooling breeze.

"I will not regret what I've done," she told herself, looking up into the comfort of the starry night. "I wanted him, and I went to him with heart and mind in unison. I only wish..." Fresh tears burned her eyes and collected in her throat.

A bobbing light stole her attention from her self-pitying thoughts. Justine rubbed her eyes and focused on the light as it bounced up the hillside, taking a snaking route from the shallow valley behind Loma de Platas. Beyond the valley was a hillock of scrub brush and cacti. As the light drew nearer, its golden glow illuminated a hand, then an arm, and finally a bouncing figure.

Ivory Sparks.

Justine leaned closer to the window, watching Ivory carry the lantern across the rough terrain. He stopped to douse the light a few yards from the house, then the faint tap of the screen door closing signaled that he was back inside. Justine left the window and sat on the bed, wondering where Ivory could have been and why.

Taking up a lantern, she spirited herself outside and took Ivory's route. Halfway down the hillside, the lantern's light fell upon a piece of evidence. Justine picked up the petals and held them to her nose for a whiff of their perfume. Roses. But where had Ivory taken them? She smiled. He must be sneaking off to deliver flowers to a woman.

The irony wasn't lost on her; one woman is given roses, she thought with a sad sigh, and another is left with the thorns.

Chapter 13

Schieffelin Hall was a grand dame. Open for only a few months, it was touted as the largest adobe building in the Southwest, and Justine had no reason to doubt it.

Standing in front of the edifice, she dreamed of someday performing on its stage. The melodrama *The Ticket-of-Leave Man*, presented by the Tombstone Dramatic Association, had just closed. Next on the playbill was a presentation of *Romeo and Juliet* by the American Stratford Company from Boston.

The Stratford Company! An answer to her prayers, she thought, growing excited at the prospect of speaking with theater people again. They'd treat her with due respect and catch her up on news of the stage: what companies were in the area, who got what role, which director was deemed the best. She craved such information, needing reassurance that she belonged in the fold. She only hoped the Stratford Company was still managed by Andrew Vixon, a man she'd met through her first acting classes. Andy might know of an opening for her, perhaps even with his company. Following the Strat-

ford Company would be the Nellie Boyd Dramatic
Company of New York to present *The Banker's Daughter*, another play with which she was familiar.

Justine smiled at the warm memory of performing
in the title role just a year ago. Only a year, but it
seemed a decade. How she missed it! Her heart
ached, and her chest tightened as homesickness
closed in. The costumes, the face paint, the applause
of patrons who admired her. The stage-door johnnys
and jeannies who wanted to rub elbows with the art-
ists. She sympathized with them, recalling her first
brush with the stage and how it had completely
transfixed her. Once she had trod the boards, she
knew she had found a new home. With Shoe Black
and Jasmine Broadwater both gone to their final re-
wards, Justine had needed a place to hang her hat,
to call her own.

Theater people never asked questions. If you were
good enough to gain a role, then you were accepted.
Nobody pried into your past or pestered you about
your parentage. Theater people lived for the moment
and for the make-believe. As soon as her business
with York was finished, she wanted to leap back into
the theater's arms and forget Tombstone and the
man who had made her dream of a life away from
the stage.

Her need for acceptance had grown strong since
her night with York. Three days had passed with no
word from him, and she berated herself for expecting anything more than his deliberate silence.

Revived by her plan to regain the stage once
more, Justine moved on with a lighter heart and care-
free steps. She checked the list of errands on which
she'd been sent by Madame Chloe and headed toward the courthouse on Toughnut Street, where she
paid for licenses for several of the girls at the Establishment. Each month Madame Chloe renewed the
girls' licenses at seven dollars each. The sum seemed
huge to Justine, but she knew through her book-

keeping that it was a fraction of the amount they brought in. Paid less than a third of what they made each month, the girls were kept dependent on Madame Chloe through stingy finances. Justine often wondered if they realized this, ignored it, or simply didn't care.

Outside the courthouse she could see Boothill, the final resting place of the good, the bad, and the unfortunate. The men killed at the OK Corral had been buried there since Justine had arrived in Tombstone, as well as a couple of red-light girls who had exchanged knife thrusts. She shook her head and turned away from the hillside graveyard. Walking in the opposite direction, she strolled toward another theater, not nearly so grand as Schieffelin Hall. It stood against a backdrop of blue sky and scudding clouds.

A couple of men on horseback trotted alongside Justine, grinning like apes and trying to make her glance their way. When she didn't, one of them flapped his hat near her face.

"You remember us, sweet thing? How's your old man? Bet he's got a real big shiner," he jeered, leaning sideways from the saddle for a close-up look under her bonnet. "Betcha she makes him a fine blanket companion. What say you, Jed?"

Justine stopped and glared at them, realizing they were the two men who had jumped York in the alley.

"Amen to that, Bud," the other chimed in, grinning and showing off his gold tooth. "No doubt she's as soft and fluffy as a goose hair pillow."

"I believe the heat has addled your think boxes. If you don't ride on and leave me be, I'll scream bloody murder and have you thrown in jail."

"For what?" the sideways one asked, righting himself.

"For beating an unarmed, innocent man."

"Can't prove it," Bud said, throwing out his chest. "Okay, then for not having anything under your hats but hair," she snapped. "That will be easy enough to prove."

"Aw, to hell with you, bitch!"

"Yeah," the other agreed, "who needs you? You ain't so fine, you know. I seen better-looking women than you in caskets."

The two laughed uproariously, and Justine tipped up her chin with the confidence of a woman who had sharpened her tongue on tougher meat than them.

"The bigger the mouth, the better it looks shut," she quipped. "And you two are carrying around cave openings on your faces."

Their laughter ceased, and they reined their horses. One made a move to dismount, his mean-spirited snarl sending a shiver down Justine's spine. Had she hurled one insult too many? She glanced around, looking for help, but she'd entered a part of town that was nearly deserted. She called herself a fool for tempting fate. Tombstone was a town of sin, sand, and bullets; a place where most of the doors swung both ways for good reason. She realized she was crazy to taunt two of its most surly residents.

"Hello, Jed. What y'all doing?"

Justine turned toward the voice, recognizing it before she saw Satin Doll stepping from the shadows of the theater's overhanging roof. The man sat back in his saddle and grinned like a drunken monkey.

"Well, hello there, honey. Now, don't you look good enough to eat."

"Hiya, Satin Doll." The other man tipped his hat, showing a headful of greasy hair. "It's Bud Townsend. Remember me?"

"Sure, hon. I'd never forget a man like you." She smiled, making it a compliment, although Justine knew it wasn't. "I'm meeting my friend here." She looked at Justine and motioned for her to come closer. "We won't keep you boys. 'Bye now."

She waved, then reached out and pulled Justine to her side. "See y'all around."

"Yeah, sure thing." Jed glared at Justine, then spurred his horse into an all-out gallop. Bud dipped his head in a farewell, and his mount lurched forward to follow Jed's.

"Girl, you've got a mouth that could use a dam," Satin said, sending Justine a scolding frown. "Take it from someone who knows, silence is golden, especially around dimwits."

Justine nodded, taking the criticism good-naturedly. "I know. My mouth gets me in plenty of trouble. Thanks for coming to my rescue."

"I know those old boys. They the ones who jumped York?" Satin asked, and Justine nodded. "Hmmm, that's just their style. Two against one."

"How is York?"

"Fine." Satin gave her a measured look. "You haven't seen him lately?"

"Not since the night he was attacked."

"Yeah, he told me about you helping him. Mighty nice of you. He's doing okay. Takes more than a couple of punches to take him out."

"He's tough, that's for sure."

"Got a minute?"

Justine nodded, and Satin pulled her toward the theater.

"I want to show you something," Satin said, sighing when Justine stopped to examine the old show posters pasted to the front of the building.

"Look at this," Justine said, pointing to one. "What is this place?" She glanced above her at the hand-painted sign swinging from the second floor and read it to herself, laughing at the misspellings. THE ORUNGE LANTURN. She looked back at the poster and read aloud, "'Alligator Al, Half-Man, Half-Reptile! Jaws Wired Shut for Your Protection! Faint-hearted Not Admitted.' Mercy me." She laughed again, shaking her head. "I hope I never have to work in another place like this. I've had my fill of sharing the stage with sword swallowers and snake charmers."

"Take a gander at this one," Satin said, tugging her around the corner to the west side and positioning her in front of a poster advertising a show girl.

Justine read it, and the name of the girl struck a hammer blow. Lizette the Flying Nymph.

"Lizzie," she whispered, moving closer to better scrutinize the fading reproduction of the woman's face.

"They put this up right before she came to town."

"Why is it still here?" Justine asked.

"This place closed down right after Lizzie performed here. It never did much business. It's for sale now, but there haven't been any takers."

Justine nodded absently, her attention caught by the image of Lizette. Hers was a child's face: small, heart shaped, with an urchin's appeal enhanced by saucer-sized eyes. Long, wheat-colored hair was parted in the middle and fell to her waist. She wore a stylish dress with a big bow at the bodice, and she held a large fabric flower in one hand. A beautiful sadness emanated from her perfect visage. Justine felt a sense of familiarity. Had she met this woman somewhere before?

"I feel as if I know her," she murmured.

"That so?" Satin asked. "Why is that, do you think?"

"Maybe I met her in a show or a theater. . . . "

"Could be."

Justine read the exclamations on the poster and derived from them that Lizette's act consisted of her flying across the stage, most likely suspended by thin wires, which were hard to see from the theater seats. "As Graceful as a Butterfly," the poster proclaimed. "As Beautiful as a Dream! Lizette the Flying Nymph Will Soar Across the Stage and into Your Hearts!"

Justine couldn't recall such an act, but the face was familiar. Where are you, Lizette? she asked silently, her fingertips smoothing a turned-up corner of the poster. Dead or alive? Did the Count break your heart and drop you somewhere in this vast wasteland?

Her thoughts moved to gruesome scenes of violence, and Justine turned away from Lizette's haunting image. Satin was staring at her, making Justine feel uneasy.

"You don't recognize her?" Satin asked.

"No, should I?"

"Guess not." Satin shrugged and started to move away, but Justine caught her arm.

"Satin, why did you want me to see this? Why is Lizzie so important to you?"

"I just thought you'd like to, that's all."

"No, that's not all." Justine studied the other woman, noting her pale coloring and the nervous twitch at one corner of her rosebud mouth. "Do you know something about her that York doesn't?"

"If I did, why would I tell you?" Satin charged.

"I don't know why, but I think you want to tell someone. Tell me. I'll listen, and I'll keep it to myself if that's what you want." Justine clutched Satin's arm, sensing she was struggling with an inner foe. "I owe you one, don't I? Tell me, do you know where Lizzie is?"

"No." Satin averted her face, and pain tightened the skin near her sloe eyes. "But I know she's not alive. I know that. And I know I could have done something to save her." She turned her back to the street, and tears spilled onto her cheeks. "I betrayed her."

"Oh, Satin, I don't believe that."

"It's true. She trusted me, told me about her regrets and how scared she was living at the Establishment. I told her to get out of there, but she was too frightened of Madame Chloe and the Count. She said they wouldn't let her go. I said I'd talk to them, set them straight, and then she could leave on the next stagecoach, but that scared her even worse." Satin wiped the tears away with the back of her kid gloves. "She made me promise not to interfere, but I ran into Chloe at the courthouse and gave her a piece of my mind. I told her she was a wicked old witch for keeping girls against their will."

"That's not betraying Lizzie," Justine said, trying to ease Satin's conscience.

"Yes, it was." Satin sniffed and gathered her composure. "No need to whitewash it. I promised her I wouldn't tip her hand to the Madame or the Count, and I broke my word. Madame Chloe knew I was talking about Lizzie, and I could tell she was anything but pleased to hear Lizzie had been shooting off her mouth around me. That woman has got snake oil in her veins." Satin shivered. "I knew in my gut that my big mouth had put Lizzie in danger, but I didn't do anything about it. I just closed my eyes to the whole thing and went about my business."

"Well, what could you have done?"

"I could have told Lizzie I'd double-crossed her," Satin said firmly. "And that's what I should have done. I saw her the next day with the Count over at the corral, but I didn't say anything to her. She looked so unhappy, so scared." Satin paused, fighting off another bout of tears. "I should have gone to her, made the Count give her up, and then shielded her from him."

"I think you're being too hard on yourself," Justine said, but Satin acted as if she hadn't heard her.

"That was the last time anybody saw her. She just disappeared like a puff of smoke. I asked Madame Chloe what happened to her, and she said the Count took Lizzie to another place where she'd be happy. She's dead. In my heart I know it."

"But it's not your fault. I'm sure York will understand if you—"

"No!" Satin whirled on her, grabbing her shoulders and giving Justine a shake. "You can't tell him! If you do, I'll . . . I'll kill—"

"Hey, hey!" Justine shook off Satin's grip. "Save your threats. I'm not going to tell York. I'm just saying that if *you* tell him, I know he'll understand."

"You're the one who doesn't understand, honey." Satin adjusted her bonnet and stood more erect. "Just keep this to yourself, huh? When I want York to know, I'll tell him."

"This thing is eating at you," Justine said. "You need to—"

"I need to get going. I've got things to do." She brushed past Justine and hurried away, her voice drifting over her shoulder. "See you around."

Justine stared after her for a minute, thinking about Satin's deeply rooted grief and Lizzie's wretched life. She remembered the way Ivory and York had said Lizette's name: lovingly. She knew Ivory had been in love with the girl, but what of York? Had she soared into his heart as well?

Justine was still wondering about Lizette when she arrived back at the Establishment.

"Jussie, at last," Madame Chloe greeted her in the front hall. "Did you get the licenses?"

"Yes, Madame." She pulled them from her drawstring purse and handed them over. "Is there a problem?"

"Yes." Madame Chloe examined the licenses, then fanned her perspiring face with them. "One problem after another today, it seems. First, one of the maids quits, and now Blanche says she's feeling too poorly to work tonight."

"What's wrong with her?"

Madame made a face of impatience and fanned herself more rapidly. "She saw the midwife yesterday and had a problem taken care of, but the medi-

cine made her sick. She should have been back on
her feet today, but she lost a lot of blood and she's
still weak."

"Blood..." Justine tried not to show how ap-
palled she was by this news. Madame acted as if the
deliberate loss of a baby was of no consequence
whatsoever. Madame might work up a sweat sometimes, but she was a block of ice. So cold, Justine
thought, examining the woman's dull eyes. So
empty inside.

"You'll have to fill in, Justine. Take off early and
get yourself gussied up. Nothing too flashy. That
mint green dress I saw you in the other day will do
fine."

"Fill in?" A bleak wind blew through her.

"Oui. You will take Blanche's place tonight."

She was shaking her head before the words tum-
bled out. "But I can't. I wasn't supposed to—"

"Cherry!" Madame Chloe pushed past Justine to
flag down Cherry before she could dash upstairs. "I
have renewed your license, so you *will* work tonight."

"But I'm cramping. I'm near my time, you know,"
Cherry complained.

"Too bad. I have lost Blanche for the evening, and
I will not lose you, too."

"It shouldn't be busy," Cherry said. "You won't
need all of us, Madame Chloe."

"Cherry, if you do not wish to work I can arrange
for you to be sent elsewhere."

"No!" Cherry's eyes grew large with panic. "I'll
work."

"Bon." Madame Chloe's lips curved into a superior smile. "Justine, I'll be in my quarters, and I don't
want to be disturbed." She put a hand to her forehead. "This turmoil has given me a headache."

"But, Madame Chloe, I can't work tonight."

"Why not?"

"Because I...well, because..." What could she

say? How could she get out of this? The thought of being a prostitute chilled her to the bone.

"You'll work." Madame Chloe's tone was as solid as a rock. She closed the door in Justine's face.

"I *can't* fill in," Justine murmured to herself as she spun around and looked up to see Cherry's sympathetic smile.

"Don't try to fight her when she's in this mood," Cherry said. "She always wins." She shrugged before running up the stairs.

"You been very bad."

Wincing at the truth, York nodded, confirming China Mary's accusation. He sat in her office, feeling like a schoolboy being punished for misbehaving. Unconsciously, he touched his bruised eye where the color had faded from deep purple to violet.

"I not talking about that," China Mary said.

"I know." He tried on a smile. "I'll be able to work tonight."

"Take one more night to heal," she suggested. "Tonight it light crowd. Tomorrow different story. Always plenty busy on Friday nights."

"Fine with me." He shrugged and studied his scraped knuckles. "It's just that I'm getting restless. I'm used to having something to do at night."

"Where you been last couple of days?"

"Bisbee."

"Why?"

He bobbed one shoulder. "I had to meet someone there. Had to pick up something."

"Not my business? I understand." She tucked her chubby hands into her wide sleeves. "Satin Doll look for you yesterday." She waited for a response that didn't come. "Why you hide from her?"

"I'm not hiding." He shifted to a more comfortable slouch in the straight-backed chair. "Have you noticed how fuzzy headed she is most of the time?

She's using too much of that faraway smoke of yours, Mary."

"She grown woman. She mess with what she like. Not my business."

"In other words, you don't give a damn."

China Mary's eyes narrowed to black slits. "If you worried, you talk to her. Don't put your burden on my back."

"You're not worried? I don't think she's had a clearheaded minute in weeks."

"Tell her. Not me."

York swiped the air with one hand in frustration, then stared moodily into the near distance, resting his chin in one palm. China Mary let him brood for a minute before she rose from behind the desk and went to refill her teacup at the ornate sideboard. She didn't return to her desk, but stood near York, sipping tea and looking down on his golden hair and furrowed brow.

"Satin Doll not who make you sore hearted. You got trouble with another woman. Jus-see, maybe?" She gave him a few moments to respond, but he didn't. "What you do, York Masters? You sleep with that virgin girl?"

He ran a hand over his face and tipped his head back to stare at the tin ceiling. China Mary made a tsk-tsking sound and he groaned, accepting her scolding. Burying his face in his hands, he waited out the regret that had been his constant companion for days. He was a failure, caught in his own loop. The other night he'd been amused by thoughts of seducing Jussie, but he'd been the one seduced. He knew he was getting too involved and that he couldn't allow his heart to rule his head. His mission came first, and only when it was over would he listen to his heart and take its advice concerning Jussie.

He'd hurt her feelings following those minutes of sheer heaven when she'd taught him the difference between pleasure and passion. And that hurt. He was disappointed in himself for taking what she gave and then giving her the back of his hand.

"York Masters, you kick yourself too much maybe," China Mary said, trying to console him. "You didn't put gun to her head, did you? She got plenty of smarts."

"I don't know what the hell I thought I was doing," he said, scrubbing his face with his hands, paying no mind to the pain it created. His outer bruises were nothing compared to the ones he suffered inside. "I promised myself I wouldn't get personal with her, but she surrendered like a willow in the wind. That's the *last* thing I need—another woman making demands, acting like I owe her something."

"Watch out, York Masters," China Mary said, her tone suddenly recondite. "You bellow like fresh-cut bull." When he sent her a baleful glare, she laughed in his face. "Like I said, she plenty smart. I don't think she expect much from you. Probably expected just what she got. Maybe you the one who expected more of yourself." China Mary bent closer to peer into his face. "You fight shame, York Masters. You no gentleman with that girl? That what take sparkle from your eyes?"

"A gentleman, I wasn't," he admitted, tenting his fingers and looking across their peak at Far East. The big cat lay sprawled on China Mary's desk, purring and preening, her pink tongue darting out for long swipes at her white fur. York wished for the cat's clear conscience. Cats had no memory of rights and wrongs. They lived from moment to moment. "The Count will be here any day now, and that's all I want to think about," he said, more to himself than to Mary.

"Maybe you should have done hard thinking instead of thinking until you got hard." China Mary grinned wickedly. "Trouble is, no man can put whiskey back in bottle after he's drunk on it. Not even you, York Masters."

Ah Lum entered the office from the saloon, looked from his wife to York, then back to China Mary. "Jus-see here to talk with York," he said. "He in or out?"

York bit back the urge to answer, "Out," catching the challenge in China Mary's eyes. "In," he said, his harsh glare directed at the infuriating Chinese woman.

Ah Lum opened the saloon door and motioned for someone to come inside. "He in. Come. Come."

York stood up as Justine entered the room. He could tell by the flustered look on her face that something had rattled her. Her bonnet was askew, reminding him of the night when she'd upended his decision not to get too involved with her. She extended only a glance toward China Mary before her naked gaze sought him.

"I'm sorry to bother you," she said, her voice taking on a nervous quiver that York knew stemmed from their night together. What he'd hoped wouldn't happen had already happened: she was uneasy around him, uncertain of how to approach him, unsure of how to talk to him. "It's just that a problem has come up, and I'm not sure how to deal with it."

"What problem?"

"Madame Chloe wants me to work tonight."

"And?" York prompted when she didn't continue.

"And I don't want to. I won't!"

York shook his head, not following her objections at first. Then he noticed the almost frantic movement of her eyes and realized she was scared.

"Oh, you mean she wants you to work upstairs?" he asked.

"Yes. She's short one girl, and she expects me to take her place. I won't do it, York. I was playacting at Big Nose Kate's, but no amount of blackmail or flattery can make me follow in my mother's footsteps."

"You not have to do this, girlie," China Mary said, speaking before York could. "I think of something. Why you look surprised?" she asked when Justine stared at her, wide-eyed. "You think I *make* my girls spread legs? China Mary never do this. You no fallen angel. I think of way out of this for you."

"*I'll* handle it," York said, taking Justine by the elbow and leading her toward the back staircase. "Let's go up to my room."

"No!" She jerked away as if his touch and suggestion were poison. "I didn't come here for that."

"For what?" he challenged, losing his temper even as he tried to hold onto it.

"You know." She looked at him through a veil of dark lashes, and her milky skin took on a pink hue. She seemed to collapse into herself with embarrassment.

"What's wrong, Jussie? Do you think I'm an animal now? That I can't control myself around you?"

Justine looked from him to China Mary, and he could see that she was adding things up and realizing China Mary knew what had happened between them. Her color deepened to rose. York reached out, straightened her bonnet, then stepped back and motioned for her to precede him.

"That's more like it," he said, scrutinizing her properly positioned bonnet, then her flushed face. "Let's go upstairs and talk this out, shall we? Mary has a business to run, and we shouldn't involve her in our problems any more than we have to." He sent the Chinese woman a quelling glare when she started to speak. "No, Mary. I'll take care of this, thanks."

China Mary turned her back to them, honoring his request, and Justine had no recourse but to go upstairs with him. Once there, he left the door to his room ajar for her peace of mind. She stood stiffly at the foot of the bed, her gaze never straying there, but York knew it was the only piece of furniture occupying her thoughts.

"So, what are you going to do about this?" she demanded, giving York the distinct impression she didn't think he was going to do a damn thing.

"You're sure Madame Chloe wasn't just joking around?"

"Madame Chloe doesn't joke."

He nodded. "Right. Well, leave it to me. I can probably sweet-talk her out of it."

"You have that kind of faith in yourself, do you?" She scoffed openly, with a breathy, unamused laugh. "She's not an impressionable maiden, you know. Breezy words won't send her spinning like a windmill."

"Like they sent you spinning?" He smiled at the way she jerked her chin with affront. "Well, that's what you meant, isn't it? That my words are what got you in my bed?"

"I don't want to talk about that. All I want from you is a way out of this mess you've thrown me into."

"All my fault, is it?"

"Yes, it is!" Her temper flared so quickly that it took York by surprise. He actually staggered backward, blown off course by the force of her anger. It was as if she'd thrown open a stove door. The heat stole his breath and shriveled his cocky attitude. "You might find this amusing, but I don't! Just because I've slept with you doesn't mean I'm a whore. I'm not! And you can't make me one! I won't let you!" A sob strangled her, robbing her of her voice. Tears made her eyes look like molten silver.

He wanted to take her in his arms and reassure her, but he knew she'd fight him like a wildcat. Running a hand through his hair, he turned aside, unable to witness the wounds he'd inflicted.

"I don't want you to go whoring," he said, his

throat so tight he could hardly speak himself. "What do you take me for, anyway?"

"Just what you've shown yourself to be—a heartless, unfeeling rake. And don't act as if I'm crazy to think you'd want me to whore for you. You've made it clear from the start that you thought I was as wild as a turpentined cat."

"That was before I got to know you better. Jussie, I'm well aware that I was your first man. Do you really think my heart is so black that I'd go back on my word? We have a deal, remember? I promised you wouldn't have to sell yourself. Believe me when I tell you that I'll handle this. Trust me?"

She stared at him long and hard before shaking her head firmly. "No, I don't."

He laughed at her honesty. "Yes, well, why should you? Look, I'll square this with Madame Chloe. You go back to the Establishment, and I'll be there within the hour to set things right."

"Well . . . okay." She started for the door.

"Hold up a minute." York went to the closet and pulled out a burlap sack. "I wanted to give this to you. Here, take it."

"What is it?" she asked, taking the sack with trepidation.

"Open it and see for yourself. Won't bite."

"Hmmm," she murmured, pointedly not comforted by his assurance, but she peeked inside and then her gaze bounced back to him. "My things! How did you? . . . oh, heavenly days!" She took the sack over to his bed and dumped out its contents.

Examining each article with loving hands, she let the tears slip down her cheeks. She picked up the silver mirror and looked at her reflection in it, smiling happily. Then she took up the ivory comb and brush and clutched them to her breasts.

"I didn't think I'd ever see these again. Jasmine Broadwater gave them to me. They're made from ivory taken from Africa."

"Who's Jasmine Broadwater?"

"A voodoo queen in New Orleans."

"You knew voodoo queens there?"

"Oh, yes." She nodded, her face serious and tear-stained. "Jasmine Broadwater was good to me. She was Shoe Black's friend first, then mine. One time she put a curse on a bad man who was trying to force me and Shoe Black out of our home."

"Your home?"

"Yes, the boat hull we lived in. Jasmine Broadwater slapped a curse on him, and he started babbling like the village idiot. We never saw him again. She had great powers." Her wide eyes told him just how great. "Nobody in his right mind crossed her." Her gaze fell to the scattered articles and she grabbed at the dog-eared, leather-bound book of Shakespeare's comedies. "Wonder of wonders! I have my William back. Oh, and this!" Tears fell more freely as she picked up a rabbit's foot suspended from a rusty chain.

"Did the voodoo queen give that to you, too?"

"No." Eyes brimming, she turned to face him. "Shoe Black did. It's all I have left of him, save my memories."

Suddenly she was in his arms, and hers were around his neck, and her tears clung to his skin. York sucked in his breath in a moment of ecstasy. If he hadn't been as tough as cowhide, he would have had to admit he had damn near swooned. As it was, he admitted to being delighted to hold her in his arms again and feel the tap of her heart so close to his.

"Thank you, thank you, thank you! You've made me so happy. I thought I'd lost these things forever and . . . and that broke my heart. How did you ever find them?" She leaned back in the circle of his arms.

"I had another agent track them down for me," he said, then had to clear his throat because his voice had been roughened by his secret longings. "I know everything's not there. Your clothes and—"

"Oh, I don't care about them," she said, leaving his embrace as suddenly as she had catapulted into it. He felt his heart lurch, as if it was trying to follow her. "Elmer and his lot can have those, and the money, too, but these things can't be replaced. Thank you, York."

"You're welcome." He thought he might again rest easy. "Glad to come through for you. You see? I'm not all bad."

She put the things back in the sack. "What shall I tell Madame Chloe if she notices these?"

"Tell her the sheriff recovered them for you."

"Very well." She went to the door, but looked over her shoulder at him. "You'll be along soon?"

"Yes."

"Thanks again for..."

He waved off her gratitude, his pride smarting from her refusal to agree with him about having a few good points. She started to say something else but must have changed her mind, then left him alone.

York went to the window, watching until she emerged from the front of the building, crossed the street, and walked briskly toward the Establishment, swinging the sack like a girl in pigtails swinging her schoolbooks.

"I'm *not* all bad," he told her departing figure. "and I *do* have a heart, damn you."

After all, his heart was what had brought him to Tombstone in the first place.

Chapter 14

When York strode into the Establishment later that evening, heroic in his white suit, he looked to Justine like Gabriel coming forth to confront Lucifer. And not a moment to spare, she thought, having already donned the mint green dress Madame Chloe preferred—the one she'd sworn never to wear again, especially in York's presence, because she'd worn it on *that* night. Anxious and worried that she'd have to cause a scene by telling Madame Chloe she had absolutely no intention of servicing any of the customers, Justine melted in the nearest chair when she caught sight of York.

Sweet Jesus, Joseph, and Mary, he'd arrived, as good as his word. She bobbed her head in relief, thinking his word was the only dependable thing about him.

Spotting Justine's limp figure on the corner settee, he returned her silent greeting before kissing the back of Madame Chloe's hand and murmuring something for Madame's ears only. Then he escorted Madame Chloe into her office and closed the door firmly behind them.

"What's that all about?" Cherry Vanilla asked, and all eyes locked on Justine.

"I haven't the slightest idea," Justine lied, forcing herself to stand and praying that her knees wouldn't buckle. "I didn't even know he was coming around this evening."

"Bet I can guess," Cherry said, bestowing a wise look on the others. Fussing with the lace edging her low-cut bodice, Cherry became coy, waiting for someone to beg the information out of her.

"What?" Justine asked, wondering what Cherry might have concocted in her simple brain. "What do you think you know?"

Cherry smiled, glad to be asked. "I'd bet a week's wages that he's in there playing right into Madame Chloe's hands," Cherry said with a mysterious smile as she sashayed aimlessly about the parlor, pausing briefly to exchange a conspiratorial grin with Ivory Sparks.

"How's that?" Blond Babette asked, and the other girls echoed the question. Everyone but Justine, who didn't think she wanted the answer.

"Why, it's simple. We all know Madame doesn't need an extra flounce around the place tonight." She directed a glance in Justine's vicinity. "It'll be as slow as molasses, always is on Thursdays. Blanche is out sick, but so what? Us girls could manage fine."

The working girls nodded, agreeing with Cherry's summation so far.

"But Madame Chloe wants Justine to work. Why?" Cherry gazed at each of her sisters-in-sin, one by one. She arched her brows in a way that implied she had all the answers and was just being stingy. When their expectation began to border on impatience, she propped her hands on her hips and drew in a deep breath as if she were preparing to blow the house down. "Because she knew York Masters wouldn't be able to stand the thought of some hairy-legged, gray-handed miner loving up to his

woman!" She laughed, delighted with her clever-
ness. "Don't y'all see? Hell's bells, she's done this
sort of thing before, ain't she? Poor York will pay
dearly to keep Jussie his and his alone. I betcha that's
what he's a doin' right this here minute." She issued
a glaring challenge at the other girls. "Don't that
make sense?"

The others murmured "Yes," some enthusiasti-
cally and others grudgingly. When they all turned
toward Justine for confirmation, she laughed nervously, uncertainly.

"That's silly . . . isn't it?" She could see by their expressions that Cherry had struck gold with her pros-
pecting. "It's not? Well, I think it's deceitful for
Madame Chloe to pull such a dirty trick—if that's
what she's doing." She cast a quick glance at the
closed doors and wondered if York had figured out
the ruse. "You said she's done this before?"

"Sure thing," Cherry assured her. "Every time a
man gets sweet on one of us, she figures some way
to turn it into more money for her. You got to remember one thing about Chloe Le Deau: she lives
only to make money. She ain't interested in love, loyalty, friendship, charity—none of that stuff. Money
is what makes her old heart pump. She'd shoot her
own mother if the price was right." Cherry pressed a
hand to her lips just as the office doors swung in.
"Shhh! Here they come. Uh oh, Madame looks
mighty pleased. You must have cost York plenty."

For a few bewildering moments, Justine felt guilty
and sorry for York, but then she reminded herself
that whatever the cost, it was worth it. York didn't
want her identity revealed, or his either. Besides, she
wouldn't put it past him to have already figured out
that Madame Chloe simply wanted him to pay her a
handsome sum to keep Justine untouched by other
men.

He smiled reassuringly, and Justine smiled back
because she was grateful. Whatever he'd done, he'd

done for her, and she wanted him to know she appreciated the gesture.

"Justine, you are to go upstairs with Monsieur Masters. He has graciously paid for you for the entire evening."

"Oui, Madame . . . upstairs?"

"Oui. Upstairs." Madame Chloe poked a finger toward the ceiling. "That is where our work is conducted, and you'll be no exception."

"Oh, of course." Justine nodded, but she didn't understand. Was Madame using this ploy to put her in her place, to make her well aware that tonight she was just a whore, like any other?

"Third door on the left." Madame made a dismissive motion just as the chimes announced a caller. "All smiles and creamy bosoms, girls. Here comes money."

York cupped a hand on Justine's elbow and steered her upstairs to the appropriate room.

"You know what the others said?" Justine asked, standing outside the room, reluctant to go inside. "They said Madame Chloe asked me to work tonight because she *knew* you'd pay handsomely to keep me for yourself. Makes sense, doesn't it? Cherry said she does that sort of thing all the time."

His brows rose and fell. "I got that impression when she negotiated a price. I felt like a fly caught in a spider's web."

"Exactly!" Justine jabbed a forefinger in his chest. "That's the same image I conjured up. Did you hear the way she spoke to the girls? And why is she making us stay up here tonight instead of in my room? It's all her way of putting us where she wants us."

"Settle down." He opened the door and stuck his head inside. "Not too bad." Looking back at her mutinous expression, he touched a fingertip to her nose and frowned playfully. "Don't get so riled up, angel. This is a draw. We *all* got what we wanted." Opening the door the rest of the way, he motioned for her to go inside. "Well... shall we?"

She took a step back, loath to enter. "A whore's room. Well, it won't be the first I've been in."

"It's old hat for us," he said, grinning wickedly. "When I saw you hiding in a corner when I first came in tonight, I was reminded of that time at Big Nose Kate's. Remember?"

"I don't think you'll let me forget."

"Awww, come on. Cheer up. Sleeping in a whore's room doesn't make you one, Jussie. Go on in. We can't stand in the hallway all night."

Sighing, she forced one foot in front of the other. The room was as small as her own, dominated by a bed and a long table on which a pitcher, bowl, whiskey, and glasses were arranged. One window, heavily curtained, broke the monotony of the climbing-rose wallpaper. When York sat on the bed, it creaked and groaned. He bounced on it, laughing at the noise it made.

"No quiet rutting in this bed," he said, still chuckling. He sobered in the face of her apprehension. "Jussie," he said, drawing out her name in a gentle rebuke, "don't be so glum. Let's make the best of the situation."

"Meaning what?" she asked, her tone changing the question into an accusation. "If you think I'm going to let you—"

"Ah-ah-ah!" He wagged a finger at her, chopping off her sentence. "Don't go putting words in my mouth or ideas in my head." He wiggled his brows, tugging a smile from her. "I only meant that we don't have to act like two awkward kids around each other. We're all grown up and we're not up here to play slap and tickle. This is all part of the job." He looked past her. "So, close the door and relax, partner."

Shrugging her acquiescence, Justine shut the door, then paced around the room, examining the sparse furnishings. "Bare necessities," she said, eyeing the chipped bowl and pitcher, two cloths, and a round of scented soap. "Have you stayed in these rooms before?"

"Why, Justine Drussard, what a leading question!" He laid a hand over his heart just as a spinster would when shocked down to her shoes.

"I bet you have," she answered for him. "My mother never wanted for customers. No matter that she was usually so besotted she could hardly stand up and didn't know who or what was on top of her. Didn't matter to those men."

"Settle down somewhere, will you?" He'd lost his sense of humor, or had it been quashed by her memories? "I'm glad you wore that dress, by the way. It looks mighty pretty on you."

"Madame Chloe made me wear it." She dropped listlessly onto the pink upholstery and bumpy springs of the only chair. "I swore I'd never wear it again, but she had it in her head that I would, and I didn't want to make things any worse by arguing with her about it. She's a tough old trail boss when she makes a decision. You get the feeling she'd just as soon put a bullet in your heart as listen to a differing opinion."

"Why didn't you want to wear the dress?"

"Because it . . ."

"Reminds you of me?" he finished with a ghost of a smile, then stood up and stretched. He put his hat on the long table and poured himself a whiskey. He checked the label and made a face of disapproval. "Madame Chloe should furnish better spirits if she wants to keep her higher-class clientele. Want a drink?"

"No, thanks, and I hope you don't drink too much of that stuff."

"You don't drink?"

"Not unless I'm forced to."

"What *do* you do, Jussie?"

"Work for a living when I'm allowed to," she shot back, making his eyes widen at her venom. "And I try to stay out of places like this." She shivered uncontrollably, hating being in a whore's workplace again. "I was raised in a series of rooms like this one. Mama put a pallet on the floor in one corner for me, and I went to sleep hearing grunts and groans. When I got old enough to figure out what my mother was doing with those men, I covered my head with a pillow to keep the sounds out. Of course, she always said we'd have a better place someday, but she didn't really want anything better. All she wanted was liquor, and she wasn't particular about brands."

With his back to her, York couldn't see her expression, but bitterness and resentment colored her voice. He closed his eyes for a few moments, aware of the flux of sympathy he felt for her. His informants had relayed a sketch of her life to him, but it had been woefully incomplete. They had said she was a "former dock rat who calls herself an actress." From that description he had filled in the empty spaces, painting her as a wily vixen with loose morals and plenty of grit.

Being exposed to the bare truth of her life shamed him. Worse, it made him want to take her into his arms and into his heart. Combating such folly, he said, "Here," and shoved a glass of whiskey in her hand. "It won't kill you, and it may even do you good. Take the shock out of your system."

"How much did you pay her for me?"

"Enough to flatter you." He tapped his glass against the one she held unsteadily. "To a quick end to this nasty business we're caught up in, and to better days ahead for both of us."

She nodded. "Cheers." Then the whiskey shriveled her tongue, scalded her throat, and set fire to her stomach. "Awwggg!" Never had such a sound escaped her, but it came from her gut and expressed her feelings perfectly. She doubled over, coughing violently, and thought she might lose her teeth and tonsils when York slammed her several times on the back.

"Stop it!" she managed to croak out, ending his inept attempt to help her. She pointed weakly to the water pitcher, and York scrambled to pour her some.

Grasping the glass of water as if it would save her from the jaws of hell, Justine drank down the cooling liquid. It doused the flames inside her, but her stomach still recoiled from the burning liquid she'd poured into it.

"Are you okay?"

Eyes watering, she shook her head. "Do I look okay? That stuff is horrid." Her voice was as attractive as a bullfrog's. "Tastes like horse piss."

He threw back his head and bellowed, laughing so loudly that Justine was afraid he might bring Madame or one of the girls to the room out of sheer curiosity.

"Hush! Not so loud!"

"Why not?" he asked, wiping moisture from his eyes. "We're supposed to be having fun, and I am. Horse piss?" He laughed again, doubling over this time. "Oh, Jussie, you *are* a treasure."

"Well, it *does* taste like that!"

"I wouldn't know," he said, still laughing. "I've never had the occasion to sample that particular brew."

"You know what I . . . oh, never mind." She smiled in spite of herself, responding to his sparkling eyes and the fact that he'd called her a treasure. When he drank down another measure of whiskey, she shook her head. "You must have a cast-iron stomach, York Masters. Tough outside and tough inside, too."

He accepted her compliment with a wink and a grin. "See, it's not so bad. We'll get a good night's

rest and continue along our merry way tomorrow,
none the worse."

"How are we going to get a good night's rest?"
she asked, looking past him to the single bed. "You
think I'm going to just climb in there and give a repeat performance?"

"No." He poured another whiskey and frowned
into the glass, irritated that she thought so little of
him. "You can have the bed, Jussie. Believe it or not,
I can sleep in the same room with you and not touch
you. In fact, I'll be most pleased to prove that to you
tonight." He hoisted the glass in a mock salute and
drank deeply from it.

"I hope you don't get drunk."

"I won't." He set the glass down and shrugged
out of his suit jacket, hanging it on the doorknob,
then he loosened his string tie. "You don't mind if I
get comfortable, do you?" He sat on the bed and
pulled off his boots, then wiggled his toes in his
socks and sighed with satisfaction. He looked at her
sitting in the chair and made a face of disgust. "Are
you going to sit there all night as stiff as a board?"

"I might."

He stood up and motioned to the bed. "Let's trade
places. I'd like to play a few games of solitaire."
Without further preamble, he grabbed her hand and
pulled her to her feet, then gave her a push toward
the bed before he sat in the chair.

"Maybe I *wanted* to sit there," she grumbled, but
sat down anyway. The bedsprings sang out, making
her flinch. She looked across at York, but he was
busy shuffling a deck of cards. "Did you play cards
before you came here?"

"No, not often."

A door closed down the hall. Justine looked from
the door in front of her to York. He grinned.

"Bet that fella didn't have to pay as much as I
did."

"I can't imagine what pleasure a man gets out of

sleeping with a woman who cares not one jot for him."

"That fella down the hall isn't looking for tender lovin' care, angel. He just wants to scratch an itch."

"Disgusting," she intoned.

"Human nature," he corrected.

"If it's so *natural*, how come women have to be *paid* before they'll oblige?"

He glanced at her, then back to his card game, but there was a smile in his eyes. "I'll have to think on that one. Maybe it's natural for a man, but not for a woman."

"Maybe women expect more than a tussle in the sheets and a slap on the behind when it's over."

"Sounds like you've been ruminating on this."

"It's not unusual for a woman to try to figure out men. Sometimes I think we couldn't have sprung from the same root."

"I think we're more alike than we are different."

"You do?"

"I do." He showed her the ace of hearts, then placed it above his seven stacks. "Instead of dwelling on the differences, ponder the ways we're alike."

"You mean things like men and women both eat and sleep?"

"Deeper than that," he said, chuckling.

"Like what?"

"Oh . . . like we all want to love and be loved."

The unguarded answer astonished her, but she fought to keep from gaping at him. Lying on her side, she stacked her hands beneath her cheek and wondered what he'd been like before coming to Tombstone. Was it possible there was a sweet-tempered, warmhearted gentleman beneath his cavalier attitude?

"Do you live in a grand house in St. Louis?" she asked, closing her eyes and picturing such a place.

"No, but my parents' house is quite lovely. I live in a guest house on my grandmother's property."

"A guest house. Your grandmother must have quite a place."

"The guest house used to be for servants, but she only has two retainers now, so I moved into the old servants' quarters."

"I bet you have a big family."

"Not big, but big enough. We're close-knit."

She smiled, liking the sound of that. Close-knit. That's the way a family should be, she thought. All for one and one for all.

"I have two brothers and a sister and lots of aunts, uncles, and cousins. Both of my grandfathers are dead, but my grandmothers are still living. Most of us live in or around St. Louis, which makes it nice at Christmas and on other holidays. Plenty of presents and mountains of good food."

Presents, good food, Christmas cheer. It was all foreign to her, the stuff of dreams. But it had been normal for him. Expected, even.

"My father is a doctor, and my mother is busy with the church and social organizations. She's president of the Literature and Edification Society. Don't ask me what they do exactly. All I know is that a bunch of women meet at my parents' home once a month and read poetry or parts of novels aloud, and sometimes they go to the theater and write essays about the plays they saw."

"How wonderful," Justine murmured, picturing herself in such a circle of women, sharing ideas and opinions about the arts. "They like the legitimate theater, do they?"

"Yes, and the opera. Sometimes my mother drags my father to performances."

"And your father's a doctor," she said, marveling at that. York Masters had been showered with opportunities. Did he understand how blessed he was?

"That's right, and one of my brothers is a doctor. The other is an attorney."

Justine assembled this, getting a clear picture. "Your family is wealthy. Upper class."

"Oh, I wouldn't say wealthy."

"I would."

She sighed as the whiskey began to seduce her, no longer burning, but smoking and sending lazy fumes to her mind. She yawned as she removed her shoes and lay back on the noisy bed. The feather mattress embraced her. She began to relax, muscle by muscle, nerve by nerve. After a while, she felt pleasantly drowsy. Turning her cheek into the pillow, she closed her eyes for a moment or two of repose.

Cherry's high-pitched giggle woke her. Justine opened her eyes, confused for a few moments about where she was and what she was doing there. Who was laughing? She listened, closing her eyes again to think. The laughter was coming from a distance, and it tapered off to silence.

By the time Justine opened her eyes again, she had remembered she was at the Establishment in a room with York. He was sitting in the pink chair, slumped into an uncomfortable position, chin in hand, eyes barely open. The deck of cards lay at his elbow. The whiskey bottle was near it, half-empty now.

"Sounds like Cherry's having fun," he mumbled.

"How long have I been asleep?"

"Not too long." He looked at his pocket watch. "It's a little after midnight."

"You look about as comfortable as a cowboy astride a wild sow," Justine said, rising up on one elbow and running a hand across her eyes. "You won't be able to get any sleep in that chair."

"That's right smart of you. Mind sharing the bed?"

The suggestion sent a bolt of alarm through her and poked her into a sitting position. She glanced at the space beside her. There wasn't much, she thought, but then this bed wasn't meant to actually be *slept* in. Looking toward York again, she figured his body would fit, but there'd be no room leftover.

"Forget it," he said, batting his hand at her. "Stupid of me to ask."

Should she? Would he behave himself? Naughtiness streaked through her, making her wonder if he could actually lie beside her and not take her into his arms. Was he really that iron-willed? Were his feelings for her so lukewarm? She couldn't imagine it. In fact, she found it insulting.

Might be fun, a voice whispered in her head. Go on. Share the bed with him. It's not as if you haven't done it already. Make him suffer a little. See what he's made of.

She shrugged casually, her insides as jittery as drops of oil on a hot skillet. "I'll share the bed."

"No fooling?" His head came up. His eyes sparkled in the dim light.

"No fooling. Just keep on your side of it."

"No problem." He wasted no time, but sprang from the chair, drew back the top sheet, and sat on the side of the bed. When he pulled his shirt from the confines of his waistband, Justine realized he was taking a step further than she'd intended.

"York, what are you doing?"

"Undressing." He glanced over his shoulder to read her expression. "Jussie, you don't think I'm going to crawl in bed fully clothed, do you? You might sleep in your finery, but I don't."

"But . . . but we're not . . . I mean, I thought you wanted to take a little nap."

"It's after midnight. I don't nap after midnight. I sleep." He shook his head, laughing under his breath. "Don't worry. I'll leave my long johns on." He chuckled again. "Besides, I'm the same man, dressed or not."

"I know that," she snapped.

"If you're smart, you'll get comfortable yourself. If I wanted to jump you, that dress wouldn't protect you."

She counseled herself not to give him the upper hand. This was *her* game, not his. He was being so nonchalant. Oooh, that really plucked her feathers! Did he honestly think she believed he was completely unshaken by the prospect of sleeping with her? Well, if he wanted to make things more difficult for himself, then she'd oblige. With that in mind, she eased off the bed and, with her back to him, began unfastening her dress.

"Of course, you're right. I'm the same woman, clothed or not. Don't worry. I'll keep on my undergarments."

"I'm not worried," he said, shucking his trousers and shrugging out of his shirt.

Justine smiled to herself, catching the unsteadiness in his voice. When she glanced over her shoulder again, he was already under the top sheet, his back to her. She removed her dress and petticoats and corset, then eased beneath the covers, trying not to to touch him, and failing. The bed was too narrow for modesty. Her knee brushed the back of his, and her shoulder rubbed his back. With each touch he stiffened, and Justine was sure he was holding his breath. Having such power over him, making him respond against his will, sent a delectable thrill shimmering through her.

Alas, poor York, I know you well, she recited in her mind, amending Shakespeare's lines. He had to be hugging the edge of the mattress because he wasn't touching her anywhere. The naughty streak widened within her. Almost against her own judgement she snuggled more completely under the covers and eliminated the whisper of space between their bodies. Her rump bumped his. Although he didn't move a muscle, she sensed the grinding of his teeth. It made her smile, but the voice of reason chased aside her delight.

He's a caged tiger right this minute, the voice said. Do you really want to open the trap door and let him out? Once he's out, you'll no longer be his mistress; you'll be his prey.

He squirmed, bringing out the mischief in her again. She just couldn't help herself.

"I'm sorry if I'm bothering you," she said, trying to keep from laughing.

"You're not." His voice was gruff.

"It must be uncomfortable for you to be so close to me and not touch me . . . I mean, *really* touch me."

"I *know* what you mean. I'm fine. Get some sleep." He sounded too nonchalant.

Justine pressed her knuckles against her smiling lips, enjoying the game of cat and mouse, especially since she was the cat and he was her mouse. Her heart went out to him because she knew his struggle intimately. They were both living, breathing contradictions, pushing each other away even as they tried to get closer.

"I'd understand perfectly if you got all hot and bothered," she teased, then realized he wasn't the only one heating up. Perspiration beaded her forehead, and the air she pulled into her lungs seemed warmer than it had been only a minute ago. She listened for a response that never came. Twisting to face him, she made sure her body slid against his. He felt as hard and as hot as a desert rock. His eyes were stubbornly closed. Dots of moisture dotted his upper lip. "Are you hot and bothered?"

"No." He drew his eyebrows together, creating vertical lines between them. "Go to sleep, will you?"

"Any *normal* man wouldn't be able to stand this. But you're not normal. We both know that."

He opened his eyes to glare at her. "What's that mean?"

"You have an iron will," she explained, amazed

that she could speak to him straight-faced when her
whole insides giggled. "You're a professional Pinkerton man."

"So?"

"So that means you're above human needs or
matters of the heart. Everybody knows Pinkerton
men have no feelings. They're trained to be as hard
as trail biscuits. Any other man would want to kiss
me, hold me, make love to me, but not a Pinkerton
man. You're not the least bit tempted, are you?"

"What if I am? Wouldn't you scream like a ban-
shee if I kissed you?"

She raised one shoulder in a shrug. "Oh, I
wouldn't *scream*, I don't think. But why wonder?
You're not going to kiss me, are you?"

He squinted one eye in a twinge of suspicion.
"Are you pulling my leg?"

"No, I'm trying not to touch you, much less pull
anything on you." She widened her eyes as if she
found such a suggestion alarming. "But then, you're
as cold-blooded as a fish, so I don't have to worry. I
could get closer, right up against you..." She snuggled into him, pressing her breasts against his chest
and rubbing her stomach on his. His body hair tick-
led through her chemise. Bending one knee, she
managed to slide her leg between his. He bared his
teeth, clearly tormented. "You're not bothered one
bit? Not tempted in the least? Not even thinking
about how soft I feel against you or how nice it
would be to wrap your arms around me and...?"
She felt him stir against her belly and lifted her
brows in mock surprise. "What's that? Is that the leg
you thought I was pulling?"

His grin was lopsided and charming. "Jussie
Drussard," he said, his voice pouring over her like
honey, "you've got the devil in you."

"Not yet," she murmured with a smile, "but from
the feel of it, I will soon."

Chapter 15

Delight made his eyes shimmer. He touched his smile to hers.

"You're a lusty little lady," he murmured, his lips moving against hers as he spoke.

"I never thought anyone would say that about me," she whispered, laughing nervously. "I never believed it of myself until you came along. I can't imagine where I . . ." The next thought propelled her from his embrace, and Justine was out of bed and standing, swaying, before him. Her eyes burned from being widened too far, and she couldn't keep her lips from trembling as the awful image of her mother and herself, side by side, arm in arm, branded her mind's eye.

"Jussie . . ." York propped himself on one elbow and reached out to her. "What's wrong, honey? You're looking at me as if I had horns shooting up through the top of my head."

"Look at me." She extended her arms, then glanced down at herself and laughed without one drop of humor. She was shaking, afraid for herself, enraged by her blindness when York was near her.

"You've paid for me, and I'm getting ready to give you your money's worth. Just like her. . . . ." Shivering, she turned her back to him, crisscrossing her arms over her chemise-covered breasts and holding tightly to her upper arms to curb the convulsions racking her body. "Just like Mama."

"Oh, Jussie . . . don't." York bounded from the bed, came up behind her, and enfolded her in his embrace. "You're not like her. I didn't pay for you."

"Yes, you did."

"No, not really. That was all a game." He swept her hair from her neck and pressed a kiss there.

"And what's this?"

"I'm not pretending anything." His lips sought and found the sensitive skin behind her ear. "We were having so much fun a minute ago. Don't let's spoil it."

"Yes, we were having fun," she agreed, wriggling from his arms. "But I remember the last time we had this kind of fun and how it wasn't much fun once you were finished with me."

"Now, don't go blaming me for everything." He dipped his head, looking for all the world like a bull ready to charge. If she hadn't been so distraught, Justine would have laughed aloud. "As I recall, you kind of went off half-cocked."

Her shivers stopped abruptly as she traded one memory for another. Glaring at him, she was astounded to see that he was serious. "Me, half-cocked? That describes you, mister, not me. All I wanted was to be treated with a little respect, and you couldn't handle it. You like me just fine on my back, but you don't want to be seen with me outside the bordello. No, siree! You've got a reputation to consider and mine be damned!"

"Now, you listen to me for a change." He extended a palm toward her, and his squared chin inclined at a self-righteous angle. "I tried to apologize for giving you the wrong idea—"

"I didn't have the wrong idea."

"Yes, you did. It was your first time, and maybe I could have been more sensitive. . . . "

"Maybe?" she scoffed, thrusting her chin forward in a stubborn challenge.

"But you didn't make it easy, ranting and raving like you did. You got your feelings hurt because I put business before pleasure."

"Only when it pleases you," she amended. "A minute ago you were putting pleasure before business."

He started to speak, then compressed his lips in a straight, stern line. Anger mounted in his eyes like thunderheads, making them a steely blue.

Justine crossed her arms and jeered at him. "It's terrible to be slapped in the face with the good, old-fashioned truth, isn't it?"

"I don't know what you're used to," he said, his tone chilling. "I've heard that those actor fellas are asshole buddies, so it's understandable you wouldn't know what to do and what not to do around a *real* man."

Impudent beyond good measure, she looked from left to right in pure puzzlement. "Could you point him out, please?"

He stepped right up to her and clamped one hand on the back of her neck, pressing the other into the small of her back. Her struggles only made him tighten his hold.

"Baiting a man in bed and then backing off isn't done, angel," he said, his voice husky. "As far as what you said about you being like your mother, we both know that's hogwash."

"Let me go," she said, squirming to no avail.

"Because what we're about to do has absolutely nothing to do with business," he finished before his mouth came down on hers, reminding her that he was the more powerful, especially when riled and aroused. She'd let the tiger out of his cage and now there was hell to pay.

He swept her up into his arms and carried her back to the noisy bed, his mouth smothering her protests, his muscles and tough skin taking her blows. Dropping her to the bed, he straddled her and pressed her fists into the mattress at the sides of her head. He looked down into her flushed face, and his smile was almost feral.

"Jussie, stop it." Amazingly, his tone was calm, even amused. "You'll wear yourself out."

"Get off me! I'm not a calf to be roped and branded, damn it!" She bucked, making him laugh again. "And stop laughing. You're a crude bully! If I were a man, you wouldn't be laughing."

"Honey, if you were a man, I wouldn't be sitting astride you in this bed."

Instead of letting her go, he stretched out on top of her and placed kisses across her collarbone and up her throat to her chin. His lips felt like warm satin sliding over her sensitive skin. He made little sucking noises, and his tongue left drops of moisture in its wake. Gradually, his grip on her wrists lessened as he sensed her rising passion. Justine thought about escaping, but not seriously. Her heart began to beat faster, and her thoughts skipped ahead, anticipating each step that would lead to that peak of passion York would take her to if she let him have his way. Let him have his way...She frowned, thinking of her mother again and how she'd lived by that creed.

"You're not her," he whispered, kissing her frowning mouth. "You're you."

"What we're doing is wrong," she said, almost moaning with indecision and weakness.

"Maybe, but neither one of us can help it."

He was right, she thought, her eyes closing as a sigh of contentment floated through her, chasing

aside the images of her mother and her mother's life.
She couldn't help the way York made her feel or her
response to his feather-light kisses and lulling voice.
Her body longed for him, directing the rest of her to
follow or be left behind. Come daylight, she'd la-
ment, but until then she wanted only to keep feeling
this way.

"I've told you I'm helpless around you," he murmured, telling her what she needed to hear. "I had
every intention of being a gentleman tonight, but
you've gone and ruined it."

"I appreciate the thought," she whispered, clasping his head in her hands and bringing his mouth to
hers. She tipped his head so that his lips met hers at
a delicious slant, a perfect fit.

He kissed her fully, his tongue surging into her
mouth to find and mate with hers. Her body heat
soared, and Justine ached to discard the rest of her
clothing and glory in skin against skin. Reading her
mind, he grappled with her laces and buttons. He
disrobed her and then himself, the clothing tossed
aside like the useless barriers they'd become. Justine
gazed upon him, unashamed, and he upon her, un-
inhibited.

"My God, look at you. Beautiful. So beautiful," he
said, his voice hoarse with passion. He ran his hands
lightly over her breasts, then watched her nipples
pucker for kisses. He obliged, and she trembled uncontrollably. "From your midnight hair to your pink
toes, you're every man's dream."

"Hush, you're embarrassing me. I swear, if you
were a peddler, you could sell fire to the devil. You
smooth-talker you."

"You don't believe me, do you?"

She frowned again before she could stop herself.
No, she didn't believe him, but that was insignificant
now. Come morning, it would torment her, but at
that moment she was tormented only by a burning
need to enfold him within the secret heart of her.

She gripped his shoulders and levered herself up to rain kisses over his breastbone and into the curling hair near his flat nipples. Like hers, they responded, tightening and becoming dusky. She kissed one, sucking gently, then the other. He growled deep in his throat, and with a strangled moan fastened his mouth on hers.

His kiss, wild and groping, sent her reeling into that world of sensory images she had known before, but she was no longer a stranger, having visited once before. Bending her knees, she made a cradle for him and the lower part of his body fit against her, warm and snug. She explored the satin walls of his mouth, tasting him with her agile tongue and tempting him with slick caresses. He tasted of whiskey, but this time she enjoyed the sips. She drank deeply of him, wanting him to make her mind stagger and whirl and buzz. His kisses seemed carnal, naughty, because he didn't just kiss, he mated, he drank, he ate, he impaled, he sucked in her soul. Was there any woman on earth who could resist a man such as this? she wondered, dazed by his onslaught. Lassoing the sun was child's play compared to refusing York Masters.

Running her hands over his shoulders, she delighted in the passion that darkened his eyes to cobalt. She draped herself around him as her mouth pledged allegiance to his and her heart drummed in rapture. He stroked her breasts and made her groan with desire, then he tucked his hands under her hips and gathered her more completely beneath him.

She bowed up, rubbing her smooth belly against his, which was corrugated with muscle and furred with gold-tipped hair. He raised up on stiff arms to gaze feverishly at the soft mounds of her breasts. Although he wore no discernible expression, his eyes burned as he bent forward to flick her throbbing nipples with the agile tip of his tongue. Her body responded by jerking, then quivering. Justine felt as if she had no power over herself. He had taken over completely, making her answer his every summons. He touched her again and again with his fire-tipped tongue, then took one of her swollen nipples into his mouth.

"Oh, York..." Her voice was strangled, but she was astounded she could speak at all.

Encouraged by her spontaneous moaning of his name, he suckled her other nipple. Heat, sharp and piercing, burned through her. She drove her fingers through his hair, holding on for dear life while the exquisite pain of pleasure speared her. He moved from one breast to the other, keeping them moist and throbbing. His teeth nipped lightly, drawing a squeak of pleasure from her. Justine began to pant instead of breathe. Just when she was sure something inside her was going to explode, he shifted his interest from her breasts to her stomach and below. When she began to thrash, he reached down, sliding his hand between her silky thighs, and pressed the heel of his hand against her femininity.

She hadn't realized the extent of her wanting until he covered her with his large hand and she felt the wetness her need had caused.

But she wasn't the only one charged by passion. His erection fascinated her, and she couldn't keep from staring once her gaze found it. Round and glistening, the tip was as dark as an overripe cherry. He pressed it against her, nestling it into her triangle of ebony hair. She thought he meant to tease her, but he surprised her by driving into her, making her gasp with pleasure. Without being aware of it, her body had once again responded. Her hips were completely off the bed, and her hands had somehow come to rest on the top of his thighs. They felt so powerful, so hot under her hands that she couldn't resist stroking and caressing them, loving the crackle of hair against her fingers. The muscles beneath his skin flexed and bunched as he moved in and out of her like a restless tide.

Gazing up into his face, she measured his expression and liked what she saw. The smile that teased one corner of his mouth, coupled with the relaxing of muscles around his eyes and across his cheekbones, conveyed his exaltation. That she could produce such feeling in him made her heart pound with joy. She lifted her hands to trace the lines in his face from cheek to chin, from one temple straight across his forehead to the other.

"You feel good inside of me," she said, tenderness welling up within her.

A smile, fleeting and self-absorbed, skipped across his mouth as he stretched carefully upon her, grinding ever so slightly against her and making her fight for breath. He laced his fingers through hers and held them on either side of her head, then moved up and back, in and out, deep and shallow. His body hair rasped on her skin, and his breath fanned her face. Stroke by delicious stroke, her body fused to his. Her breathing grew rapid and so did his. After a few minutes, he stopped all movement. Examining his expressive face with anxious eyes, Justine saw that he was collecting himself. He attempted to regulate his breathing, then caught her watching him and smiled reassuringly.

"I don't want to finish yet. This is too good to stop now," he said breathlessly, disjointedly. "Don't move, Jussie. Not one muscle. Give me another minute."

"But I want to move," she said, sighing.

"Don't." He pressed his forehead to hers, his body tense and quivering. "Please."

Justine forced herself to lie perfectly still, but she couldn't command her insides not to tremble. York

gathered a long breath and began surging and ebb-
ing again, sweeping her easily into the age-old
rhythm. She smiled, released an "ahhh" of intense
joy, and lifted her hips to meet each thrust.

His movements became less practiced and more
spasmodic, uncontrolled. With a grimace he
pressed his face against her shoulder, and her
name was torn from him, ripped from his very
soul. His release was a shower of fiery sparks,
making her glow inside. She clung to him, eyes
wide with wonder, lips parted by her ragged
breathing. Treasuring the last minute of their joining, Justine closed her eyes and knew she'd never
feel like this with any other man. Something about
York appeased something in her that she didn't
even know was there unless he nudged it into ex-
istence.

This is right, a calm voice said within her. *This man
is right for you. This man is your destiny.*

"Hold on, Jussie."

York's hand moved between their hot, slick
bodies. Slipping into the folds, his fingers massaged
and delved until he found the place he sought. Justine cried out, driven out of her head with the desire
his touch created.

His mouth melted over hers, taking in her
sounds of wonder and self-involvement and luring
her tongue into a writhing dance of passion. He
had the most demanding mouth, insisting that hers
pay attention and respond. Even as her passion
peaked and split into a million pinpoints, she delivered long, thrusting kisses, and as her passion
subsided, she received his thirsty tongue strokes.

She flattened her hands on his shoulders and then
down to the arch of his back. He felt like a sleek
animal. He made love like a demon.

"If this is sin, then I'm doomed to hell's fire." She
kissed his earlobe, and he chuckled. "I just wish
you...I mean, I wish..." She sighed, exasperated

with her inability to say what she felt. "I wish we really loved each other," she said, not really telling the truth. What she wished was that he loved her— even a little bit. "Wouldn't it be lovely to make plans . . . to talk about important things like children and making a good home for them?"

He rolled off her in a single, fluid motion that left her blinking in surprise. By the time she realized she was alone in the bed, he was already standing by the window, holding back the heavy drape to see outside. The stars bathed his face in a milky light. His profile was so classically perfect—like a statue in a museum—that it took her breath away. She wanted him back in bed, but she knew it was too late. She'd chased him away.

"I guess I should have kept my thoughts to myself and my mouth shut," Justine said, struggling against the loneliness that tried to squeeze the love from her heart. "Every time we make love, I open my big mouth and lose you."

He smiled but didn't look at her, preferring to gaze at the distant light. "Sometimes it's best not to talk when your emotions are so close to the surface."

Standing in the pale light, he was so exquisite that to look upon him was almost too much to bear. Tears blurred her vision as she let her gaze float from his square jawline to the casual slope of his shoulder, the shelf of muscle across his chest, the light filtering through the curling hair running down the center of him and pooling above that part that made him unmistakably male. Even now it was not tamed, but strained outward from the rest of his body, as if seeking the warmth she had provided.

"May I say one more thing before I lace up my lips?"

Still smiling, he nodded. "Just one more thing. What is it?"

She took a deep, satisfying breath. "You are the most beautiful man I've ever seen."

Points of light glittered across his blue eyes when he shifted them toward her. "And how many have you seen?"

Wrinkling her nose playfully, she wiggled more deeply into the feather mattress. "Don't ruin my flattery by pointing out my shortcomings." Reaching for the edge of the sheet, she started to pull it across her hips.

"No, don't." York extended a hand, stopping her, and moved to the bed. "Don't hide yourself from me. I love to look at you."

"You just don't like to talk to me."

"No, it's not that." He sat on the edge of the mattress and placed his hand on her stomach, a smile edging his wide mouth. "I want to be honest with you, Jussie. I don't want to say things I'm not certain of, or things you might misunderstand." He leaned back again, sliding on his side and pulling her to him. "I know I'm your first man, and that carries certain responsibilities with it."

"No, it doesn't. I don't want you to feel beholden . . . obliged."

He smiled and kissed the valley between her breasts. "I know. But I *do* feel responsible. I'm teaching you how to pleasure a man and be pleasured by one. That's a responsibility, Jussie, whether you know it or not."

"Am I a good student, Mr. Masters?" she asked, grinning.

"Superb." He slid lower so that he could rest his cheek on her stomach. She felt him relax against her, as if her touch steadied him. "I know you were disappointed last time. I disappointed myself. But we shouldn't get too involved with each other. We have to remember why we're together in the first place."

"The Count."

"That's right. First and foremost, I'm on company time. I'm here to track a man, to gather clues, to find answers. You're assisting me. I don't go to bed with everyone who assists me in my work."

"That's a relief."

"You're different, Jussie. I can't keep away from you." He turned his head to kiss her navel. "You're just too sweet, and I've got a mighty big sweet tooth, angel."

She ran her fingers through his silky hair, watching it shimmer against her hand. She understood him more than he knew because she was as shamelessly weak around him as he was around her. It was as if they were drawn to each other by a spell more powerful than anything Jasmine Broadwater could have conjured up. No matter how much they protested or how hotly they argued, they ended up in bed, her clinging to her dream of belonging and him clinging to his solitude.

"I suppose this sort of thing is going on all around us," she said after a while. "But it's not as noisy as it was earlier. Maybe the clients have all gone home or passed out. I suppose we have Madame Chloe to thank for this night." She stroked his hair again, remembering the poster and the lovely Lizette. "I saw something interesting today."

"What?" He sounded sleepy.

"I was checking up on the shows coming to town. *Romeo and Juliet* will be presented in a few days. I'd love to go."

"So, go."

"No, I—"

"I'll take you."

"You'd escort me to the theater?" She held her breath, caught off guard by his gesture.

"Sure. Remind me, though, or I'll forget."

She nodded, but she couldn't make herself believe he really meant to take her out in public.

"That's what you thought was so interesting?"

"What?" She had to think a moment before she remembered what she'd been talking about. "Oh, I saw an old poster of Lizette." When she didn't go on, he rolled onto his back to look up into her face.

"And?"

"The Flying Nymph?"

"Yes, I know. What was so interesting about that?"

Although he looked as innocent as a lamb, Justine could tell he was holding something back from her. The whole story had not been revealed, and he was loath to lay it out for her inspection.

"She's beautiful."

Getting no response, Justine scooted off the bed and grabbed the top sheet, draping it around her like a billowing cloak. She went to the window and looked out at the dark night. I should have kept quiet, she told herself, then shook her head. No, it was best to get everything out in the open. Sunlight was more comforting than shadows.

The window gave the same view as the one in her room. The hillside sloped into a narrow valley, then the land surged up again into foothills and mountains. But the night obscured most of the details, giving only the sense of hulking shadows and pools of gray and black.

A yellow light blinked, then blinked again. Justine flattened one cheek against the cool glass, glad for the diversion. The light bobbed, ducked into shadows, flew back out. It was being carried.

Ivory, she thought. He'd been visiting his lady again. Who was she? Where did she live? Was he keeping her a secret because she was married or maybe a half-breed? There was something forbidden about the liaison or he wouldn't be sneaking around. She felt a kindred spirit with Ivory, having a secret love of her own. Justine looked back at York. He sat stoop shouldered and brooding. She wanted to give him a good shake.

I want so much to get close to you, don't shut me out, she wanted to scream at him. *Don't you know you can tell me anything? Nothing could make me betray you.*

"So you won't talk about her?" Justine asked.

He raised his head and looked at her. "I've told you about her. I followed her trail here, but she vanished. I don't believe she became a whore because she had her heart set on it. I think she loved the Count—or thought she did—and she thought he loved her."

"The ruin of many a softhearted woman." Justine smiled, feeling sadness weigh her down. "York, have you told me everything?" She stared directly into his eyes, begging him to trust her. "I mean, Satin Doll acted as if Lizzie was important and—"

"I've told you everything you need to know."

"You don't trust me."

"It's got nothing to do with trust." He stood up and began dressing, his movements jerky. "I'm the detective, not you."

"Oh, we're back to that. Equal in bed, but not out of it."

"And I don't want you talking with Satin." The finger he pointed at her shook with anger.

"I'll talk with anyone I want!"

He glared at her, and she glared back in a silent standoff. Finally, he turned away from her to finish dressing, and Justine stared out the window as her feeble hopes crumbled. Her lord and master, she thought bitterly. And like any good master, he wanted her obedience and loyalty, not her love.

"You just buddy up to the girls at the Establishment and find out what they know. Leave the rest to me."

"Yes, sir," she snapped. "Whatever you say, sir."

"And spare me your sassy mouth."

She gave him her back and watched the sun rise on a new day. In the gray distance she could see Schieffelin Hall. Her thoughts moved to her old life . . . her theater life. The theater. That's where she belonged. That's where she was mistress, ruled by no one and loved by many.

Chapter 16

"**D**id you enjoy last night, cherie?" Madame Chloe languished in the white-and-gold-edged chair behind her delicate desk. Her smile was feline. "You have not thanked me for arranging the evening for you."

Justine pushed aside her paperwork and turned in her chair to regard Madame squarely. She didn't like the woman's smile or her presumptuousness. "Madame Chloe, I don't wish to offend, but you needn't have gone to such trouble. York Masters doesn't have to pay for my company. I give it to him freely."

Madame's eyes glittered like wet stones. "Then you are a foolish girl. You should always make a man pay for your favors." She took a bite of cream-filled pastry, then dabbed at the corners of her painted mouth with a linen napkin. "I sensed that you were —how do you say?—uncomfortable with being asked to work that night. If that is the case, then I'm sorry to inform you that this is a brothel, and all the women under this roof work for a living."

"And I'm sorry to inform you that I was hired as a

228

bookkeeper," Justine parried before she could curb
her sharp tongue.

"That could change, ma'm'selle." Madame Chloe
picked up the remaining pastry and shook it at Justine. Powdered sugar fell like snow. She swept the
white stuff off her desk, then popped the last bite
into her mouth and swallowed with relish. "When
the Count arrives, things change. Girls come"—her
wicked, cold eyes sent shivers down Justine's spine
—"and girls go."

Refusing to be intimidated, Justine marched over
to the other woman's desk. "I'm temporary, remember? You may want me to jump when you snap
your fingers and do whatever you ask without question, but I'm not one of your girls."

"You are on my payroll!"

"As a bookkeeper. Anything else costs extra."

Madame rose slowly, seething with anger. "You
do not tell me what to do."

The white spider, Justine thought, glancing at her
mass of spun-sugar hair. The woman wasn't satisfied
unless she had everyone in her web, securely under
her power.

"I hope you're not thinking of leaving here to go
off with York Masters. I won't stand for it!" She narrowed her eyes and leaned into Justine's face. "The
little bitch you replaced tried to sneak off, but she
wasn't as smart as—" Madame pressed her lips together, as if realizing she'd said too much.

"I thought she *did* sneak off, with a miner or
somebody."

"She did."

"But you just said—"

"I'm busy!" Madame sat down and grabbed her
coffee cup. "Get back to work and leave me alone."
She pointed a long, daggerlike nail at Justine. "Just
bear in mind that I know many people—powerful
people, who owe me favors. If you run, I'll have
them follow you and force you to your knees."

Justine took a few moments to digest the threat, then another few to decide on her reaction. Deciding on nonchalance, she shrugged and smiled at her employer to restore her confidence. "I'm not going anywhere. I like it here, and I'm guarding no romantic notions about York Masters. I enjoy his company, but not enough to pack my bags and run off with him."

Madame Chloe nodded. "I thought you had a good head on your shoulders, and now I am sure of it."

"Madame, does Ivory have a girlfriend?"

"Ivory?" Madame Chloe patted her white hair, feeling to make sure each curl was in place. "Not that I know of. He used to like Lizzie."

"Lizzie?" Justine's heart kicked, but she remained calm on the outside.

"She used to work here. The Count took her away."

"Why?"

"She was too much trouble."

"Where did he take her?"

"How should I know?" Madame threw out her hands, then narrowed one eye as she gave Justine a quick once-over. "Why should you care? Why all these questions?"

"I'm curious. Ivory is a nice man, and I wondered if he had anyone special, that's all."

"You'd do well to keep away from Ivory. He's not playing with a full deck."

"He's not? He seems perfectly fine to me."

"He's fine enough to play the piano, but beyond that he's an imbecile. He falls in love with every girl who befriends him, and that makes trouble for me." Her expression hardened. "Trouble I do not need. Do you understand?"

Justine nodded, but refused to let go. "What about Shelley?"

"Shelley?" The look Madame Chloe directed at

Justine sent a shaft of fear through her. "What has
that fool Ivory been telling you?"

"Nothing, except that he loved Shelley and she
was taken away by the Count. Shelley and Lizzie,
both of them taken away and both of them loved by
Ivory. It seems odd."

"What is odd is that you are so curious about
strangers. What does it matter to you where these
women are? Did you know either of them?"

"No . . . I don't think so." Justine sighed and
turned away, trying to appear blind to Madame
Chloe's cold fury. "I'm just softhearted when it
comes to sad love stories. Poor Ivory seems to be
unlucky in love."

"Poor Ivory is going to find himself out in the
streets if he doesn't keep his mouth shut."

"If you don't like him, why keep him on? I'm sure
you could find someone else to play the piano . . . if
you really need a piano player all that much."

"I want to keep an eye on him. When he's under
my roof, I can control him. If I send him away, he'll
spread his stupid stories all over town, and fools like
you will believe him."

"But he's telling the truth. He loved Shelley and
Lizzie, and the Count took them away from him."

"They weren't taken away from Ivory," Madame
said with a weary sigh. "It was decided that they
would do better in another town. They were spending too much time gossiping with Ivory instead of
attracting business." She sent a black glare toward
Justine. "There is no room here for gossips. I expect
the people under this roof to be discreet. Men come
here because they can trust my girls not to embarrass
them with loose tongues and thoughtless gestures."

"You mentioned other towns . . ." Justine sat at
her own desk and tried to keep her voice from trembling, although her insides were shaking like jelly.
She knew she was treading a thin line, but she had
to go on. York wanted results, and she wanted to

hand them over and end this charade. The sooner she got on with her life, the sooner she could mend her broken heart and continue with her theater work. "What other towns? Where does the Count take the girls? Phoenix? Tucson?"

"Cherie, why are you testing me?"

"I'm not. I'm just asking—"

"Are you deaf today? Have you not heard me telling you that I don't like gossip?"

"How is that gossip?"

"How is it any of your business? Would knowing these things help you balance my ledgers?"

"No, but—"

"Then keep your thoughts on your work and your questions to yourself!" An evil look fell over her face like a veil. "Heed my word, and I'll take care of you."

Justine opened the ledgers and bent over them, averting her face from Madame Chloe as an inner voice whispered, That's what I'm afraid of.

Justine was growing more and more frightened. Jasmine Broadwater had once told her that she had a strong sixth sense and should take heed when it ran a cold finger down her spine . . . as it was doing now.

Justine moved along the dusty street, hardly noticing the other people or the horse and buggies. Glad to be away from the Establishment and its white-spider mistress, she tried to put her misgivings behind her, but she was finding she couldn't.

Maybe she was spooked because of what had happened between her and York. Making love was still a new experience for her, so it was natural that she'd be apprehensive, especially after he'd shut her out so completely. It was almost as if he'd been looking for a reason to disillusion her, to make her want to keep her distance from him. Well, he'd succeeded. While she still desired him and, yes, still loved him, she wanted no more of his bossy, overbearing arrogance. If he chose to keep secrets, fine! She didn't want to know. All she wanted was to get far, far away from him.

If only that were true, she thought, feeling the lie in her heart. If only she could help him, could reach out and touch his heart. But he was too strong to fight, so she had to run.

The banner fluttering across the front of Schieffelin Hall signaled that her trip was not in vain. The theater company had arrived, and *Romeo and Juliet* would soon grace this Tombstone stage.

Her mood brightened at the sight of the gay banner waving at her in the dry breeze. Justine went to the stage door. As soon as she opened it, she smelled the theater and heard its sounds.

Hammers banging away, someone testing a baritone voice, someone else reciting well-remembered lines from the play, the smell of fresh paint, the aroma of new lumber, shouts and orders and general mayhem—it was all so dear to her that she had to blink back tears of joy.

It was cool inside. The ceilings were so high that Justine could barely discern the rafters above her. A man rounded a corner and came straight toward her, then stopped and stared as if she were an apparition.

"Jussie? Godamighty, it can't be. Not out here in the middle of the desert!"

Justine smiled and held out her gloved hands to him. "It's me, Andy." When he didn't take her hands, she stomped a foot in frustration. "Andrew Vixon, are you going to give me a big hug or not?"

"I am!" The short, round man gathered her into his arms. "Jussie, it's so wonderful to see you again. Where on earth have you been hiding?"

"Here, I'm afraid. Oh, I was with a dreadful company that dumped me in this godforsaken place and..." She shook her head, flinging aside the rest of her sordid history. "That's not important. What *is* important is that you've lost more hair!" She ran a hand over his bald pate. Andrew was in his early thirties, but he had only a rim of sable hair running round the back of his head from ear to ear.

"The wigs fit better this way," he joked, laughing with her at his predicament. "But, you! You're more beautiful than you were the last time I saw you. What company are you with now?"

"I'm not. Would you believe I'm bookkeeping for a pleasure palace?"

"You're joking."

"I wish." She grimaced at Andrew's expression of shock. "It's true, but I'm anxious to get back into theater work. I don't suppose you know of any openings?"

"Maybe." He placed an arm around her shoulders. "Let's have some tea and renew acquaintances. Martha Cox and Winnie Dalton are with this company now."

"No! Oh, it's been ages since I've seen them."

"Well, come along then. You've got some catching up to do, my sweet Jussie."

He took her behind paint barrels and stacks of lumber to a room at the back of the cathedrallike theater. Costumes hung along one wall, and packing crates served as dressing tables. A trunk had been transformed into a table on which was laid a tea service. Two brunets and a towheaded young man sat around it. The taller brunet, a woman in her forties with a handsome but horsey face, shot up like a sunflower when she spotted Justine.

"Winnie, look who's here!" She grabbed the other woman's shoulder and gave it a good shake as she released a braying laugh.

The other woman, apple cheeked and pug-nosed, let out a shriek of recognition, and the towheaded man looked from one of his companions to the other with confused amusement.

"Jussie!" Martha, the tall one, embraced Justine, then turned her over to Winnie. "Oh, it's good to see you. Leonard, let me introduce you to a fine actress, one of the best Juliets in the country. Leonard Crandall, may I present Miss Justine Drussard."

"Oh, Martha, stop it." Justine laughed to cover her embarrassment and shook Leonard's hand. "Pleased to meet you. You're one of the actors?"

"Benvolio, at your service," he said, bowing low.

"Ah, a good role," Justine said, then looked at the two women. "And which are you?"

"I'm Lady Capulet this time around," Winnie said, "and Martha is playing the Nurse."

"I hope to see one of your performances while you're here," Justine said, remembering York's offer but telling herself he only meant to be kind, not to be taken seriously. "I can't tell you how much I miss all of this." Removing her gloves, she went to the costumes rack and prop table to touch a ruffled collar, a mock sword, a bejeweled cup. "This must be the lovers' cup."

"That's right," Andrew said. "Sit down and have some tea with us, Jussie. You don't have to rush off, do you?"

"No, but I'm sure you're busy."

"Not too busy for an old friend and fellow thespian," Andrew said, indicating one of the pillows circling the tea table. "This one is nice and soft. Have a seat."

Justine sat on the goose-feather pillow and arranged her skirts around her. Looking from one familiar face to the other, she smiled and her eyes teared. "Oh, dear. I don't want to blubber and bluster. Pour the tea, Martha, before I break into sobs."

"I know how you feel," Winnie said. "Seeing you brings back so many wonderful memories. What are you doing here?"

"Bookkeeping for a brothel," Andrew answered for her, sitting down opposite her and nodding when Martha offered to pour him some tea. "Can you believe that? Shame on you for wasting your talent."

"Yes, shame on you," Martha agreed. "You're such a good actress." She turned to speak to Leonard. "We're not fooling, Lenny. Jussie is the best Juliet any of us have seen."

"And her Katharina," Winnie exclaimed, "in *The Taming of the Shrew*? Nobody plays that role with as much spirit as Jussie."

Overcome with the praise and acceptance, Justine let the tears flow. "You all make me so happy," she said, explaining her sudden outpouring. "I've missed you . . . I've missed this." She looked around at the props and other theater property. "I don't seem to belong anywhere except in a theater."

"Then why are you working in a brothel?" Andrew asked.

"I fell in with bad company. The troupe I was with left me here after stealing me blind." She waved a hand, warding off their questions and concern. "As soon as I've made some money, I'm heading back to where I belong." She sighed, looking at the dear faces of her friends. "The theater."

"We don't have any openings at the moment," Andrew said, "but there might be something in a few weeks."

"What? I'll do anything!"

"Are you thinking about Sandra?" Winnie asked Andrew.

"Yes, that's right. Sandra Taylor is with our company. She's got the Lady Montague role in this production, but she's planning to leave us when we reach San Antonio in a couple of weeks. She's marrying her childhood sweetheart there."

"Lady Montague," Justine said, recalling the lines and the composition of that character. "Yes, that would be lovely. I could take over that role, Andrew?"

"If you can be in San Antonio in two weeks, the role is yours."

"Two weeks..." Justine chewed on her lower lip, lost in thought, but her life was such a jumble of ifs and maybes that she couldn't make hide nor hair of it. "Can I get back to you before you leave Tombstone? I have to sort things out first."

"Sure, Jussie." Andrew reached across the shawl-draped trunk to grasp her hand. "I understand. We'll be here for the rest of the week."

"I know." She sipped the tea, letting it restore her inner calm. "This is a grand theater, isn't it?"

"It is, it is," Andrew agreed. "First time for us. This place is brand new."

"Yes, and the townspeople are excited about the shows coming here. I've heard there are quite a few upper-class folks in Tombstone, although I haven't seen anyone but miners, drunks, gunslingers, and saloon girls. Would you believe that I was almost gunned down in the street!"

"Oh, Jussie!" Winnie, sitting next to her, slipped an arm around her shoulders. "You weren't hurt, were you?"

"No, a man shoved me out of the way before I was shot. You should all take care, though. This place is rife with outlaws and hired guns. Have you heard of the Earps?"

"Yes!" Martha's eyes grew large with sudden animation. "They were in the middle of that gunfight at some corral in town."

"The OK Corral," Justine said, amazed that Martha would know of it. "That's the gunfight I stepped into the middle of, but how on earth did you hear about it?"

"It was in all the papers," Martha said.

"And Martha just loves to read about outlaws and brave lawmen," Leonard said, chuckling. "Her dream is to meet a Pinkerton detective someday."

"There's nothing wrong with that," Martha said

indignantly, then looked to Justine for support. "Is there, Jussie?"

"No. There's nothing wrong with dreaming... nothing at all." She sipped the tea, thinking of her own dreams about her own Pinkerton man. She wanted York to confess that he did love her, that he shared some small corner of his heart with her, although why it was so important that he voice this baffled her. She knew only that it was her most constant dream nowadays, her most fervent hope.

"Why did you join such a tarnished acting troupe in the first place?" Andrew asked, and Justine had to think a moment before following his change of subject.

"I heard there was a lot of work out this way and"—she shrugged off her excuse—"I needed the job. I got myself into a tight place and had to have a steady income quick."

"We've all been in that tight place," Winnie said, embracing her again. "Hunger makes for many a poor decision."

"What production did you all act in together?" Leonard asked.

"We met in class." Andrew smiled at a memory, sharing the smile all around. "We were young pups ready to set the theater world on its ear."

"Maybe we still will," Justine said, hoping. "It's not too late for any of us. Besides, y'all are doing well for yourselves. This company has a fine reputation. You should be proud, Andy."

"I am. I hope you'll think seriously about joining us."

"I want to, I really do." She accepted a refill of tea, loving the company and hating to leave it. "Do any of you recall seeing an act called Lizette the Flying Nymph? Maybe you might have met her?"

"Oh, I remember her," Martha said, then mirrored Justine's shocked expression. "Why are you looking at me like that?"

"You remember Lizette? Are you sure?"

"Yes. I met her in St. Louis. She lived there. My people are from that area."

Justine set aside the teacup and saucer, eager for any news. "What do you recall about her?"

"Why are you so interested?" Winnie asked.

"Because . . . a friend of mine knew her and was wondering what became of her."

"Can't help you there," Martha said. "I don't know where she is now. I saw her last about a year ago. We were both taking dance lessons from the same instructor. Lizzie was head over heels in love with a Frenchman and talked about running away with him. She said he had lots of money and had promised to hire the best acting coaches in the country to tutor her." Martha shrugged, rolling her round eyes comically. "I thought it sounded too good to be true, and I told her just that, but you know how we women are when we get starry-eyed. There's no talking sense to any of us."

"Do you recall the Frenchman's name?"

"No, but he was a shady character. Nobody knew much about him. I think he had some kind of fake title. You know, like lord or duke."

"The Count," Andrew said with a wide grin. "I remember her now. I auditioned for a play with her in Kansas City. That Count fellow was with her. She told me he was managing her career and where she'd be playing. I caught her act—the flying nymph one—in Phoenix. It wasn't bad, but it wasn't acting. Her count didn't do much for her, I guess."

"I never knew anything about this flying nymph act," Martha said. "I figured she'd get into a mess of trouble with the Frenchman. There was all kinds of gossip about her when she left St. Louis with him."

"I remember she was pretty, but not very talented," Andrew said. "Lizette . . . what was her last name?"

"Let me think . . ." Martha closed her eyes, thinking hard. "Lizette Masters . . . no *Le*Masters. That's it. Lizette LeMasters."

"Right, right." Andrew nodded, then frowned at Justine's startled expression and quick intake of breath. "Something wrong, Jussie?"

"No." Justine knew she looked stricken, but she couldn't help it. Masters. LeMasters. It was too much of a coincidence. A question trembled on her lips and she let it fly. "You never heard if she was married, did you?"

"Lizzie? Could be," Martha said with a positive air. "Not to the Count though. He wasn't the marrying kind."

"She wasn't married when I met her," Andrew said. "Why did you think she was?"

"I was just wondering. The way you talked, it sounded as if she ran off with the Frenchman. But if she wasn't married, why would she run?"

"People were whispering," Martha said. "There was something wrong about the whole thing. Maybe she was married."

Justine smiled at the others. "Oh, well. It's nothing to me. Tell me about the rest of your tour. How much longer do you plan to be on the road?"

She listened, but only in spots. The image of Lizette kept floating into her mind, then York's shuttered expression whenever she mentioned the woman. Why had he kept this secret from her? Did he sense she wouldn't sleep with him if she knew he was married? Well, he was right, she thought. She wouldn't have even let him kiss her if she'd known! She should have seen through him, but love had blinded her.

You're just a pawn, she told herself. Like Madame Chloe spinning webs to trap people she could use, York Masters was wooing and seducing and flattering people he needed to help him find his wayward wife. If a heart was broken along the way, so be it.

He thinks no more highly of me than he does of

Satin Doll, she told herself, making herself face the terrible truth. We're just pillow companions. He doesn't really give a good goddamn about any of us. No wonder his wife left him! He probably isn't even with Pinkerton. He's one big fraud.

Lord, she'd been a fool! Just like Lizette following the shady Count's orders, she had followed York's. Two silly women looking for love and finding heartache instead.

Sensing a lull in the conversation, Justine made ready to leave. "I've kept y'all away from your work long enough. I know how busy things are when you hit town and are getting ready for a show." She stood up, brushing the wrinkles from her dark jade skirt.

"Y'all . . ." Andrew kissed her cheek. "Spoken like a gal from New Orleans."

Looking around at her friends, she knew she could count on them. She had to get back to where she belonged and away from York and his dark, distrustful world. "Give me a hug . . . all of you." She held out her arms, embracing Andrew, then Martha, Winnie, and even Leonard. "I'll be in touch before you leave Tombstone, and I hope to get around and see one of your performances."

"If you can't afford a ticket, we'll let you watch from the wings," Andrew promised, seeing her to the door as the others chorused farewells to her.

"Thank you, Andy." She hugged him again and kissed him on the cheek. "You don't know how much this visit has meant to me. I feel like myself again."

"Come back to us, Jussie."

"I will." She nodded firmly, tugging on her gloves. "I must."

She left by the stage door and went around to the front of the theater, so lost in thought that she was no more than a couple of feet from York before she noticed him. She stopped, then surged forward, intent on passing him by.

"Hey, hey!" He grabbed her elbow and spun her around to face him. "What's wrong with you?"

"What's wrong with *you?*" she shouted at him, so furious her face felt like a stove lid and her chest was heaving as if she'd run a mile. She jerked her arm from his grasp and puffed upward at a stray curl that had fallen onto her forehead. "What did you do, follow me?"

"Now why in hell would I do that?"

"I don't know why you do anything, and I'm tired of trying to figure it out. I've got a life of my own, believe it or not. Why should I worry about your troubles, anyway, when you don't give a damn about mine!"

"Whoa!"

"And don't speak to me as if I'm your faithful mare because I'm not."

"Not what? Faithful or my mare?"

That he found her so amusing sent galling anger shooting through her. She was taking a swing at him before she could stop herself. York intercepted her fist before it reached his jaw. Gripping her wrist and holding it steady, her knuckles a bare inch from his face, he lost his sense of humor.

"I don't know why you're as sore as a broke-tailed cat, but I *do* know you'd better simmer down before I let go of you because if you punch me, I swear I'll give your backside a good swipe. Now, do we understand each other?"

"Yes, now let go of me." She was pleased that her voice was as calm and cold as the Mississippi in December. When he released her, she rubbed the circulation back into her wrist. "I was offered a job with this acting troupe, and I'm going to take it."

"Ride that past me again, 'cause I'm sure I didn't hear you right."

"You heard me."

"You can't, Jussie. We've got a deal."

"To hell with our deal. I'm tired of being used by you."

"What's happened?"

"I got smart, that's what's happened."

"Let's talk about this. I'm sure, given enough time, you'll eventually make some sense." He pulled his pocket watch from his vest pocket and flipped open the gold lid. "Meet me at China Mary's for dinner. Say in an hour? That'll be around six."

"My time isn't yours anymore," she said, and started to flounce away, but he stepped in front of her, and she bumped into him. She flinched when his thumb poked her chin up so that her gaze met his.

"Jussie, meet me at China Mary's. Six o'clock. Either you show up or I'll come get you. Your choice." He stepped around her, his shoulder brushing against hers hard enough to make her stumble, then strode away, as arrogant as a prize steer.

Chapter 17

Refusing to be dictated to, Justine gave in to her impish streak and followed him, but she kept well back so he wouldn't know she was dogging his footsteps.

He'll spit bullets when he gets to China Mary's, turns around, and finds me right on his heels, she thought with a mischievous grin. And it'll serve him right.

Maybe he was from a highfalutin family and she was the product of a whore, but that was their pasts. All that mattered was what they were doing with their lives now, and in that respect she was just as good as he was—better even! She entertained people, and he hunted them down. She certainly wouldn't trade places with him. Her life was an open book, but he wouldn't know the truth if it hit him in the face and blackened his other eye!

Realizing her thoughts had lent her energy and she was trotting almost right behind York, she curbed her momentum and straightened her bonnet, which had slipped to a lopsided angle. Taking a few moments to get her bearings, she noticed that York wasn't going right to China Mary's, but was taking the long way there through Hop Town's collection of rambling rooming houses and Chinese shops.

She remembered the last time she'd ventured into this pocket of town and how conspicuous she'd felt. Staying close to the buildings so she wouldn't be seen easily should York suddenly turn around, she dodged skinny dogs and sloe-eyed children. A vegetable stand jutted out to the street, forcing her to scamper around it. The seller gave her a curious look and held out a big, sweet onion.

"Cook up good, Missy. You buy?"

Pressing a finger to her lips, Justine shook her head and moved on, seeking the shadows again and hoping York wouldn't look behind him. He's going to Satin Doll's, she thought. He passed a potion-and-herb shop, and the proprietor called out to him. He ducked inside to speak to the man. Justine scurried into an alley to hide. Ten minutes dragged by before York left the shop and strode along the packed-dirt street to Satin Doll's humble room. Whatever had transpired inside the shop had upset him. Even from a distance, Justine could make out his fury-tinted features. Satin Doll's door opened directly into the dusty street, but it was closed, and York knocked hard on it.

"Satin? It's York. Satin, I know you're in there. I've just spoken to Tsu Chang, and he says you haven't been out of there in two days."

Justine found a hiding place behind a wagon loaded with baskets of clothes and linens that was hitched outside a laundry. Satin's door swung open. Justine caught only a glimpse of her before York strode inside and slammed the door behind him. Skirting the wagon, Justine stalked closer until she was standing to one side of the rickety door. It was made of wide, irregular planks that left gaps. Justine could see movement through the cracks, so she leaned sideways to peer through the widest separation. She could see the back of York's white jacket and the exotic oval of Satin Doll's face. But Satin didn't look so good, Justine thought, noticing the girl's heavy-lidded eyes.

"You're a mess," York said, his tone sharp with irritation.

"You're looking better," Satin said, her voice as lazy as a honey-laden bee. "Can't hardly see your bruises anymore. What do you want? Must be important. You nearly knocked my door down. What are you doing out so early this morning?"

"Satin, it's not morning. It's evening."

"Is it?" She laughed. "Time flies."

York turned sideways so that Justine could see his profile. He frowned, glancing around the cluttered room. Taking off his hat, he ran a hand through his hair, holding it off his forehead for a few moments while he studied Satin.

"What am I going to do with you?"

"I've been under the weather, that's all." She shrugged and fell back on the bed, arms outstretched and hair flowing across the pink satin pillow. "No need to get so huffy."

York moved to block Justine's view. All she could see was his broad back as he stood over Satin. "That poison you smoke is making you sick. China Mary says you haven't shown up for work in two days. We're all worried about you. You're killing yourself."

"How sweet of you to worry." Satin reached up to grasp his hand. "But I'm fine. Don't worry about me, hon. I've just got the don't-cares, and I think I picked up a little cold. Tell Mary I'll dress and come to work tonight."

"She said not to bother if you're fuzzy headed, which you are." He sat on the bed, giving Justine a view of both him and Satin. He touched Satin's cheek, and she rubbed against his hand like a cat against a table leg. "Baby, don't do this to yourself. What's wrong, huh? Why are you so unhappy?"

Justine held her breath, wondering if Satin would finally tell York and rid herself of her burden. Satin opened her mouth, her eyes filled with tears, then turned away, hiding her face in the pillow.

"Go away, York. I can't st-stand to look at you. Go to Frenchy. She deserves you. Not me. Not m-me."

"Satin, what in hell are you talking about? We're friends, aren't we? You can talk to me. You can trust me."

Justine closed her eyes for a second and wished hard that Satin would tell York about Lizzie. Don't keep holding on to it, she thought. Please, Satin. He'll understand. And if he doesn't it won't be the end of the world.

York gathered Satin into his arms. She was limp, boneless. "Satin, Satin, Satin," he chanted against her sleek hair. "Promise me you'll stop spending so much time with that opium pipe. Please, promise me."

"Don't..." Satin struggled against York's comforting arms. "I don't deserve this. Don't touch me. Don't!"

"Settle down. You're out of your head—"

"Let go!" Satin wrenched free, and there was a wild look in her eyes. "For your own good and mine, get out of here now. No!" She pulled back when York tried to touch her shoulder. "I mean it."

"Come on, Satin," York consoled. "I'm not leaving until you're yourself again. You mean too much to me. You're still my best friend, aren't you? Satin... Satin, honey..."

Justine turned to find a couple of black-outfitted children staring at her. They giggled, then darted away. Feeling foolish for having been caught snooping, Justine walked on toward China Mary's. She stood outside York's room for nearly half an hour before she heard his footsteps on the stairs. When he saw her, his steps faltered and his brows shot up to mingle with the blond hair that swept across his forehead under his black hat. He took off the hat and pushed his hair off his brow, but it fell across it again.

"You're early." He opened the door and motioned for her to go inside. "You should have gone on in instead of standing out here in the hallway."

She'd thought about it, but had decided she'd probably trespassed on his territory enough for one day. He looked tired, wrung out. She knew a wild moment when she almost reached out to him, offering comfort and soothing words of encouragement, just as he'd done for Satin. I must be out of my mind, she thought, gaining distance from him by moving across the room. She couldn't trust herself around him. Trust, she thought with a wry smile. It all boiled down to that.

"So, what's all this nonsense about your joining an acting troupe?" he said, hanging his hat on the tree but keeping his suit jacket on. He tipped his head to one side, waiting for her explanation.

"It's not nonsense. I'm an actress. I need work. I was offered a job, and I'm going to take it." Justine swept her skirts to one side and sat in one of the wing chairs. She wondered why this prospect didn't make her heart race. I should be more excited, she thought. I should be *aching* to get back on stage. But there was so much left unfinished, unsaid, unresolved. "The troupe will be short one actress once it reaches San Antonio in a couple of weeks. I want you to pay me what you promised before then so I can get to Texas in time to take over the role."

"Fine, providing your work for me is completed by that time. Otherwise, you'll have to stay right here and let some other show girl have that job."

"I'm not going to argue with you. I'm just telling you my plans." She pulled off her gloves, striving to appear resolute.

"I see." He ran a hand thoughtfully along his jaw. "So, you're going to welsh on our deal? I never figured you for a cheat."

"I'm not." She bristled, stung by his claim. "I've done enough. I say we're even." She felt uneasy, knowing he'd just come from a difficult time with Satin and was probably in no mood to be charitable. She sensed the frustration boiling in him, ready to overflow.

"You think we're even?" He threw back his head and released a short, ringing laugh. His expression of contempt sent a bolt of misgiving through her. "Not by a long shot. You haven't given me anything to go on. Most of what you've found out, I already knew."

"If you're not satisfied, then maybe you should point the finger at yourself." She folded her arms under her breasts and shifted sideways a little, angling away from him. He laughed, making her blood boil.

"Now how do you figure that? Why should I take the blame for your failures?"

"Because you've been keeping important information from me."

"Now we're getting to the heart of the matter." He sat on the bed, falling so heavily that he bounced a few times before coming to rest. "You know everything you need to know."

"Is that so?"

"Yes. You should just dig deeper. Get some answers for me. Have you gotten close to any of the girls? Have you done *anything* useful?"

"Yes, I have." She ran her damp palms down her skirt. Outside she presented a picture of indifference; inside she trembled with the sting of one betrayed and beguiled. "I'm not stupid, York. I've done enough detecting on my own to figure out that Lizzie isn't just some woman who's missing. She's your wife. And that makes me your mistress —or am I just a poorly paid whore?" She knew a moment of triumph when his head jerked up and his mouth dropped open. "Just one thing puzzles me. Why didn't you want me to know? Did you think I wouldn't sleep with you if there was a chance your wife was still alive?" She arched one brow in reproach when he tore his eyes from her and ground his teeth, making muscles twitch along his jawline.

Hurting inside but refusing to let him see it, Justine stood up and paced aimlessly, finally coming to stand before him. She looked down at his blond head and wondered if he felt any remorse or if this was all an act. He could have made a good living on the stage, she thought, then prepared to drive in the verbal knife and give it a good twist. No mercy. He'd shown her none.

"It's no wonder she left you. Is there anyone you *don't* use for your own purposes? Did you lie to her, too?"

He winced as if struck by a sudden pain. Did the truth hurt? Justine wondered with a vindictive twinge. He stood up, making her step back, and gathered in a great gulp of air, then released it in a labored sigh.

"Let me explain—"

"Try. Just try."

"I will!" He patted the air with one hand, tapping down his anger and hers. "I admit I haven't told you the whole story, but I realized I was wrong to do that. I was going to tell you—"

"Oh, were you? How nice."

"You don't have it all figured out, not by a long shot." His smile was unpleasant. "I'm not, nor have I ever been, married."

Justine started to argue, to call him a liar, and tell

him to go to hell, but something in his eyes stopped
her. "Are you telling the truth?"

"Yes."

"Then who is Lizzie? I know she's something to
you. I know."

He dipped his head, gathering strength. When
he looked up again his eyes shimmered with sorrow. "My sister. Lizette is my sister, not my wife."

"Your sis—" Justine shook her head, then felt
overwhelming relief, followed by confusion. "Then
why didn't you tell me about her? Why keep it a
secret? Are you ashamed to be her brother?"

"No, of course not."

"Then what?" Justine grabbed his arm, and he
winced. "Tell me."

"I didn't trust you. It wasn't any of your damn
business. I didn't want to tell you about how she
ran off with a criminal and whored for him. I want
to see the Count swing. I want to kill him with my
bare hands. And not because he's a suspect, but
because he turned my sister into a whore. She was
innocent, sweet, untouched, and then he came to
town." His upper lip curled in distaste. "He's slick.
He wooed her, made her believe every word he
said, and she turned her back on her family. My
parents . . . they've gone through more than you
can imagine." He paused to draw a deep breath.
"It's painful, personal. It's not something I talk
about to strangers."

"I thought I was more than that."

"You are. But I didn't want you to let your guard
down. One slip could put you in danger."

"Oh, so this was all for my benefit?" She crossed
her arms and tapped one foot with irritation. "I
should be grateful that you lied to me, is that it? Brilliant, York, brilliant. Lying is an art with you." She
flung up one hand. "You're the Michelangelo of de-
ceit!"

He ran a hand down his face, wiping away a thin

veil of perspiration, but there was wry amusement in his eyes. He shook his head and laughed at himself, and Justine realized not only had she bested him, but he knew it.

"You're right," he said, shrugging. "You're absolutely right. In my work, you master lying or you don't work for Pinkerton very long. But I had reconsidered, Jussie, and I *was* going to come clean tomorrow night and beg your forgiveness."

"Tomorrow night," she said with a smile that told him she didn't believe a word. "Why wait?"

"Because I was going to tell you after we'd been to the theater." His smile was sheepish. "I admit, I was going to soften you up a little before I confessed." He massaged the back of his neck with one hand and crossed to the window. "Oh, hell! I've stepped in a pile of it this time. I know you think I've got the character of a coyote, and I don't blame you. I was stupid to let you go on—"

"You were going to take me to the theater?" she asked, hearing nothing of what he'd said beyond that. "Which one?"

He looked perplexed for a few seconds as he buttoned his jacket with fingers that trembled slightly. "Schieffelin Hall. You said you wanted to see *Romeo and Juliet*, and I told you I'd take you. Remember?"

"Yes, but . . ." She lifted a hand as a piece of the puzzle fell into place. "Is that why you were outside the theater earlier?"

He nodded, reached into the inside pocket of his jacket, and pulled out two tickets. "Sixth row, center."

She took them, saw that they were exactly what he reported them to be, and shoved them back into his hand. "Oh, you make me so—so damned mad!" Tears sprang to her eyes, and she turned so he couldn't see her cry. She fought to keep from sobbing with frustration, her throat raw and burning. The man was infuriating, she railed. Just when she was on the verge of hating him forever, he did something like buy tickets for a theater performance she longed to see. How dare he!

"I want to escort you to it, Jussie. Will you go with me? We'll have dinner and ... and I'll try to explain ... oh, hell! I don't blame you for being mad. I'm mad at myself for being such a goddamned fool."

She wiped the tears from her cheeks before she spun to face him again. "I never thought you actually meant to take me out in public."

"In public? What does that have to do with anything?"

"I thought you'd be too ashamed to be seen in public with me, so I didn't dare dream—"

"Damn it, Jussie!" He grabbed her shoulders and gave her a gentle shake. Gritting his teeth, he made a comically impassioned face of exasperation at her. "Why in hell would I give a damn what the people in this town think of me or who I'm seen with?" He bent his knees until he could look straight into her eyes. "I'm ashamed of myself, not of you."

"But you've always talked bad about actors," she reminded him. "You let me know right away that you thought I was low class because I worked in the theater."

He shrugged and let her go. "Look what the theater did to my sister." He stuffed his hands into his jacket pockets and rounded his shoulders.

"The Count did that, not the theater."

He spun lightly on the ball of one foot and walked stiffly to the table where a whiskey bottle waited. "Lizzie was a sane, levelheaded girl until she went backstage and met some actors a couple of years ago," he said, pouring himself a double shot. "From that moment on she became a different person. Then she met up with the Count, and nobody could talk any sense into her. All she thought about was being famous. The Count said this, and the Count said that...." He shook his head and drank down half the whiskey. "I got sick of hearing about the Count and his castle-in-the-air promises. Lizzie was blinded by all his pretty talk, but not me. Mother thought the Count would move on to another girl, leaving Lizzie wounded but wiser." He laughed gruffly and finished his drink. "He left all right. But he took Lizzie with him, the son of a bitch." He set the glass down hard. "If he killed her...I won't rest until I see him dangling from the end of a rope."

She studied him for a few moments before she ventured, "You think she's dead, don't you?"

He hung his head and squeezed his eyes shut. "Yes," he said, his tone low and hurting, then poured another drink. "I want to know why, when, and where she's buried. My family deserves that much, don't you think? As it is we're living in limbo. We can't grieve for our lost Lizzie. We can't even pay our respects to her grave." He drank the whiskey and his eyes watered, but Justine wasn't sure it was from the kick of the liquor. The eye that had been blackened sported only a pale blue tint, made more obvious now that the color had drained from his face. "For awhile we didn't try to follow her or find her. We—my family and I— were trying to save face. Everyone knew our Lizzie had run off with a scoundrel, and we went about our lives, missing her, but not enough to reach out to her." He laughed mirthlessly. "Saving face. My family sometimes treasures the wrong things. I should have gone after Lizzie right away instead of waiting weeks, months."

"Well, she had a right to make up her own mind. You couldn't very well drag her back home if she didn't want to go."

"Why can't a woman find a good man, make a

good match, and be satisfied with that?"

Her burst of laughter was meant to insult, but he seemed immune, caught up in his own ideas of how life should be lived.

"You know," he said, "if you're smart, you'll take the money I give you when this is all over and use it to set yourself up in a nice place so that you'll attract a respectable man and get married. Don't waste it by going from place to place, auditioning in one theater after another. In a few years you'll be sorry because you'll have nothing to show for your life except wasted time."

"Hold on," she said, breaking into his sermon by poking a finger in his chest. It pained her that he'd send her into another man's arms, but she didn't want him to know it. "I'm not your little sister, so rein in the brotherly advice. I don't need it. As for wasting my life, maybe I want something more to show for my life than a few children and a clean house."

"What's wrong with that?"

"Nothing, but I want more. Why shouldn't I go after everything I want instead of settling for part of it?"

"Women have it so easy in this world. Men are put here to take care of them, so why fight that? I'd love it if someone would take me in and accept responsibility for me. Why would you want to strike out on your own and take life's punches on the chin? If Lizzie had stayed home and concentrated on being courted well, she'd be alive and happy today."

"Well, she might be alive, but I don't think she'd be happy. She obviously loved the theater and wanted very much to be part of it. But that's not why she left St. Louis."

"Why then?"

"She was in love. She wanted to please her man. I suspect theater was her second love, don't you?"

Justine rested her hands on his sleeves, making him look at her. "She fell in love with the wrong man. The theater didn't betray her, the Count did. Put the blame where it belongs, York."

"What made you think Lizzie and I were related?"

"Simple addition... adding two plus two." She became aware that his hands had somehow found their way to her waist and that they were perilously close to an embrace. She stepped sideways and moved out of reach. "My friends with the theater troupe remembered a few things about her. Nothing you don't already know," she hastened to add, "but when they said her last name was LeMasters, it all fell into place for me. Are you Masters or LeMasters?"

"LeMasters. We're from French soil, one generation back."

"Well, at least we have that in common."

"I'm glad it's all out in the open." He squared his shoulders. "Would you like to eat? Let's have something brought here. I'm not hungry, but—"

"I can't." She picked up her purse and moved to the door. "I need to get back to the Establishment."

"Why?"

"Because I want to." She faced him, hoping he wouldn't pester her further. "I'm in no mood for a night out or in with you. I want to be by my lonesome."

He smiled crookedly. "I understand."

"Besides, you should go downstairs and get ready for work. You're still a faro dealer, aren't you?"

"More or less." He curled his fingers around her forearm, keeping her from opening the door. "Before you go, tell me whether or not I should come around for you tomorrow evening." Something in her eyes made him plead his case further. "Jussie, I know you want to go. If you won't let me take you to the theater, then I'll hand over the tickets and

you can ask someone else." He went to the bed
where he'd dropped the tickets and held them out
to her. "Here. I bought them for you, so take
them."

She reached for them, but didn't want them without York attached. Giving a reluctant sigh, she shook
her head. "No. I'll go with you tomorrow night.
What time?"

"The curtain rises at eight. I'll come for you at
six."

"Six? Why so early?"

"We'll have dinner first at the Wagon Wheel. It's
just across the street from Schieffelin Hall."

"Yes, I've seen it. You don't have to—"

"I *want* to." He took her hand and lifted it to his
lips for a brief kiss. "Are you going to leave me in the
lurch, Jussie?"

"I don't know," she confessed, torn between
needing to get away from him and wanting to be
near him. "I'll think about it and let you know."

"That's fair." He opened the door for her. "Be
careful walking back to Madame Chloe's. Tombstone's streets are dangerous after dark."

"It's not dark yet, but I'll be careful. Good night,
York." She left him quickly, before she was
tempted to stay or ask him to walk with her to
Madame Chloe's. She was halfway there before she
remembered she hadn't told York about Madame's
slip concerning the former bookkeeper.

Alone in his room, York grabbed the whiskey
bottle, dropped into the nearest chair, and raised
the bottle to his lips. The liquor went down hard,
like a fist. He coughed, his limp body heaving and
shuddering. With some effort he shrugged out of
his jacket and peeled off his shirt. One side was
wet with fresh blood. Pushing out of the chair, he
stood before the mirror and examined the place
where Satin's knife had sliced off a piece of skin. It

wasn't a deep cut, but it pained him something fierce.

"Satin, you crazy little witch." He poured water into the shallow bowl and prepared to cleanse the wound. Satin was out of her mind from opium. When he'd tried to console her, she'd grabbed a knife and started swinging. He had to do something to help her, but what? He took another long drink from the whiskey bottle to fortify himself while he dressed the surface wound and tried to figure out a way to save Satin from herself.

Chapter 18

⁓◝◞◟◝⁓

"**I**'ve worn this dress only once," Cherry Vanilla said as she fussed with the silver satin that fell in folds to Justine's gray kid shoes. "It didn't do a thing for my coloring, but on you"—she stood back to examine the whole effect and brought her hands together under her chin in a moment of jubilation— "on you it's simply heaven!"

Justine whirled in a circle, testing the weight of the skirt and its movement against her stiff petticoats. The satin whispered over her silk undergarments. "This is the most beautiful dress I've ever worn. Ever!"

"If York Masters isn't in love with you already, he will be after he sees you in this."

Justine shrugged off the woman's comments, not wanting to indulge in such fantasy. "Should I wear my hair up?"

"Yes, let me do it." Cherry took Justine by the shoulders and turned her around, then fashioned Justine's dark hair into a braid, which she then coiled on top of her head like a crown.

"You're very kind to be helping me," Justine said, waiting patiently for Cherry to finish.

"I enjoy it. I feel like you're one of the girls. Family, you know."

Justine smiled, glad to have gained Cherry's confidence. She'd been trying to get closer to the other women, but it wasn't as easy as she'd anticipated. They were tight-lipped when the discussion included the Count or his visits. The main rule of the house was that they were to keep their mouths shut, and so far they had obeyed it to the letter.

"Nobody at the theater will look any better than you," Cherry said.

"Have you ever been to Schieffelin Hall?"

"Oh, no. This backwater town would have me tarred and feathered if I showed up among the wives of the men I pleasure. It just ain't done."

"Then maybe I shouldn't—"

"You're different. You keep the books. Everyone understands that."

"I don't know," she said doubtfully.

"I *do* know. Besides, it'll be good for Tombstone's high and mighty to rub elbows with the working class." Cherry turned her around so that Justine faced her again and flicked at a few loose curls clinging to Justine's temples. "Pretty as a picture."

Someone knocked on the door, and Cherry opened it to find Babette.

"Oh, my!" Babette stared at Justine, her eyes bright with envy. "You look grand. Just grand!" She wrinkled her button nose. "I brought you something." She held out a necklace of silver and pearls. "Won't this look nice?"

"I couldn't wear your jewelry," Justine protested. "My earrings will do." She fingered her earbobs.

"This isn't mine." Babette giggled and glanced at Cherry. "It belongs to Madame Chloe. I took it from her room."

"What?" Cherry's eyes grew as large as summer

pansies. "You stole it? Girl, you're plumb nuts!"

"She won't miss it," Babette said. "I've done it lots of times and never even returned them. Madame has trunks of this stuff. Take it." She pressed the necklace into Justine's hand.

"I don't know..." Justine admired the necklace, but was afraid to wear it. "Madame Chloe's already not too happy about me going out with York. She thinks I'm going to run off with him."

"Who'd blame you?" Babette said, then took the necklace from Justine and moved behind her to fasten it. "Madame Chloe's in such a state, she won't notice a thing. She's been buzzing around here today like a mad bee."

"Yes, I noticed. Why is she so fidgety?" Justine asked.

"Well, I figure the Count must be heading this way," Babette said. Justine tried not to react, but her heart soared into her throat. "She gets this way when he's coming. Everything has to be just so. No dust anywhere, everything shining, and all his favorite food in the pantry."

"So, she caters to him," Justine observed.

"Lordy, yes," Cherry broke in. "Everybody around here does. He's the boss, honey."

"Even Madame Chloe's boss?"

"You bet," Cherry said. "I think Madame Chloe is stuck on him, too." Cherry caught Babette's sharp glance and turned away. "But it's not my place to spread tales."

Babette sighed with irritation. "Oh, well. I guess you're one of us girls now, aren't you?" She gave Justine a long, thoughtful appraisal.

"Well, I feel as if you're my friends, if that's what you mean."

"Right, we're all friends. Got to stick together, don't we? Madame Chloe treats us like we're her house slaves, but we get back at her in our own ways. You'll see...." Babette's gaze drifted to the necklace. "Like that jewelry. Every time the old bat gets my dander up, I sneak into her room and take something."

"I don't know about this," Justine said again, touching the necklace and wondering if she should tempt fate.

"Wear it," Cherry said, flapping a hand at her. "Babette's right. The old gal's not going to miss it. It was most likely given to her by a customer. Means nothing to her."

Justine went to stand before the mirror and admired the borrowed gown and necklace. If York Masters's eyes didn't pop out when he saw her, she'd blacken both of them.

"Okay, I'll wear it, but I'll return it to you. There's no way I'll keep this."

"Do what you want," Babette said. "And have a grand time tonight."

"I plan to."

Justine cleared her throat nervously and saw in the mirror that Babette was heading for the door. "Did either of you know the bookkeeper before me?"

"Sure." Cherry said. "We both knew her."

"Did she run off with a miner?"

"That's the story we were told," Babette murmured, sending Cherry a furtive glance.

"The story..." Justine shrugged. "Oh, well, I guess I'm wrong."

"About what?" Babette asked.

"Well, I thought Madame Chloe said something about the woman being taken away instead of going off with the miner. Did the Count take her or did a miner?"

Babette looked at Cherry, then shrugged. "Well, none of us heard anything about this miner until a week or so after Donna left. That was her name, Donna. It sounded fishy to me, didn't it to you, Cherry?"

"Hmmm?" Cherry jumped as if she'd been

pinched. "Uh, well, yeah. I don't think she ran off with a rich miner, but the Count didn't have nothing to do with it either. He wasn't in town then." Cherry's gaze drifted to the necklace Justine wore. "If somebody did something to Donna, it was Madame Chloe."

"That's my thinking on it, too," Babette said with a firm nod. "I wouldn't put anything past Madame Chloe once she gets riled up."

"Did you know Madame Chloe and Donna were messing with each other?"

"Cherry!" Babette pressed a finger to her lips. "You don't know that for sure ... do you?" Her eyes twinkled with delight.

"No." Cherry shivered. "But I saw her and Donna touching each other once—and not like two ladies should touch. Made my skin crawl. I think Madame Chloe is a witch."

"Pooh! She's no witch." Babette laughed and lightly slapped Cherry's shoulder. "She's got you spooked, don't she? Simmer down, gal. She can't put a hex on you." Babette spun around and went toward the door to the office. "But we'd better quit gabbing. These walls might have ears, for all we know. Have a grand time, Jussie, and give York a kiss for me." She opened the door, then stepped back inside. "He just came in the front door. I heard him."

"Tell him I'll be out in a minute," Justine said, suddenly trembling with nervous anticipation. "Make him wait in the office."

"Okay." Babette winked.

"Good luck, honey." Cherry kissed Justine's cheek. "I hope the evening is like a dream."

"Thanks, Cherry. Thanks for everything, both of you."

The other women left Justine to struggle with her nerves. She checked her hair and her makeup once more before pulling on her dark gray gloves and picking up her small evening purse, which was beaded in silver and gray. She chose a mask of cool repose before swinging open the door and walking regally into the office.

York sat in the chair at her desk, but he stood when she entered. Elegant beyond compare in his black, double-breasted evening suit which was piped with matching ribbons of satin, and his blindingly white shirt, he didn't disappoint her with his reaction.

"Ah, so you're ready—" His mouth dropped open, and his eyes took on a sheen of admiration she'd never seen before. "My God," he breathed in a whisper. He shook his head as a grin claimed his wide mouth. "What a vision."

She stared back, enamored of the sight of him in evening attire. "You look like a prince."

He glanced down at himself and laughed. "Yes, but I forgot my sword and white steed." He grinned. "And you are a princess, dressed in a gown that matches your eyes. Those bewitchingly silver eyes." He came forward and took both of her hands in his. "You look lovely, Jussie." He kissed her cheek lightly, politely. "I'm most proud to have you at my side." Sidestepping, he positioned himself there and tucked her hand in the crook of his arm. "Shall we, Miss Justine?"

She swept her lashes downward in a moment of pleasure. "Yes, York, I'm ready."

"I have a buggy waiting outside."

"A buggy? But it's only a short distance. We can walk."

"Walk?" He feigned horror. "And take a chance on getting dirt on that lovely gown? No, Miss Justine, we will ride in style to the theater."

She looked into his handsome face and wanted to pinch herself to make sure she wasn't dreaming. "This is a side of you I've never seen."

"Do you like it?"

"I think I do."

"Good. Tonight I'm on my best behavior."

He escorted her along the hallway, winking at Madame's girls, who gushed and twittered at the sight of them. "Good evening, girls," he called, sweeping Justine outside and helping her into the two-seater buggy. Taking up the reins, he flicked the sorrel into a walk.

"Did you rent this rig?"

"I did, and the horse, too."

"You don't have your own horse?"

"Not at the moment." He glanced back, making sure the way was clear before he urged the sorrel past a slower wagon. "In this town a gun is more valuable than a horse."

"I suppose that's true." As she looked around, Tombstone didn't seem so ugly to her. Even the lights streaming from the saloons seemed brighter and cleaner. "I'm all jittery inside I'm so excited," Justine admitted with a laugh that fluttered from her like a startled bird.

"We're going to have a wonderful time. The time of your life," he promised, and Justine believed him.

" 'What's in a name? That which we call a rose by any other name would smell as sweet. . . .' " Justine moved off into the night as a spirited breeze billowed her silvery skirts behind her like satin sails.

York set the brake and jumped down from the buggy, intent on keeping near her. The dinner and theater had put her in a mood he found irresistibly attractive. Emerging from the theater dreamy eyed and breathless, she'd enchanted him and made him want to extend the evening, so he'd driven them outside of Tombstone to a place he knew. A semicircle of rocks and outcroppings provided seclusion while giving a view of the vast desert terrain and a night sky studded with stars.

And through the night she drifted. Like an angel

in silver, Justine commanded the desert as she would a stage. Snatches of Shakespeare's *Romeo and Juliet* fell trippingly from her rosy lips. On the journey out of town she'd entertained him with her favorite speeches from act 1. Now she was into act 2, the balcony scene.

After the performance, she'd taken him backstage to meet her friends. Each and every one had regaled him with stories of how Justine had impressed directors and audiences alike. She didn't know how good she was, they all told him confidentially. She kept thinking she wasn't good enough for legitimate theater, so she joined lesser acting troupes to gain more experience.

"But she was ready to take the stage at the best theater in this country the minute she decided to act," Andrew Vixon had assured him. "Justine is a natural. Everyone but her knows it."

A natural, he thought, watching her dance across the rugged terrain, dodging scrub brush and towering saguaros. When she'd begun speaking the lines on the ride there, he'd found himself engrossed, for she put the Juliet he'd seen that night at Schieffelin Hall to shame. And here without stage, costume, or direction, she recited Shakespeare by heart, not in a singsong, poetic fashion, but as natural speech. He had seen many renditions of the balcony scene, but he'd never heard Juliet speak in such plain English. Justine made Shakespeare's words her very own, and thus brand new.

"'. . . doff thy name; and for thy name, which is no part of thee, take all myself,'" the desert Juliet said, turning to face him so that her words rode the breeze to where he stood.

"'I take thee at thy word,'" York quoted, recalling only that line and no others. "I'm sorry, but I don't know the rest."

"You would remember *that* line," she said, teasing. "No matter." Tipping back her head and ex-

tending her arms from her sides, Justine whirled and
laughed up at the stars. "Oh, what a night! Poor
Romeo. Poor Juliet. Names and families can be both
a blessing and a curse." She stopped spinning to
look at him. "Remember when we first went into the
theater, and I thought people were scowling at us
because they disapproved of low-class me being
escorted by high-class you?"

"Yes, I remember, but you were wrong."

"I know, I know. You were right. To the people of
Tombstone we're *both* a couple of lowlifes. A whore's
bookkeeper and a China woman's faro dealer, that's
all we are. But it made me realize how quick I am to
feel unworthy. It's a struggle for me. I have to keep
reminding myself that I'm a good person and that I
should have more self-confidence."

"Yes, you should."

"Well, you're partly to blame," she said, arms
akimbo. "You did your level best to keep me under
your heel."

"Forgive me?"

"Do you think of me as your equal?"

He came toward her and laid a hand on her
cheek. "Yes, maybe even my better."

She shook her head. "Now you're resorting to
false flattery. Tonight, York, tell me the truth instead
of what you think I want to hear."

Feeling the spell had been broken by his rash
compliment, she moved away from him. York balled
his hands into fists, aching to hold her and keep her
against him. Like a cloud, she was hard to pin down
tonight, but that was part of her appeal.

Looking up at the blazing night and following the
light to where it swam upon her silvery gown, York
recalled another of Romeo's lines with which to
tempt his ephemeral Juliet back into the magic of the
moment.

" 'Lady, by yonder blessèd moon I swear, that tips
with silver all these fruit-tree tops . . . ' " he called to

her, and smiled when she whirled and became his Juliet again.

"'O, swear not by the moon, the inconstant moon, that monthly changes in her circled orb, lest that thy love prove likewise variable.'" Her voice throbbed with meaning, making York listen not only with his ears, but also with his heart. The woman wasn't just quoting from memory. She was speaking directly to him, and he knew it.

"'What shall I swear by?'" he asked, as if the words had come to him by themselves and not by a playwright's pen.

"'Do not swear at all; or if thou wilt, swear by thy gracious self, which is the god of my idolatry, and I'll believe thee.'" She smiled sadly, helplessly.

Another line or two popped into his head. "'O, wilt thou leave me so unsatisfied?'"

Her smile sweetened. "You skipped some lines." Then she shrugged, glanced up as if for guidance, and said, "'What satisfaction canst thou have tonight?'"

"Hmmm, uh, wait a second." He fumbled for the lines and found them. "'The exchange of thy love's faithful vow for mine.'"

"Very good," she congratulated. "That's enough."

"No, go on. A little more."

"I'm sure you're quite bored by now."

"Please . . ." He didn't know why he wanted to hear more, but he couldn't let her stop. Something urgent rose in him. He wanted to hear—he *had* to hear more. It was important. "'The exchange of thy love,'" he prompted, motioning urgently that she continue.

"'I gave thee mine before thou didst request it,'" Justine said, lowering her voice to make him listen to each word and comprehend its meaning. "'My bounty is as boundless as the sea,'" she said, seeming to float instead of walk toward him. "'My love as deep.'" She stood before him and tipped her face up to the moonlight, up for his pleasure should he want to take it. "'The more I give to thee, the more I have, for both are infinite.'"

"Jussie..." He breathed her name as if evoking a goddess and then dropped a feathery kiss upon her lips. "No wonder you want to get back to the theater. You're marvelous."

Her expressive eyes widened. "You think so?"

"I know it. I've never *felt* Romeo and Juliet's love, or their sorrow, until now."

She stared deeply into his eyes, making his heart race. "To be honest, neither have I. Not to this extent, anyway." She brushed her hands across the shoulders of his borrowed coat. "Maybe our costumes and the setting have something to do with it."

"And our circumstances?"

"Yes, those, too. Have you ever wondered how we would have reacted to each other if we'd met at another time and in another place?"

"Endlessly."

She smiled, slipping from his embrace. "You are the charmer tonight." Moving with natural grace, she made a trip along the semicircle of rocks and boulders, running the fingertips of one hand along the rough surfaces. "When I lived in New Orleans and before I earned my first stage role, I would go to the theater and watch the people arrive. I loved seeing them in their buggies, wearing their finery and jewelry. Tonight, I was one of them."

York hitched up his trouser legs and sat on a low boulder. "Tell me about your life back then, Jussie. Tell me about Old Shoe Black and Jasmine Broadwater. What became of them?"

"Dead. They're dead." The light was blown out of her eyes.

"Yes, but how? Tell me."

"Why should you care?"

"I don't know, but I do." He held out a hand, but she averted her face, refusing him, and he let his hand drop back to his bent knee. "Okay, if you don't want to talk about it, if it's too painful..."

"I loved them both." She glanced at him, and he saw the shimmer of tears in her eyes. "Jasmine Broadwater went first. Her throat was cut from ear to ear, but we never knew who did it or why. It was mean where we lived. People were always killing each other over nothing." She leaned back against the rock wall, tilting her face up to the starlight so that it sparkled in her eyes and across her dress. York couldn't recall a time when she was more hauntingly beautiful.

"And Old Shoe Black, did he meet a similar end?"

"He died for me." Her eyes became pools of liquid silver. "Two men attacked me. Drunks. Drunk and amorous and not about to take no for an answer. They jumped me, threw me to the ground, and ripped my clothes. Old Shoe Black came charging out of nowhere. I swear, I don't know where he got the strength. He was old and feeble, but he found enough muscle to pull those men off me. He yelled for me to run and I did, but I looked back and I saw the men knock him down and smash his head with a piece of an anchor."

"You were in the shipyards?"

She nodded. "Later, when the men were gone, I came back. Old Shoe Black was dead. The police were there, and they took his body away. I never found out where they buried him. A pauper's grave somewhere in the area, no doubt, because there wasn't any money. Without him, I knew I had to find a life for myself."

"How old were you?"

"Seventeen."

He hung his head, picturing her as a frightened seventeen-year-old on her own in the streets of New Orleans. Only her high ideals had kept her from her mother's fate.

"I couldn't live on the docks or in the streets for

much longer or I'd end up dead like Jasmine and Old Shoe Black. There was so much wickedness going on, you just couldn't outrun it."

"So what did you do?"

"I worked as a chambermaid and washed dishes in restaurants. I rented a room and started taking acting classes. Before long I landed my first role, and I never looked back."

"I bet you missed your friends."

"Oh, my heart aches for them even now." Her hands pressed against the front of her dress, and York swore she sobbed. "They sheltered me from many a storm. I guess they were as close to a family as I've ever had. They died within two weeks of each other."

"My God," he whispered, hurting for her. "You must have thought the world had turned ugly on you."

"Yes, well, I was used to it. The world has never been a pretty place to me—except in the theater."

The truth of her words sent him to her. He flattened his hands on the rock at either side of her head and let his arms accept his weight as he leaned close, drawn to her gray eyes as if they were magnets.

"You deserved better," he whispered. "And God knows you deserved better treatment from me. I assumed you were a rough-and-tumble girl from the bad side of town, and I let my imagination overrule my good sense. I'm afraid my imagination is jaded. I don't expect goodness in people anymore; I expect bad things like greed and jealousy and treachery. That's what I see in my business."

"Then you're in the wrong business," she said, laying her fingertips against his mouth.

"That's what my mother keeps telling me." He kissed her fingers. "Maybe I should listen."

"Maybe you should. Did you ever see Lizette act?"

"Yes, a couple of times. Only in small roles. She

wasn't anything near as good as you. She *acted*. You *are*."

"I think I'll make you top stage-door johnnie," she teased. "Be careful, you're turning my head."

He cupped her chin in one hand and turned her head so that he could kiss her flushed cheek. "Was there no man in your life who turned your head before me?"

"No, though a few tried."

He chuckled and kissed her neck.

"And you're the first to quote Shakespeare to me in the middle of the desert. How did you know so much? Did you playact with your sister?"

"No, but I've seen my share of stage plays. Remember, my mother is a supporter of the arts."

"Would she approve of you escorting me tonight?"

"Why wouldn't she?"

"Why did Juliet's parents frown upon Romeo?"

He swayed back to examine her expression. "Jussie, you have a twisted view of my family."

"Are you the only one who disapproved of Lizette's choice?"

"No, but it wasn't only the theater we disapproved of. The Count was our main objection."

"But you *did* disapprove of having your sister perform in a theater."

"Yes, yes." He pushed away from her, seeing that romance was not to be. "But Lizette isn't like you. She's frail, and she has a tiny, soft voice that isn't meant for projection." He said the last with gusto, demonstrating his power so well that his voice echoed back to them. "And she doesn't have your talent. She had stars in her eyes, but that was it. I think you're right. She loved the Count a hell of a lot more than she did the stage. In fact, she told me once that she shook like a cat passing prune pits each time she stood before an audience."

"Then why did she do it?"

"That's what I asked her, and she said that acting made her feel important. She dreamed of being pampered and cared for, of traveling to exotic places and being adored by countless men. It was the life-style she loved, but not the work." He touched a forefinger to his temple in a thoughtful pose. "But I believe you love the work. There was no audience here tonight, save me. No adoring masses or gushing directors or promises of wealth and fame, yet you gave a performance I'll never forget. In fact, I can't imagine any Juliet being as spellbinding as you."

She blushed, and York couldn't keep his distance. Not with her skin tinted rosy, her lashes swept down to shadow her cheeks, and her lips parted in sweet invitation.

He took her in his arms and captured her mouth with his. Her arms circled his neck, and her body, soft and pliant, fit against him. He'd never kissed a woman who tasted as sweet as Jussie. In his dreams he could taste her—that clean, springlike taste of her, as if her mouth were virgin territory, unspoiled by any man. Each time his tongue surged past her lips, she seemed to flower, coming to life in a burst of loving devotion that made him feel as important as the sun to all budding things. In loving, she was his creation, and that pleased him no end.

"Jussie, Jussie, you take my breath away," he confessed between hungry kisses.

She raked her hands through his hair over and over again and strained upward to meet his mouth. Finally she tore her lips from his and rested her forehead against his chin, her breathing as ragged as his.

"Tonight has been a dream," she whispered against his shirt, her breath warming the fabric and reaching through it to his skin. "Thank you, York."

"It's been a dream for me too, so don't thank me." He held her away, intent on keeping his promise to himself that he would be a gentleman. "I should get you back home now."

"Home?" She frowned. "That place isn't my home."

"Well, anyway, we should be getting back."

"Why?"

"Because it's time for all respectable young ladies to be in their own rooms," he said, putting starch into his voice, just as his father would have. "It must be close to midnight."

"Really?" She sighed wistfully. "So, the night is truly over."

"There will be others."

"Not like this one."

He kissed her lightly again, then clasped her hand and led her toward the buggy. "Take it from a faro dealer, Miss Justine, and don't bet on that unless you want to lose. You have many magical nights ahead of you. Any woman with your fire is destined to light up the world."

"My, my!" She pressed a hand over her heart. "I swear, you are a silver-tongued devil when you put on a tailcoat. But I wonder . . ."

"What?" he asked, lifting her into the buggy.

She craned forward, leaning into his upturned face. "Will you be your old, surly self tomorrow?"

He laughed and delivered a quick kiss to the tip of her nose. "After tonight, Jussie, I don't think either one of us will be the same again." He stepped into the buggy and over her legs and feet to take his place next to her. "Besides," he said, releasing the brake and clucking the sorrel into a trot, "I think you like it when we fuss and quarrel."

She was quiet for a full minute before her voice emerged, soft and thoughtful. "Perhaps, but I think I like it better when we don't."

He glanced at her but couldn't read her expression in the dark. Her eyes glittered like jewels, making him wonder if there were tears in them. Melancholy settled over her, and after a while it covered him as well. By the time the buggy rolled into Tombstone's rowdy streets, he dreaded the end of the evening that had brought him ever closer to the mystique of Justine Drussard.

Outside the back entrance to the Establishment, he kissed her good night and saw that there *were* tears in her eyes.

"Why are you crying?"

"Oh, I just hate for this evening to end."

"Me, too," he said, resting his forehead against hers and holding her hands.

"You do? Then why not come inside?" She gave his hands a tug.

"No, let's leave it at this." He took a deep breath, beating down the desire building in him. "A gentleman saying adieu to his lady by the light of the moon, not by the glare of the sun."

"You're right," she said, smiling and moving inside, leaving him to stand alone in the cold light of the moon. When the shadows had swallowed her, her disembodied voice floated out to him. "'Good night, good night! Parting is such sweet sorrow that I shall say good night till it be morrow.'"

He spun away, unwilling to share the intensity of his feelings with her. A fierce passion squeezed his heart, and as he climbed into the buggy, his very aloneness insulted him. It was at that moment, when he wanted to cry out from the pain of his lonely heart, that he knew beyond any doubt that he'd fallen in love with her.

Chapter 19

Leaving Justine at the Establishment, York directed the sorrel toward the OK Corral, where he
left the rig, then went on foot toward China Mary's,
taking the route through Hop Town.

"Hey, Masters!"

He slowed, looking toward the familiar voice.
Wyatt Earp lifted a hand in greeting as he walked
out of the saloon, flanked by his brother Morgan and
Doc Holliday.

"Howdy, fellas. Did you win or lose tonight?"

"Both," Wyatt admitted. "I think I made out better
than Doc, though."

"That's not saying much," Doc said. "Everybody
knows I'm not lucky at cards. Just women." Doc
grinned at his own joke, his ice blue eyes twinkling.

"You look like a damned fool dressed like that,"
Morgan drawled, running his gaze up and down
York, his mouth working into a sneer.

"What's got into you tonight?" York asked, sensing Morgan's bad mood. "Looks to me like that sour
mash you've been drinking has leaked into your
veins."

276

"Where you been?" Wyatt asked, angling for safer ground.

"Schieffelin Hall. I took Justine Drussard to see *Romeo and Juliet.*"

Doc wiggled his brows and smiled, but Morgan barked a laugh that grated on York's nerves.

"Ain't that interesting," Wyatt said, with a broad wink.

"Yeah, yeah." Morgan hooked his thumbs in his vest pockets and rocked back on his boot heels. "Real interesting if your taste runs to whores trying to pass themselves off as respectable."

Fury flashed through York like a lightning bolt, propelling his fist like a ball shot from a cannon. He struck Morgan in the mouth before the man could defend himself. Morgan fell back, butt first, onto the dirt-packed street.

"Damn you. Don't you *ever* call her a whore again or I'll knock you into next month!"

"You son of a bitch!" Morgan screamed, scrambling to his feet. "I'll kill you!" But before he could get a good swing going, Wyatt pinned Morgan's arms behind him. "Let go of me! I'm going to kill that bastard!"

"Simmer down." Wyatt jerked Morgan's arms, bumping elbow to elbow behind his back. Morgan howled in pain.

"Morgan, you're going to let your mouth stampede your brain once too often and get yourself killed," Doc drawled, running a finger lightly over his full mustache. He was looking past Morgan to the calmer Wyatt.

"Don't pay him no mind," Wyatt said, flinging his brother sideways and sending him stumbling down the street. "He was got in the morning and he's half piss."

Wyatt's droll humor penetrated York's fury, and he had to laugh along with Doc. Morgan started to lurch toward York, but Wyatt cuffed him again.

"Morgan, you're my brother and I love you, but don't keep testing me or I'll have to shoot you. Now get along." Wyatt touched the brim of his hat. "I'll take my brother home now. Y'all have a quiet evening."

"We'll do our damnedest," Doc assured him. "See you tomorrow, Wyatt."

"Tomorrow, Doc. Come on now, Morgan. York busted you because you asked for it. No need in wanting to kill a man for that. Hell, you ought to thank him." Wyatt draped an arm across Morgan's shoulders and forced him away from Doc and York.

"Damn fool," York said. "You're right about him, Doc. He's going to pop off to the wrong man and get his head shot off."

"Maybe Wyatt can make him keep his fool thoughts to himself. Where you headed?"

"Back to China Mary's, but I thought I'd check in on Satin Doll. She didn't show up for work again today. Come with me, if you want. I know where there's a fine bottle of bourbon hid in Mary's office."

"Sounds appetizing." Doc fell into step beside him, shoulder to shoulder, as tall as York. "So you've been to the theater with your lady, have you."

"That's right."

"Don't go setting your jaw," Doc chided. "I'm not going to say anything against her. I think she's right pretty and no more a whore than Morgan Earp is a genius."

Grinning, York shrugged. "So, how you been lately? How's that cough?"

"Okay, I guess."

York nodded, knowing full well Doc wasn't okay. Everybody knew he was dying from tuberculosis. He'd come to Arizona on doctor's orders, having been told the air was easier to breathe in the Southwest. The air wasn't doing him much good, but he kept himself plied with whiskey to dull the pain.

"So Satin Doll's still acting up?"

"Yes." York sighed, shaking his head. "I don't know what to do about her, Doc. She's been holed up in that room with her opium pipe for days."

"Did you tell China Mary?"

"Yes, and Mary has talked to her until she's blue in the face. She's given up, I think, but I keep thinking I can help Satin. I don't know what's wrong with her lately. She's sad all the time."

"I heard something interesting tonight over at the Crystal Palace," Doc said as he and York entered Hop Town. "Heard the Count was seen in Bisbee yesterday."

"Holy hell!" Excitement arched through York. "Who said?"

"A couple of fellas. You don't know them, but they knew what they were talking about. That means he'll be here in a day or two, York. Better tell Jussie. She ought to be prepared."

"Right. I'll tell her tomorrow." He smacked a fist into his open palm. "Damn! He's finally on his way, the bastard. Did you hear anything else?"

"Nope. For that information you ought to hand over the whole bottle of bourbon."

"It's yours, pal." York patted Doc on the back. "All yours. Let me just check on Satin, and we'll be on our way." York knocked on Satin's door, but there was no answer. "Come on, Satin," he called, irritated. "It's York, so open the door." He glanced at Doc and frowned. "She's been doing this lately—not coming to the door when you knock—and I'm getting damned tired of it."

"Go on in then," Doc said, giving the door a shove. It opened, creaking and groaning, inch by inch. "Satin Doll? Guess who's come to visit...." Doc stepped forward, then froze and reached back to block York. "Jesus!" He spun around, his face white and filled with horror. York shoved Doc aside, panic pumping through him.

Satin hung from the rafters, her head tipped to

one side at an impossible angle. The coarse noose ran around her thin neck, leaving red-and-blue marks. Her feet dangled a foot off the ground, and she was as still as death is final. Two or three flies clung to her expression of pain and surprise. Her eyes, like two buttons stuck in her head, stared out at him, as lifeless as the rest of her.

"Satin!" A sob cut his voice in two as York rushed forward and grabbed her around the hips. She was stiff. "Cut her down, Doc," he cried, his voice breaking. Desperation knifed him, slicing through his heart. "For God's sake, cut her down." He pressed his face into her cotton dress and squeezed his eyes shut, trying to block out her horrific expression. He felt a jolt, and then her weight was his to manage. She didn't feel like Satin anymore. He held only a body, stiff and unnatural, which he lowered to the floor. Pushing her hair from her face, he looked up at Doc.

"Jesus, oh, Jesus," Doc muttered, his icy eyes glittering with moisture. "Why did she . . . Oh, Jesus."

York tried to close her eyes, but it was too late, so he picked a silk scarf off the floor and laid it over her face. Grief filled him until he thought he might burst open. "Go get Dr. Goodfellow."

"What for?"

"Just get him!" York ordered through clenched teeth. "Please, get him."

Doc nodded and went to the door. York gathered Satin closer, trying to hold on to her memory and sort out what had happened.

"Why, Satin?" he moaned, lowering his head to her shoulder. She smelled of death, no longer his sweet-smelling Satin Doll. "Oh, Satin, look what I've done to you."

"I'm leaving now," Peachy announced. The Establishment's cook, chocolate skinned and always smiling, picked up the wicker basket she used as a handbag and started for the back door. "See you tomorrow morning, child. I'll be here by sunup."

"Why so early?" Justine asked.

Peachy's iron gray head shot up with surprise. "Because I gots lots to do, being it's Thanksgiving tomorrow."

"Thanksgiving?" Justine stilled, caught off guard. "My, my, so it is. To be honest, I never celebrated holidays much."

"Well, it's celebrated around here. The doors is locked all day and night, and the girls is treated to a day off and a big Thanksgiving feast. Madame Chloe makes sure there's enough for everybody who lives or works under this here roof."

"That's nice of her," Justine said, surprised by Madame Chloe's gesture, but then everyone deserved a day off. Maybe that was why the madame had been so scarce today.

"Yes siree, I gots lots to do tomorrow, so I best be getting home." Out the back door Peachy went, smiling to beat the band.

Justine peeked inside the teapot to check on the color of the brew. It was caramel and smelled of orange and spice. She poured herself a cup and added a measure of rich cream, stirring it and watching a finger of steam curl upward.

"Is that tea I smell?"

She turned and waved Ivory closer. "Sure is, and there's enough for you if you want some."

"I do," Ivory assured her. "I'll even let you pour." He backed up to the waist-high counter and hitched himself up to sit on it. "I like it when it's quiet like this—this hour between dinner and opening our doors to all the lonely hearts." He swung his feet, and Justine thought he looked like a little boy sitting on a tree limb. "I wish I could have seen you last night. Everybody said you were pretty as a picture."

Justine smiled her thanks. "Here's your tea." She leaned against the counter next to him, sharing the time. "I had a wonderful evening. Schieffelin Hall is a beautiful theater. I had no idea Tombstone had so many cultured people. That place was packed last night. Wall-to-wall money."

"Honey chile, why do you think they're working in them silver mines? There's money in them thar hills, and more than a few people around here are making a shit pile of it." He ducked his head, and his face colored pink, making his freckles stand out even more. "'Scuse my French."

"You're excused."

"Schieffelin Hall was built with silver money."

"Was it?"

"Sure, old Al Schieffelin built it. His brother, Ed, is the town founder. Ed was told he wouldn't find anything of value in this area 'cept maybe his own tombstone, but he struck it rich. As a joke, he named the place Tombstone."

"Not so funny," Justine observed. "Just take a look at Boothill. It's filling up fast."

"Ain't that the God's honest truth."

"Well, I've got to see Babette before the doors open."

"Why do you need to see her? Got a problem?"

"No, nothing like that." She reached into her skirt pocket and withdrew the borrowed necklace. "I have to return this to her. She let me wear it last night. Isn't it pretty?"

Ivory snatched the necklace from her fingers and stared at it, his eyes becoming red rimmed as his mouth worked, but no words came out.

"Ivory, what's wrong? Ivory..." Justine clutched his forearm, making him tear his gaze from the necklace to look at her. "What's the matter?"

"Babette lent this to you?" His voice was a whisper, hoarse and full of pain.

"Yes. Why?"

"Because it's not hers. She had no right." He

closed his fingers around the pearls and silver, and his fist trembled. "No right."

"Well . . ." Justine sighed, realizing she'd stepped into a pile of trouble. "Yes, I know it's not hers. She took it from Madame Chloe's room, but I'm sure she'll return it. Babette's a good person deep down. She just has sticky fingers, and she—"

"Madame Chloe? *She* had it?" Ivory cut in. He choked back a sob before he answered. "I gave this to Liz. To my Liz!" He brought the necklace to his lips and kissed it. "That bitch. How did Madame Chloe get it? I know Liz wouldn't have given it to her, so she must have stolen it."

"Liz? Are you sure? This is an expensive piece of jewelry."

"Don't I know." He wiped the tears from his eyes and gave a mighty sniff. "I'd saved my money a couple of years back, thinking I'd buy me a house or a plot of land somewhere. I was in love with this girl—"

"Shelley?"

"Yes. I loved Liz as a friend, but Shelley and me . . . well, we talked about getting married." He wiped more tears from his eyes, sniffed, and shook his head. "Liz was so lost and lonely, and I wanted to do something nice for her, so I gave her this necklace I'd bought for Shelley with my nest egg. She wanted to leave town, so I thought she could take the necklace and maybe get some money for it. She cried with joy when I gave it to her." His eyes teared again, and he blinked, wetting his stubby lashes. "I 'member she asked me why I was bein' so good to her, and I said, 'You deserve something beautiful,' and she just broke into sobs." So did he, burying his face in his hand.

Justine touched his baby-soft hair, then squeezed one of his bony shoulders. "There, there. What a sweet man you are, Ivory. You've got the heart of a saint." Wrapping her arms around him, she pulled him to her so that he could rest his head on her shoulder. "I don't know how Madame Chloe got this necklace, but I'm not giving it back. You keep it."

"What if Babette asks for it?" He raised his tear-stained face.

"She won't. She told me to keep it, but I didn't feel right about it. It's yours, Ivory." Justine chewed her upper lip thoughtfully. "Liz wouldn't have given this to Madame Chloe, would she?"

"No, never. I tell you, this was her ticket away from Madame Chloe."

"I believe you," Justine said, comforting him and wondering if she should go to China Mary's tonight and tell York about the necklace. But it was already growing dark outside, and she didn't like to walk the streets alone. Tomorrow would be soon enough. She'd have the day off for Thanksgiving, so she'd have plenty of time to see him and discuss this new revelation.

"Thanks for letting me keep this," Ivory said, dropping the necklace into his shirt pocket.

"You might want to give it to the girl you're courting now," Justine suggested.

"I'm not courting anyone."

"You don't have a girl?"

"No." His denial was firm, unyielding.

Justine shrugged, her curiosity triggered. If he had no sweetheart, who in the world was he sneaking off to see carrying flowers?

"I've got to be getting to my piano," Ivory said, sliding off the counter. "Can I have a refill before I go?"

"Sure." Justine poured more tea. I'll be going to my room now."

"What do you do in there every evening?"

"Read," Justine admitted. "Sometimes I sew or simply daydream. I've always been able to amuse myself."

"Why not?" Ivory gave her a timid peck on the

cheek. "You're mighty good company, honey chile."

"Have a good evening, Ivory," Justine said as he left the kitchen. She finished her tea, poured some more, and took it with her to her room. She relished the evenings, when she could be herself, and not watch every move she made and everything she said for fear she might slip up and cast suspicion her way.

"Thanksgiving," she whispered as she sat in the chair by the window, enjoying her tea. Her thoughts returned to her night at the theater with York. She'd felt as if she were living out a dream. Even now she glowed inside. She'd never felt so alive. With every heartbeat she thought of York and wondered if and what he thought of her.

A gentle tapping shook her from her thoughts, and she looked toward her closed door, unsure whether or not someone had knocked. Then the sound was repeated, tentative and furtive. Justine set the saucer on the end table and tiptoed to the door. She pressed her cheek against it.

"Who's there?" she whispered, feeling as if the caller wanted the visit kept secret. "Ivory, is that you?"

A man cleared his throat on the other side of the door. "It's John Henry Holliday, ma'am."

Justine had to think before she realized it was Doc Holliday who had come calling. "Doc, is that you?"

"Yes, ma'am. I'd like to talk with you if I could."

Opening the door, Justine confronted the tall, mustached man. He was good-looking, lean and long faced, with eyes that seemed to gaze right through to her soul. He wore a blue handkerchief, the same shade as his eyes, around his neck.

"Yes? What can I do for you?"

"Well, ma'am—"

"Justine or Jussie is fine, really."

"Miss Justine," he said, walking his fingers around the brim of his hat. He kept his head down, as if he were too shy to look at her. "You remember me, don't you?"

"Of course. I never forget a kindness, and you were very kind to me. I'm just surprised to see you here."

"Well, Miss Justine, it's about York Masters."

"York." She swallowed the fear that jumped into her throat. "What about him? Is he hurt? Did someone sh-shoot him or something?"

"He's not hurt, Miss Justine, but he's hurting." Doc lifted his blue eyes to her silver ones. "He's been drunk since last night, and I'm getting kinda worried about him."

"Drunk? Since last night?" She shook her head. "No, that's not possible. I was with him last night, and he was stone-cold sober."

"After he left you, ma'am, he got drunk."

"But why? It doesn't make sense."

"He's grieving over Satin Doll."

"Satin?" A chill clawed its way up her spine, and she knew bad news was coming. She gripped Doc Holliday's coat sleeve. "What's happened to her?"

"She's dead."

"Oh, no!" Justine's fingers tightened on Doc's sleeve while her other hand flew up to cover her mouth. "How?"

"Me and York found her last night. We went around to her place to check on her, and . . . well, ma'am, she hung herself."

"Hung herself?" Justine realized she was repeating everything he said, but she couldn't take it all in. "York . . . he's been drinking?"

"Yes, ma'am. It's like something bad is eating him from the inside out, and he's trying to kill it with liquor." He glanced behind him, checking to see if they were still alone, then lowered his voice to a whisper. "I'm a hard-drinking man, Miss Justine. Ask anybody and they'll tell you I can put pert near any man under the drinking table, but York has me beat hands down. He's drunk a gallon of the stuff, and he's getting sick, Miss Justine, but he keeps on drinking. I'm afraid he's going to kill himself."

"Then keep the liquor away from him," Justine said, grasping the most simple answer she could find.

"He's a grown man," Doc explained. "And he don't take kindly to being told what to do. But if you could come and talk to him, maybe he'll listen. I've tried and so has Wyatt, but he just sits and drinks. Even old Dr. Goodfellow tried to get him to eat something, but he threw the food across the room. He's getting our goats, if you know what I mean."

"Yes, Doc, I know." She turned from him and reached for her bonnet and handbag. "If you'll be so kind as to take me to him, I'll see what I can do."

"Yes, ma'am. Be glad to."

"Where is Satin? Have they buried her?"

"Yes, ma'am. This afternoon, up on Boothill. York wouldn't even go to the funeral."

"I suppose China Mary is beside herself."

"Yes, ma'am."

"Poor thing." Justine closed the door to her room. "I was afraid something like this would happen. We'll go out the back way."

"Yes, ma'am. After you."

She led the way outside, then accepted Doc's offered arm and went with him toward China Mary's, but a few blocks later he took a wrong turn.

"Where are we going?"

"To the Crystal Palace."

"York's not at China Mary's?"

"No, ma'am. He's in my room above the Crystal Palace."

"But why didn't you take him to his room?"

Doc grimaced, then released a choppy sigh. "He didn't want China Mary to see him this way. He's not a pretty sight."

"I see. Well, thanks for preparing me." She

squared her shoulders, determined to see York through the storm.

"Don't be in such a hurry to thank me," Doc said, his eyes shining with wry amusement. "You might want to kick my butt once you've rassled with him."

Chapter 20

$\sim\!\!\infty\!\!\sim$

They went in the back door of the Crystal Palace and up a dark staircase. Rowdy shouts and lusty laughter drifted to them from the main floor, where Tombstone's revelers were in full swing.

"Is he alone?" Justine asked, climbing the stairs behind Doc.

"No, Wyatt's with him," Doc said, glancing back at her. "Dr. Goodfellow's right next door should we need him."

"I hope we won't." She reached the landing to the second floor, and Doc led her along the wide hallway to the end where a huge window was open to the cool night breeze.

"Hot days are over for the year," Doc observed, angling his face to the breeze. "Nights are already getting right cool."

"Tomorrow's Thanksgiving."

"So it is."

"I have the day off, so I can stay with him if you'd like."

Doc looked down at her from his superior height, and his eyes smiled at her. "Do what *you* like, Miss

Justine." He wrapped one hand around the door-knob and gave a sharp rap with the knuckles of the other. "Wyatt, I have Miss Justine with me, and we're coming in."

"Come on," Wyatt called from within, but Doc hesitated.

"Take a deep breath and get ready for a hellish sight, Miss Justine," Doc warned, as serious as a funeral director. "You haven't ever seen York like this before." Then he opened the door and went inside first, moving to one side to let Justine enter at her will.

". . . told her to come here? I don't want to see her. Let go of me, goddamn it!"

Justine didn't recognize York's voice, all scratchy and filled with loss. Wyatt Earp stood leaning over a narrow bed and struggled with a whiskered, wild-eyed, sour-faced man. The lawman turned to glance at Justine and Doc, and his expression begged them to interfere.

"Too late now. She's already here," Wyatt said, tight lipped and impatient. "Damn it, York! No, don't . . . aw, to hell with you. I'm tired of playing nursemaid to a jackass." He straightened and flung his hands out at York in a dismissive gesture. "He's all yours. I've got to get out of here before I start taking apart the furniture and chewing up the wall-paper."

"Good, who asked you here anyway?" York jeered, then brought the whiskey bottle to his swollen lips and drank the stuff as if it were well water.

Wyatt snatched a brown hat off the tree by the door and rocked it onto his head. "Good luck, Miss Drussard," he said, giving her a brief nod of encouragement. "He's about as cooperative as a bee-stung bear."

"Thank you for all you've done for him," Justine said, breaking through the surface of her shock long enough to be polite.

"Yeah, well, that's not much." Wyatt laid a hand on Doc's shoulder as he went out. "I'll save you a bottle of the good stuff downstairs, pard."

"Do that. I'll be needing it." Doc closed the door, shutting them in with what York had become. "There he is, ma'am." Doc extended a hand toward the drunk. "Not a pretty sight."

"No, he's not." Justine made a face at him, wanting him to know just how disgusted she was by his condition. Did he jump into a whiskey barrel every time something didn't go his way?

"Quit talkin' 'bout me like I'm not here," York said. "I'm here." He jabbed a thumb into the center of his chest.

"Yes, we know." Justine said, taking off her bonnet. "We can smell you—all the way down the street."

Doc laughed, turning his back to York and covering his mouth with his hand.

"I want you"—York pointed a shaking finger at her—"outta here, now."

"I'm not leaving," Justine said, calmly placing her bonnet and handbag on the bureau.

"Get out!" He raised up, then fell back and groped for a pillow, which he flung at her. It missed by a foot.

Justine gave the pillow only a cursory glance as she studied the room where Doc Holliday lived. It was good sized, with big windows and comfortable furniture. Family pictures covered a table. They looked out of place beside the two empty whiskey bottles.

"What can I do to help?" Doc asked.

"Would you leave me alone with him, please?"

"Well, now, Miss Justine, I don't think that's a wise idea. He's as strong as a bull and not half as pleasant. He might hurt you."

She smiled and shook her head. "He won't. I'll be fine. Please, give me an hour or so with him." She directed the next to York, who glared at her with eyes that looked painful. "You won't lay a finger on me, will you?"

"I might if you don't leave me be."

Justine made a chiding face at him. "He's just being ornery."

"If you say so." Doc shrugged and left.

Justine leaned against the door and took stock of the lump of humanity before her. The room reeked of stale liquor and sour sweat, and in the middle of it was York. He wore nothing but a pair of trousers and suspenders stretched over his broad, gleaming shoulders. His hair looked gummy, his eyes were bloodshot, and he hadn't shaved since she'd last seen him. His upper lip was frozen in a permanent sneer.

"Why don't you leave me the hell alone?" he demanded, his eyes and voice hollow.

"She didn't kill herself over you, so don't flatter yourself." Justine purposefully made her tone flat and merciless, wanting to cut through his self-pity as quickly as possible. It worked. His sneer took on an evil edge and he peered at her, eyes narrowed suspiciously.

"What do you know about it?"

"She didn't kill herself because of anything you did or didn't do. She killed herself because of something *she* didn't do."

"You don't know anything about it." He took another swig of whiskey and rested the bottle on his bent knee.

She threw back the draperies and opened the window to let in air that wasn't laden with the stench of whiskey and sweat. "I thought you'd finally learned that I'm smarter than you. Guess the whiskey has pickled your brain and made you forget."

"You're full of beans."

Justine stood beside the bed, hands on hips, and

regarded him squarely. "I'm in love with you, and you not loving me back isn't reason easy enough for me to kill myself. I'd cry and feel sorry for poor little me, but I wouldn't end it all." She rushed on, seeing that she had his attention. "You weren't her first man, York, so you couldn't have been as important to Satin as you are to me. Don't you see? If I wouldn't kill myself over you, then Satin Doll wouldn't either." She went to the window on the other side of the bed and lifted it for more ventilation. She thought of Shakespeare's star-crossed lovers. "People do die for love—perhaps your sister did—but not Satin Doll."

"What makes you think you know so damned much?"

"I know more about life getting too ugly to face than you'll ever know, mister." She picked up the pillow he'd thrown at her and tossed it right back at him, then she grabbed the neck of the whiskey bottle. "Now, let me have this."

"No." He wrenched the bottle from her grasp and sprang from the bed, but he was none too steady on his feet. He swayed and staggered like a newborn colt. "I don't need lectures from a dock rat. Get out before I throw you out."

She flinched at his insult. "Look at yourself. You're pathetic." She gave him a once-over, hoping to make him feel as dirty as he looked. "Moping around here like a lovesick rummy, and for what? For Satin? For all you know she had more lovers than you can shake a stick at. It's just like a man to think he was the only one who came acalling."

He growled like an animal and moved faster than Justine thought he could, liquor laden as he was. Grabbing her arm, he slung her at the door. She fell against it shoulder first and stared at him with shock. A mean drunk, she thought, then hardened herself for a bumpy ride as he advanced toward her. His fingers felt like bands of steel around her upper arms as he shoved her to one side, opened the door, and pushed her over the threshold.

She darted past him, back inside the room, before he could close the door in her face. "I'll leave when I'm good and ready."

"You'll leave now. I didn't invite you, and I sure as hell don't need you." He gripped her wrist and yanked her toward the door, but she dug in and made it doubly difficult. When she started fighting him off, clawing at his hand and wriggling like a nest of snakes, he fought back by shoving her roughly up against the wall.

Justine stumbled, almost falling to her knees, but kept her balance. She flung her hair from her eyes and glared at him, her expression so full of venom that it made him pause.

"Well, come on!" she challenged, bracing herself. "You think you're the first drunk I've fought with? Not by a mile, buddy. My mother taught me how to handle mean drunks, so come on, big man. Show your muscle. Liquor makes a fighter out of the most lily-livered coward."

The hard light in his eyes dimmed, then went out. All the color drained from his face, and sweat shone on his forehead. He started to speak, but then he heaved and whirled away to release the meager contents of his stomach. He dropped to his knees, weakened by sickness, and retched, shoulders shaking and head sinking between them.

"Oh, God . . ." He moaned, then coughed up another mouthful of bitterness. "God almighty, I'm ruined. I'm a worthless sack of shit."

"No, you're not." Justine took him by the shoulders, then pulled and tugged him to his feet. "Lie down," she instructed, guiding him back to bed. "No more whiskey for you."

"I want more. I want to drink until I can't remember a damned thing."

"There's not enough whiskey for that." She

pushed him down onto the bed, then onto his side.
"Stay there. Close your eyes, York."

"No, I can't sleep. I keep seeing Satin..."

"Close your eyes," she urged, placing one hand
across them. When she pulled her hand away, his
eyes were closed. "Good."

"I've made a mess."

"Nothing that can't be cleaned up."

"Don't." His eyes flew open. "Leave it. You're
crazy to clean up my mess. I'll...I'll tend to it later."

"Close your eyes." She waited for him to obey,
then went to the washstand and filled the bowl with
water. When she returned, bowl and washcloth in
hand, York had passed out. "Believe me, York Le-
Masters, I wouldn't spend one minute with you like
this if I wasn't already crazy in love with you."

"Oh, good, you're awake. Time to shave." Justine
jumped up from the chair where she'd been nap-
ping, off and on, for almost three hours. She'd been
waiting for York to rouse from his drunken death,
and now that he'd opened his bloodshot eyes again,
it was time to restore him to the world of the clean
and sober.

"Whaaa..." He swallowed whatever obstructed
his voice and tried again. "Still here? Why don't you
leave me alone? Where's Doc? Get him in here. Tell
him to take you back to the Establishment. Madame
Chloe will be looking for you."

"No, she won't. Doc has been here and gone. I
sent him to the Establishment to tell Madame Chloe
I'll be spending Thanksgiving with China Mary, then
he's going to China Mary's to tell her to cover for you
and me." She poured water into the washbowl and
laid out his shaving tools. "Then Doc's bedding
down in your room while you're laid up in his.
Everything's taken care of," she said brightly as she
turned to face him, crooking a come-hither finger.

"Time to shave, York. I'm told a man always feels better after a close shave."

He made a low, disgusted sound and didn't move from the bed.

"You want me to shave you?"

"No, I want you to get the hell out of here. How loud do I have to shout before you can hear me?"

"You're as grumpy as an old bear."

"I get that way after I've seen a good friend dangling from a noose."

Justine sighed wearily. "It's terrible, yes, but getting stinking drunk isn't going to—"

"*Go! Get out!*"

She blinked and stumbled back, stunned by the sharp rap of his voice, then furious that he'd speak to her as if she were no better than a dog. Acting on pure fury, she picked up the bowl and pitched the water into his lap. It was his turn to be stunned. He started to spring off the bed at her, but she picked up a ladder-back chair and held him off.

"If you're going to act like an animal, I'll treat you like one. Get back, beast. Back, back." She stabbed him with the chair's legs.

"Put that damned thing down," he grumbled, slumping back onto the bed, the fire gone out of him. "You look stupid."

"If I look bad, just imagine how you look to me." She put the chair down, then refilled the bowl from the bucket of water Doc had brought. "Shall we try this again?"

"Oh, hell." He pushed himself to his feet and lurched to the washstand. "If I shave, will you leave?"

"Shave and we'll see."

While he lathered his face and pulled the razor through the inch of foamy soap, Justine changed the bed linens and laid out his fresh clothes. York turned to examine the shirt, trousers, and long johns.

"Who brought those?"

"Wyatt Earp. You have a lot of friends who are worried about you." She straightened from smoothing the wrinkles from the fresh, cotton sheet and locked her gaze on his bandage. "What happened there?"

He glanced over his shoulder to catch the direction of her gaze. "Oh, that. Satin did that. She cut me."

"When?"

"The other day after I saw you outside the theater."

She retraced that day in her mind. "Were you . . . you mean you were bleeding when I saw you in your room? You didn't let on. We talked and you never—"

"It's no big thing. Just a scratch."

"A scratch doesn't require a bandage that size."

"It's nothing, okay?" He turned sideways to glare at her before facing the mirror again. "You are the world's worst at harping on things that don't amount to a hill of beans." He finished and toweled off the rest of the soap, then slumped into the chair as if that small amount of exercise had exhausted him. "I'm clean shaven, but you're still here."

She smiled. "Didn't work, I guess."

He ran a hand down his face and kept it across the lower half, studying her as if she were a trap he wanted to avoid. "About what you said earlier. . ." He laced his fingers against his abdomen and pulled his lower lip between his teeth.

"What I said about Satin Doll?"

"No, about you, uh, being in love with me. You didn't mean that, I hope."

Lifting her chin higher, Justine stared at him, making him look away first. "Why, can't you take it?"

"Now? No." He ran a hand through his hair, then winced when he felt the stickiness of it. "Right now I can't face myself, much less your bloated expectations of me."

"Bloated. That's a good word for it." She arched a brow, refusing to be subdued or shamed by the likes of him. "You also stink. I've been to feed lots that smelled better than you." Angling a glance at the washtub in the corner of the room, she made a suggestion with her eyes.

"I hear you," he said, standing up and unfastening his trousers.

Justine dipped her fingers into the water. "It's tepid, but it'll do. Jump in."

He'd shucked his suspenders and trousers, but hesitated in removing his red long johns. He gave her a rapscallion's grin. "Are you going to wash me . . . even the good places?"

"I didn't know you had any, but the answer is no." She flounced past him, and turned the chair around, giving the tub its back, then sat in it. "I'm going to sit here and wait. When you're clean you can eat the cold supper Doc left for you, and then we'll talk."

"I'll eat, but I'm not talking."

"Fine." She crossed her ankles, tucking her legs to one side in a ladylike pose. "I'll talk and you can listen."

The water sloshed as he lowered his rangy body into it. "I don't want to listen either."

"Tough luck, partner." She closed her eyes and heard the sounds of sloshing water, imagining . . . ah yes. She remembered that body in detail. The sensual side of her responded to the memories, but the practical side reminded her that he didn't want her love. The bastard, she thought with a burst of frustration. Self-centered, selfish, arrogant, proud, deceitful . . .

"Penny for your thoughts, angel."

Her smile was downright wicked. "They're worth a lot more than that, believe me."

A mighty swoosh was followed by, "You can turn around now."

She did, then gasped at his nakedness. He stood in the tub, towel in hand but covering nothing except his thumb and forefinger. "You . . . ooh!" She gave him her back again while he laughed uproariously at her embarrassment.

"Why so red faced, angel? You've not only seen it all, you've touched it all. In fact, your mouth has been—"

"Stop it!" She covered her ears with her hands, pressing hard and squeezing her eyes shut. Nonetheless, she heard his voice faintly.

". . . can leave now because I'm not going to be a good boy." He mumbled something she couldn't hear, and she took away her hands in time to catch, ". . . order up another bottle."

"Oh, no, you're not." She leaped from the chair and placed herself between him and the door. He'd put on his trousers again, leaving his chest bare. Droplets of water clung to his chest hair, arresting her gaze for a few shattering moments.

"Get out of my way."

"No." She pointed to the tray near her feet. "You eat that and then I'll go. No liquor. Not until I'm gone." She saw the stubborn set of his jaw and decided wheedling was in order. "Please, York. For me. Do this one thing for me."

He rolled his eyes and spun around on one foot in a broad show of exasperation. Clutching his wet head in his hands, he staggered to the bed and plopped down on it. "Bring the food. Anything to get you out of my hair."

She brought in the tray and lifted off the red-and-white checked napkin to reveal cold biscuits, bacon, and a bowl of grits. He tucked into the meal like the starving man he was, and since he was busy shoveling in the food and chewing, Justine seized the opportunity to talk to him uninterrupted. Bringing the chair over to the bed, she sat down in it, facing him.

"You're not really going to buy another bottle of whiskey, are you? Oh, don't give me that ugly look. I know you don't hate me. You resent my interfering, but you don't hate me. You've been on your drunk, and it was a dandy, but let it go at that. Sooner or later, you'll have to stay sober and get on with living. I'm sure it was terrible to find Satin—"

"That's for damned sure."

"—but there wasn't anything you could do. When she cut you, was that the last time you saw her alive? Just nod, don't talk." He nodded. "That's what I thought. One more reason for her to feel guilty. Just eat and don't argue," she warned when he drew in a breath to pitch words at her. "If you think you could have forced her to stop smoking that opium, that you could have *made* her be happy, then you're a damned fool, York LeMasters."

"Masters, to you."

"Whatever you're calling yourself today," she said, jabbing verbally at one of his soft spots.

"I should have gone to see her more often, stayed the night when she asked me to, but I told her I was busy and couldn't."

"You think you're such a great lover that you can give a woman a reason to live? Whew! You think a lot of yourself, don't you?"

He stared at her with a scorching intensity that dried the rest of the words on her tongue. Setting the almost-cleared tray to one side, he placed his hands on his knees and continued to glare at her. After almost a full minute he drew in and blew out a noisy breath. "You're a bitch," he said, almost politely. Then he stood up and went to stand by the window, where a breeze caressed his bare skin.

Justine ducked her head, smiling at her small victory. He hated to admit it, but he was beginning to see that she was right. She knew it hurt him to realize he couldn't have helped Satin Doll, that his friend was doomed with or without his gestures. She lifted her head to look at him, glad for the chance to admire the starlight dancing upon his skin and glimmering in his damp hair.

"How did you meet Satin?" Justine asked, sensing his need to talk.

"She knew Lizzie."

Justine watched the expressions flit across his face and wondered what thoughts were responsible for them. "And you liked her right away?"

"Sure, I guess so. I felt I could trust Satin and China Mary. I told them everything . . . why I was in town and who I was looking for and why."

"Oh, so you were honest with them, huh?" She crossed her arms and arched one brow. "Rare for you."

The venom was back, curling his lip. "I've eaten that slop, so why don't you vamoose like you promised?"

She eyed him, regretting her sharp tongue because she had no intention of leaving him alone. "Tell me about how Satin knew Lizzie, and then I'll go."

He propped one hand high on the window facing and threw his weight off center. "Lizzie admired Satin's show, and one night she told her so. The two of them became friends. They had a lot in common, I guess, both being show girls. But Satin hates . . . *hated* the Count. I think she flirted with him once, and he insulted her. Something like that, anyway, because Satin despised him. When I told her I was out to get him, she was thrilled and wanted to help."

Lifting the window higher, he sat on the ledge, bracing his back against the facing. "My plan was to get Satin Doll into the Establishment, but Madame Chloe doesn't hire Orientals. She likes them French or French looking."

"This is where I enter, stage right."

His smile was rueful, but he still didn't look at

her. He stared out the window, listening to the distant drumming of the mines and the tinkle of whiskey glasses and money chips from down below.

"York, Satin died of a guilty conscience."

He swung his gaze to her, frowning. "Guilty? of what?"

Justine hesitated, feeling she was betraying Satin but knowing she had to give York back his peace of mind. "You see, Satin wasn't completely honest with you. She knew something about Lizzie that she could never bring herself to tell you."

"What?" He straightened from his slouch. "What are you talking about?"

"Lizzie confided in Satin that she was scared of the Count, that she hated the Establishment and wanted to leave. Satin told her to go, but Lizzie said she couldn't. When Satin said she'd talk to Madame Chloe and the Count about letting her go, Lizzie made her promise to keep quiet. I found out that Ivory was helping Lizzie. He gave her an expensive necklace, and I think she was going to sell it and buy a stagecoach ticket."

"When did you learn all this?" York asked, standing up and looking decidedly irritated.

"Just lately. I was going to tell you, but you've been rip-roaring drunk." Her reasoning made him resume his seat on the window ledge. "Just listen, will you? Satin told me she bawled out Madame Chloe for keeping girls against their wills, then felt awful later about breaking her word to Lizzie. I think she could have lived with it if you hadn't come along. She fell in love with you, York, and because she loved you, she couldn't bring herself to tell you that she might have brought about Lizzie's murder."

"Murder? You mean, you know for sure—"

"No, not for sure. But Satin felt certain Lizzie was killed and that she was indirectly responsible."

"Why the hell didn't she tell me?" He ran a hand through his hair, looking shaken and confused. "She was supposed to be my friend. She was supposed to be helping me."

"You just answered your own question. Satin felt like a cheat, and she couldn't bear having you hate her, so she hated herself until she finally couldn't stand it. I bet the last straw for her was when she lost control and attacked you."

"Oh, God." He hung his head and was silent while he sorted through everything. "I knew something was bothering her, but she wouldn't talk to me. She turned to that damn opium pipe." He directed a sharp glance Justine's way. "Why did she tell you?"

Justine shrugged helplessly. "Who knows for sure why anyone does anything? She needed to talk about it, and I was there. We had things in common, you know—both entertainers on our own and... well, we had your best interests at heart. She knew how important it was for you to find out what happened to Lizzie and the others—oh!" She snapped her fingers. "Another thing. About the bookkeeper I replaced..."

"Yes, what about her?"

"I don't think she ran off with a miner. I think she's missing just like Lizzie and Shelley."

"God almighty! Why do you think that?"

"Because of something Madame Chloe said. She hinted that the bookkeeper—Donna was her name —*tried* to run off with a fellow. You see? I've been pulling my weight."

His smile was quick and a little sad. "I know, I know. I've made a horse's ass of myself, but Satin Doll's death..." He shook his head. "And now you're telling me she felt she had something to do with Lizzie dy—uh, disappearing."

Justine dipped her head, touched that he still couldn't admit his sister might be dead.

"The Count was spotted recently in Bisbee," he said. "He'll be here any time now."

"Then you'd better stay sober," she cautioned. "How do you feel?"

"Empty." He closed his eyes with effort. "My head is pounding like a death march."

"You should get some sleep."

"They buried her on Boothill, didn't they?"

Justine nodded. "Yes."

"I couldn't go. I..." He pulled his lips between his teeth for a second, and then his Adam's apple bobbed as he swallowed hard. "She must have been hanging there for hours. She was stiff. There were flies on her face, and..." He shuddered.

Justine went to him, slipping an arm around his shoulders and pressing a kiss and then her cheek high on his arm. "York, quit torturing yourself. Satin wanted to tell you, but she just couldn't do it. I don't think it mattered to her until she fell in love with you, and then it was too late. She couldn't bear to have you hate her."

"That's why it's always a mistake to get personally involved when you're in the middle of an investigation," he murmured. "Once your heart gets into it, it's a lost cause."

Justine regarded him, sensing that he was drawing away from her even as she clung to him. "Well, tomorrow will be here soon, and it'll look better if you get some sleep before you have to face it." She tugged on his arm. "Come on," she pleaded. "Please? I know you're done in." She let out a resigned sigh. "If you get back into bed, I promise to leave. Cross my heart," she said, illustrating it with a forefinger slashing diagonally one way and then the other across her breasts. His gaze followed the movement of her finger and he smiled wanly.

"Done." He pushed off the window ledge and crossed to the bed. It creaked and groaned as he fell upon it.

Satisfied, Justine picked up the supper tray and placed it outside the door.

"Jussie."

"Yes?"

"You're not really going to leave me, are you?"

"No."

"Good. Come here. Right here." He smoothed the sheet alongside him. "You don't have to tell me I'm way too tired to be amorous. I just want to hold you. I want to feel life, to feel alive."

"But I thought you wanted to be left alone," she said, reminding him of his contradictions.

"So did I." He let his head drop back to the pillow and closed his eyes. "I was wrong...about a lot of things."

She cursed her weakness as she went to the bed, removed her shoes, and stretched out beside him, her back to his front. He curved an arm around her waist, pulling her backside into his lap, and breathed a sigh of satisfaction into her hair.

"York, did you love Satin Doll?"

"Love her? In what way?"

"You know what I mean."

"Oh, you mean *love* her."

"Yes, that's what I mean." She waited, giving him a minute to fashion an answer. When she heard him begin to snore softly, she realized he'd wriggled out of another tight place. "Coward," she whispered. The man was about as easy to pin down as greased lightning.

Chapter 21

She had the prettiest profile he'd ever come across. York propped his head in his hand and traced the wave in Justine's hair. Her lashes were thick and long and curled at the tips. He recalled the first time he spotted her on the street near the OK Corral. Arms pumping and petticoats flying, she'd hustled along the street with murder in her eyes. For a few moments, he thought she was hell-bent on jumping right in the middle of the gun battle, but then he noticed she wore no gun. That's when he tried to motion her back, and she gave him one of her now-familiar scowls for his trouble.

Little hellcat, he thought, chuckling at the memory. He hadn't meant to send her sailing, but the electricity in the air had warned him that the gunfight was a hairsbreadth away, and the little hellcat was mighty close to meeting her maker. He just couldn't stand by and let such a fine example of womanhood go to waste.

So he'd rescued her, but she was like a shadow. He couldn't run fast enough to leave her behind, and

lately, he didn't want to. He liked having her close
... real close.

He kissed her shoulder, wishing she'd undressed
so that he could taste skin instead of material. She
amazed him with the way she took charge of situa-
tions. Like last night when she'd swept in, ordered
him around like his prison guard, and even shamed
him when he lost his head and got too rough with
her.

You're a prize I'm not sure I deserve, he told her
silently, drinking in her beauty and admiring her
blazing spirit. A pesky fly swooped in through the
open window and came to rest on Justine's dewy
cheek. Satin Doll's final expression burned into
being, a vision so horrid that York jerked violently
and closed his eyes, warding off the inner terror. His
movement sent the fly winging back outside, but the
haunting memory and its message remained.

First Lizzie and then Satin... But not Jussie, he
thought, his passion changing the plea to a prayer.
Never Jussie. He had placed her in harm's way, but it
wasn't too late to pluck her out of its path, and he'd
do it. He *had* to do it. He hadn't saved her precious
life once just to throw her onto death's doorstep.
Especially now that she owned a big piece of his
heart.

"My angel," he whispered against her neck,
thinking how she'd rescued him last night from his
self-pity. "My guardian angel."

"York..." She shifted onto her back to gaze up at
him with sleepy gray eyes. "What time is it?"

"Time to go back to China Mary's." He swung his
legs over the side of the bed before he could surrender to his sexual urges. "And time for you to go back
to Madame Chloe's."

"Net yet. I want to go to China Mary's with you
first, then I'll go back to the Establishment." She sat
up, pushing her hair from her face. "You remember
my mentioning the necklace Ivory gave your sister?"

He stood up to put on a clean shirt. "Yes, what about it?"

"It's the one I wore to the theater. Babette *borrowed* it from Madame Chloe." She smiled. "In other words, she took it. Anyway, Ivory said Lizzie would never have given it to Madame Chloe."

"How did she get it, then?"

"We don't know. I let Ivory keep it because Babette said she steals jewelry from Madame Chloe all the time, and Madame has never said a thing about it. Babette says Chloe doesn't care a jot for the jewels because she has trunks of them."

"Is that so?" He sat on the edge of the bed and pulled on his boots. "Madame Chloe either took it from Lizzie or...someone else did and gave it to her." He stood up again to tuck his shirt into his trousers. "Jussie, I think you'd better move out of there. I know the Count's on his way, and you've given me enough to go on."

"What are you talking about?"

"I mean it. You've done enough."

"What brought this on?" Justine asked, giving him a dubious glare. "Not more than a few hours ago you were telling me the opposite. You said I hadn't done enough! What changed your mind?"

"Well, you told me about Satin's secret and now about this necklace—"

"And it all adds up to nothing definite," she cut in. "No, I'm just now getting my foot in the door. Babette and Cherry Vanilla are beginning to open up, and Ivory trusts me." She stood on her knees in the middle of the bed and clutched his forearms to win his complete attention. "Are you trying to get rid of me just because I said I've fallen in love with you?"

"No." He gritted his teeth as he teetered on the edge of desperation. "I don't want yours to be the next funeral I can't go to because I'm too drunk!" He framed her face between his hands and rested his forehead against hers. "I've lost two women to the Count. I don't want to lose another one. You should get clear of this while you're still breathing. It's time you left Tombstone."

"You want me to leave because you love me?" she asked, clearly disbelieving him. "Or is it because you *don't* want to love me? Aren't I good enough for you, York?"

"Don't start that again, Jussie, I'm only thinking of you—"

"Thanks a pants load, York." She sat back on her heels and stared at him so intently that he felt trapped. "You can't go home a hero with a two-bit actress—a whore's daughter!—on your arm, can you? Muh-tha and Fah-tha wouldn't approve!"

"It's not that," he argued. "I don't give a good damn what my 'Muh-tha and Fah-tha' think of you. Your insecurity is showing, Jussie, and it's not a pretty sight." He matched her frown and wondered if she was listening. From the look on her face she'd already decided he was a blue-blooded snob, and she wasn't about to change her opinion. Women! Couldn't they understand that a man couldn't think straight when his heart got in the way? He had thought he could protect her, but he was a damn fool. "Once your feelings get caught up in it, you lose your edge," he said, finding it hard to express himself. Words stuck in his throat. Emotion lodged in his gut. He kept seeing Satin's face, her lifeless body. "I'm losing it now. I'm thinking more about keeping you safe than about finding my sister's killer."

She tipped her head to one side. "I'm surprised the agency would let you trail the Count, seeing as how your sister is the one missing and all."

He swung away from her, trying to hide, then realized he couldn't. "Pinkerton took me off the case." From the corner of his eye, he saw her face go quite still. "I'm on my own time, Jussie."

"Are you with Pinkerton, or is that a lie, too?"

"I work for them, but not now. I'm on leave." He saw the disappointment on her face. It cut him to the quick.

"Is there anything you've told me that isn't a lie?"

He looked away, feeling small. "I don't want anything to happen to you. That's no lie."

"I've gone too far to turn back now. I want to meet the Count. I want to know what happened to your sister."

"I'll tell you all about it when it's over."

"When it's over you'll be long gone, and I'll be left in the dust."

"That's not true, Jussie."

"I'm supposed to believe you?"

"Jussie," he cajoled, reaching for her, but she scooted off the bed and away from him. "Where are you going?"

"Back to the Establishment," she said, tying on her bonnet. "You've dried out, so I've done my good deed. It's back to work for me."

"I thought you were going to spend the day with me at China Mary's."

"Changed my mind."

"Why?"

She rounded on him, a woman wronged. "Because you're a chicken-livered, lying jackass!" Her lips quivered, and her eyes sparkled with unshed tears. She brushed away his touch of concern. "Leave me alone. You can't understand. I don't expect you to love me back, but you don't have to act like I socked you in the gut, and you're still punch-drunk."

"I'm not . . . I didn't . . ."

"And you don't have to boot me out of town either. I won't make any trouble for you. I'm not the type to hang on a man and beg for crumbs."

He hooked his fingers around her arm, trying to

find a handhold before she could storm out of the room.

"Don't!" She glared at him as if he'd spit on her, then she visibly controlled her temper and lowered her voice. "You're off the hook. I don't expect a damned thing from you. Believe me, I know what people like you think of people like me. Working with you made me think you'd grown to care something about me, but I know that's—"

"Jussie, you're not listening to me. I'm trying to tell you that I *do* care for you, and that's why I want you to leave town."

She smiled bitterly. "Is that what you're trying to tell me? See you around, boss man."

"Don't be this way, Jussie. Let's put aside how we feel—"

"Or don't feel."

"Okay, okay." He opened the door. "I've hurt your feelings. When you've simmered down, we'll talk."

She rested a hand on his chest and delivered a vinegary smile. "Don't hold your breath, honey." Her hand slipped down his front, barely brushed his fly, then she sashayed out. York slammed the door behind her, releasing a string of choice words that turned the air blue.

Stepping into the front foyer of the Establishment, Justine sensed something was different. The laughter drifting from the back of the house sounded genuine, not the forced, fake gaiety that usually echoed in the halls. She heard a man's voice and knew the Count had arrived. Anticipation gripped her, catching her breath.

Justine went to her room, whipped off her bonnet, and placed it and her handbag on the bed. She faced the mirror to brush her hair, taming it into a sleek chignon. Running her hands down her navy blue dress, she checked her appearance, not wanting to look like a woman who had grabbed only a wink or two of sleep last night. Then she let her curiosity tug her toward those polite, chattering voices. They floated to her from the dining room, and Justine knew before she rounded the corner that she was stumbling into the middle of Madame Chloe's Thanksgiving feast. Aware of the other faces turning her way, Justine saw only one. The Count.

He was younger than she'd expected, having fancied him older than Madame Chloe, perhaps in his forties. But he was clearly in his thirties. About York's age, she guessed. His hair was blue-black with a center part that corresponded with the center part of his trimmed mustache. His eyes, so darkly brown they appeared black, were alive with twinkles and sparkles as he gave her a sweeping assessment. They reminded her of a midnight sky full of stars. He smiled, displaying clean but slightly irregular-shaped teeth. He wasn't as good-looking as York, but he would turn his share of feminine heads, she thought, because he had something else, something indefinable. Observing his proud carriage as he rose to his feet, Justine was reminded of a maned lion moving with heavy grace and a rearing stallion pawing the air with flashing hoofs.

Wearing an impeccable butterscotch suit, the Count was undoubtedly a man of expensive tastes. He wore gold and diamond rings on both hands, and his necktie sported a gold-and-ruby pin in the shape of a horseshoe.

When her gaze met his directly, Justine knew a moment of trancelike intensity. Yes, there was something about him, something that made her heart beat hard and fast and her knees weaken. The rest of the world receded, and he became the focal point. He had a power, a force—what Jasmine Broadwater had called "a innard rattler." "Youse feels it insteads of hearin' it," she'd said.

"Excuse me for interrupting," Justine said, tearing

her gaze from his and glancing over the table laden with turkey and fixings.

"Happy Thanksgiving," Madame Chloe said. "I was told you'd be spending today with China Mary."

"My plans have changed, but don't let me interrupt you."

"You are not interrupting." Madame Chloe motioned toward the sideboard. "Get yourself a plate and join us. Besides, you haven't met our guest. Justine Drussard, allow me to introduce your employer."

"Charmed," the Count said, inclining his head.

"The Count. Is that what I should call you? Count...?"

"Yes, that will do," he said, and his smile was so warm Justine was reminded of summer days.

"Nice to meet you." She extended her hand. He kissed the back of it lightly, his glittering eyes never leaving her face. Justine let her hand linger a moment longer in his, then pulled away, feeling shy and shaken. She went to the sideboard, glad for the diversion. "It smells delicious."

"It is," Cherry Vanilla piped up. "I'm stuffing myself like a turkey."

Justine counted heads, noticing that Ivory Sparks was missing. "May I squeeze in beside you, Cherry?"

"Sure, hon."

"No." The Count glanced to his right at Babette. "Would you make room for Justine, pretty one?"

Babette looked from him to Justine, then shrugged and everyone on that side of the table shifted to make room. The Count seized a chair and politely held it out for Justine.

"I don't mean to be so much trouble," she murmured, taking the seat.

"You are anything but that," the Count whispered softly as he assisted her in moving closer to the table.

"How is China Mary?" Madame Chloe asked.

"She's very upset."

"So I thought. Well, let's not speak of death at the dinner table." Madame Chloe lifted her wineglass. "We have much to be thankful for today." Her gaze met the Count's and held. "We're so happy you arrived in time to celebrate Thanksgiving with us."

"So am I. Actually, I thought about not coming until after the holidays, but something—" he turned his powerful eyes on Justine—"something drew me here. Chloe told me you're good with numbers, but she failed to mention you're also a beauty." He bathed Chloe in his smile. "Shame on you, cherie."

Justine took portions of turkey and dressing, uneasy with the attention. "It's kind of you to—"

"No, I'm not being kind. I'm being honest." He shifted toward Madame Chloe, thus dismissing Justine. "So, Chloe, you were telling me about York Masters."

Justine stiffened, then jumped when the Count's hand landed heavily on hers. His enigmatic gaze swept her, pinning her and making her squirm inside.

"You should find this interesting, cherie," he said with a velvety voice that should have been soothing but wasn't.

Justine realized she wasn't breathing: she made a conscious effort to do so. She felt as if everyone at the table was aware of her pounding heart and damp palms, but as she glanced around, she saw that no one was paying her any mind.

". . . and I believe he was her lover at one time. Do you know anything about that, Jussie?"

Justine blinked and cleared her head. "I'm sorry. I was so . . . I didn't quite hear." She shrugged and gave herself firm instructions not to fall apart.

"About Satin Doll," Madame Chloe said. "Wasn't York Masters her lover once upon a time? Before you came into town, I believe."

"Oh, yes. I-I know they were friends. Maybe they

were lovers." She tried to smile. "I've never discussed it with York."

"*Oui*, well, he is the one who found her dead, or so I heard," Madame said.

"That's right," Cherry agreed. "I heard the same thing. Didn't York find her, Jussie?"

"Yes. He and Doc Holliday found her. I thought we weren't going to talk about that now."

"Yes, she's right," the Count said. "Tell me less about Satin Doll's death and more about York Masters's interest in our new bookkeeper." He swung his gaze to Justine and squeezed her hand. "Is he in love with you?"

"No," Justine said, managing a laugh. "I don't know what you've heard, but York and I are only friends."

"Didn't look like only friends the night y'all went to the theater," Cherry said. "You two looked like lovebirds to me. Couldn't keep your eyes off each other."

Justine wished she could wring Cherry's neck. "That was a nice evening, but as I said, we're only friends." She made herself eat, but the food stuck in her throat. When it seemed that everyone was waiting for her to say something else, she abandoned any pretense of appetite. "Why are you all so interested in York?"

"We're not." The Count turned to face Madame Chloe again. "Are we interested in him, Chloe?"

"Not in the least." Madame Chloe's supercilious smile annoyed Justine. "Frankly, I don't care whether he lives or dies."

Justine set her fork down with a clatter, tired of the baiting. If she had enemies, she wanted to face them. Staring hard at Madame Chloe and then at the Count, she gathered her courage and chose her words carefully. "Is there something you want to say to me? Is this a reprimand of some sort? Because if it is, then please state it, and let's quit playing with words."

Madame Chloe arched a brow, but before she could respond the Count rose from his chair and extended a hand to his hostess.

"I see that you're finished, Chloe. Shall we have a sherry in your quarters?" His gaze swept the others. "You'll excuse us. As usual, Chloe and I have business to discuss."

"Oui." Madame Chloe put her hand in his and allowed him to escort her from the room, but not before she tossed a feline smile at the women she left behind.

"Who does she think she's fooling?" Babette said, helping the others clear the table and stack the dishes in the kitchen for Peachy to wrestle with tomorrow. "The Count belongs to nobody, Madame Chloe included."

"Aw, you're just jealous," Cherry teased. "Don't worry. He'll pay attention to you later. You know how him and Madame Chloe like to get off to themselves and count money."

"Yes, but she tries to act like she's his one true love or something, and that's pure hog slop," Babette said with a huff.

"Wasn't that a pretty suit he had on?" Cherry asked. "And did you get a good look at that horseshoe pin? Lordy, that cost a few dollars."

"And we helped pay for it," Blanche pointed out as she sauntered from the dining room. She was a slow-moving girl with a voice to match. "You never hear Madame Chloe or the Count thanking us for making money enough for those shiners."

"Where's Ivory?" Justine broke in, following Cherry into the kitchen.

"I dunno. He makes himself scarce when the Count's around. He hates him."

"Cherry, do you remember a girl Ivory liked by the name of Shelley?"

"Sure. I didn't know her, but I heard of her. Hey, Babette, you knew Shelley, didn't you?"

Babette nodded her blond head. "Yeah, what of it?"

Justine shrugged, trying to show only a casual interest. "Oh, nothing. Ivory mentioned her, that's all. He said he was in love with her," she explained, standing over a sink full of dirty dishes. "Should we fill this with water so these dishes will be easier for Peachy to wash up tomorrow?"

"Do what you want," Cherry said, breezing toward the door. "I don't have to wash them, so I don't have to worry about them."

Babette primed the pump beside the sink. "Good idea, Jussie. Cherry just doesn't care about helping anyone but herself." She looked at Justine. "So, Ivory was talking to you about Shelley."

"Yes. You knew her?"

"She was a sweet girl. Ivory fell head over heels for her, and that caused a problem." Babette lowered her voice to a whisper. "Madame Chloe and the Count don't take kindly to us messing with the piano player. Ivory got real crazy about Shelley and didn't want her to bed anybody else."

"What happened to her?"

"The Count finally had to take her off to another town to get her away from Ivory." Babette pumped some water into the sink before she continued. "Just like he had to do with Liz. Take my advice, honey, and don't get too friendly with Ivory. You might get hurt. The Count even told Ivory that if he starts up with another girl, he'll fire him. He's got Ivory so spooked that he carries a pistol around with him when the Count's in town because he thinks the Count wants to kill him."

"Ivory is packing a gun?" Justine shook her head, finding this news hard to reconcile.

"He sure is. He showed it to me. I told him I pity the person who taps him on the shoulder some night and gets a bellyful of lead for his trouble." She laughed at the thought. "I'd keep my distance if I was you. That poor boy's about half a bubble off plumb."

"I'll keep that in mind. What about the Count? You think he and Madame Chloe have something going on between them?"

"Maybe, but nothing regular. Madame Chloe likes to make everybody think she's got the Count under her thumb, but that's bull. The Count spreads it around." Babette dropped an eyelid. "He gets around to all of us sooner or later."

"H-he does?"

"Sure. He samples all us girls before he puts us to work. I guess it's part of his salary." She giggled and poked a playful finger into Justine's side. "Maybe he'll give you a go. He's good, honey. He'll curl your hair." She patted her frizzy mop. "Just look what he did to mine!"

Laughing, Justine waved Babette out of the kitchen and sat at the table to think about the Count and what his questions about York could mean. The prey was getting closer to the trap, but was the hunter really the hunted? Did the Count know York was hot on his trail? Had he known all along that Lizette's big brother was out for his hide? If he did, then she and York were in some mighty hot water.

The Count *must* know something, she thought. Why else would he have directed those questions about York as if they were darts? He was tipping his hand to her, giving her a glimpse of his full house, then waiting for her to up the ante like a damned fool or fold and accept her losses.

Justine dropped her head in her hands. She had to tell York! God, she hoped he was sober. She needed him to be steady as a rock!

A movement outside the back door sent a jolt through Justine, and she covered her leaping heart with one hand as her gaze swung to the glass in the door. Ivory peered in at her, grinning like a jack-o'-lantern. Justine motioned for him to come inside.

"What are you doing lurking out there?"

"Making sure it's all clear," Ivory said, dropping into one of the chairs around the rough-hewn table. "The Count's back, d'ya hear?"

"Yes, I met him at dinner."

"You'd best watch out, honey chile."

"Why?"

"Because he's not what he seems. Don't get blinded by his good looks and elegant clothes. Underneath all that he's a monster."

"Ivory, who do you take flowers to at night?"

"Nobody." He glared at her, daring her to refute him.

"I've seen you. Out there. Who is it? Why do you sneak off like that? Are you afraid she might disappear like Shelley if Madame Chloe or the Count finds out you've got another girl?"

He shot to his feet, his limbs jangling like a Halloween skeleton's. "I don't know what you're talkin' about. I'm not sneaking off to see no one." He shook a bony finger in her face. "You need to mind your own bees wax, honey chile. It's dangerous to go spouting things you don't know nothing about. Best keep your lip buttoned or you might end up very, very..." He paused long enough to swallow and make his Adam's apple jerk in his long throat.

"Very, very what?" Justine asked, feeling in her bones that he was about to say *dead*.

"Sorry," Ivory finished, then whirled and strode to the door, long legs stretching in front of him. "Very sorry." He pulled open the door, glanced back at her, then flung himself into the darkness. But before he disappeared his coattail flapped up to reveal a pearl handle sticking out of his trouser pocket.

"A pistol," Justine whispered to herself. "He *is* armed." Could Ivory have killed Shelley and Lizette? Maybe he acted in a jealous rage because "his" girls

had sported with other men. Was it possible that
Ivory Sparks was as crazy as a bedbug?

She fashioned a scene in her mind of Ivory falling
in love with Shelley and then Lizette and feeling betrayed when they kept sleeping with other men. Or
perhaps the straw that broke the camel's back was
when they remained faithful to the Count.

No, she thought, shaking her head. Everyone said
the Count had taken the girls away from Ivory. She
groaned, realizing she was so confused that her
mind was running in circles and getting her nowhere
except to the edge of exhaustion.

Justine closed her eyes and took a long, deep
breath. She exhaled, making herself relax. Don't
panic and don't look for wolves behind every tree,
she told herself. One thing was certain: Ivory was
lying about his evening trips. He was taking flowers
to someone—a secret love, perhaps—but who? Did
it have anything to do with Lizette or Shelley?

Pushing from the chair, she went to her room and
lit the signal lantern, placing it in the window for
York to see. The Establishment's location on top of a
hill made it visible from nearly every part of town,
but Justine thought York might have some lookouts
who reported to him. He was a sneaky little devil,
she had to admit, and there were many layers to
him.

Someone knocked softly at her door, making Justine jump. Could York have seen and responded to
her signal within barely a minute? Impossible, she
told herself.

"Who is it?"

"The Count, Jussie. Would you come out into the
office?"

"I . . . *oui.*" She gathered in a deep breath and took
the startled look off her face before opening the door
and stepping into the office.

The Count was sitting behind Madame Chloe's
desk, and he extended a hand, silently bidding her

to sit in the chair on the other side of it. He poured
brandy into two snifters and handed her one.

"I thought we might use this time to become better acquainted," he said, leaning back and breathing
in the brandy aroma. "Chloe is impressed with your
work."

Justine couldn't decide which was more silky, the
brandy or the Count's voice. "I'm glad. I like my
work here. I understand, however, that my position
is temporary."

"Only until I give my approval," he said, smiling
against the rim of the glass. "Where is your home?"

"Here." She shrugged. "I've moved around the
country quite a bit. I grew up mostly in New Orleans."

"But you are French?"

"Yes, both my parents were from France. I learned
French before I learned English."

He seemed pleased as he continued to sip the liquor. "Tell me about yourself."

"What do you want to know?"

"Everything."

She laughed, giving herself a few moments to select a past. "Everything? My life is an open book, but
not a very exciting one. My father was a sailor, my
mother was . . . a seamstress. I'm an only child, and
my parents spent most of their money on me. They
dressed me up like a little doll and paid for all kinds
of lessons for me—dance, piano, finishing school."
She took a drink of the brandy and felt it spread heat
through her as she warmed to her counterfeit history. "I'm a restless spirit, and when I left finishing
school, I never looked back."

"And since that time what have you done?"

"This and that . . . I've been an actress, bookkeeper, show girl, piano teacher." She shrugged and
drank some more brandy. "Whatever was necessary
and available."

"I'm puzzled." He set the snifter on the desk and

tented his fingers, looking across the tips to her. "Usually women with experience are easy for me to spot, but not you. From you I get no sense of a woman who has traveled many different roads with many different companions."

"I don't recall mentioning companions," she said, pleased that he had failed to trap her. "I've traveled alone and not so many roads as you seem to think. In fact, this is my first trip to the Southwest."

"What brought you here?"

"An acting troupe." She laughed, giving him time to appreciate the sound of it, husky and fetching. "A horrendous group of would-be actors led by a sweaty, oily man who called himself 'Monsieur Bonsoir.' He put his hands on me once too often, and I gave him a good swift kick. The next morning I woke up to find the troupe had left without me, taking all my personal belongings."

"You were robbed?"

"Yes, and left with nowhere to go. I was lucky to be taken in here."

"I feel you've left out large pieces of your past."

"Not really."

"You have no lover? No men who have claimed your heart?"

"In the past, a few. None now. Why are you smiling?"

"Because a woman of your beauty always has a suitor."

"York Masters, is that the name you want to hear? Why are you so interested in him? What's he done to you?"

"Nothing that I know of, but I'm curious as to why you deny having feelings for him when it's obvious to everyone else that you do."

"I told you he's a friend," she said, making her voice hard. "Are you calling me a liar?"

He said nothing, just smiled, and Justine found his smile just this side of sardonic.

"Well, are you?"

"You're a beautiful woman," he said, almost to himself. "Your eyes are like smoke. And where there is smoke, there is fire, yes?"

She sat back and laughed to herself. "You're a smooth talker, but I know when I've been steered onto a different path." She made herself hold his direct gaze, although something about it made her insides quiver. "Count, if you want me to stop seeing York Masters, then I wish you would just say so."

"And you would? Just like that?" He tipped back his head and laughed. "How accommodating! I like that in a woman."

"Yes, most men do," she parried with a smile. "Don't you have any other name to go with your, uh, title?"

"Yes, but none I care to share with you." His expression suggested he knew he was being rude and didn't care.

"Fine with me. I can assure you I won't lose sleep over it." She was proud of her courage, but soon felt it falter as he narrowed his black eyes in a slow burn. Justine called upon her acting talent and raised one brow in reproach, determined to impress the Count with her spirit. She sensed he was a man who welcomed a challenge, and she was determined to be one.

"Has anyone ever told you that you're a rash young woman who might do well to curb her tongue?"

"No. Would you like to be the first?"

His smile was slow in coming but worth the wait. Despite herself, Justine glowed inside when his smile hit her full force. It was beautiful, wide and cunning, reaching into his eyes to transform them into glittering pools. He poured himself another measure of brandy and lifted the glass in a silent toast.

"Has anyone ever told you you're ravishing?"

"Sorry, others have beat you to the draw on that one."

He laughed, the sound low and throaty like a purr. "So I thought. Would you do me the honor of having dinner with me tomorrow night?"

"Where?"

"In my room."

"Your room," she repeated.

"Up there." His gaze lifted. "In the attic."

She looked up at the tin ceiling. "Oh. I thought the only things that lived up there were bats."

"Will you?" he asked again.

"Yes, I'd like that. What time?"

"Seven. Just you and me." He stood and came around the desk, taking one of her hands and pulling her up from the chair. He kissed her hand, then turned it over and examined her palm.

"You are a passionate woman," he said, running his thumb across her skin. "But you have many faces, many moods."

"You read palms?"

"Yes."

Justine nodded, silently encouraging him to go on. It was nothing new to her. Jasmine Broadwater had taught her how to read palms and tea leaves, as well as to decipher the birth signs and read the "bones" of the voodoo magic.

"You put your faith in the wrong people. You're easily led. Someone is angling for your trust but will misuse it." His brow puckered. "You should be careful, Jussie. I see danger and death."

"My, my!" She shivered and withdrew her hand, but inside she laughed at him, knowing one couldn't read such things in a palm. "You're scaring me."

"I'm sorry." He chuckled and touched a fingertip to her lips, sliding it across them in a brief caress. "You don't believe in such nonsense, do you? Then you *are* easily led! How disappointing." He released her hand and strode from the office. He paused on the threshold and smiled. "Seven. On the dot. Don't make me wait." He started to close the doors, but then hesitated long enough to deliver one last parting shot. "Oh, and let's not lie to each other tomorrow night, hmmm?" He was gone before she could think of a retort.

"Well!" Justine propped her hands on her hips and retraced the conversation. When had she lost her balance? That man was slippery! One moment she was mentally congratulating herself, and the next she was being told she was easy prey and a liar!

In her room with the door closed firmly behind her, she wondered what the Count had in store for her tomorrow night. Just dinner, or did he expect something more? Babette had said he bedded all the girls. Was she considered one of them?

Somewhere in the back of her mind came a warning, and Justine realized that the lamp she'd lit earlier was dark. Only moonlight changed black to gray. She tensed, wondering if she might not be alone after all. Her mouth went dry, and she tasted coppery fear on her tongue. The shadows in the far corner split in two, one moving out from the other. Justine parted her lips to scream, but her heart was in her mouth. Before she could make a sound, a voice reached out to her.

"Honey, you'd better saddle your hoss before you sass the boss."

Chapter 22

The heartbeats drumming in her ears impaired her hearing. Justine plastered herself against the door, one hand groping for the knob. "Ivory?" she whispered, amazed she could speak at all. As soon as the outline of a man's broad shoulders came into focus, she knew she was wrong. Releasing her pent-up breath, she batted a hand at the intruder in a burst of aggravation.

"Ivory?" York's chuckle grated on her nerves. "My, my, isn't that telling? What would Ivory Sparks be doing in your bedroom? Have you been doling out your favors behind my back?"

She remembered that she was mad at him and drew on that. "You're not the least bit funny. You scared the life out of me." Cutting her eyes to the door, she raised a finger to her lips. "The Count could still be outside," she whispered.

"I know," he whispered back. "I've been eaves-dropping." He came closer until she could see the sparkle of his eyes and the gleam of his teeth. He bent down, and his lips brushed her ear. "I saw your signal and came running." He nipped lightly at the

326

lobe, his lips tugging playfully on her earbob.

Justine raised her shoulder, warding off his tick-ling caress. "How did you get in here?"

"The window."

Then his mouth found hers, surprising her. Jus-tine pushed against his shoulders, more in shock than anger, but he devoured her lips as if he were starving for her, and his flattery overruled her irrita-tion. She circled his neck with her arms and arched into him. Her middle pressed into his belt buckle, and she felt something different about him. Justine reached down, and her fingers closed over the gun butt. She struggled away from his drugging mouth.

"Why have you got that?"

"What? This?" He bumped against her, making her aware of something else besides his gun.

"No," she whispered, blushing hotly. "The gun, you fool. You've never worn it before."

"Yes, I have."

"Not around me."

"Now that the Count's in town, you can't be too careful."

"So you already knew he was here?"

"You smell good. What have you got on?" His hands covered her breasts, and his thumbs moved over the centers.

"What's gotten into you all of a sudden?" She slapped aside his wandering hands and slipped away from him. "A few hours ago you couldn't wait to see the last of me."

"That's a damn lie, Jussie." He glowered at her, but she could tell he wasn't really mad. "I'm trying to save your sweet life." He jerked a thumb behind him. "That piece of filth in there would just as soon cut your throat as take you to bed."

"I think he wants to do the latter first."

"You think that's funny?" He reached out, grabbed a handful of her hair, and brought her up against him. "I'm not laughing." He angled her mouth to his and arrowed his tongue inside, tasting the slick walls and making her moan. He kissed her until she was breathless and growing dizzy. When he lifted his mouth, she sucked in a huge breath and rested her forehead against his chin.

"Don't be mad at me, Jussie. This has nothing to do with you being an actress or what your mother did for a living. I just want you to be safe. After Satin . . . well, now I think I was wrong to make you help me."

"You're confusing me," she admitted. "You want me on your terms and only if I do as you ask, but I've been taking care of myself and making my own decisions for a long time, York."

She escaped his embrace and went to the door. Opening it a crack, she peeked out and was glad to see no one was there. They could talk safely. She closed the door and crossed the room to light the lamp again.

"The signal was because I needed to talk with you." She lost her train of thought when the light revealed his low-slung gun belt and the gun she'd felt earlier. "I can't get used to seeing you with one of those strapped on. It's not like you."

"I wear a gun most of the time. A man would be stupid not to in a town like Tombstone with animals like the Count roaming loose. It's just that I didn't think I needed one around you, but you're getting mighty dangerous." His eyes sparkled with devilish lights. "I figured I'd better arm myself." He laughed at her miffed expression. "Why did you think I was Ivory?"

"Because he's been acting strange," she said. He swayed toward her, and she staved him off by planting her hands on his chest and locking her elbows. She gave him a dubious look. "And he's not the only one who's acting strange around here." She tried to be serious, but he was making it a chore. "I want to talk to you about Ivory and the Count and Madame

Chloe." She sat on the bed and patted the place next to her. "Sit." Her glance was meant to gently scold. "And behave, please."

"A hard request to honor." He sat, making her bounce on the feather mattress. "Tell me what you know, then I'll tell you why I think tomorrow would be a good time to disappear—without the Count's help."

She sat straight, folding her hands in her lap. "We'll see." She felt her stubborn streak widen. Now that she'd met the Count, she wanted a chance to trip him up, but she'd save that for later. First, she had to make York see that she was clever enough for the job ahead. "About Ivory—he carries a gun." Her glance fell on his pistol again. "Seems like everyone does lately. Babette told me tonight that Ivory thinks the Count might try to kill him."

"Probably true."

"And the Count has warned him that if he messes with another Establishment girl, he'll fire him."

"Kill him, most likely. Ivory had better watch his back."

"You, too."

"Are you worried about me?" he asked, grinning as he tucked a finger under her chin and brought her face to his.

"The Count wanted to know about you." She saw the shock register on York's face and knew she finally had his full attention. "That's right. Both he and Madame Chloe questioned me about you tonight. If I was stupid, I'd think they just wanted to see how I felt about you because they supposedly lost their last bookkeeper to a secret lover, but I'm not stupid." She gripped his hand. "York, I think the Count knows you've been following him. The way he asked about you . . . well, he must suspect something. I think he wants to see me tomorrow night to find out what I know about your business here."

York sat back on the bed and stared up at the

shadowy ceiling before he heaved a sigh. "I find it hard to believe he *knows* I'm hot on his trail. I mean, when the hell did he find out? Has he known for days, weeks, months?"

"Does it matter? He knows. Enough said. That's why we *must* act quickly, or he'll slip through our fingers."

"Whoa, little lady." He sat up and twisted to face her. "That's my job, not yours. I wanted you to find out what you could from Madame's other girls *before* the Count arrived. He's here now, Jussie, so you can leave. I'll give you the money I promised, and you can get yourself clear of this mess. It's my worry, not yours."

"No!" she whispered fiercely, rising from the bed to pace.

"Jussie, honey—"

"And don't sweet-talk me," she rasped. "It's too late for that. I didn't want any part of this puzzle but you forced me into it. I tried to get what I could from the girls—"

"You've done fine."

"Just listen!" She pointed a finger at him and he grinned. "Listen," she warned, and he sobered. "I'm dead serious. You needed someone on the inside to gain everyone's confidence. Well, here I am!" She spread out her arms, beseeching him to see her as an asset instead of a problem. "The Count has asked me to dine with him alone—"

"That's what worries me," he interrupted.

"Why? It's perfect. I'll go, and I'll be on my toes. This time around I won't let him have the upper hand. I won't be jerked around. I'll give him a taste of his own medicine."

"Hold on." York stood up, gripping her shoulders to make her stand still. "The Count isn't stupid. He's had more women than a dog has fleas, and there's nothing about them he doesn't know. If you think you can wrap him around your little finger, angel, you're wrong. When it comes to getting what he wants, he holds every card, so don't try to beat him at his own game."

"York, I *know* he killed your sister and the others, and I *think* Madame Chloe might have killed that other bookkeeper, Donna." She gripped his lapels and pulled herself up on her tiptoes. "Give me a chance to bring him out for you. Tell me how to do it. Tell me how to make him run from cover so you can expose him for what he is. I want to help."

"Why? You've been kicking and screaming about leaving for weeks. Why are you so all-fired determined to stick around now? And don't say it's because you love me. If you did, you'd do what I'm asking and skedaddle while you're still in one piece."

She let go of him and sat on the bed again, her head bowed as her thoughts took shape.

"Well?" he persisted. "I'm waiting. Give me one good reason why I shouldn't pack your bags and get you out of here right this minute."

Her head came up. "Because I can't run away this time. I've got to *do* something. All my life I've stood by and watched the users and the takers run over people like me . . . and Lizzie and Satin. I hid in the shadows and let it happen. Monsters like Madame Chloe and the Count." She shook her head, remembering details about Chloe and how it all added up to one thing—the woman was evil through and through. "I know you're after the Count, but Madame Chloe's soul is just as black as his. She and that bookkeeper were more than friendly, and everything was fine and dandy until Donna met up with a lucky miner and decided it was time to leave Chloe behind for greener pastures." As she warmed to her story, she saw that York was hooked as well. "Do you think Chloe would let anyone use her? Hell, no! Chloe is the user around here. She works these girls and takes the money they make—just gives them enough to get by—and then she spends the money on chocolates and clothes and other fancy things for herself. When she got wind that Donna was getting ready to hit the road, Chloe decided she couldn't allow that to happen. She'd given Donna a job, a room, little gifts, and this was her thanks? Chloe isn't satisfied unless she owns you. Until your life is hers." Justine went to the sideboard to pour herself a glass of water.

"And she killed Donna?" York asked as Justine drank thirstily. "That's what you're getting at? Well, I agree, she probably did. But she'll fall right along with the Count. I'll see to it."

Justine set the glass down and faced York again. "I know what she was thinking at the time: the Count had gotten away with killing people who were no longer useful to him or were too much trouble, so Chloe decided she'd follow his lead. She killed Donna and got away with it!" She balled her hands into tight fists. "I'm sick of it! Sick of watching people like them use the downtrodden, the poor, the simpleminded, the frightened, the weak, and not be punished for it!"

"I'll get them. Don't you worry."

"But I want to help, York. I've stood in the shadows too long. I've turned the other cheek too often. Satin was right—it's not enough to look after yourself while people around you are hurting, suffering, dying."

Concerned, he took her fists in his hands, and his touch made her relax. She laced her fingers through his. "Jussie, you sound guilty and there's no need for that. You've done more than—"

"I haven't done anything. When Jasmine Broadwater died I didn't try to find out who killed her. I just ducked into the shadows and watched my back. And when Old Shoe Black was killed—saving my life—I cried, but I didn't do anything. I knew the men who killed him. They hung around the docks all the time. I should have gone to the law, but I didn't. I just cowered. I let my fear, my weakness, win over my love for him. When I think about it now"—tears burned her eyes—"I'm . . . so ashamed."

"Honey, there's no need for that." York drew her against him and held her tightly. "You're being way too tough on yourself. I think Satin Doll's death has rattled both of us more than we know."

"It's not just that." She rubbed her cheek against the front of his shirt. The flat mother-of-pearl buttons felt cool against her hot skin. "Her death started me thinking . . . it kind of dredged up the shame and helplessness I felt when Old Shoe Black was killed." She pulled back to look into York's eyes. "Not caring enough to stand up for what's right is why there are towns like Tombstone, dangerous towns. How many people are buried at Boothill because nobody would give them a helping hand? The Count and Madame Chloe have gotten away with murder, York. This time I can help because I have you standing beside me." She stood on tiptoe and kissed his lean cheek. "I can help draw the Count out so you can trap him."

"How?"

"By telling him about that necklace—that I know it's Lizzie's and I know Lizzie wasn't taken to any town but was most likely murdered by him."

"No, no, no," he chanted, moving away from her. He held his hair from his forehead for a second, then let it fall in its usual disarray. "That kind of confession will get you strangled, angel."

"Then what?" she pleaded, hands outstretched. "I've got a golden opportunity tomorrow night. Let me use it!"

"Hold up . . ." He lifted his hands, warding off her pleas. "Let me think a minute." He sat on the bed and cradled his head in his hands. Minutes ticked by before he pulled his head from his hands and looked at her. "What will keep him from bedding you or hurting you?"

"You."

"Me? How?"

"You can be close by." She glanced at the window. "Outside."

"How can I do anything for you out there?"

"You can see the attic window from the street."

"Yes," he allowed.

"Then if anything happens, if I feel I'm in danger, I'll signal from that window, and you can break in and rescue me." She propped her hands on her hips and smiled, feeling satisfied with her plan. York grinned back at her.

"You know how long it takes to kill someone?" He snapped his fingers. "That long, honey. I can't run that fast."

"York," she said, groaning, "don't make this so impossible. If I make the Count think he's about to get caught, he'll make a run for it."

"And what will that prove?"

"I don't know!" She flung out her arms, exasperated. "You're the detective, not me!"

York paced, absorbed in thought. "So, the Count knows I'm trailing him. I figured something like this might happen. I've asked a lot of questions along the way. Somebody tipped him off." He shrugged. "But what's done is done. Now that he suspects, I should force a face-to-face meeting while there's still time. If he gets too suspicious, he'll hightail it back to France and stay low until things cool off. I can't let him slip the noose."

"No, we can't let that happen. That's why—"

"Jussie, shut your trap a minute, will you?" He smiled then, taking the edge off his brusque request. "We're not going into this with guns blazing and our eyes shut. You can go tomorrow night, but I don't want you spouting a bunch of accusations at him.

He'll slit your throat before I can get the front door open."

"Then what? What can I do?"

"Drop crumbs that will lead him to me." He smiled. "Like that fairy tale. Tell him you don't think I'm a faro dealer. Tell him I'm closemouthed about where I came from and why I landed in Tombstone." His smile became nearly sinister. "Tell him I've been asking lots of questions about him, Madame Chloe, and their business." He held up a warning finger. "But make sure he understands you haven't given me any information. Tell him I asked about things like when he was coming to town and where he took Lizzie and the others when they left Tombstone. You understand?"

"Yes, I see. You want me to make him think I'm not as charmed with you as everyone thinks."

"That's right. Run me down."

"Shouldn't be hard," she teased. "I'll tell him you think you're more handsome than a four-hundred-acre spread. I'll tell him you just don't lift my skirts high enough."

He laughed and looped an arm around her waist. "Don't pour it on too thick, but you've got the right idea. Can you handle it?"

"With my eyes closed."

"Keep them open—wide open—around the Count. If he tries to make you sleep with him, then what?"

"I'll signal you somehow."

"No." He shook his head. "Not good enough. Tell you what. I'll give you exactly one hour to set your trap, then—"

"One hour? That's not long enough. I'm going to have dinner with him and—"

"And I don't want you to be his dessert. One hour, then I'll arrange some kind of interruption."

"What?"

"Leave that to me. I'll think of something. You

just drop those crumbs within an hour, okay?"

"But what good will crumbs do?"

"They'll either make him come to me or run from me. Either way, I'll be one step ahead of him."

"And what will you do?"

"Never you mind." He framed her face in his hands and kissed her. "I'll get him. I'll get both of them."

"How?"

"You just concentrate on doing your job. Promise me you'll follow my orders to the letter? You won't say anything more than what I've told you to say. Give him a little rope, and he'll hang himself; too much and he'll hang you and me, understand?"

"Yes."

"I have your promise that you'll do as I told you?"

"Yes," she said, nodding impatiently. "But what about afterward? What do you think will happen? A gunfight? Will he call you out?"

"No, that's what brave men do. Cowards aim at your back. That's what I'm expecting from the Count." He kissed her, his lips lingering on hers. "Why don't I stay the night?"

"No." She pressed away from him, tempted but wary. He wanted her, and she wanted him, but what would come of it? Their final good-bye loomed, and she had to guard her heart. It was going to break, but there was no use in having it shattered completely. "I think you should leave. Let's not take any chances on being caught."

"You're still sore at me."

"I'm not. I . . . I'm just not in the mood."

"I could get you in the mood," he offered with a smile.

"York, please." She pushed his hands away and moved to the other side of the bed. "Will you just leave?"

He was quiet for a few moments, then shrugged.

"Okay. If that's what you want." He went toward the window to make his exit.

"York!"

"Yes?"

She wanted to hold him, to get him to love her back, but she said, "You won't try to be a hero and get yourself shot full of holes, will you?"

"I'll dodge every one of them." He grinned and blew her a kiss. "If you need me before tomorrow night, put the lantern in the window and I'll be here in a flash. And remember that your days under this roof are numbered. I'm not going to take any back talk on that, Jussie. After tomorrow night, you're out of here."

"I'll leave peacefully," she assured him.

He threw one leg over the windowsill and dropped out of sight.

Chapter 23

Ascending the narrow staircase to the attic room, Justine felt her chest tighten with apprehension. She went over what she should say and how to say it, then knocked on the door. It swung open to reveal a more casually dressed Count than she'd seen before. He wore white trousers, a white shirt, and a deep plum smoking jacket.

"You are prompt. I respect that in a woman," he said, taking her hand and leading her across the threshold. His sweeping gaze took in her cream-colored dress's simple lines and minimum of bows and ruffles.

Supper had arrived before her and was laid out on a round table just big enough for two and covered with a lace cloth. Two tall candles threw flickering light across the fine china and polished silver.

"Let's have a glass of wine first," the Count said, already pouring. "Wine is such a civilized drink, don't you agree? Animosity simply can't exist in the same room with it."

"Were you expecting animosity from me?"

"No, should I?" He handed her a crystal glass. "To

a delightful evening," the Count intoned, and tapped his glass against hers. He pulled out one of the leather wing chairs at the table. "Won't you sit down?"

"Thank you." She did, then made a slow survey of the room. The attic was spacious, with exposed rafters and a smooth wood floor. One corner was partitioned off by an Oriental screen, and Justine guessed that behind it was the Count's bed—and the blasted window. It wouldn't be easy to get to, but she'd do it if necessary. York was supposed to be out there watching, waiting.

The Count sat in the other wing chair, crossing one leg over the other. His white clothes accentuated his dark good looks.

"So you have befriended the piano player."

She was thankful she wasn't sipping her wine because his question constricted her throat. Justine's gaze snapped to his, and she saw that he wasn't as casual as he appeared.

"Ivory Sparks?" she asked, then lifted one shoulder in a halfhearted shrug. "He's a sweet man. Kind of melancholy, don't you think?"

"I think he is sometimes strange."

"Strange?" Justine smiled, thinking this was certainly an instance of calling the kettle black. "How do you mean?"

"You are best friends with him, non?" he asked, ignoring her questions.

"Not best friends, no. I think he's funny. There's nothing going on between us, if that's what you mean. In fact, I think Ivory has a girl."

"Who?"

Justine went cold all over. What had she done? Betrayal stabbed her heart. Had her carelessness placed Ivory in danger? "No one here at the Establishment," she said, trying to smooth over her blunder.

"Why do you think this? He's told you?"

"No, but I've seen him taking flowers to someone. It's nothing." She moved her hand as if to dismiss the thought, and some of the wine spilled over the side of her glass. "Oh, dear." She took the napkin the Count offered and wiped the wine from her hand. "Could we eat now? I'm hungry." And in a hurry, she tacked on mentally.

"But of course."

While he uncovered bowls of fried chicken, green peas, and Mexican corn, Justine got herself back on track. Don't panic, she told herself. Stay calm. Make him dance to *your* tune and quit reacting to everything he says. She accepted the plate of food he prepared and decided to knock him off balance a bit.

"Let's pray," she announced curtly. She bent her head and folded her hands before the Count could beg off. "Dear Lord," Justine intoned, peeking through her lashes to witness the Count's momentary confusion before he bent his head. He kept his eyes wide open and staring into his lap. "We thank you for this food and for the roof over our heads. Keep us safe from those who would break your commandments, and for those who do go against your will, may they burn in hell with no mercy," she finished harshly, then added sweetly, "Amen." She looked up expectantly, her gaze challenging.

"Amen," he whispered, and irony floated in his black eyes. "You are religious?"

"Well, I could do a sight better, but I give thanks where thanks is due."

"Shall we eat now? All finished with your rituals?"

She smiled and turned her attention to the food, though she had no appetite. Mentally, she congratulated herself and endeavored to keep the Count off guard. Now for those crumbs. . . .

"So, Ivory takes bouquets to someone," the Count said, returning to the very subject Justine hoped to avoid.

"Yes." Justine drew a deep breath, determined to make him follow her lead and not the other way around. It occurred to her that this wasn't a dinner engagement, but a contest of wills. "There's no reason to worry about Ivory. Let's talk about you. For instance, why—"

"May I be frank?"

"Please," she said, puzzled.

"I'm afraid Ivory might have done something regretful. He might be in trouble—again."

"Again?" she asked, then wished she could kick herself. Ivory wasn't the man of the hour, York was! She had a message to deliver, a gauntlet to throw down, and the Count was keeping her from it, damn him!

He settled back and drummed his fingers on the tablecloth. "You see, Ivory Sparks doesn't just fall in love, he becomes obsessed. That is why it troubles me to hear that he might be seeing another woman. He's too shaky in the head to handle a relationship. You must not entice him, *ma petite.* Even befriending him is flirting with disaster."

"Oh, I'm not worried," she said nonchalantly.

"I had to remove one of the girls because she'd grown afraid of Ivory Sparks. He was obsessed with her, as I've said, and she begged me to take her far away from him, which I did. He hasn't forgiven me for that, but I know I did the right thing. Before that, one of the girls Ivory courted disappeared." He looked away, then swung his gaze back to Justine with a suddenness that made her heart slam into her throat. "I believe Ivory killed her. You see, no one ever heard from her again. She vanished. When I questioned Ivory, he flew into a rage."

"Her name..." Justine swallowed, feeling as if her mouth were stuffed with cotton. "What was her name?"

"Shelley."

"And the other? The one you had to remove?"

"Lizette."

The names resounded in her head. "Lizette's doing all right? I mean, she's happy now that she's away from Ivory?"

"She was."

"Was?" She's dead, Justine thought. Dead. I knew it.

"The last time I saw her..." He shrugged. "She left my employ a couple of months ago."

"Where did she go?"

He tilted his head to one side, and she knew she'd gone too far, asked one question too many.

"Ivory wouldn't track her down, would he?" she asked, trying to cover up her pesky interrogation. "Could he be taking flowers to *her*?"

"To her?..." The Count's eyelids drooped, and he seemed to look into himself for several seconds, then he shook his head ever so slightly and laughed. "Could be, but it's doubtful." He frowned. "My talk has upset you." His lower lip protruded in a forced pout. "I am sorry, Jussie."

"No, it's just that..." She shook off the diversion. "I was thinking about York Masters."

Got you, she thought when the Count's head rocked back as if he'd been punched.

"What about him?"

"You were asking about him before, and something struck me." She leaned forward as if to divulge a secret, and the Count followed suit. "I don't think he's really a faro dealer." She sat back to smile smugly at his arched brows.

"Why not?"

"Well, because he only works when he's good and ready. I've asked him about where he comes from and how he ended up here, and he just buttons up. If I nag him for answers, he gets mad and says it's none of my business."

"I admire a man who values his privacy."

"I'm glad you're an admirer of his because he sure is interested in you."

The Count laid his fork aside, dabbed at the corner of his mustache with the linen napkin, and sat back, obviously giving up any pretense of eating. "He has asked questions concerning me?"

"A wagonload of them," she confirmed, glad to have him dancing on her strings for a change.

"What questions exactly, cherie?"

"Exactly? . . ." She pretended to mull this over. "When you were expected in town, where you take the girls after they leave here, if the girls act scared of you—things like that."

"And your answers?"

"Answers?" She shrugged. "What answers? I didn't know when you were coming or what other towns you go to. As far as anybody around here acting scared"—she let go of another huge shrug—"I never saw it. He got mad at me for being such a dummy, but that's his problem. Besides, I never have thought he cared much for me. He's too full of himself. Whew! I've never known a man more bewitched by his own reflection in my whole life!" She laughed, winning a smile from the Count. "I know everyone around here thinks I'm head over heels for him, but it's just not true."

The Count traced the design in the tablecloth and smiled thoughtfully. "I wonder if I should believe any of what you've just told me."

Justine felt her courage waver. She'd thought she had him hooked, but he was only teasing her. Looking directly into his eyes, she gave him her coldest, boldest glare.

"Count, you can believe what you want. It's nothing to me. I just thought you might want to know that somebody in town is interested in your whereabouts, that's all." She flung her napkin down in a huff. "You'll have to excuse me. Being called a liar is just not my cup of tea."

She would have risen, but his hand clamped down on hers, and his glittering black gaze made her stay put. His touch gentled into a caress, showing her that he was pleased she'd obeyed his silent command.

"There, there," he cajoled. "Forgive my rash ways. I'm glad you've told me about York Masters and his questions. I just don't understand it all. Why would this stranger be asking about me?"

"I'll tell you what I told him," she said, smiling. "I don't know."

He laughed at that, making her laugh with him. "Maybe he's a detective on the trail of his sister's killer."

She had no mirror in which to gauge her reaction, but Justine felt sure she was successful in reflecting only confusion, although her heart stopped momentarily and fear corkscrewed through her stomach. "A detective?" She smiled, feeling it on her lips but nowhere else. "That sounds exciting! Do you think so? And what did you say about his sister? She was killed?"

"You take me literally," the Count said, laughing at her. "I was only weaving a story." He laughed again and squeezed her hand. "There you go again, being easily led."

"Yes, well..." She shrugged. "I guess I am a little gullible at times, especially when there's an adventure afoot."

"I believe you might work out fine here. Just fine."

"But my position is only temporary," she reminded him.

"Unless I approve of you, which I do."

"You do?" she asked, holding her breath. Had she really fooled him? Did he believe her to be no threat to his business?

"Oui, very much so. Would you like to stay on here at the Establishment?"

"Oui, very much so." Her parroting made him laugh again. Laugh hard, Count, she thought, it may be your last.

"I see no reason why you shouldn't stay on," he said. "There's just one small problem. . . ."

"There is?" She waited for the other shoe to fall.

"Madame Chloe told me you didn't like it when she asked you to work upstairs one evening."

Ah! She knew Chloe would come into this somehow. The white spider and her black count. Justine sighed and put an expression of remorse on her face. "I've tried that sort of thing and found I'm not any good at it. Besides, I was hired as a bookkeeper. There was never any mention of my being anything else."

His smile was no longer attractive, his eyes no longer warm. "I'm telling you now, ma petite, if you stay here you must learn to enjoy the work—all of the work that's required of you." His hold on her hand tightened, and Justine glanced toward the window. Now? Should she make a run for it? "This is a house of pleasure," he said, capturing her other hand as well. "And you will be expected to pleasure your share when you're called upon. I will instruct you."

"Instruct me?" She stilled, feeling only the thud-thudding of her labored heart.

"Oui." He said the single word slowly, letting his lips purse around it before he let it go. His thumbs massaged the insides of her wrists where her pulse fluttered. "I do this for all my girls. I am a good teacher, ask any of them. When I am finished with you, you will be able to pleasure each and every man you are with. Two, three at a time, even."

The thought of that drained the color from her face, and she had to struggle not to turn away from his powerful gaze.

"Sex is my specialty," he went on. "I know every position, every trick of the trade. I will show you how to please a man and how to arouse him with your hands and mouth. *Est-ce que vous comprenez?*"

She nodded that she understood him, unable to speak past her disgust. He leaned forward, raising her hands to place feathery kisses on them. It was all she could do to endure them.

"When I'm through with you, you'll be the best whore at the Establishment. I promise you."

Justine stared into his eyes and saw that she'd mistaken warmth for the black flames of hell.

A voice, loud and raucous, broke through the tension. Justine looked toward the door, wondering if this was York's diversion. Other voices sounded, feminine ones, and then gunshots split the air.

"What is that?" the Count said, almost growling. He crossed to the door and threw it open, letting the sounds of panic into the attic. From below came shouts, screams, and another gunshot. "Damn it. What's going on down there?"

Seizing the moment, Justine slithered past him and hustled down the stairs.

"Come back here!"

She paused, looking over her shoulder. "Don't you want to see who's causing all the commotion? I do!" She went on, nearly flying down the stairs to the lower floors, feeling as if she'd escaped in the nick of time.

The shouting came from the foyer, but the voice wasn't York's. Running down the last flight of stairs, Justine was amazed to find a staggering, cussing, gun-toting Doc Holliday. Like frenzied bees, the Establishment girls flew around him, trying to take the gun away before he could blow another hole in the ceiling. The queen bee, Madame Chloe, stood off to one side, her hands clutched under her chin and her eyes wide with hysteria.

"Get it away from him!" Madame screamed. "Next he'll shoot somebody instead of just my ceiling!" She looked toward Justine. "You! Get that gun away from him!"

"M-me?" Justine asked.

"No, me."

Justine whirled to find Wyatt Earp behind her. He smiled and gently pushed her to one side.

"Excuse me, ma'am."

"Of course," Justine murmured as he went past. He was tucking in his shirttails, leading her to understand that he'd paid for his time and had been interrupted by Doc's uproar.

"I want a woman, and I want one now!" Doc yelled, hooking an arm around Cherry Vanilla's waist. "You'll do, honey bunch."

"Doc, give me that gun." Wyatt reached up and twisted it out of his hand. "What are you shooting up this place for?"

"That witch said I couldn't have a woman," Doc said, slurring his words and glaring at Madame Chloe.

"Not for free," Madame amended. "You said you had no money."

"I don't. Lost it all at the gaming table tonight. That's why I need some comforting." He grinned at Cherry and gave her a smacking kiss. "I feel better already."

"Get him out of here," Madame said, her voice rising. "Look what he's done to my property. You're going to pay for this!" Her voice was shrill, her eyes bright with fury. "You can't come in here and shoot up my place without paying dearly."

"What will you do?" Wyatt asked with a jeering grin. "Kill him?"

"Maybe I will!" Madame shot back. "Don't tempt me."

"That is quite enough, Chloe."

Justine pressed against the wall, giving the Count free access to the foyer.

"Count," Wyatt said, still grinning. "Back in town again, I see."

"You figured that out all by yourself, did you? I'm impressed," the Count said, barely glancing at Wyatt, directing his black gaze at Doc instead. "If this man is a friend of yours, I advise you to take him away. Otherwise, I'm sending for the sheriff."

"That makes me and Doc shake in our boots," Wyatt returned with a laugh, but he yanked Doc away from Cherry. "Let's go, pard. There are friendlier pleasure palaces in town."

"Don't come back here unless you have money in hand," Chloe ordered, her voice still nearly a shriek. "Better yet, don't come back at all!" She stared at the plaster on the floor. "Look what he's done!"

Wyatt escorted Doc from the house, glancing back once at Justine and sending her a cheery message with his eyes. The Count slammed the door behind them and turned toward Chloe. She sniffed, then rested a limp wrist against her forehead.

"This has upset me so," she whined. "I won't be able to sleep now."

"You girls go back to your rooms," the Count said, shooing them with impatient hands. He met Justine's gaze and smiled. "You, too, cherie. There will be other nights for us." He took Chloe's hand. "Come, my dear, let's have a drink to settle your nerves. A little gunplay is no reason for you to fall apart."

"I never liked Doc Holliday or that Wyatt Earp," she groused as he led her toward her quarters. "And they don't like me. They think they own this town and I'm tired of it! Tired, you hear? Something must be done about them. I wish you would..." Her voice faded as the Count shut the door, sealing them off.

"Glory be!" Cherry rolled her eyes in exasperation. "Madame Chloe thinks everybody's out to ruin her business. You okay, hon?"

Justine started, realizing she was frozen to the spot. "Yes, I'm fine. Good night, everyone." She went to her room, closed the door, and silently thanked all concerned for the interruption. Moments later, something moved outside her window, then she saw Wyatt's face. Crossing the room, Justine opened the window.

"Evening, ma'am. Enjoy the show?"

"Yes, very much. Your timing was perfect." She glanced past him into the dark. "Where's York?"

"Nearby. He says for you to pack your things. He'll be around in an hour or so to take you to China Mary's. You'll be ready?"

"Yes."

"I'll tell him."

Justine closed the window, then dug her valise out of the closet and started stuffing her few belongings into it. The sooner she was away from the Establishment the better, she thought. She recalled Doc Holliday's performance and smiled. How much did he and Wyatt know about York and his business in Tombstone? Had they been helping him all along?

York would need all the help he could muster, Justine thought. The Count and Madame Chloe were a dangerous duo. A match most certainly made in hell.

*lined up. The Count, if he could, would see that that happened to her. Or him.

Where the Next? Was the place she'd escaped into—*

Chapter 24

⌢⌣◯◯⌢⌣

Fifteen minutes later Justine stood at the window, packed and ready to go. Anxiety nudged her, making her edgy. York, where are you? she wondered, wishing he would come early. She wanted to leave . . . now!

The moon was a lantern in the sky, illuminating the heavens and washing out the stars near it. A movement caught her eye and set her heart to pounding. York? He'd come early! Her vision sharpened to reveal a figure scampering down the hillside and into the valley's shadow. The bobbing walk could only belong to Ivory Sparks.

"Where are you going?" she whispered into the dark, then felt guilty again as she recalled her earlier slip when she'd told the Count about Ivory's midnight visits. "Who do you sneak off to see?" she asked.

The Count had tried to make her think Ivory was a lunatic, but she'd seen through that ruse easily enough. The Count was a lot closer to lunacy than openhearted Ivory Sparks. Ivory was flighty and full of hatred for the Count, but who could blame him? He'd lost two women to that vile man.

Staring at the place where Ivory had merged into the shadows, Justine thought her eyes were playing tricks on her when a ghostly image floated into view. She blinked hard, but the white figure remained constant. Someone else was taking Ivory's path, following in his footsteps. Someone wearing white. Justine gulped, and her heart froze solid for a few seconds. The Count. He'd been wearing white. Good Lord, he was following Ivory!

Guilt slapped her hard, making her heart start beating again and her mind start whirling. Oh, hurry, York, she pleaded. Hurry! Ivory's in danger and I need you to—

She silenced the inner plea, realizing she was depending on someone else to do the honorable thing. Don't make that same mistake, she told herself. *You* caused this, and *you* must do something about it! You can't wait for York. It'll be too late.

She raced from the room and out the back door, holding up her skirts for unencumbered flight. Pebbles slipped under her inadequate shoes, and she had to fight to keep from rolling like a tumbleweed down the hillside. Her heightened senses made her progress sound like a freight train in her ears, and she envisioned the two men ahead of her stopping to listen to the racket.

She tried to be quiet, but rocks and pebbles scuttled before her, sending others in their wake. Bramble branches whacked against her skirt, and her breath rattled in her throat, sounding for all the world like a blacksmith's bellows. Whoosh-*whoosh!* Whoosh-*whoosh!* Justine tried to hold her breath, but that made her dizzy, so she concentrated on not falling head over heels down the hill.

Reaching the sheltering shadows, Justine was glad to be out of the moon's spotlight. She paused to get her bearings and peer ahead at the makeshift path that crossed the narrow valley and then snaked up the next hill. Her head throbbed along with her hammering heart. Sweat beaded on her forehead, and the desert breeze made her shiver. It wasn't a warm night, but her agitation made her body temperature soar, and it felt like a summer day to her instead of a late-fall evening that was cooling toward dawn.

Her shoes sank into the sandy soil, making it all the more difficult to keep her footing. How far along the path was the Count, and how far was he behind Ivory? Should she call out and alert Ivory? No, a voice warned her, keep quiet.

If nothing else she'd discover Ivory's destination, she thought, hurrying across the flat valley floor. She hitched her skirts higher to take the swell of the land as it swooped up to form the next foothill. But she'd gone only a few feet upward when gunshots rang out. One sounded first, followed quickly by another.

Terrified, she fell, landing with a jarring thump on her backside. Her breath escaped in a rush, and she could only gasp, and blink into the blackness while her lungs screamed for oxygen. When she hauled in a life-giving breath, her head cleared, and she knew she was sitting in danger's path. That's when one more shot rang out. It sounded final—a killing bullet.

Scrambling to her feet, she raced back across the valley floor, then gathered up handfuls of her skirts and plowed up the hillside, her knees pumping hard.

A low-growing cactus caught her skirt, causing a mighty rip, but Justine kept grinding up the hillside, her flowering imagination convincing her the Count was right behind her, gun in hand and his heart set on more bloodshed. It *could* be Ivory, she thought. Ivory might have killed the Count. But her intuition said otherwise. In her heart, she knew the Count was alive and kicking.

And if he spotted her dashing through the moon-light, he'd know that she knew, and he'd have no choice but to silence her. Have to get away . . . have to get to York . . . run, run, run!

Prickly bushes and scrub brush dug their tiny fingers into her clothing, trying to trip her, slow her down, but she ran on with an energy rooted in un-adulterated fear. For once the Establishment looked like a haven to her, and she burst through the back door, tiptoed to her room, and closed the door be-hind her. Hurrying to the window, she glanced out and saw nothing but moonlit ground.

Pressing a hand to her laboring heart, she waited to catch her breath and gather her senses. Glancing around the room to make sure she wasn't leaving anything behind, she realized these might be her last few moments in the Establishment. She sighed, see-ing the end in sight. But first she must report to York, she thought, grabbing her valise and taking a determined step toward the door.

It swung open with a sinister *swoosh*.

Justine smothered a scream as Madame Chloe slammed the door and blocked the exit. The other woman's gaze locked on the valise, her smile hate-ful.

"All packed up and ready to hit the trail with your Pinkerton detective?" Madame Chloe asked, almost purring. "Are you surprised I know all about your pathetic little plan?" She laughed low in her throat. "The Count saw right through you, cherie. He said you'd run away tonight—or try to." Her gaze slipped to Justine's torn dress and the briars clinging along the hem. "But it seems you've already been outside once. I must be just in time."

"Get out of my way," Justine ordered.

"You will not run from me. I warned you."

"And I'm warning you. Move!"

"I was good to you, and this is how you show your gratitude? You must be taught some manners."

One of the madam's hands slipped down her skirt toward her bulging pocket.

Realizing that Madame Chloe was reaching for a gun, Justine surged forward. She tried to push the other woman aside, but Madame Chloe was stronger than she looked. Suddenly her hands clutched Justine's hair. She yanked Justine's head back, making her howl with pain. Justine caught the woman's wrists, and it took all her strength to hold Madame Chloe away from her.

Still out of breath from her race back to the house, Justine felt her arms tremble from the effort. Madame Chloe got one hand free and clawed at Justine's cheek, drawing blood. Anger and frustration pumped through Justine. She kicked the woman in the leg, throwing her off balance, then shoved her clear off her feet.

"You witch! You can't bully me like you do the others. I'm leaving, and you can't stop me!"

She started for the door, but Madame Chloe grabbed her ankle and she fell forward, striking her chin on the bed frame as she went down. She saw stars, then pain shot through her head. Before she could think clearly or react, Madame Chloe pounced, straddling her and fastening her cold hands around Justine's throat. Her fingers felt like bands of steel pressing in on her, crushing her neck. Choking, Justine tried to upend Chloe, but she couldn't. She hadn't the strength. Blackness threatened, and her lungs began to collapse. Her eyes closed of their own accord.

Then there was blinding light. Air suddenly rushed down her throat to inflate her lungs. She rolled onto her side, no longer pinned by the heavy weight. She clutched her aching throat and coughed violently, gripped by the need to breathe again, to live again. She blinked away her tears, and her eyes focused.

"Don't you go pulling a gun on me, you silly bitch," a man said.

She heard a smart slap, a strangled cry, then Chloe fell a few feet from her, obviously sent to the floor by a blow. She clutched a six-shooter in one hand, but she was no longer in any condition to use it.

Justine looked up into Wyatt Earp's lean face and sighed.

"You all right, darlin'?" he asked her.

She nodded, smiled, and promptly fainted.

"What are you doing here?" York asked when Wyatt stepped out on the front porch of the Establishment.

"I thought you'd be at China Mary's by now," Doc added.

"There was some gunfire a little while ago, and I came to check into it." Wyatt hitched a thumb over his shoulder. "Behind here in those foothills. Y'all go. I'm staying with Jussie."

"Jussie?" York started up the porch steps, but Wyatt held him back. "Go see who got shot. Jussie's okay."

"Come on." Doc grabbed York's sleeve and tugged him along. "Maybe somebody blew a hole through the Count and saved you the trouble."

"I hope not. I want that bastard myself." York broke into a run, heading back behind the Establishment and down the incline to the valley floor. Heart pounding, boots rapping, breath rasping, he struggled to keep his footing. He could hear Doc behind him, puffing like a train coming into a station.

It seemed to take hours instead of minutes to cover the few yards of ground. Dodging cactus and low shrubs, York tried to see ahead through the dense brush as he ascended the next hill. He could hear Doc struggling for breath, but he didn't dare slow down. He'd caught the scent of his prey, and there was no turning back for him.

Whoever might be ahead could surely hear them, he thought. Then he tripped and went sailing. He landed on something softer than hard earth. When his vision cleared, he found he was staring into Ivory Sparks's lifeless eyes.

"Christ!" York rolled off the body and scrambled to his feet. "Look, Doc, it's Ivory."

Doc went down on one knee and turned the body over. Ivory Sparks had been shot in the back and then through the head. Flowers lay scattered around his body.

"The Count," Doc said, rising to his feet. "He must be ahead of us." Doc wheezed and gasped.

"I'll go on. You hang back and get your breath."

"I'm okay," Doc grumbled, then released a hacking cough.

"I know, but pull Ivory out of the path, then catch up with me." York forged ahead before Doc could object.

Trying to be quiet but finding it impossible, York ducked and scuttled from one shadow to the next until he reached a grassy knoll broken up by heaps of stones and...he squinted. What were those structures? Remnants of a burned house? His eyes widened when he realized he'd stumbled upon an old graveyard. The stilted frames were Indian funeral pyres. It must not be used anymore, he thought. He'd never heard of a cemetery up here.

He started to skirt around it when he noticed the fresh flowers on two of the graves. Flowers... bouquets. York looked back over his shoulder, thinking of Ivory and those flowers scattered around him. He'd been bringing flowers here to these graves.

"Oh, my God," York whispered, staring at the mound nearest him. Lizette? All this time Ivory had known where she was.... A change in the light put him on guard.

York rested his hand on the butt of his gun, thumbing aside the backstrap for a quick draw. For a moment he thought his eyes had fooled him, then he sensed a presence behind him and knew he'd been caught in the old circle-behind-and-ambush-'em ploy. Whoever had been in front of him was now placing the cold tip of a revolver against the base of his neck.

"Good evening, Masters," the Count said pleasantly. "Or should I say, LeMasters? Now, turn around very slowly. That's right. Slow . . . very slow."

When he'd turned only halfway around York saw the gun. It was within his reach! In one fluid motion he sent his elbow up high as he whipped around, slamming it into the Count's gun. The Count fired, but his aim was ruined, and the bullet ripped the sky, then the gun sailed out of his hand and landed with a thump somewhere nearby.

The Count moved more quickly, and before York could draw on him, the Count bent double and rammed his head into York's stomach. The force of the blow sent York backward. He fell hard with the Count in tow. Fingers of iron wrapped around York's throat and began cutting off his air. York wrestled one fist free and smashed the Count's chin, rocking him back long enough for York to get in another blow, this one landing just under the man's left eye.

York bucked, trying to dislodge him. He landed another fist alongside the Count's head, making him grunt with pain, then grappled for a better hold, seizing the Count's shirt collar. Dust rose up as the two fought, bit, kicked, and wrestled for superiority. York managed to roll to his hands and knees and was on the verge of springing to his feet when he felt a mighty tug, swiftly followed by the gut-burning realization that the Count had removed his own gun from his holster.

"Stop right there," the Count said between heaving gasps. "Stay on your knees, Pinkerton man. I like you that way."

Aggravated, York felt like a damned fool. Stupid! Letting that man get your gun. Stupid, stupid. Then his aggravation melted in the heat of his fear as he became aware that he was facing the last minutes of his life. He looked down and saw he was kneeling on one of the graves, one with a wilted bouquet. Beyond it, too far to easily reach, the Count's gun glinted in the moonlight. So close, but so far away. A lifetime away.

"Is this Lizzie's grave?" he asked, hoping for more time.

"No, that's Shelley. Lizzie is next to her, I think."

York narrowed his eyes, straining to see beyond his sister's grave. "There are more, aren't there? Those others aren't Indian graves. They're too new."

"Yes, there are others. Ten, maybe more. I lose count. Lizzie was your sister, am I right?"

"Yes, you bastard, she *was* my sister." York gritted his teeth, sick that he couldn't get his hands around the Count's neck. "Why couldn't you have let her go? Why did you have to kill her?"

The Count made a regretful sound. "Loose ends, Pinkerton man. The people I work for don't like loose ends. We hire the girls and give them a good life as long as they pull their own weight. When they cease to do so, then we must . . . eliminate them." There was a smile in his voice. "If your sister had only done what was requested of her, she'd be alive today."

"Murdering son of a bitch," York muttered, staring at the gun in the moonlight. God, if only . . .

"Say your prayers now—"

"What about Ivory?" York swallowed hard. His mouth was dry, his tongue a dead weight. "He knew you'd killed them, so why didn't you get rid of Ivory before now?"

The Count sighed. "I wanted to, but Ivory had

made himself part of this community. He'd be missed. Nobody paid any attention when the fallen angels left town suddenly, but Ivory's leaving would draw notice. He told everyone who'd listen that he'd *never* leave Tombstone of his own free will." The Count sighed, disgusted. "He even played piano in church every Sunday. All the little old ladies of the town doted on him."

York's estimation of Ivory increased. "Smart fella. Bought him some time, didn't he?"

"His time ran out tonight, and so has yours." The voice was cold, deadly.

"At least have the guts to face me when you pull the trigger."

"I don't think so," the Count said, laughing under his breath. "That's how gentlemen do it, and I'm no gentleman. Be happy, Pinkerton man. I'm sending you to join your dear sister. . . ."

York stiffened and looked up at the starry heavens. He told himself to pray for his soul, but the only word that whispered past his lips was, "Jussie."

The wheezing cough sounded like a dynamite blast in the deathly quiet. Sensing the Count's stunned alarm, York ducked and rolled in the direction of the other gun. A bullet plowed into the dirt near him, sending up a spray of pebbles and grit, but it didn't break his momentum. Before the Count could squeeze off another shot, York had the other gun in hand and was on his feet facing his sister's murderer.

Time slowed, clearly showing the Count's shocked expression as he stared at the last face he'd ever see. York smiled with satisfaction, and the gun kicked in his hand once, twice, three times before the Count went down on his knees, blood oozing from his wounds, his black eyes wide and unbelieving. Then all the life went out of his face, and he pitched forward into the dirt. Smoke curled from the

tip of the gun York held, and the smell of gun-
powder filled his head.

York raised his gaze from the Count's lifeless body
to the man stepping from the shadows along the
edge of the graveyard.

"You're damned lucky I move fast," York said. "If
I didn't, the Count would have blown your head off
by now and mine, too."

Doc Holliday smiled lazily and stopped beside the
body. He gave it a kick. "Oh, I wasn't worried. I
sized up the situation and figured you had enough
sense to take advantage of any diversion." His blue
eyes twinkled at York.

"You coughed on purpose?" York asked, then
laughed and slapped Doc on the back. "You old fox."
He sobered, realizing Doc could have gunned down
the Count easily, but had given York the opportunity. "Thanks, Doc." York held out his hand, and
Doc shook it. The two men stared at each other,
sharing the moment of triumph and savoring the relief that came with it. It was over.

York released Doc's hand and looked across the
cemetery. Ten? More? How many were buried here,
hidden here? "Let's go check on Wyatt and Jussie,
then I'll need some other men to help me open these
graves." He glanced at Doc. "I'm not taking that bastard's word for it. I've got to know for sure."

Hardly a breeze stirred, but it was cold. Winter's
breath tightened the flesh and seeped into the
bones. York grabbed the sides of his long coat and
yanked them around it. Behind him the men worked
with their shovels, but York stood apart from them
and looked up at the moon on its final descent. In
another hour it would be dawn.

He'd once told Lizzie that he'd lasso the moon for
her if he could, and she'd said he was more full of
gas than Uncle Zeb after a supper of beans. But he'd
meant it. From the time he was old enough to feel

protective, he'd guarded his sister because, for all her spunk and sassing, she was frail and simpleminded.

Months of investigating had all come to this—a windy hilltop and a graveyard of secrets. Soon it would be done with, put behind him, and he could decide how to spend the rest of his life.

He thought of Jussie, safe and sound at China Mary's. He'd put her through her paces, he thought with a grimace. Yes, she'd gotten more than she'd bargained for. Was she glad to be done with it, done with him? He sure wouldn't blame her if she never wanted to look at him again, but he'd miss her. He sighed, feeling the stab of pain near his heart. Lord, he'd miss her!

"Got this one uncovered," Wyatt said, loud enough for York to hear and join him. "The Count said this one was Shelley?" Wyatt lowered the lantern he held.

"Yes." York looked down into the shallow hole, then shut his eyes to the gruesome sight. "No casket."

"Nope," Wyatt said. "Damn shame. We should move them all, I guess, and give them decent burials. This one's got black hair."

York released his breath and whirled away. He took in great gulps of air, feeling as if he'd been on the verge of passing out. It wasn't Lizzie.

"Yep, this here is Shelley," Wyatt said, bending closer. "I recognize this dress. She was wearing it the last time I saw her at the Establishment. I remember them fabric roses along the hem of it."

"Got this other one dug up," Doc said softly, almost regretfully.

The first thing York saw was the cloud of long, blond hair, filthy with dirt. Then he saw the ring. His great-grandmother's beaten-silver ring, given to Lizzie on her sixteenth birthday.

York sobbed, turning away as tears filled his eyes

and grief struck a blow so fierce that it drove him to his knees. The world around him ceased to exist, and he was left with only an empty heart. He squeezed his eyes shut as a tiny part of him reeled with surprise. He'd thought he was ready for the truth, but he'd been a fool. He felt a hand on his shoulder and looked up into Doc Holliday's comforting blue eyes.

"Sorry, son."

York nodded and pushed to his feet again. "The ring ... the silver one. It was Lizette's."

"You okay, pard?" Wyatt asked.

"Yes. I'm taking her ... her remains back to St. Louis with me. We have a family plot there and—" He stopped, afraid his voice would break, then forged on. "Anyway, I'll buy a casket and all."

"Sure," Doc said, patting him on the back. "I'll talk to a friend of mine who's a carpenter. He'll build you a right nice one. You'll be leaving soon?"

York looked toward China Mary's. "In a few days. I've got some things to square away first."

Chapter 25

❧❧❧

Only the constant purring of Far East broke the tense silence as Justine, China Mary, and Ah Lum sat in Mary's office and waited for York to return. When the knock sounded on the alley door, they all jumped, then smiled sheepishly.

"I answer," Ah Lum said, going to the door and opening it a crack. He glanced over his shoulder. "Not York. Just Wyatt Earp."

"Let him in," China Mary said, waving impatiently.

Wyatt stepped inside and removed his hat. "Morning." He frowned. "Or is it afternoon?"

"Afternoon. Why you come? Where's York?"

"He's seeing a man about a casket for his sister. He'll be here soon." Wyatt glanced down in reverence. "Damn shame about his sister."

"But York..." Justine wrung her hands. "He's fine, isn't he? When he was here earlier he...well, he wasn't hurt, was he?" Tears stung her eyes, and she knew it was because she was on the brink of exhaustion.

"Now, Miss Jussie, he's right fit," Wyatt said.

363

"Like you, he's a little sore and worn out from everything that's happened, but he's holding up all the same." Wyatt ran a hand down his face. "It's been a long night for all of us—and a long morning."

"I want to thank you again for saving my life," Justine said. "Another few seconds and..." She shook her head, unable to go on.

"My pleasure, ma'am." He cleared his throat and looked embarrassed, then squared his shoulders. "I've been talking to the girls at the Establishment. Once they found out the Count was dead and Madame Chloe was in jail, they opened up."

"About what?" Justine asked, rising from the chair. She put a hand to her throat. It was so sore she couldn't manage anything above a hoarse whisper.

"They told me there was a body buried in the basement, and sure enough there was."

"Donna," Justine said, sighing and feeling a wave of relief. "I knew I was right. Madame Chloe killed her, didn't she?"

"That's what the girls say. Nobody saw her do it, but Babette saw her drag a rug down into the basement, then take a shovel down there. After that the basement door was locked." Wyatt shrugged. "The girls were all too scared to say anything for fear they'd end up down there, too. But now that Chloe's in jail, they want to keep her there."

"I don't blame them." Justine sat down again, limp with fatigue. "I'm glad Madame Chloe's going to get what she deserves. I was afraid she might get away with it."

"No, ma'am." Wyatt gave a wink. "I'll personally see to it that she spends some years behind bars." He glanced at China Mary and Ah Lum. "Well, I'll be on my way. Just thought y'all would want to know about Madame Chloe."

"You better man than I thought," China Mary said. "You come back one night, and I let you drink all night for free."

"Well, now"—Wyatt's eyes lit up—"that's mighty nice! I'll just do that. Good day, y'all." He let himself out the back door.

Justine stood up and paced restlessly. "Poor York," she whispered, her heart going out to him. "This must be terrible for him." She glanced at the Chinese couple. "If you don't mind, I think I'll go upstairs and wait for him in his room."

"Go, go." China Mary nodded. "You rest, too. You tired out."

"Yes, I am."

York's room smelled of him. Justine curled into a ball on the bed and closed her eyes, but the memory of Madame Chloe's evil expression and the feel of the woman's fingers around her neck kept her from sleep. If only York were here, she thought. She'd feel safe then.

It seemed like hours before she heard footsteps. She sat up as the door swung open.

"York!" She sprang off the bed and into his arms. "Are you all right?" Leaning back, she framed his face in her hands.

He smiled. "As well as can be expected. What about you? You sure you don't want the doctor to have a look at those bruises?" He gingerly touched her neck where Madame Chloe's fingers had left marks. "I know how it feels, and it's not good."

"We both just about got our necks wrung, didn't we?" She stepped from his embrace as her tussle with Madame Chloe invaded her thoughts again. "Wyatt was here. Did you know about the girls spilling the beans?"

"Yes. You were right about that bookkeeper." He sighed, suddenly looking weary. "She makes twelve. Twelve bodies. That's how many we found." He shook his head. "Most of them we can't even identify. We'll have to bury them in unmarked graves."

"It's horrible." She sat on the bed. "But it's behind us."

"That's right, angel." He crossed to the bureau. "And I've got something for you."

"What?" A present? she wondered, beginning to smile.

"The money I promised you." He held out an envelope. "You earned it, so here you go."

Justine stared at the envelope, and her brief happiness withered and died. Disappointment made her heart fall. She seized the envelope and looked at York, then at the envelope again. With a cry of disgust, she threw it at him. He ducked and it hit the wall behind him. Currency littered the floor.

"Why the hell did you do that?"

"You certainly know how to lift a girl's spirits, don't you?" she asked in her hoarse, aching voice. "Why'd you come back here anyway? Why didn't you just ride off into the sunset like any other self-respecting cad?"

"What brought this on? I'm honoring our deal, and you're snapping at me like a turtle!"

"I don't want your money. I didn't risk my neck for an envelope full of bills."

"Then why *did* you risk your neck?"

"Because I—" She stopped short of confessing and delivered a smoldering glare. "I suppose you'll be leaving soon."

"I'm taking my sister's remains back to St. Louis, yes." He picked up the money and the envelope. "I have to admit I was hoping you wouldn't take this."

"Why?" She tipped up her chin. "I *did* earn it."

"I know, but I like having you in my debt."

She reached out and snatched the envelope from him. "Well, I don't. I think it would be nice if, for once, we were on equal footing."

"You don't think we have been?"

"No. You've always treated me as if I were your servant girl."

"Jussie . . ." He growled her name and wagged a finger at her. "That's not true."

In no mood to be cajoled, she crossed her arms over her chest and flashed a glinty stare. "I know you think you're better than me, and why shouldn't you? You live in fine style in St. Louis while I'm a gypsy, moving from one town to another."

"Oh, is that how I see you?" He mimicked her, crossing his arms.

"Yes." She glared at him, hating him for paying her off. "You've given me the money, so you can go now."

"You can't wait to see the last of me, is that it?"

"It's . . . it's not that," she demurred, not wanting him to think she was kicking him out of her life.

"Then what is it?"

"I hate crying, wailing farewells!"

"So do I." He sat beside her. "I haven't made your life a bundle of joy, have I?"

"That's not entirely true."

"Isn't it?"

"No. It's been exciting." She waved a hand dismissively. "I'm a grown woman. If I hadn't wanted to help, I wouldn't have. You gave me a chance to get clear, but I decided to hang on for the whole ride. It got bumpy at the end, but I'll mend. No real harm was done." She held out her hand to him. "Let's shake and part friends."

"I thought we'd gotten past that."

He stared at her hand, and his eyes glazed over with a sheen that might have been tears. Before she could decide for certain, he had her in his arms and was kissing her with such ferocity she could do nothing but submit. She couldn't count the kisses, they came with such lightning speed, one after the other. Fiery kisses. Smoking kisses. Wet kisses.

"Jussie, Jussie . . ." He held her face between his hands and stared into her eyes. "I know I have no right . . . no claim on you. Oh, Jussie." He kissed her again, and his tongue slipped between her trembling lips and caressed the inside of her mouth with feathery strokes.

Justine moaned, overtaken by her love for him. Her pulse pounded out his name as he placed sweet kisses on her cheekbones and eyelids.

"When I thought the Count was going to kill me, I should have been thinking about my family... and Lizzie... but all I could think about was you."

"Oh, York." She sighed, wondering if this were a dream.

"All I could think about was that I wanted to see you once more and tell you... that is, I wanted to express my gratitude for what you—"

"No, wait." She swayed back, holding him off, then stood up. "That's not what you were going to say. What did you want to tell me, York?"

"That I was sorry," he said, rising to his feet.

She looked him up and down, wanting to give him a good, swift kick. "I can see that you're sorry, but there's something else." She inched her face closer to his, grabbed him by the shirt, and yanked him down to her eye level. "What did you want to say to me?" She could see it in his eyes and feel it in her heart, but she *had* to hear him say it before she could believe it. Sensing his dilemma, she nodded encouragement. "Go on, tell me. What did you *really* want to say, York?"

"I... it's just that..." He swallowed hard and winced. "Oh, hell. I love you, Jussie."

She smiled, then laughed with jubilation. "Now, why was that so hard to say?"

"Because... because I don't see how... oh, Jussie. I can't ask you to be part of my life. I just can't."

She let go of him. Her burst of joy flickered and died. "I know that," she said, turning aside and flinching from the sting of knowing she wasn't good enough. Would she ever escape it? Would she ever be worthy enough to be loved by someone like York? "Don't you think I already knew that? I'm not stupid." She hardened her heart, not wanting him to see how much he hurt her. "You've made it clear how you and your family feel about theater people. "We're trash to you, so—"

"That's not what I meant."

"—of course you can't possibly tell your folks you have your heart set on some floozy actress from the New Orleans docks, the daughter of a whore, raised up by darkies who—"

"Hey, hey!" He grabbed her shoulders and gave her a gentle shake. "Listen to me, will you? This hasn't got a damned thing to do with my family or yours."

"Of course it does. It has everything to do—"

"Listen!" He shook her again, playfully. "Your mouth is running like a stream again, Jussie. I can't ask you to hitch your wagon to my star because I don't know where I'll be going after I leave St. Louis. All I know for sure is that I won't be working for Pinkerton anymore."

She stared at him, dumb with amazement.

"You've told me how much acting means to you, and I've listened. I'm not stupid, either, and I understand you've got to ply your trade in places bigger and finer than Tombstone or Bisbee or . . . or Contention City. But I've lived my whole life in St. Louis and Chicago, and I'm not happy in big towns anymore." He took a deep breath, his swelling chest straining the buttons on his shirt. "I want room to breathe. I want to settle somewhere for a spell. With Pinkerton, I was running here and there, never staying anywhere long enough to leave my mark."

"Have you told your family of your decision?"

"Not yet, but I think they know I won't be coming back to them permanently. They know I've been unhappy for quite a while. They tried matchmaking, tried to get me interested in a girl they had picked for me. . . ."

"Was she pretty?"

"Yes, but I don't love her, and she certainly wouldn't move off to the great unknown with me. Not many women would, and I—"

"I would."

He grew still, but his eyes were alert and anticipation hung in the air.

Justine shrugged. "That is, I would if the right man asked me."

"What about your acting? You said it was the only thing that made you happy. I saw that on your face the night in the desert when you were Juliet. I saw how wonderful you are, Jussie. And those actors in the troupe, they said you were the best. You wouldn't give that up"—he swallowed, hard—"would you?"

She whirled away, her skirt twisting around her slim form before it fell into place over her petticoats. "York, when I met Old Shoe Black, he was playing a Jew's harp and his banjo on a street corner for pocket change. I started dancing and singing along, and more and more people stopped, clapped, and pitched money into Old Shoe Black's derby hat. We decided we had a good thing going, so we went into business together on that street corner. I liked the money and the attention." She hesitated, remembering. "But mostly I loved Old Shoe Black, and he loved me."

Pausing in her roundabout explanation, she looked at York. He was standing, legs braced apart, arms folded across his chest, impatiently hearing her out. She smiled, loving him for all his good points and willing to tolerate his bad ones.

"When he was taken from me, I was a lost lamb. The only thing I had left was my ability to escape through the theater. I could be somebody else and not have to face myself too often or look too closely at my wretched life. Yes, I'm good at acting. You know why?" she asked and he shook his head. "Because the only time I was happy was when I was pretending I was Juliet or some other character, usually loved by a handsome man and cherished by a family. Acting gave me what I didn't have in my own life." Emotion built within her, filling her chest and constricting her throat. "But if you're offering me the real thing..." She blinked and her lashes grew wet with tears. Seconds ticked by, and she thought he might turn and walk out of her life, but when he started walking, it was toward her.

"Jussie, do you mean it?" His voice was hoarse, and Justine realized he was just as overwrought as she. "You'd go with me? I can't promise a damned thing except that I'll be good to you, and I'll make a living for you somehow. You'll never be hungry, and you'll always have a roof over your head. I'm a good provider and—"

"You don't have to sell yourself, York LeMasters," she interrupted, holding out her arms to him. "I already think you're the cat's meow."

"Well, why didn't you say that the minute I walked in the door instead of putting me through hell?" Grinning, he grabbed her around the waist and hauled her to him. "You'd really follow me to some small town and be my wife?"

"I didn't say anything about *following*, but I'll go with you. Side by side, me and my man."

"That sounds like heaven to me, angel."

She spread her hands across the front of his shirt. "What do you think you'll do? Farm, maybe work in a bank?"

"I was thinking of being a sheriff in some place like Contention City."

"A sheriff?" She looked up into his face, the idea tickling her fancy and bringing on a smile. "You'd make a good one."

He kissed her, quick and hard. "If you think so, then I'm willing to give it a try. But are you sure you won't hanker for the stage?"

"I'm sure. I'll be too busy being your wife to miss

it. Besides, I'll have lots of things to do. I want to teach Sunday School and help out at the school. Maybe I'll even start a club like your mother's—a reading circle or an arts appreciation society. I might start my own community theater group!"

He threw back his head and laughed. "Living with you isn't going to be dull, is it?"

"You can bet on it, faro dealer." She put her hands at the back of his head and brought his lips down to hers for a tempting nibble, then a full kiss. "I love you," she whispered against his mouth. "Thinking I'd never make love to you again made me sad right down to my toes."

He cupped her buttocks and pulled her lower body against his. "I should have known the minute I laid eyes on you that my bachelor days were numbered. You were all smoke and fire that day you went looking for the sheriff and almost became part of that gunfight at the OK Corral."

"My hero," she twittered playfully, then grew serious as she looked up into eyes that rivaled the bluest sky. "My everything." She stood on tiptoe and kissed him. "But will your family accept me?"

"Of course, they will. Once they hear about how brave you were in helping me uncover the Count and Madame Chloe's horrible scheme, they'll love you just as much as I do." He bussed her nose. "They're not as bad as you've made them out to be, angel. All they want is for their son to be happy. Once they see that you're the only woman I could ever love, they'll welcome you with open arms."

She touched the blue marks on his neck and unbuttoned his shirt. "I hope so. You must be tuckered out." She looked up at him through her thick lashes. "Remember when you gave me that lecture on how virgins fall in love with the first men who bed them?" she asked, pushing the shirt down his muscled arms.

"I seem to recall that," he murmured with a chuckle. "Guess I was right about something after all."

"You loved me then, but you were too mule headed to admit it."

"You know, Jussie, when you're about to make love to a man, you shouldn't be calling him names." His hands spanned her waist, and he lifted her straight up until her feet dangled inches from the floor. "I reckon you've still got a lot to learn about bed manners and the like."

"You don't mind schooling me, do you?"

"I think I can tolerate it."

She ran her fingertips lightly over the healing knife wound in his side, knowing the scarring would always remind them of poor Satin Doll. Not that they'd need reminding. Their tempestuous time in Tombstone was already carved in their hearts and minds, never to be forgotten.

York's kisses were rays of sunlight. Everywhere he touched her, Justine's senses bloomed. She closed her eyes as he swept her into his arms and took her to bed. They clung to each other, neither wanting to let go for even one second.

Suddenly the import of it all swept through Justine. He loved her. He wasn't going to leave her behind. They were one—body, soul, and spirit. She released a tiny sob of elation.

"What's this?" York examined her liquid eyes. "Why are you crying?"

"Because I'm so happy. So happy it scares me."

"Why?"

"Oh, I guess because I've waited for this, dreamed of being loved by a special man, and now that it's come true I'm afraid it will disappear. Dreams usually do."

"I'm not a dream," he assured her. "I'm a man, a

man who loves you and wants nothing more than your love in return."

His kiss was celestial, making her heart take wing. Their bond was heaven-sent, the stuff of guardian angels and wishes come true and happily ever after. All those things impossible except when combined with love.

Author's Note

In the latter part of the 1800s, Tombstone, Arizona, played a colorful role in history. Not only did the gunfight at the OK Corral become legendary, but the people inhabiting the town became bigger than life. Wyatt Earp, Morgan Earp, Doc Holliday, China Mary, Ah Lum, Madame Chloe Le Deau, Big Nose Kate Fisher, Dr. George Goodfellow, Lizette the Flying Nymph, and the infamous Count all lived in Tombstone during this time.

Wyatt lived to be a crusty old man with plenty of tales to tell, but his brother Morgan wasn't so lucky. He was gunned down in 1882. Doc died of consumption in 1887. While no one really knows what became of Madame Chloe, Lizette, or the Count, I've embellished the truth and given my fictional version of what *might* have happened to these fascinating characters.

If you ever visit "the town too tough to die," stop by Boothill and pay your respects at the graves of China Mary and Ah Lum. As for Jussie and York, we can only assume that they lived happily ever after.

—Deborah Camp

DEAR READER:

More exciting, more distinctive—
these are the trademarks of the AVON
ROMANCE! And now, we at AVON
BOOKS promise you even more of
what you love, with even more stunning covers and, of course, even more
passionate involving stories.

In August 1989, award-winning
author Judith French returns to
the Chesapeake Bay with SCARLET
RIBBONS, a tender love story set amid
the tempest of the Revolutionary War.
This one is fascinating and filled
with action.

And look for SILVER SPLENDOR,
Barbara Dawson Smith's glorious tale
of a free-spirited American beauty
who captivates a British lord's heart.
He's traditional, she's unconven-
tional...they're irresistible!

Remember, when you reach for the
best in romantic reading, don't miss
the AVON ROMANCE—two tales every
month, month after month!

Warm wishes,

Ellen Edwards

Ellen Edwards
Editor, the AVON ROMANCE Program

Coming in October 1989:
Laura Kinsale's

SEIZE
THE
FIRE

More passion and adventure
from this talented spinner of
romantic tales!

Available in paperback
at your favorite bookstore.

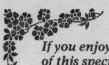

If you enjoyed this book, take advantage
of this special offer. Subscribe now and . . .

GET A *FREE*
HISTORICAL ROMANCE
── NO OBLIGATION(a $3.95 value) ──

Each month the editors of True Value will select the four best historical
romance novels from America's leading publishers. Preview them in
your home Free for 10 days. And we'll send you a FREE book as our
introductory gift. No obligation. If for any reason you decide not to keep
them, just return them and owe nothing. But if you like them you'll pay
just $3.50 each and save at least $.45 each off the cover price. (Your
savings are a minimum of $1.80 a month.) There is no shipping and
handling or other hidden charges. There are no minimum number of
books to buy and you may cancel at any time.

send in the coupon below

Mail to:
True Value Home Subscription Services, Inc.
P.O. Box 5235
120 Brighton Road
Clifton, New Jersey 07015-1234

YES! I want to start previewing the very best historical romances being published today. Send
me my FREE book along with the first month's selections. I understand that I may look them
over FREE for 10 days. If I'm not absolutely delighted I may return them and owe nothing.
Otherwise I will pay the low price of just $3.50 each; a total of $14.00 (at least a $15.80 value)
and save at least $1.80. Then each month I will receive four brand new novels to preview as
soon as they are published for the same low price. I can always return a shipment and I may
cancel this subscription at any time with no obligation to buy even a single book. In any event
the FREE book is mine to keep regardless.

Name _____

Address _____ Apt. _____

City _____ State _____ Zip _____

Signature _____
                    (if under 18 parent or guardian must sign)
Terms and prices subject to change.
                                                    75741-9A